P9-DEG-036

DREAM SCIENCE

Books by
Thomas Palmer

THE TRANSFER

DREAM SCIENCE

THOMAS
PALMER

DREAM SCIENCE

TICKNOR & FIELDS
NEW YORK
1990

For information about permission to reproduce selections from this book, write to Permissions, Ticknor & Fields, 215 Park Avenue South, New York, New York 10003.

Library of Congress Cataloging-in-Publication Data

Palmer, Thomas, date.
Dream science / Thomas Palmer.
p. cm.
ISBN 0-89919-858-9
I. Title.
PS3566.A544D7 1990 89-20457
813'.54—dc20 CIP

Printed in the United States of America

WAK 10 9 8 7 6 5 4 3 2 1

For Linda

Let me begin anew; let me teach
the finite to know its master.

— EMERSON
Journals

THE BALTED ALTAR

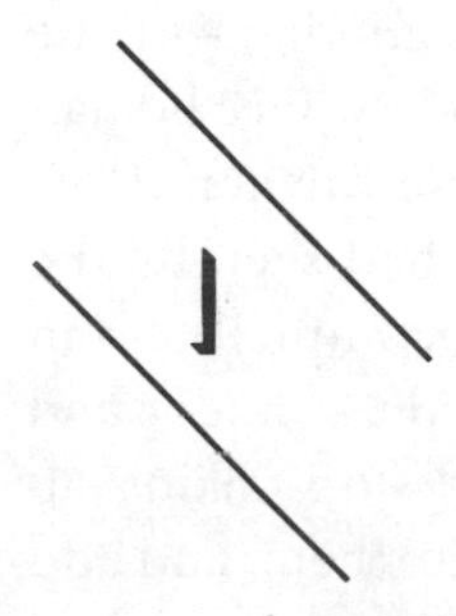

POOLE had begun to give an ironic inflection to the phrase "in my former life." Sitting at the long laminated-plastic table in his socks and blue pajamas (even though he wore them all day, they were still pajamas), he would glance at Mac, who was working across the room at the terminal, and begin some casual reminiscence with these four words—then pause significantly, as if the idea itself were a doubtful one and did not deserve its habitual introductory status. Having made his point, he would go on to talk about his wife, his job, the small coastline town where he lived; at other times he concentrated on his childhood, his family, or his years in school. It was hard to tell if Mac was listening, since he continued punching keys with his blunt, thick-nailed fingers, dropping his head down between his heavy shoulders to peer at the screen. He would make a comment now and then but he never offered any stories of his own. Mac was more likely to talk to the machine, pushing his wheeled chair back against the wall and cursing it steadily under his breath or banging the ivory-colored case with his meaty hand. He was a powerful man. Poole had fought with him several times without inflicting any damage, though he himself had been beaten almost senseless.

Poole reminisced to pass the time. He was amazed by how much he could remember. One thing led to another—if he could see, for instance, a motel cottage in Florida where he had spent two nights at the age of nine, then a little further effort might bring back a woman in a straw hat he had seen by the pool, or maybe the exact shade of red of the vinyl upholstery in his family's rented car. And so his stories tended to wander and lose themselves in detail; sometimes he would stop talking altogether. He wanted to catch these memories, fix them, and add them to the growing edifice of his past. Some, he suspected, had been sweetened and rubbed smooth by the intervening years, and his determination to identify them and dig out the truth in them occasionally struck him as quixotic, even perverse, in the light of his current circumstances — after all, if Mac had chosen to argue that he had no past at all, how could he have proven him wrong? He had no photographs, no letters, nothing — only the memories themselves, which hardly proved anything, as comforting as they might be.

For now, however, the world was nothing like what he remembered. To begin with, it was much smaller — it had shrunk to a single room. This room was built like an interior office, with bare white walls, yellow-green carpeting, fluorescent lights, and a bathroom at one end. It was about the size of a small conference room and contained the sort of furniture familiar to Poole from his days as a fund manager for a Connecticut bank — two office desks, two black vinyl chairs on casters, the long, bare table, a file cabinet, and various smaller items: wastebaskets, ashtrays, staplers, and a telephone. Pushed into one corner was the large bed on a hospital-type frame where Poole slept on bleached white sheets.

He and Mac were the sole inhabitants, and Mac was there

only during working hours. Poole guessed he was ten or fifteen years older than himself — maybe in his late forties. He wore jeans, work boots, and knit shirts in various solid colors — not typical business attire, but Mac looked more like a bus driver than an executive. Balding, he had a few dried-out clumps of pale gray hair that he slicked back from his forehead and a dour, fleshy face with lots of color. His eyes were small, blue, and weary. When he stood after sitting for a long time, he would spread his feet, press both hands into the base of his spine, and rock from side to side, with an evil look on his face, his bones audibly cracking.

Mac was Poole's tie to a larger world — a world he still believed in, though he never saw it. The office had no windows; the only door was in the center of the longest wall. It opened onto a corridor that went completely around the office. This corridor was unique in Poole's experience in that it had no exit — no fire door, no elevator, not even a heating duct. After months, Poole had still not discovered how Mac got in and out of it.

The critical area was the long stretch farthest from the door to the office. When Mac left for the day he went back there and vanished; he was big enough to keep Poole from following him. And when he arrived in the morning at a quarter to nine, Poole had to be at least as far away as the front corridor or he wouldn't come in at all.

This situation was deeply frustrating for Poole; he could not accept it. Why should Mac be able to come and go but not him? In his more energetic days he had spent much of his time in the rear corridor looking for a way out. He had pried back the wall panels and shone a flashlight behind them; he had dug up the linoleum and chopped holes in the plywood underneath. Whenever he penetrated more than an inch or two he came up against a solid wall of cinder blocks set in mortar. He had picked away at them also — he had laboriously carved his way through an entire block with a pair of scissors only to find another one behind it.

Poole now saw this belief in a hidden or secret exit as a remnant of certain mental habits that were no longer useful to him. The hours he had spent searching for it had been wasted in a futile attempt to deny the truth of what had happened to him. That truth, plainly stated, was that his life had changed; there was no reason to expect that prior assumptions should apply. It was easier, in fact, to suppose that Mac simply vanished into thin air than to dream up theories about trap doors and concealed passages, theories that couldn't stop there but had to go on to explain why someone would build and operate this elaborate prison — in short, theories that had to force rationality on an irrational situation.

Yes, it must be admitted — Poole had lost faith in actuality. He regarded his surroundings as a function of his own mental condition rather than as a separate and independent background. He was like a balloon that had slipped through a child's grasp — the world where he had spent his first three decades, the world he had shared with millions, had floated away when he wasn't looking. It wasn't enough, he now knew, to live in that world — you had to embrace it, you had to hold it close, or you would lose it.

Poole often tried to think back to the exact moment when he had departed from his former life. Had he been in a car wreck? Was his body in a coma somewhere? Unfortunately, he couldn't pin down the time with any certainty; there was no clean break. All he could remember was that it was sometime in the early spring — the lawns were cold and green, the streets were full of potholes, and he'd been spending his evenings working on IRS forms. The last specific event he felt sure of was a five-mile road race on the last Saturday in March. He also had the impression, hard to account for, that much time had passed between that day and his arrival here — time when he had perhaps hurried, barely conscious, through other possible worlds.

At any rate, time had a different meaning for him now. The watch Mac had given him — a digital one, on which the hour and minute appeared in figures made of black, bacilli-like rods that showed dark against a smooth, oyster-gray background — did not display either the day or the month. This was an ominous sign. It suggested that every week turned back on itself, that each of them started from the same eternal Monday morning. Poole had counted seventeen of these identical weeks since he landed in this place. Even so, he found it hard to convince himself that time was passing. How could it, when there was no change? In his former life time had carried him forward into the future; now he had gotten stuck somewhere and it was slowly wearing him away.

Occasionally, after Mac had left, he would turn out all the lights and wander. He would reach out for the wall and follow it like a blind man in a maze, imagining that he could go places and explore areas that were denied to him otherwise; he even hoped that he might stumble across a narrow chink where a light shone through. Who could say? The dark had no depth to it and therefore no boundaries; the walls he could no longer see might cease to exist. He shuffled along the corridor in his socks, barely breathing, the blackness thick around his eyes. Sometimes he would see things — pale, elusive thinnings of the air. Sometimes, pursuing them, he would move too quickly and bump into the walls. He often got caught up in long, cloudy discussions of his fate, which he addressed to an imaginary listener, a listener who did not choose to answer but who heard him just the same. When he had had enough he would find his way back to the switches and turn them on. He slept with at least a few lights.

Mac always arrived in the morning with a cafeteria-style plastic tray loaded with two large polystyrene cups of coffee and some sort of breakfast for Poole — doughnuts, grapefruit, oatmeal, eggs. At noon he went out again and came back an hour later with sandwiches and soup, chili, or some other hot food. Poole could ask for whatever he liked, but the selection was limited. He could get cigarettes but no liquor, candy bars but no newspapers or magazines. The only books Mac would bring him were cheap paperbacks with the covers torn off — war stories, astrological guides, pornographic fantasies, celebrity bios — twenty or thirty at a time.

At first Mac's apparent indifference to his predicament had outraged Poole. "I fail to understand," he remembered saying, "how anyone who claims to be human can stand by and allow this to continue." On some occasions he had gone on in this vein, his voice rising, until he shouted himself hoarse. Mac remained bent over the terminal and pretended not to hear. At the time, Poole had not realized that he was working himself up for more drastic measures — that he was in effect giving off warning signals. He soon learned that he could get better results by sudden, unexpected outbursts — hurling objects against the walls and screaming choice obscenities. Mac's shoulders would stiffen as his fingers stopped moving on the keyboard. He would lift his head slightly and look up at Poole from under his gray eyebrows. That look made Poole's heart swell with fear and pride. If he had gone too far — if the chair or stapler or whatever he had thrown had come too close — Mac would get up slowly, back him into a corner, and administer a thorough and methodical beating with his fists that centered on Poole's midsection and continued long past the point where any resistance had ceased. Poole had discovered that he could escape into the corridor, but he didn't like being run out of the office and there was something horribly satisfying about the inevitability of his fate once Mac got hold of him.

So they became enemies. Poole convinced himself that Mac was responsible for all his troubles and learned to hate his wrinkled, leathery eyelids, the click of his teeth as he chewed a sandwich, the sagging slope of his round, thick shoulders, his muffled belches, his aches and pains, his sour breath, even the ashy smudges on the toes of his work shoes. He looked back on that period now with a mixture of remorse and embarrassment; he felt that it had cost him Mac's trust. It ended with an event he classed with the five-mile road race in that it immediately preceded a foggy interval of uncertain duration. One morning he had crouched in wait just inside the door to the office with a long, daggerlike splinter of glass that he had broken out of the mirror in the bathroom, its blunt end wrapped in a towel. He intended to learn all of Mac's secrets. It was time, he thought, to show that he would not shrink from extreme measures.

As it happened, he was more successful than he had anticipated. Mac was still drowsy and went down hard when Poole hit him from the side, hot coffee soaking his chest and collar. For a few critical instants he was on his back and powerless, with Poole's knee holding him down, the shard of glass poised at his throat. But Poole had lost his nerve and couldn't go on. It was that sense of unreality again; it seemed to him that his situation was too bizarre and unsettled for murder to be an appropriate response. So he hesitated, and that hesitation was decisive; it was nearly the last thing he remembered.

The most painful aspect of his recovery — he still didn't know whether it had taken a few days or many — was his gradual realization that nothing had changed. At first the pallid, bare walls and the recessed fluorescent panels of the office seemed to him only one view, one window out of many that he looked through on his travels, and not one of the most attractive. Later he became aware that he was lying in bed and that he was often in pain. As his better dreams receded — dreams where these four walls couldn't hold him — he tried to withdraw with them, to inhabit them rather than observe them from a distance. It was a losing struggle. He was less and less able to disregard the sight of Mac working across the room or the tray of food on the floor by the bed. One day, at last, he surrendered — he pushed the covers aside, sat up, and let his feet down onto the carpet.

Poole was changed. The idea of escape no longer quickened him. All his feelings lost their sharpness. He would lie in bed for hours, smoking, or sit at the table and study his hands. He lost his appetite; he couldn't read. He craved sleep but it didn't restore him; he looked forward to it only because it reduced his waking hours. He stopped trying to talk to Mac. Every motion required enormous effort — even the tally he kept of the passing weeks seemed to him too difficult to maintain. At night he lay in the bathtub for hours with his head on a pillow and the water running.

He spent much of his time in the back corridor, though he no longer tried to dig his way out. Instead, he would sit against the wall with his eyes shut and his blue-and-white-striped quilt wrapped around him. The idea that this was perhaps the place where he had come into this world comforted him. Now and then he would hear Mac swearing at the terminal.

Though they rarely spoke, he was always glad to see Mac arrive in the morning. If he was more than a few minutes late Poole got restless and hung around the door, listening — not because he was hungry, but because the day could not begin until he came. If he didn't, as sometimes happened, Poole would spend hours pacing the corridor and trying to calm himself. His great fear, which he was reluctant to admit to himself, was that Mac wouldn't come back at all and he would be left alone.

This is not to say that he had lost hope. He thought of his reduced existence as a sort of hibernation, a waiting period, a necessary adaptation to an environment where action led nowhere. He had too much pride to involve himself with the toys provided for him here — paper and pencil, sleeping and waking, eating and crapping. They weren't enough; he remembered a larger world.

He often wondered what he had done wrong. Until his arrival here he had been a success by most standards. The people he came from — long-time citizens of the USA, Yankees and German Protestants, salesmen, sailors, lawyers, and engineers — had found themselves, toward the end of the century, belonging to a nation that in its size and collective power had come to dominate the world. Who threatened them? Who was likely to dislodge them? It seemed to Poole that as their heir he had reason for confidence and might be excused for not expecting to wind up where he was now.

His own history was, he believed, quite typical. He had grown up in a large, tree-shaded house in a wealthy suburb of New York with his parents, his brother, and his sister, and he had weathered all the challenges this life had offered — he had left at eighteen to go to college and within ten years he had an M.B.A. and a healthy salary and was living in a similar house just up the Connecticut shore with a wife and their child. He had not achieved all this by accident. He gave himself credit; he had worked for it. When you were as tightly wedged in as that, surrounded by family, willingly bound by a mortgage and marriage vows, strapped down with your whole life's baggage packed in beside you, it ought to take a good hard kick to spring you loose — a bad illness, say, a divorce, a death. There was nothing like that. There was no forewarning. Here he was.

There was something then that he had not accounted for — some weakness or soft spot in his assumptions. He had been too literal-minded. He had put too much trust in appearances. The world he had accepted without question as a constant, an independent factor — the world of day and night, summer and winter, rain and sunshine — had not survived him. He was still here; it was gone.

News like this could not be absorbed all at once. Poole believed that he was just beginning to realize how bad it was. To think that he was not bound by time and place — to think that he could vanish without warning and reappear in any imaginable heaven or hell — this was enough to make you wonder whether life was truly a gift.

Poole started leaving on the office lights at all hours. At night he tried to make his dreams go to work for him. Lying in bed, half awake, he would imagine that he was back in his own home on a Saturday morning and that he could smell the fresh coffee Carmen, his wife, was making downstairs; he could see the sun glowing on the yellow curtains and the blue sky outside. And while he pretended to sleep, there was a struggle going on, a struggle to make that imaginary world linger and grow. What he hoped for was the moment when the skin on his carefully blown bubble would find a life of its own and swell outward dramatically, gathering strength as it took in walls, furniture, the entire house, the neighborhood, and more. Always, however, the wish failed — the dream that survived and became real was the one containing this hateful box and the corridor around it. These efforts exhausted him and he rarely got up after Mac came in without a feeling of defeat.

Mac had grown warier since Poole's attempt to ambush him. He had set up his desk so that it blocked the entrance to the nook alongside the bathroom; from his seat behind it he could see the entire room and he stood up if Poole got too close. He also seemed to be under pressure from the higher-ups — the phone hooked up to the terminal rang several times a day and he was always making excuses to someone on the other end. During these calls his face reddened and he squeezed the edge of the desk between his thumb and knuckles; it was plain that he took his job seriously. Poole always listened in but he never heard himself mentioned.

Every now and then Poole convinced himself that he could use that phone to get help, even though he had long since discovered that both it and the terminal were protected by a nine-digit access code that Mac was careful to keep hidden from him. On evenings and weekends he whiled away hours taking the phone apart and putting it back together again. He made a list of all the numbers he could remember and tried each of them in turn; he never succeeded in getting so much as a dial tone.

One afternoon the phone rang while Mac was in the bathroom. Poole answered immediately.

"Mac?" a bored voice said.

"Yeah." Poole did his best to mimic Mac's scratchy growl. "Listen, it's good you called. I need help. The kid went nuts — he's bleeding all over the place. I can't get near him. Send me some help, quick."

After a long pause the voice said evenly, "Call it yourself."

"I can't. I tried; I can't get through."

"So let him bleed. What do you care?" A click; the line went dead.

Mac was snickering and shaking his head as he came out of the bathroom. By then Poole had tried and failed to get the operator, the police emergency number, and a few others. "Here, like this," Mac said. He punched a few quick numbers. Poole still had the receiver to his ear; he heard two rings, and the same impatient voice answered.

"Who's this?" Poole said in his own voice.

" 'Who's this?' " the voice echoed, incredulous. "Are you kidding?" The line went dead again.

"I'm in trouble now," Mac said, punching up the sequence again, his face grim and amused.

Poole listened for two rings. When the voice answered, he said, as calmly as he could, "You've got to help me."

"Why should I?"

"Because" — he ground his teeth together — "because I *need* help."

"Yeah, yeah. Let me talk to Mac."

"No — *listen* to me. There's been a mistake. I'm not supposed to be here. My name is Poole and I'm from Rowayton, Connecticut."

"How do you spell that?"

"R-O-W-A . . ." Poole had turned toward the wall and was holding the receiver tight against his ear.

"Not that. Your name."

"P-O-O-L-E."

"What makes you think you're in the wrong place?"

"I didn't do anything. I don't want to be here."

"Why didn't you tell me this before?"

"I couldn't. Mac won't let me use the phone."

"Put him on."

Poole started to obey and then hesitated. "What're you going to do?"

"I said put him on."

Poole gave up the receiver.

Mac held it to his ear, his other arm crossed on his shirt. He leaned back on one leg and looked at the ceiling. "Yeah?" He nodded. "OK . . . yeah, OK . . . all right." He pushed out his lower lip, shook his head, and hung up. Then he turned to Poole, his large face bland and thoughtful. "Dial 292," he said. After a moment he turned and went out.

Poole stood motionless for a few seconds and then dashed after him, shouting. He was too late. As he cut around the first corner he saw Mac turning at the second; by the time he reached that one Mac was gone and the corridor was empty. Groaning deep in his chest, Poole lurched back to the office and punched 292, stabbing the buttons with a stiff finger.

It was the same voice again, sharp and unmusical. "Yeah?"

"This is Poole."

"OK, good. I've got some questions for you. Would you mind telling me what kind of work experience you've had?"

"Wait a minute," Poole said. "First of all, what am I doing here?"

"How should I know?"

"There's been a mistake. I can't stay—I've got responsibilities."

He heard papers rustling in the background. "What's your first name, Poole?"

"Rockland." Poole though he heard the voice talking to someone else but couldn't make out the words.

"Rockland, Rockland . . . Well, I was going to say that I might have a job for you, but you don't sound like you want it."

"Do you know where I am right now?"

"What?"

"Right now—do you know where I am?"

"You're in Mac's office."

"Yes—have you ever been here?"

"Uh—no, I haven't."

"Then could you do me a big favor? Could you come over and talk to me here?"

"Why?"

"It's very important. I'll tell you then."

Poole was staring, as he had been throughout the conversation, at the screen of Mac's terminal. Three unbroken columns of bluish numbers were marching upward, entering at the bottom and disappearing at the top.

"I'm all tied up right now," the voice said.

"I promise you it'll be worth your while."

"What do you mean by that?"

The voice had dropped a bit. Poole twisted one of the broad, flat buttons on his pajama top. "I'd rather see you in person," he said.

After a silence the voice said, "What exactly is going on there?"

Poole had run out of ideas; the truth itself seemed to him

lacking in credibility. "Look," he said, "I want to talk to you — I am *eager* to talk to you — because I have been living in this office for over four months. Were you aware of that?"

"No, I wasn't."

"That figure is only an estimate. I've been cut off completely from the outside. I haven't seen a newspaper or a TV broadcast. I eat only what Mac brings me. I don't know why I was brought here — I don't know when I'll get out. Mac is my keeper — he takes out the trash, brings me my laundry, and leaves on weekends. I've heard him talk to you — I assume it was you — about his work. Am I clear so far?"

"Uh-huh."

"Then can you see why I'm dissatisfied? Would you agree that I have a legitimate grievance?"

"Just a second."

Poole heard him put the phone down. This time he was sure there was a conversation. His heart was racing; he crushed the receiver against his ear.

"Mr. Poole?"

"Yes."

"Would you consent to answer a few questions?"

"Why?"

"We're trying to straighten things out here. It's possible, as you said, that there's been a mistake."

"What kind of mistake?"

"We don't know yet." He cleared his throat. "You are troubled, you say, by your confinement."

"Yes."

"You remember an earlier time, a period of relative freedom and happiness. Your present life seems empty and frustrating by comparison."

"That's right."

"You had not expected this change and you resent it — it seems unfair to you."

Poole was losing patience. "Listen," he said, "aren't you missing the point? It seems to me that — "

"Just a few more," the voice said, cutting him off. "Now, in reference to this change, this transformation we were talking about, do you know why it happened? Something you did, maybe? Something you didn't do? You've had time to think it over, right?"

Poole sat down heavily in Mac's chair. "I'm still working on that one."

"So you don't have any idea."

"No, I don't."

"All right, Mr. Poole. Hold on — I'll get back to you."

Poole listened to the line hiss faintly. His hands were sweating; his moist breath bounced back from the receiver. Please, he thought, let this be the one. Let the doors open for me now. On the terminal the three columns of numbers kept jigging upward.

"Mr. Poole." The voice had a new edge of authority.

"Yes."

"We can't account for you. We haven't been able to trace you."

"What do you mean by that?"

"I mean that as far as we're concerned, you're on your own — your problem is outside our jurisdiction."

"So?"

"So we've got nothing to talk about. I'm sorry, but that's the way it is."

"Wait a minute." Poole's voice cracked as he hunched over, sheltering the receiver. "You said — "

"You said yourself that you didn't know why you were here. We don't know either. Therefore it's our view that you ought to seek help elsewhere."

Poole was stunned. His eyes turned hot and salty. "Elsewhere?" he said. "There isn't any elsewhere."

"Maybe not. Goodbye, Mr. Poole." He hung up.

Poole immediately punched the three numbers again. The voice answered. "I can't let you do this," Poole said.

"I heard you before. You don't seem to understand—there's nothing to be done."

"What's your name?" Poole asked.

There was no answer except for a faint clicking. "You hear that?" the voice said. "I'm changing the number here. You won't be able to call us anymore."

The line went dead again and didn't ring when Poole tried it. He punched it in again—nothing. It seemed to him impossible that the episode was already over; it had barely begun. He sat still for a moment, then slammed the receiver down and jumped to his feet. "No!" he shouted, his head thrown back. "No!" he bellowed again, drawing it out, assaulting the silence. The walls drank up his voice without echo. He yelled again, filling the room with sound, his gut tightening and his bent legs trembling. He had a sense, however, that it was just noise, just an exercise, since his mind was already working in another direction.

Mac didn't come in until almost an hour later. Poole was sitting at the long table with a spiral-bound notebook, writing down an account of the conversation. Mac looked subdued. He trudged over to the terminal and sat down, though he seemed in no hurry to log himself in. Instead, he rubbed his face slowly with one hand, pulling his cheeks back with the heel of his palm.

Poole tossed down his pen and turned to him. "Mac," he said, "I've got to talk to you. Now."

"So talk."

Poole pulled his chair closer. "I've been blind, Mac. I couldn't see a damn thing. I thought that you were against me—that you were keeping me prisoner." He leaned forward, his hands on his knees, his eyes hungrily searching the other man's face.

After a moment he went on. "I know better now, Mac. Now I'm asking for your help."

Mac braided his fingers behind his head and tilted up his large face. "Sure, OK," he said, his eyelids closing briefly.

"Show me the first step, Mac. Show me the way out."

Mac coughed behind closed lips, then sighed, his chest sagging. His powerful arms hung from his laced fingers. "I wouldn't do it before. Why should I now?"

"I wasn't ready. I would have been lost out there."

"Out where?" Mac said.

Poole hesitated. "Out there," he said, "where you're alone with yourself."

Mac shook his head as if disappointed. "You think I don't want you out of here? You're nothing but trouble."

"That's just it, Mac. It wouldn't have worked even if you'd tried to show me. But it's different now. I can do it."

Mac was eyeing Poole critically when the phone rang. He made a sour face and picked it up. "Yeah," he said, "he's still here . . . No, that's all right . . . The what?" His voice rose. "What do you want, you want my fucking head? . . . All right, I'll tell him." He hung up, sat back, and crossed his arms. "They got their eye on you now, kid," he said. "They're coming after you — they're gonna wear you down." He scratched an eyebrow with his thumbnail and clapped his hand on his arm. "Maybe you'll wish you never picked up that phone."

"I don't get it," Poole said.

"It was the guy you talked to before. He says he changed his mind — he says maybe he has a job for you after all."

"What kind of job?"

Mac nodded at the terminal with his chin. "Something like that."

The phone rang again. Mac didn't move. "Don't answer it," he said.

Poole had to fight to keep still. After five rings the phone was quiet.

"They got your scent now," Mac said. "They're gonna run you down."

"But why?"

"For this." Mac tapped the terminal with two fingers. "Forty hours a week. Bodies are scarce around here."

Poole was confused. "But you work for them, right?"

"I need the money."

Poole looked to one side. "I thought — "

"You thought," Mac said softly. "Tell me what you thought."

The mockery in his tone discouraged Poole, but he went ahead anyway. "All right," he said. "I asked for your help — I'll tell you why." He was excited; in the last hour he had built up an argument that he hoped would change everything.

"While you were gone," he began, "I was talking to that guy on the phone — your boss, I guess. I was describing my situation to him. After all this time, to talk to someone outside this room, someone besides you . . . anyway, he wasn't interested in my problems. He couldn't care less."

Poole was watching Mac closely. Though his face was almost expressionless, he looked as if he was listening.

"He sounded," Poole continued, "as if he'd heard it all before." He leaned closer. "*Before,* Mac! As if what happened to me had happened to other people around here. As if it was strictly routine."

Poole wanted a Winston. He patted his pajama pocket, found none, and crossed the room to get one, lighting it on his way back. "OK," he said, sitting down again, "so I said to myself, let's suppose everybody — I say everybody even though I haven't met any of them — let's suppose everybody gets dumped in here by surprise just like I did. It's a different world. The rules are different. The boundaries are different. Take this office, for example — it looks ordinary enough. But it's not — it's very strange. When you go out to the back of the hallway, there's a door there — you can come and go. When I go back there — nothing. I know; I looked. I'm convinced that even if I had a jackhammer, a cutting torch, and fifty pounds of quality explosives, I still wouldn't be able to find a door back there. You with me so far?"

Mac looked thoughtful. He shifted in his seat.

"Good," Poole said. "Now how is it that you can come and go and I can't? This is the question that was killing me. And the reason I couldn't get past it was that I was too dumb to see what was staring me in the face the whole time — namely, that all this crap about doors and openings was beside the point. *I* was the problem. *I* was the one who couldn't get out. And the reason I couldn't was that I had locked myself in!"

Poole was on the threshold of his main argument. He crushed out his half-smoked cigarette. "When I first came here," he said, "it didn't seem real to me — I thought it was a bad dream and I was waiting to wake up. I thought that you, for instance, weren't genuine, but just something I imagined. Now I know better. Now I know that the main difference between this place and the place I came from is that there is no big picture. Get it? There's no setting, there's no background that's the same for all of us — there's just you and me. It's like the world has been chopped up into little bits. Each of us has one — each of us lives in one. This office is mine; that's why I can't follow you when you go out. We can be here together but we can't meet anywhere else, because this office is the only place where your world and mine overlap."

Poole sat back, a little dizzy. His heart was thumping. He looked up at Mac. "That's how it is, isn't it?"

Mac took a toothpick out of a white cardboard box beside the terminal and started cleaning his teeth at a slow, methodical pace that was torture for Poole.

"It happened to you too, didn't it?" Poole asked. "You used to live in the big world."

Mac pulled the toothpick from his mouth and peered at the end, then leaned down and tossed it in the wastebasket.

"I know this is true," Poole said, lying.

"Suppose it was?" Mac said. "Then what?"

"I know you can help me, Mac. I want to make my world bigger. You've got to show me how."

Mac sat still and stared at him for a moment. "Let me get this straight," he said. "You think it's different here. You think we've lost touch. You think we're all locked up in our heads, or something."

"That's right, Mac. Remember the real world? It's gone." Poole rapped on the desk with his knuckles. "Hear that? That's a ghost knocking on a windowpane. We've been changed into spooks and we're living on memories. This place isn't real, Mac — it wouldn't be here if we hadn't imagined it."

Mac creaked back in his chair. "So you think we're dead, then."

"Something like that."

Mac shook his head and looked away.

"Admit it," Poole said. "You've been acting as if there's nothing peculiar about this place. But when you leave here I *know* you don't go back to some little house you bought twenty years ago. You're a ghost, too. Confess."

Mac seemed reluctant to answer, and Poole sensed an advantage. "Look," he said, "I know it hasn't been easy to put up with me. A new arrival, a nobody. Why should you have to clue me in? Until this moment I probably wouldn't have believed you. But I'm letting go, Mac — I can handle it now. You've got nothing to hide."

Poole gathered from the other man's silence that he was on the right track. "If I had to guess what you're thinking," he said, "I'd say you're wondering what the guy on the phone will say when he finds out I'm gone. He wants to nail me down, right?

He wants to hook me up to one of these goddamn boxes." He slapped the plastic side of the terminal. "Well, I don't want to join his operation. I want to travel — I want to stretch my legs. I know you can help me."

He was barely conscious of what he was saying. He didn't care; all that mattered was whether Mac agreed. He felt, now, that he had said all he could. "So what about it? Are you listening? You want to give me a fighting chance?"

Mac glanced around the room, then leaned forward and shut off the machine. His voice was low and distinct. "I think you're in trouble, kid. I think you're becoming unbalanced."

"One more reason to help me, Mac."

"What makes you think I can?"

Poole lowered his voice also. "I know you, Mac. I can tell you've made your peace — you've settled for what you have. But if you decided to change things, I can tell you'd know where to start. Give me some of that knowledge, Mac. I need it. I'm asking you. Give it to me."

Poole rejoiced at the signs of conflict in Mac's face: the pushed-down brow, the frozen jaw, the restless eyes. He felt he had the upper hand. He was afraid to give Mac that one last shove; it might be one too many. So he waited, afraid to breathe, his chest tight as a fist.

"You better hope it works," Mac said quietly. "Things can go wrong."

"Then you'll do it?" Poole said, his voice rising.

Mac ignored him. "And if it does," he went on, "you may be sorry. I can think of worse places than this. This may look like heaven next to where you're going."

"And where might that be?" Poole asked, giddy in spite of himself.

"I don't know." Mac had a doleful look. He got to his feet, his eyes avoiding Poole's, and went through his rocking motion, making his bones creak. "I'll come back in the morning, we'll eat breakfast, and we'll do it." He slid past and stopped a few steps away, his back to the doorway, his shoulders slumped.

Poole had turned in his seat and was looking at him; he had never studied Mac so closely. There was something new in his blunt, weatherbeaten face, something he had not seen even at the moment when he had him down on the carpet, helpless, with the shard of glass inches from his throat. The sight of it subdued him. "Why are you afraid?" he asked.

"I'm not afraid," Mac said. "There's nobody to be afraid for." He turned and went out.

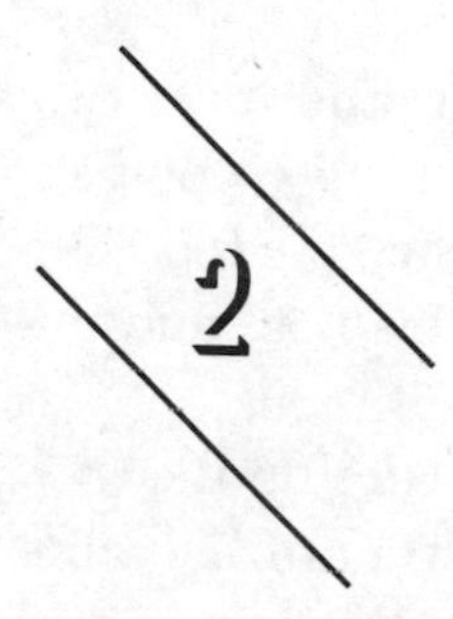

POOLE had a restless night. He left all the lights on; he spent hours wandering through the hallway. According to his calendar, which he checked two or three times, he had now spent at least nineteen weeks in the office. Quite a while—by his count it must be September. How would he explain his absence? In spite of Mac's warning, in spite of all his own talk about ghosts and mental prisons, he still believed that the way was open for him to go home.

Although Mac had made repairs, there were still signs of his escape attempts all along the back hallway—dusty bits of mortar, holes in the baseboards, a missing ceiling panel. These were what he would leave behind—these and a few thousand fingerprints and a couple of cigarette burns in the carpet.

He finally settled in the left-hand corner of the back corridor, with his pajama-clad legs stretched out and his watch beside him; it was almost three in the morning. In a few hours, he believed, he was going to leave this place and reappear somewhere else, maybe even in his old life. But what confidence could he have in it now?

The long night passed. When Mac came in with breakfast at a

quarter to nine he had a large bundle wrapped in brown paper under his arm. Poole was already up and sitting at the long table with a cigarette. He hadn't slept much and his joints felt stiff and brittle.

They ate in silence, sitting across from each other over two plates full of still-hot scrambled eggs and greasy potatoes flecked with browned onions. Poole barely touched the food but was grateful for the coffee; he held it under his nose and inhaled its rich warmth between swallows.

When they were finished Mac stacked the plates on the tray and pushed it aside, then slid the package in front of him and unwrapped it. Inside was a worn-looking dirty-white canvas bag with reinforced straps and a zipper running along the top. He opened it and pulled out a heavy, gray-green leather jacket. It too had seen a lot of wear; the shoulders and elbows had lost their sheen and were speckled and creased. He shoved it across the table at Poole. "Try this on," he said.

Poole stood up and pulled it onto his shoulders. The leather was soft, thick, and weighty; the fit roomy but not loose. A green knit lining had been sewn into the cuffs and collar. The jacket had a faint odor, he thought, of wood smoke and machine oil. Though it was not something Poole would have worn in his former life — it was too rough, too old, too poorly matched with his brainy job and his silvery steel-and-plastic Japanese car — he wanted it now.

"I'm giving you that," Mac said. "Now try the rest of this stuff."

In five minutes Poole was dressed for the first time since he had come to the office. He wore, in addition to the jacket, a gray long-sleeved sweat shirt, heavyweight khaki pants, a brown leather belt, wool socks, and high-topped work boots like Mac's with thick synthetic soles. He held out his arms and gazed down at himself.

"Forget how they look," Mac said. "Those are good clothes —

the best I could get." He dug into the bag again and started smacking objects down on the table, naming them as he did so. "A knife. Cigarettes. Butane lighters. Sunglasses. Aspirin. Cash." When he was finished he held the open bag up to the edge of the table and slid everything back in.

"Where am I going?" Poole asked.

"I couldn't tell you." He zipped up the bag, lowered it to the floor, and pointed to the chair across from him. "Sit down."

The stiff uppers of Poole's new shoes creaked as he did so.

"All right," Mac said quickly, as if hurrying through an unpleasant task, "I'm going to try to get you out of here. It may not work, but we'll try. You ready?"

Poole hesitated for a moment, then nodded. The nod seemed insufficient to him; he said, "Yes."

"OK. Take anything you want from here and put it in the bag." Mac stood up and slapped the back of the chair. "And take your chair, too. I'll be waiting in the hall." He picked up his chair and carried it out the door.

For a queasy instant Poole wanted to pull off the unfamiliar clothes and get back into his pajamas. His stomach gurgled on a rising, querulous note. He leaned back and glanced around the room, taking in the white walls, the thin, yellow-green carpet, the soft, even light. It looked almost comfortable to him now.

He got up and collected his watch from the bedside table, his razor and toothbrush from the bathroom. Head bowed, he hesitated over the stack of yellow legal pads he had scribbled full of comments and complaints on his condition. He took only a blank one and a few ballpoints. The homemade calendar went with him.

At the door, bag in hand, chair under one arm, he stopped for a last look. His new shoes added at least an inch to his height and made the office seem deeper and oddly vertiginous. In a better world, he thought, I would put a match to it. He turned and went out.

Mac was sitting in his chair in the corner of the back corridor. He motioned for Poole to sit down beside him.

"All right," Mac said. "Watch me." He got up and walked down the hall.

He vanished halfway through it. One moment his heavy body blocked Poole's view; the next, it was gone. He didn't break stride or slow down or push anything aside. He didn't go all at once either; Poole had the distinct impression that his trailing heel was visible for an instant longer than the rest of him. It was as if he had sunk out of sight in a transparent, invisible liquid that dissolved him on contact. Poole had been afraid it would be something like this, something obviously impossible — one more proof that his old life was over. He felt vaguely nauseated; he lit a cigarette and blew a long plume of smoke down the hallway.

In a moment Mac repeated the stunt in reverse, strolling effortlessly out of nowhere. Poole was ready for him this time and thought he saw him ripple or waver at the moment of emergence, like a reflection in water. Mac had a sober, preoccupied look in his eyes. He sat down beside Poole.

Neither of them spoke for a few moments. Then Mac capped his knees with his broad, pale hands and glanced over at him. "You saw it?" he asked.

"Yeah, I saw it," Poole said.

"Well then you know." He sounded almost apologetic.

"I've walked down there a million times," Poole said, "without doing anything like that."

Mac didn't answer.

Poole was restless; he got up and leaned one shoulder against the wall a few steps down the corridor, blocking Mac's way. The leather jacket felt hot; he pulled it off and tossed it onto his seat.

"Look down the hall," Mac said. "Tell me what you see."

Poole turned and glanced over his shoulder. He took time to make sure. "Same as always."

"There's a trick to this. It takes practice."

These last words, delivered in Mac's somber, matter-of-fact tone, made Poole impatient. "So let's get started," he said.

What followed was a long, frustrating exercise in which Mac attempted to make Poole see a door at the other end of the corridor — not halfway down, where he had vanished, but on the far wall. He described it in detail; it was a cheap, machine-made, floor-to-ceiling office door, its steel skin coated with a fake walnut veneer. It had a round, brushed-metal knob and opened to the left.

Poole tried to make it appear but couldn't; the opposite wall remained stubbornly blank.

"That's the door you're going to walk through," Mac said. "If you can't see it then you'll never find it."

Poole tried squints, unfocused stares, sidelong glances — nothing. The effort made his head ache. He began to dislike Mac again. "Tell me this," he said finally. "Do you always see it?"

"No — it depends. If I don't look for it, it's not there." Mac got up and walked down the hall and back. "See? Nothing happens." He sat down again. "It's the same on the other side. When I come through that door I have to look for this hallway instead of the one I'm in." He seemed to consider something for a moment, then leaned down and unzipped the canvas bag, pulling out a pair of gray socks. "Worth a try, maybe," he muttered.

In a few moments Poole was standing beside his chair with a sock tied around his head like a blindfold. According to Mac's instructions, he was to walk down the hall to the door and open it. Mac, with one hand inside his upper arm, would lead him there.

Sightless, Poole shuffled down the hall, letting the pressure of Mac's grip pull him along. What would it feel like, he wondered — a tingling, maybe? A cold draft? A sizzling in his ears? About halfway down he felt Mac let go of him and he stopped where he was. "Mac?" he said. When there was no answer he tore off the blindfold. He was alone in the corridor.

This might be funny, Poole thought, if I was in the mood. After a moment he retreated to the chairs.

When Mac reappeared, Poole didn't give him a chance to speak. "Now I want to try something," he said. Standing just behind the bigger man, he guided him slowly down the hall again and stopped him when he began to vanish. At that point Mac looked like a drowned man floating face down in the water; all that showed were his shoulders, his heels, and the back of his head. Poole went around in front of him and saw a group of quivering, metallic puddles, like disturbed pools of mercury, corresponding exactly to those parts of Mac's body which were still visible — the head an oval, the next one a vertical section through Mac's chest and shoulders. Overcoming his fear, he reached out and touched the lower one. It felt cool, flat, slick as ice, but not at all wet. It left nothing on his fingers. Poole reached out again and gave the gleaming puddle a good shove. It didn't move.

Crossing to Mac's side, Poole persuaded him to turn in place by tugging on his shirt. Now he was facing Poole, or at least half of him was — he was split right down the middle. He had a skeptical look in his remaining eye.

I can get used to this, Poole thought, feeling weak. He took Mac's hand in his own and pulled it toward the dividing line. The hand disappeared when he tried to take it across; a moment later it swung back to Mac's side.

Poole stooped and picked up the sock that had been his blindfold. He pressed it into Mac's hand and then, holding Mac's arm by the elbow, poked it toward the boundary. Both hand and sock vanished on the other side; both came back just as easily. He repeated the motion a few times and then decided that he'd had enough. Mac's divided face troubled him; he pulled him back into the corridor. "I hope it doesn't get any worse than this," he said.

Mac stood with his weight on one leg, his hands on his hips, his sizable gut hanging over his jeans, and gazed at the floor. "OK, let's take a break," he said.

They returned to the chairs. Poole didn't say much, hoping that the time had come for some explanations.

"This is not good," Mac said finally, "not good at all."

"Why not?"

"A recluse," Mac said. "You might be a recluse."

"What's that?"

"They're people who can't get across lines. They're pretty scarce, supposedly. But since they can't travel, there could be a lot more of them than people think; there could be millions that nobody's ever seen" — he looked away — "all sewn up in their little boxes for shit knows how long."

"What's travel?" Poole asked.

"Travel is when you come to a line and cross it. It's easy to do, but it's dangerous — the lines don't always last. Sometimes you can't get back again."

"That's what that is, a line?" Poole asked, bobbing his chin at the corridor.

"Uh-huh. It feels pretty fresh; it's probably good for a while longer."

"How long?"

"Weeks, probably."

"Mac," Poole began, "you heard me ramble on for hours about my former life. You knew what I was talking about, didn't you?"

"Yeah, I did."

"So what happened to it? Where is it now?"

"You already know — it's gone."

"What do you mean, gone?"

Mac cocked his arm over the back of the chair and rested his head on his hand. "The world's different now, my friend. Everybody here came from someplace. No one ever goes back."

"So you don't think I will?"

Mac sat motionless, his eyes flicking over the bare walls. They suddenly returned to Poole. "Son, you'll be lucky if you ever get out of that room." He nodded toward the office.

Poole could tell he meant it. "I don't believe you."

"Suit yourself."

"Why me?" Poole asked.

"That's not a good question."

"Why not?"

After a moment Poole knew he wasn't going to answer. He tried another tack. "Where do you live now?"

"I've got a place of my own out in the woods. I grow tomatoes in the summertime."

"Where exactly?"

"You know Jersey at all?"

"A little."

"Sussex County — way up the river near the New York line. At least I think that's where it is."

"You're not sure?"

"Look," Mac said, his voice quickening, "when I leave here I get in my car and drive home. I don't want to know what's down the road. There's lines all over the place — you cross one and you don't know what you're going to find. Maybe you're not paying attention; maybe you had a few beers and you cross one by mistake. I hate that shit — I truly do. I hate it worse than . . . " He shook his head. "If you've got any brains at all there's only one way to go: you find a place you like and you stay with it."

"Then why," Poole asked, "do you come through here?"

"It's a job."

The phone started ringing around the bend in the office. Mac swore under his breath. "Fuck 'em," he said. "I'm not here."

The sound seemed to annoy him; he kept glancing around and shifting his feet. After eight or nine rings it stopped. Mac's shoulders sagged and he slumped back in his seat, his face slack and thoughtful.

"Suppose," Poole said slowly, "you stopped coming and bringing me food?"

"You'd either get out or you'd starve."

"Then how is it that you can cross the line and I can't?"

"It's just the way it is—some people travel better than others." He spread his hands on his knees and took a deep breath, as if he had to overcome an inner reluctance. "It's like you said yesterday—there used to be one big world and everybody lived in it. Now it's broken into a million pieces—this office is one of them—and the only way to go between them is to cross a line. If there's no lines, then you can't travel—simple as that." He held Poole's gaze for a moment. "Now the place you came from—Connecticut, right?—I wouldn't say it's completely gone, just scattered in pieces. If you did enough traveling, you'd probably come across some of them. You could almost bet on it. Travel, see, is sort of like remembering: there's not that many surprises. Any place you go is going to look a little bit familiar."

"How do you recognize a line?" Poole asked.

"You get a feel for them. Say you're riding down the road in the rain and you look off to one side and see the sun shining real bright on something—now that's got to be a line. Usually they're not so obvious. You see a difference in the light—you come closer and it looks a little blurry, sort of. You keep looking at it and maybe you'll start to see what's on the other side."

Somehow Poole knew that Mac was telling the truth. It seemed to him that his whole life had been nothing more than a lengthy preparation for this moment, and now that it had come, he was struck by the humor of it. Everything he had counted on, everything that mattered to him—his life, his past, his future — where were they now? He had bet on the wrong players; he had been watching the wrong game. He started snickering and shaking his head. Where was the sorrow, the anguish? Though it was possible that he had lost his mind, he suspected that the real problem was nothing more than a few mistaken assumptions — the same sort of erroneous givens that had so often spoiled the financial projections he had once made for a living.

"Mac," he said, "did you laugh, too? Did it seem funny to you?"

"For a while, yeah."

"But not anymore?"

He shook his head. "You never forget. You're always going to remember."

"Remember what?"

Mac was staring at the door at the other end, the door Poole couldn't see. "It's a goddamn shame," he said.

They talked for another twenty minutes. Poole learned that Mac had been a state liquor store manager in North Philadelphia for fifteen years before he made what he called the "jump." Like Poole, he couldn't remember the exact date. Carter was in the White House; Rizzo was mayor. Even so, he knew about Reagan and Bush and Gorbachev; the barrier that sealed off the real world was full of holes, and news leaked through all the time.

"The real world" — he cautioned Poole against careless use of the phrase. It stamped you as a worn-out and backward-looking person. People took it as a criticism of their current status; they didn't like to be told that they had lost anything by coming here. In this view the jump was nothing less than a reward; those who had shown mastery of life were granted a release from their earthly prison and brought here to pursue a freer, less cluttered existence.

Mac had no use for these arguments; he had never believed them. Any idiot could see that this was no paradise. People tried to make it look better than it was because they knew they couldn't go back; if they were honest with themselves they'd admit that they'd lost plenty in coming here. Mothers lost daughters. Fathers lost sons. Children lost their parents; husbands and wives lost each other. You could start over again, but everyone knew it wasn't the same.

Some arrivals, he said, were so bewildered by the change that they spent the rest of their lives trying to find their way back. For them every line was a door that might lead them closer to home. They never stayed in one place for more than a day or two; you saw them once and you never saw them again. Wanderers, they took what you gave them and moved on.

Poole was still thinking about the shimmering, metallic puddles he had seen a few minutes earlier. Rubbing his fingers together, he tried to remember what they had felt like — cool, hard, dry as glass but slick as ice.

Mac coughed roughly into his fist. "I'm going to tell you something now that may surprise you. I haven't been coming here all this time just to mess around on that terminal. No, I was sent here for one very specific reason — to keep an eye on you."

Poole turned and looked into Mac's pale blue irises.

"That's right," Mac said. "You had it right the first time."

Poole didn't answer. As far as he knew, Mac had never lied to him.

"You've been noticed," Mac said. "You were noticed the day you came here. Believe it or not, you are the highly prized object of a major research effort." He sat back in his chair and looked down the corridor. "If you give me a minute I'll try to explain."

Take as long as you want, Poole thought.

"In the place I come from," Mac said, "just across that line, there are people who have gotten together in order to find out what happened to the real world. They left it just like we did.

"In their former lives they were scientists, businessmen, engineers. They've already had successes. They were the ones who discovered how to send signals across lines — this was a tremendous thing.

"Think of it this way. The world, the real world, used to be a round ball spinning in space. You've seen pictures — satellite pictures. But it's not like that now. It's not round — nobody even knows what shape it is." He leaned his head back and looked up.

"Think of a big building," he continued, "with thousands of little rooms. None of these rooms has a door or a window — they're completely sealed off. If you're inside one of them, there's no way you can tell who your neighbors are or even whether you have any. But suppose that inside many of these rooms there's a collection of holes or openings, and if you step through one of them it's like stepping through a door into any other room. Nobody can tell how many rooms there are. Nobody can tell what the building looks like. Nobody even knows how many holes there are in each room."

He stopped for a minute; he had been choosing his words carefully. "Now there are some people," he went on, "who say the real world is still out there somewhere. They say each little room is a piece of it — they point to people like you who are dribbling in from it all the time. What they're trying to do — what they'd like to do if they could — is to put all the pieces back together again. These are the people I've been working for."

He dug deep into his pocket, pulled out a plastic card, and handed it to Poole.

There was a picture of Mac on one side, a head-and-shoulders color snapshot against a light blue background. His chin was tilted up, his eyes looked small and dark, and his shiny nose and cheekbones reflected the flash. To the left of the photo, arranged vertically against a straw-colored ground, were the notations

PANLOGO
Research and Development
Edmond D. McPhatter
5/19/31
F3068

The back of the card was blank.

"It's not a for-profit outfit," Mac said. "It's more like a police station in a bad neighborhood. You have to cross a lot of lines before you run into people who haven't heard of Panlogo."

Poole handed the card back to him.

"The world isn't what it used to be," Mac said, pocketing it. "A lot of things didn't last. The U.S. government, for instance. Why should anybody take orders from Washington? They don't even know where it is."

After a moment Poole said, "You said something about a research project."

"I'm getting to it." He gazed down the length of the hallway. "Tell me this," he said. "Did you ever think there was anything particularly special about yourself?"

"Like what?"

"Anything — some particular talent, maybe something that happened to you."

"I showed up here, didn't I?"

"Besides that."

Poole didn't want to slow Mac down by talking about himself. "It's hard to say."

"Well, you could get an argument about that. The people I work for are very interested in you — they think you're the greatest thing since bottled beer."

"Why?"

"Because of where you are." Mac looked at Poole as if he expected him to understand. "Listen," he said quickly, "this office is what's known as a 'locale'—it's like one of the rooms in the big building I was talking about. There're millions of them, I hear. You get from one to another by crossing a line. Some of them are good-sized—the real world is the biggest one of all.

"But this one is in a class by itself. First, because it's so small. I measured it once while you were napping—about eighteen hundred cubic yards. Believe me, that's tiny. Second, because of this line here—it's a very special kind of line. Most lines are like crocodiles—they'll snap at anything. But this one's different. It's small, it's bashful—it's almost not even there. One of the main reasons you haven't seen anyone else in here is that I'm the only one who's been able to cross it."

Poole found himself staring into Mac's blunt, ordinary face.

"Let me go back a little," Mac said. "You think you got here about five months ago, right? You probably did. That was your jump. What usually happens is that you wake up and find yourself in a place that looks vaguely familiar except that there's hardly anybody around. You get worried—you start looking for people you know, and you can't find any. You cross a line or two by mistake. Finally you break down and tell someone your troubles—they try to explain it and you don't believe them.

"But it was different for you. You jumped farther. You jumped almost completely out of reach. So the people I work for—the researchers—think you've got the worst case of what they call 'reality failure' they've ever seen. They want to get a close look at you. They think it could be important."

He couldn't be making this up, Poole thought.

"So my job was to come in every day and bring you food and pretend that nothing unusual was going on. I was also supposed to make sure you didn't find out about the line. They were afraid you'd cross it and they'd lose you."

"So why are you telling me now?"

Mac looked away. "I just got tired of it, I guess. I thought you could use a break."

"You thought I could get out."

"I still think you can."

The phone rang again. "I better get it this time," Mac said, standing up. Poole watched him go around the corner.

In the days that followed, Poole began to wonder whether he really wanted to get out of the office.

He had spent nearly a week in the back hallway with no success; the door at the far end refused to appear. Though Mac said it was too early to get discouraged, Poole privately doubted that another week, even another year, would make any difference. This admission wasn't nearly as crushing as he'd thought it would be. Just the opposite: he felt lighter, more buoyant, less weighed down by false hopes.

Mac had tried to show him a way out of the office. What he'd shown him, instead, was that the office was everything — that there never was and never would be anything but the office. Had he, Poole, ever really believed that he could leave it and reappear somewhere else simply by wishing?

For Mac's sake he maintained the pretense of an interest in entrances and exits. Most mornings he carried his chair out to the hallway and sat down to wait for Mac's arrival. He was nearly always on time.

A person moving at a normal walking speed passes through any given vertical plane in less than a second; that was how long it took Mac to get into the hallway, though he was slower in the morning since he was carrying hot coffee. The edge of the tray appeared first, then his hands on its sides and the scuffed toe of his work boot down below, then all the rest of him nearly at once. If Poole was watching from behind, this action took place on the far side of the shining, metallic membrane — the line itself, visible only in use. Poole had discovered its exact location by stretching threads across the hallway at narrow intervals and noting which ones snapped when Mac crossed over. He had extended its borders to the walls and ceiling with a soft pencil. As far as he could tell, it never moved.

Now and then it seemed unfair to Poole that Mac could come and go as he pleased while he could not, just as it had once seemed unfair that a man he knew at college was sleeping with a certain woman and he was not. But he didn't hold it against Mac. They were two different sorts of beings. Because Mac had this special talent, Poole naturally tended to exaggerate its importance — but what good was flying if you didn't have wings?

Since Poole no longer held Mac responsible for his predicament, they got along much better than before. Mac seemed relieved to be able to tell Poole about the world on the other side of the line. One morning he called Poole over to the terminal to show him that the so-called work he had been so careful to keep private was nothing more than a smorgasbord of video pastimes to keep him occupied while he watched Poole. He had a choice of crosswords, computer chess, various puzzles and games, programs that taught French, algebra, or astronomy, and a news wire. The wire in particular intrigued Poole; it looked like one of those headline services on cable TV. It was dated September 13; according to his own calendar that was more or less correct. Mideast tensions, summit meetings, baseball scores — exactly the sort of news you would expect, and no mention of the world having fallen to pieces. Mac said it was another instance of how the real world leaked through here and there. The Panlogo researchers had picked up the signal but were unable to trace it. Apparently it was more or less ubiquitous.

Poole watched the wire for a few days but soon lost interest. The office was his entire world; he was beginning to feel as if he had always lived in it. He took a certain pride in its neatness, its vacancy. Mac couldn't hope to understand this feeling. He was a visitor. He had another life.

Mac brought him new toys now and then — drawing paper, a deck of cards, a nail clipper, one day a Polaroid camera and film. Poole now had one of the prints taped to the wall over his bed. It was a shot of the back hallway, empty except for a small object hanging in the air about halfway down. If you looked closely you could see that it was a large, fleshy nose — Mac's nose, to be exact. He also had a few disappointing shots of the metallic membrane. It looked merely gray; the flash had bleached out the chains of light snaking across its surface.

As time went on Poole settled into a new, more static existence. If he was restless, he got up and walked around; if he was sleepy, he dozed; if he was bored, he permitted himself to be bored. The days passed quickly without his urging; it was really quite remarkable, how they melted into each other and left nothing behind. And though he still knew who he was and where he had come from, it seemed to him that this was the least of the story; that his name, weight, and date of birth were arbitrary and barely relevant details; in short, that the most truly astonishing thing about him was neither his loss of his former life nor his arrival in this office but simply that he had ever happened to exist in the first place.

Yes, it was an interesting fate, this business of being alive, of being what you were and not something else. The phrase Mac had used to describe his condition — reality failure — seemed inadequate to him. Reality hadn't failed; if anything, it had asserted itself with a vengeance, proving once and for all that it wasn't answerable to his limited notions. What had failed, rather, was his sense of balance. Everything he had taken for granted now seemed to him enigmatic, mysterious. He was embarrassed by this persistent feeling that things were even stranger than they looked. He could foresee a day when the mere sight of the fine hairs on his forearm could take his breath away — to see them there, dark, slightly curved, fully emerged from the nothingness that surrounded everything, the nothingness of the not-real, as if by their very existence they proclaimed that it must be thus and not otherwise!

He also had an uncomfortable sense that he was particularly suited to this tiny room, that it reflected his own character and was somehow entirely appropriate for a person like him — no great sinner, skeptical and prudent, a compromiser, ever content to melt into the crowd, with no larger ambition than to live his life like other people and to accept with gratitude what was given to him (sometimes troubled that he had been given more than most but by no means unwilling to accommodate himself) — in short, an individual not entirely complacent but still aware that for most of his life neither history nor circumstance had put any great obstacles in his way. Therefore this office, this prison, this bland, cozy, and colorless nowhere.

He mentioned this feeling to Mac one day while they were sitting over their coffee after lunch. Mac swept a few doughnut crumbs off the table with the edge of his hand. "Just because you live here," he said, "doesn't mean you invented the place."

"So you don't think I'm being punished?"

"For what?"

"For being what I am."

"Well . . ." He shook his head. "To tell you the truth, I wouldn't rule anything out."

It soon became obvious that this sort of talk made Mac uncomfortable, though if Poole persisted, he wouldn't back away; it was as if he felt duty-bound to say what he knew. He was clearly disappointed that he hadn't been able to get Poole across the line, though he rarely spoke about it. Oddly enough, Poole himself found that he was less and less troubled by his failure. He had never been able to walk through walls; it seemed to him childish to resent it now. Mac could do it, but Mac was different. Poole had secretly begun to suspect that although Mac looked ordinary enough, he was not strictly human anymore, that he had turned into a sort of lugubrious angel, a celestial mailman assigned to carry messages between here and the beyond.

At the same time he sensed that a change was coming over him, a change he had not expected and was almost reluctant to admit. He felt it in the evenings after Mac left, at that hour when he liked to lie in bed, smoking. He felt it while he stood at the sink and watched the water run over his hand. What he felt was that this office was no longer the cramped and smothering box he had thought it was. What he felt was that he had never been freer in his life.

He had thought at one time that there were certain iron laws of time and place — apparently not. He had thought that his own life had achieved a certain momentum and stable trajectory — wrong again. The strange thing was that he missed his old assumptions so little; in fact, he felt almost relieved to see them go. Had he really been so weakly attached to his own life?

When he was alone, either after Mac left or on the weekends, he sometimes played a little game with himself. Whatever he was doing — reading, trying to remember, tossing paper balls into the wastebasket across the room, or just staring into space — he would stop for a moment and listen.

He could always hear the blower in the ceiling. It was necessary to cancel it out, just as it was essential to blot out the room around him if he wanted to continue playing. Poole was uncomfortable in the dark, and it often took him a few moments to summon up the courage to turn off the lights. The blower seemed much louder then. He would stand leaning against the doorway with his hand on the switches, the blackness seeping behind his eyes like a thick, penetrating dye.

If he stood there long enough, he would start to hear other sounds. They all seemed to come from inside him. Moist gurglings and suckings in his stomach; the steady, shuddering boom of his own heart, loudest where his pulse beat against his temples. Sometimes he heard a faint mutter like a tide trickling over a gravel beach — millions of blood cells, he suspected, squeezing into capillaries by twos and threes. These sounds came up out of the silence, made themselves known, and stepped aside — they weren't what he was looking for.

The last thing he noticed was a sort of low hiss underneath them all, like the tape hiss on an expensive amplifier. He didn't know what made it; it seemed to come from inside his ears. It had scared him when he first heard it; he had somehow known that it was the last barrier, that on the other side of it was the emptiness that was the purpose of the game. At that point he was tempted to ease himself backward, to follow the sequence in reverse until the blower got loud again and he could turn on the lights. He took that path several times.

But if he kept listening, sooner or later even the hiss began to fade. Then there was silence, a silence like death. He respected it. At one time, not so long ago, he would have argued with it, made rude remarks, dared it to talk back. He couldn't do that now.

And what he discovered — what he went back again and again to rediscover, each time more certain that he was right — was that this silence was not the silence of emptiness, of vacancy. Not at all — this silence was almost human. It was the silence of a withheld voice. He wasn't alone anymore.

Poole didn't feel as if he had sought out this confrontation. If anything, he had done his best to avoid it, always having insisted on his own privacy and in turn believing that if there was any sort of mind or will concealed behind appearances, then it had hidden itself for a reason.

And now this — a bare white room, a hallway turning back on itself, and silence.

No room here for materialists. A different world, and not easily explained. It was hard to imagine a more appropriate setting.

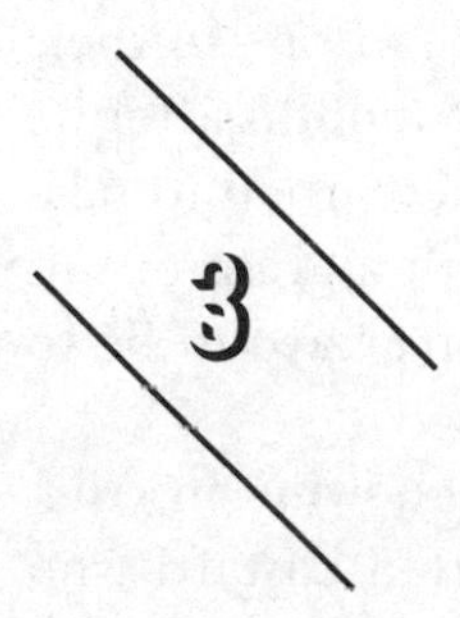

3

ACCORDING TO MAC, Poole was becoming something of a legend in Panlogo. Everybody talked about him. They recognized that his predicament reflected their own in a more intense light; like him, they had all been pulled up by the roots and forced to start their lives over again in a different world. They had adapted, they had solved the immediate problem of food and shelter, they had built a community and made it work, but even so they had never fully recovered from that initial shock, that terrifying lesson in the weakness of appearances. And though they were now, if anything, even more hardheaded about the day-to-day business of living, they didn't give themselves to it with the same abandon — an element of trust was gone.

When word leaked out that the investigators in charge of Poole's case had elected to give him no help in finding the line — that they had decided to conceal it from him — an opposition developed rapidly. In a hastily convened meeting the project director, a man named Wolpers, argued that there was no effort to keep Poole locked up, that a rescue had been planned from the beginning, and that the delay was attributable solely to the need for a few preliminary analyses. Though Wolpers remained in charge, the group voted for an immediate attempt to get Poole over the line.

Mac sprang this news on Poole in the middle of one of their daily afternoon rummy games; it was about two months after he made the same decision on his own. Poole had learned to take everything he heard about Mac's other life with a grain of salt and didn't forget to draw a card. "So you don't have to lie to them anymore."

"I've already taken plenty of heat just for following instructions. Now I'm the bad guy. I'm the coldhearted bastard who did what he was told."

"You could tell the truth now."

"Nope. I want to keep my job." Mac peered over his hand at Poole's discard, the four of diamonds.

"So they think all I needed was a few pointers," Poole said. He was back in his light blue pajamas; the clothes Mac had brought him were washed and neatly folded under the bed.

"As a matter of fact," Mac said, "today was the day I was supposed to get you across. There's a small welcoming committee just outside — they've been there since eight this morning."

"They could wait a long time."

Mac didn't argue. He drew a card and scratched under his ear with one finger. "Things will be a little different now. You'll be able to talk on the phone."

"Could be nice."

"Well, you'll probably get asked a lot of questions — you can count on it."

Dandy, Poole thought. Talk to the mysterious disembodied man! Talk to the man who isn't there!

They finished the hand and started another one. "You know," Poole said, "it'd be OK with me if you just came in every now and then with my meals. I don't see why you should have to spend all day in here."

Mac nodded. "I'm glad you mentioned that. I've been thinking about it."

"It was different when you had a job to do."

Mac looked up, grinning. "When I had to beat the shit out of you twice a week?" After a moment the grin faded; he rapped his cards on the table and fanned them again. "To tell you the truth, I've gotten to like this place. It's quiet here. You don't have to worry about somebody charging through the nearest line."

"That's for sure."

"Last week some looters attacked a storehouse on the edge of town. They were armed. Nobody knows where they came from."

"Oh yeah?"

"It was a hit-and-run. People are getting nervous."

"What did they get?"

"A little food — not much. They tried to torch the whole building."

"I thought there was plenty to go around."

"If you want to live off the land, you have to keep moving. They probably stumbled on it and decided to have some fun. I heard they had some women with them."

"Is that unusual?"

"Yeah, to have them on a raid like that."

"It sounds like an exciting life."

Mac frowned at his cards. "It's bad enough that the world went to pieces. That shit isn't going to help any."

Poole could tell from Mac's bottled-up look that a sermon was on the way. He had heard quite a few in the last several weeks and he knew which one was brewing now: it was an attack on the nomadic life.

Mac often complained that people who were content to live off what was left of the real world — cleaning out supermarkets, pumping the tanks dry at gas stations, slaughtering whatever livestock they came across — were only guaranteeing misery for everybody who came after. When he was traveling for Panlogo, he had seen dozens of locales that were completely burned out by roving human parasites. Those places wouldn't heal by themselves. Sooner or later people would have to do more than just cross a line or two to dig up a meal. By that time they would have forgotten everything they ever knew about getting one for themselves. They'd be huddled around fires in the snow with nothing to eat.

Whenever Mac got going on this gloomy prophecy Poole reminded him, just for the sake of argument, that he himself had said that nobody knew how many lines there were and that each of them led off in a different direction; therefore, it was possible that no matter how many locales were looted, there would always be fresh ones to exploit, so long as you stayed in front of the pack. And wasn't that what people had always done? Was there really any difference between pumping out a gas station and pumping out an undersea oil field?

These lively and pointless debates had become a regular pastime. Poole had the advantage of disinterestedness; he could say what he pleased, since his isolation removed any question of his acting on his opinions. Mac, however, was committed to the Panlogo outlook. He didn't criticize Wolpers for keeping Poole in the dark; he said if Poole hadn't grabbed the phone that time, he might never have told him anything. Panlogo, he maintained, was powerful not because of the number of citizens it had attracted or the trade routes it had opened or the farms and machine shops it operated or the attackers it had beaten off, but because it offered a way out of the despair, restlessness, and nostalgia that infected everybody who jumped out of the real world. "Don't tell me you don't know what I'm talking about," he said. "You and your pajamas — I've seen that faraway look you get, as if you couldn't give a shit whether you ever get out of here. Don't kid yourself. Suffer a little. Use your head. God help me, I'm not going to let you turn into a goddamn mushroom."

This was a recent and, to Poole's thinking, unsportsmanlike gambit: to remind him of his helplessness under the cover of specious promises. So far he had let it pass, though he no longer believed that Mac could do anything of substance for him. This wasn't to say that he had given up on the future. He had patience; he was convinced that he had been chosen for a singular fate. There were signs, he suspected, all around him, if he could only read their meaning.

And so part of the attraction of Mac's on-the-spot dispatches from the outside world was their basic irrelevance; they offered an occasional respite from his own cloudy imaginings. He had to admit that this honeycomb of alternate realities that Mac claimed to inhabit sounded like an interesting place to live. Like the real world, it was both limitless and mysterious; unlike it, however, these qualities were right there on the surface. The point was brought home to him at the end of the card game, when Mac reached into his shirt pocket, pulled out a small white envelope, and tossed it onto the table in front of Poole.

"What's that?" he asked.

"Open it."

Poole got a shock when he did so. Inside were a half-dozen color photos of his house.

He spread them out on the table in front of him. There was his name in white letters on the mailbox by the driveway. There was his sailboat and trailer under a tarp in the back yard; there was the vegetable garden, the two cars, even the morning paper on the front lawn. The pictures were dim and bluish, as if they had been taken before sunrise. But in one of them, the only one showing the front of the house, there was a soft glow in the bedroom window.

"Those are just a day or two old," Mac said. "One of our best scouts brought them in."

"Wrong," Poole said. He had noticed the pale green of the trees, the bare earth in the garden bed, the absence of the lawn chairs, still stored away, and incredibly, forsythia in bloom. "This is sometime in April."

"I'm telling you those shots are just a few hours old."

Poole glanced up at Mac. "Impossible."

"Looks are deceiving. That's not really your house."

Poole went back to the photos. They were flawless. He could count the shingles on the roof. It was that light in the bedroom, however, that really hurt. He knew who had turned it on — who ought to have turned it on. It was Carmen; she had gotten up to feed their daughter. "I want to talk to this guy. Right now."

"He's gone. He's on another assignment."

The pictures were shadowless, soaked in blue. Poole knew what time it was. It was the hour of birdsong, of whispers, of bare feet, and dogs whining at the door. "Tell me this," he said finally. "Did he speak to her?"

"Listen to me carefully," Mac said. "He couldn't have seen her. There's nobody there. No one. After he took those shots, he went inside — he cruised the whole neighborhood. Not a soul."

Poole was still staring at the glow in the window. The photos had loosened something in him. I'm lying on my stomach, he thought; I'm half asleep. The light goes on in the bathroom. I hear water running.

Mac's chair creaked as he shifted his weight. He pointed at one of the photos. "I was told that the date on that newspaper is April twelfth."

Poole stared at the small white bundle lying in the grass near the front door.

"That's right," Mac said. "The day you left."

A few minutes later Mac admitted that he had perhaps dropped the pictures on him too quickly. He had just gotten them that morning. They were a classic example, he said, of moonlight.

Moonlight, he explained, was the name for the uncanny resemblance certain locales had to their counterparts in the real world. It was cruel, in a way — it forced you to remember.

The scout from Panlogo, Mac said, was in the locale for less than an hour. There were no signs that anyone else had ever been there. After he took the pictures, he broke into the house. The clock on the kitchen wall said twenty minutes to six. Therefore it was reasonable to suppose that on April 12 sometime before 5:30 A.M. he, Poole, had jumped out of the real world.

"And that locale has been sitting there ever since," Mac said. "You left it there like a footprint on your way out. The whole place is like one big still photo. Time stopped dead there; it didn't start moving again until the scout showed up. If you could travel, you could go there yourself — you could even live there if you wanted. That's moonlight. But the thing to keep in mind is that even though these pictures are accurate in every detail, that locale is actually no closer to the place you came from than the room we're sitting in. It's a million miles away."

Poole felt drained. "So why did he bother to go there?"

"Wolpers sent him. They're still trying to figure you out."

"How did he find it?"

"I think they've already opened some places nearby — but it still took him three days. Most of a day to get back."

"Did he bring anything else?"

"I don't know — I didn't read the report."

"So," Poole said slowly, "every time someone makes the jump, he leaves a locale behind . . . a locale that copies the place he was when he jumped."

"That's right. Some people think all locales get started that way."

It all fit together. It was sickening, Poole thought, how it always fit together. "So my wife and daughter were never there."

"Nope. Chances are they never jumped. Not many people do."

Poole leaned over the pictures again. He had laid them out in a row. The bark on the trees was darker than usual, as if it had rained. Now the grass would start to grow again — it would get long and tangled. The garden would run to weeds. No one, but no one, would ever turn off that light upstairs. "Can I keep these?" he asked.

Mac nodded. He was sitting sideways and doodling on the piece of paper they had used to keep score. His chest rose as he took a deep breath. "Me and my wife," he said, "were going to retire to the country. Buy some land, build a house. We were going to raise dogs."

"Have you got pictures?"

"Hell no. I know what she looked like."

They played a few more hands of rummy. Poole spread the photos on the table by his elbow and turned to them now and then; the first strangeness had worn off.

Mac couldn't keep his mind on the game. He stood up and went through his rocking routine and then walked out to the corridor; he came back muttering. "Must think I'm some kind of Houdini . . . six months you can't find the line, and now you're going to trip over it."

Shortly after four he was standing next to Poole at the bend in the hallway. "I'm going to have to do a little play-acting here," he said.

Poole leaned against the wall and watched the line swallow Mac up and spit him out several times in succession. He always crossed with the same careful, measured step, his head level and his eyes blank. After a few passes he rejoined Poole. His face was flushed; he kept glancing back at the line. "I'm drawing a crowd," he said. "There's barely room to turn around. They're all rooting for you."

Just to be polite, Poole leaned forward and looked down the hall. It was as empty as ever.

"Try it again," Mac said. "Just for fun. All those people — it might make a difference."

Poole looked at him for a moment, wondering if he was serious.

"Do it for me," Mac said. "What the hell?"

Not much to ask, Poole decided. He stepped away from the wall and faced down the corridor, his hands at his sides. As usual, there was no sign of a door at the far end. After a moment he walked down past the line and back.

Head bowed, Mac was tapping his upper lip with his thumbnail; he stopped long enough to say "Try it again." He didn't glance up.

Poole dutifully repeated his promenade, stepping directly on the line this time. He had done it hundreds of times.

Mac was waiting for him at the far end. After a moment Poole shrugged.

That shrug, however, wasn't entirely honest. Something had happened. Nothing definite; it was little more than the suspicion that he had missed something, that he had been distracted for a moment and had not given the effort the attention it deserved, fully believing that if he had, he would not have noticed anything at all.

He walked down and back again. The sensation repeated itself. It was still elusive, barely perceptible. But he was sure of it now. It happened just as he was stepping over the line.

It was as if he had stopped for a moment. It was as if he had frozen in midstride while something flashed by him at tremendous speed. It made no sound. It had caught him between one instant and another. The interval it occupied was so narrow that it didn't even register until it was over.

But it left him with a picture — fading but unmistakable. It was his bedroom at home. It was just before dawn. He saw the empty bed, its covers turned back, the mattress still showing the imprint of two bodies in the glow from the lamp on the night table. Darkness was thinning on the windowpanes. Raindrops pattered in the tree outside as a breeze came up. He remembered the damp air in a chilly pool on the floor. All of it was familiar to him. And though there was no one there, the room wasn't empty. There was something else — an odor, a presence. It didn't belong there and it frightened him.

"What is it?" Mac said.

"I don't know — I thought I saw something."

"Try it again. I wasn't looking."

Poole knew that he really didn't have any choice.

Mac stayed where he was. Poole set himself on a spot about three strides from the line. He straightened his shoulders and shook his hands at the wrist.

Then, as if a hand had pushed him from behind, he started down the hall.

4

IT WAS his last moment in the office. As he stepped across the line, he stepped into his own bedroom. He looked around quickly. The lamp was on. The bed was empty and the covers pulled back. It was dark outside; he could smell that dampness in the air.

He turned, facing in the direction he had come, and leaned forward on one foot. "Mac?" he said softly. He was standing only a step away from the wall. Barefoot, he edged forward and touched its grainy surface with his fingertips. It felt solid enough.

He straightened up. He couldn't hear anything but a few birds singing. He had barely moved.

Dawn filtered in from the other rooms at the top of the stairs. The door to Lucinda's room opened onto a soft grayness. Poole approached so quietly that Carmen didn't look up when he stopped at the threshold. She was leaning over the crib with her robe open. "OK then," she said softly, pulling the edge of the blanket up. When she yawned, she tilted her head back and saw him.

Poole came up beside her and put his hands on the rail, inhaling her warmth and odor of sleep. He was afraid to speak.

"Time is it," she said.

He didn't answer. She turned and tramped away to the bathroom.

Cinda was lying on her cheek, her eyes closed and one hand balled at her throat. She moved a little. He heard a car door clap shut and an engine turn over.

Let it be true, he thought. *Let it be true.*

He was still standing there when Carmen left the bathroom and went downstairs, her bare heels slapping the wood.

He followed quiet as a burglar. His head seemed too high off the floor. Halfway down he looked out and saw the streetlight still shining over the corner of Marsh Road three lots away — a fading greenish ball.

At the bottom he heard the kettle go on the stove. He hesitated, then unlocked the front door and stepped onto the cold brick stoop. The cars were still in the driveway. The street had a dull wet sheen. He saw a light behind a window at the Mattesis' down the block.

But the sign he was looking for lay rolled up on the lawn in a clear plastic bag. The wet grass was icy under his feet as he bent down to pick it up. He shook off the dew and peered through the wrapping at the date on the front page: April 12.

Poole stood there, in spite of the cold, for a good five minutes. A car went by, then another. He had returned; he knew it now. His euphoria gave way to a chilly sort of relief. There was still plenty he didn't know, plenty no one could tell him, plenty that he would be wise to keep to himself. But he didn't doubt for a moment the truth of what had happened to him.

The kitchen was too bright. He stopped in the doorway and saw Carmen pouring from the kettle, her face still clotted with sleep. She took the paper from him, then shuffled over to the table in her gray robe and switched on the radio. "Once *we* get up," she said, "then she can sleep."

Poole didn't answer. He listened to the announcer warn that extra delays due to construction could be expected near Exit 40 on the Merritt Parkway, his voice light and amiable. Carmen spread out the front page and leaned over it, her arms crossed in her lap. After a moment she tucked her chin down and brushed at the corner of her eye.

Poole went to the cupboard and carefully took down a mug and a tea bag, put the bag in the mug, and poured from the kettle. "I had a bad dream," he said.

"Oh?"

"I was trapped in an office. I couldn't get out."

"Huh."

"There was another guy there — he could come and go. I'd never seen him before."

"So what happened?"

"I woke up."

"Huh."

She had found something to read and didn't continue. Poole let the tea bag steep for a minute or so, then fished it out and brought the mug to the table.

The tea was hot and he drank it slowly. In the meantime he reacquainted himself with the room around him. It looked genuine enough. What was more, the woman across from him seemed virtually flawless.

As Carmen reached for her mug again she glanced up at him and let her arm drop to the table. The tea had revived her; she was awake now. Poole noticed that she was looking at him strangely.

"Where," she asked, "did you get those pajamas?"

He looked down at himself. The light blue cotton flannel, the flat buttons the size of quarters, the drawstring — it was one of the pairs he had worn in the office. "The bottom of the drawer," he lied.

"I don't recognize them." She reached out and rubbed a bit of the sleeve between her thumb and finger. "They don't look new."

"They're not, I don't think."

After a moment she shrugged and returned to her tea.

Poole spent the next minute or so watching her. She had put on weight over the winter, he remembered; even her hair looked heavier, though it may have lost a little color. But she still had her narrow, plunging shoulders and her father's fine dark eyes, the eyes she held her eighth graders with while she taught them about salt marshes, dinosaurs, atoms, and other mysteries. Now, as she bent over the paper, all he could see of them were the smooth dove-gray lids, also perfect in their way, given back to him on this wet morning like the paleness at her throat, the beginning swell of her breasts — in short, his own life.

He opened up the sports section and pretended to read. Some unknown benefactor, he felt, had taken great pains to make him feel at home; the scenery was accurate to the last detail, an absolute tour de force. And yet he had a nagging feeling that the effort had been largely wasted, that no amount of realistic decor could restore his former confidence. What was Mac's word? Moonlight.

He watched her lift her mug and tilt it under her nose; her throat bobbed as she swallowed. She happened to glance at him over the rim, and her focus sharpened. "Are you feeling all right?" she asked.

"I guess so. Why?"

"You look funny." She reached over and laid her hand on his forehead. "Maybe you're coming down with something."

"I hope not."

"Do me a favor — don't go running this morning. I'll make you some breakfast."

He sat quietly while she went from the fridge to the cupboards, the cupboards to the stove, the stove to the drawers, the skirt of her robe swinging as she moved. She cracked three eggs in a bowl; bacon sizzled in a skillet. He had found a nearly full carton of his Winstons and was smoking one slowly, looking out the window at the back yard. You pretend, he thought, that this is really your life — you pretend and you make it come true.

An hour later he was tooling down 95 in his late-model Nissan with the rest of the morning traffic, his briefcase on the seat beside him, his tie snug against his neck. The day looked dark and blue under a high roof of clouds. Though he had made this trip hundreds of times and knew every billboard, every bridge, every dip and curve in the road, he was still astonished by the sweep and clarity of the oceans of air overhead.

Another smooth, descending turn and he was whisking across Stamford at rooftop level. In the distance the old brick and stone of the neighborhoods gave way to the steel-and-glass towers of the corporate elite. He belonged to one of those organizations, a large commercial bank. From the highway he could see the window of his own office, eighteen stories high.

When he got there he sat down at his desk and dropped his keys in the top drawer. It was not yet eight, and the phones were still quiet. He took out his daybook and read the notes he had written to himself the night before, six months earlier. "Call RW at DST," one of them said. He had no idea what it meant.

Now and then he heard footsteps in the hall outside, greetings, bits of whistled tunes. The coffee cart was making its rounds, mugs clinking. Here, as at home, everything was soaked in the queer scent of normality.

He was threatened, he knew. His mind was going to make certain demands. As time went on, as new layers of ordinary experience built up around him, he would discover that he had enough to do without constantly harking back to the Riddle of the Pajamas, to the dream that wasn't a dream, to . . . to whatever it was that had happened to him.

So he would be tempted. Not that he would forget — no, say

rather that he would choose to behave as if it had never happened — at least for the time being. Because the life he had made for himself was more valuable to him than the truth, whatever it might be.

A difficult road, yes, but if he didn't build that wall inside himself, it would surely be built around him. Carmen would believe the story for his sake — would believe that he believed it — but it would hurt her to do so. He doubted that the bank would let him continue to manage a $20 million mutual fund when it became known that he took six-month vacations in the spirit world; it wasn't, as the division president would say, "serious."

But there was a third path, was there not? He could begin his own investigation. An inquiry, an attempt at reconstruction — he had already thought of several starting points.

He took out a yellow pad and wrote down a list:

1) Orioles beat A's for AL pennant and lose to Dodgers in six.
2) Qaddafi assassinated in attempted coup.
3) Bridge collapse in Seattle.
4) Prime rate drops below 9%.
5) Lee Iacocca enters Senate race.

This was as much as he was sure of. There was a lot more, he knew, that he couldn't remember; he had already been in the office for months before Mac showed him the headline service and by then he had ceased to have much interest in the outside world. But these facts were solid.

What else? He doubted he would learn anything by poking around the bedroom at home. A painful pressure was starting to build behind his eyes. He went out to the water fountain and swallowed two aspirins.

On the way back he nodded to a couple of people — Sanker, a programmer, and Foreman's new secretary, an Italian girl, name unknown. He was startled to recognize them, though they belonged here, of course.

He rolled his chair into the corner and faced the window. He could easily see twenty miles — Long Island Sound looked no bigger than a puddle. Far off to the southwest he could make out the ghostly skyline of Manhattan.

Just because you know that there is something beyond this, Poole thought, that this is not all, doesn't mean that it is any less true and genuine. Compromised, maybe, but still worth his allegiance. The question reversed itself; it was not his surroundings that needed to be defined again but himself.

Maybe it was no accident that he had started out on his strange journey from his own bed at that hour, just before waking, when his dreams were most vivid. Maybe he had gotten stuck inside one of them; maybe there was a different kind, a tougher beast that bit you once and didn't let go. A dream like this was infinitely more dangerous.

The more Poole thought about it, the more he became convinced that it was just such a dream that had taken hold of him the night before. And by *dream* he didn't mean something that occupied a lesser or subordinate level of reality; no, he meant a live, kicking animal. And what had happened once could happen again.

When Johanna, his secretary, came in, he asked her if she could dig up a Philadelphia phone book and a map of the city. She came back a few minutes later with both of them.

Mac, he remembered, had said he used to work at a state liquor store just north of Market Street. It didn't take him long to track down the number. A woman answered after six rings and he asked for the manager. After a short wait a man's voice came on. "I'd like to talk to Mac," Poole said.

"Who?"

"Mac. Ed McPhatter."

A silence; then "He hasn't worked here for years."

Another pause.

"Hello?" the voice said.

"He was an old friend of my dad's," Poole said. "I'm trying to get in touch with him."

"Good luck. I heard he left town."

End of call; the man hung up. Poole put the receiver back gently.

Ten minutes later he shut his door and told Johanna he would be out for the rest of the day.

Though it took him over three hours to get to Philadelphia, he wasn't conscious of the time. There was only one thought in his mind. Mac was a person — Mac had lived.

He parked outside an unprepossessing row house in a cramped and treeless neighborhood a few miles from downtown. There were geraniums in the window box and a fresh layer of green paint on the door. An old man in a pastel shirt and a wool jacket was standing at the end of the block with both hands resting on the head of his cane.

According to the phone book the only Mrs. Edmond D. McPhatter in the city lived at Number 46. Poole locked the car and rang the doorbell.

She was a sturdy, tall, and wide-hipped woman in a floral print dress with a sweater over her shoulders. When he told her he wanted to talk to her about her husband, she stared at him for a moment before she said, "Come in, then," and led him down a short hallway into a dim room with white walls, a dark carpet, and modest, well-kept furniture at least as old as he was. A large dog lifted its head from a corner near the front window, its tags clinking. Poole sat in a stuffed armchair near the fireplace, and she let herself down onto the edge of the high-legged couch opposite.

He began by saying that he had recently spent several weeks in the company of someone who might have been her husband.

He didn't use the word dream. He didn't qualify it in any way. He repeated the little he knew about Mac's former life and asked her if it could be the same person.

She didn't commit herself. She seemed reluctant to speak at all. She sat up straight on the couch with her hands in her lap, her legs crossed at the ankles and tucked back. There were no magazines in the room, no TV, no radio. It looked to Poole as if nothing in it had been moved for a long time.

He quickly added that if it was her husband, he had no way to get in touch with him and didn't expect to see him again. He also said that he had no message for her, because Mac had never had any reason to think he would see her. It had been his own decision to come.

When she spoke at last she asked him where he lived, how old he was, what sort of work he did. Then she said that she didn't yet know whether to believe him or not but that he could go on.

By then Poole had decided to tell her the whole story. It was quiet in the curtained room, and he didn't hurry. An antique wooden clock ticked away on the mantelpiece. At one point the dog groaned, got up stiffly, and hobbled over to sniff Poole's hands before it limped away; he heard it lapping water in the next room. He went into detail about the office and the line in the corridor. And as he continued, now and then looking up at her large and deep-set eyes, he began to feel that the roles had been reversed, that he was playing Mac's part and she his, and that this tidy and airless room, with its swept-out hearth and its aura of stillness and memory, had become for her what the office had been for him — a prison without exit, accessible only to the rare outsider who brought news of a place so distant that it hardly mattered whether it was true.

In the end he said he had no idea where he had been or why he had come back but that he had felt obligated to find out what he could; this was why he had come to see her.

An hour had passed; she had said barely three words. He

looked at her hands and saw that she was gently stroking one with the other. He began to think that she wouldn't say anything at all, that he had frightened her, that she would sit quietly and wait until he got up and left. She hadn't taken her eyes off him since they had sat down.

Then she leaned forward slightly and touched the small of her back with one hand. "Show me this," she said.

It took Poole a moment to understand. He hesitated; he knew it would hurt her. But he got up anyway, spread his feet wide, dug the heels of his palms into the base of his spine, and rocked from side to side, grimacing, his head rolling on his shoulders, just the way he had seen Mac do it so many times, finishing by stretching his arms straight up, fingers spread, and letting them drop to his sides. His bones didn't creak like Mac's, but when he looked at her he could tell that he had reached her.

"Young man," she said, gazing now at the heavily curtained window, "my husband has been dead for nearly twelve years."

Poole saw the dog in the doorway to the next room watching him. He sat down again. "I'm sorry, ma'am," he said, wondering if he had made a mistake.

"I didn't bury him," she went on, still looking at the window, her voice controlled and emphatic. "I believe he was killed. He had made enemies. He was involved in the unions. He shot a man who came to rob the store." She paused. "We were married twenty-three years. I know he would never have left me." She turned to him, her eyes bright and damning.

"I don't think he was killed," Poole said. "I think the same thing happened to him that happened to me."

"Then why didn't he come back?"

All he could say was that Mac had wanted to and would have done so if he could.

Poole wrote his name and address on a slip of paper and put it on the table near the arm of the couch. He told her that he was going out but would be back in an hour; if she wanted to talk to him again, she should open the curtains in the front window. She seemed very calm. She didn't get up. She sat stiffly with her sweater still over her shoulders and didn't look at him as he put away his pen. Once again he had the feeling that there was no way out of this room for her. The dog was whining and clicking its nails on the floor. Poole let himself out; when he drove by an hour later the curtains were still drawn and the old man with the wool jacket was standing at the corner again.

A half hour later Poole was out of the city and heading north on the Jersey Turnpike under a wide, dirty sky. He had found what he had come for. It was no longer possible to dismiss his experience as a mental aberration, a disease peculiar to himself. But he was anything but reassured.

Two weeks passed. He lost a lot of sleep in the first few days, since he suspected that the door to that other world was still lurking somewhere in the bedroom. He stayed awake late into the night, a book on his chest, Carmen breathing evenly beside him. The slightest noise made his heart beat faster. At long last he would give in, begin to doze, and start awake, rigid and trembling; even the mildest dream now seemed dangerous to him. When this happened three or four times a night, he would get up and go downstairs to make himself something hot to drink, bring it back up, and straddle a chair by the window, the sash open, the cool night flowing in over the sill. If he waited long enough he could usually get a little rest sometime toward morning.

He made a few more inquiries. A neighbor in the insurance business told him something about the statistics on missing persons. The rates were highest for adolescents, single men, and people with criminal records. About fifty percent were never located; claims were paid on fewer than a tenth of those insured, and then only after they had been declared legally dead. The overall incidence was higher than death by snakebite or lightning but lower than death by any of the major diseases.

Of course, in a technical sense he had never been missing at all. Poole was aware from reading the papers that there were numerous otherwise solid citizens who freely confessed to having been sucked up by spaceships or whisked out of their bodies to tour the cosmos. He had always dismissed them as crackpots and still did, in spite of his recent experience. The only person he really wanted to talk to was Mac.

He had never been particularly adventurous. Although he was very much interested in himself, he didn't see why anyone else should be, and was willing to lead a conventional life in a conventional setting, knowing that the essential freedom, the freedom of mind, could flourish behind any number of disguises. He liked his job well enough. He was a specialist, paid to keep close watch over the medical electronics industry. It was his business to know which companies would perform well and which would stagnate, so that his bank, which invested heavily in the field, could spread its cash accordingly. There were pleasures in the work. It was a guessing game, a quest after secrets, a digging into the future. Success meant capital flowing toward its most efficient use; failure meant write-offs and rumblings from above. He sat in his office and poked his feelers deep into the surrounding organism, a complex industry dispersed through forty cities, and tried to pick up every quiver.

Naturally there was a lot of nonsense associated with working near the top of any large organization: matters of style and personality, the endless jockeying for advantage, the ostensible hierarchy versus the actual flow of power. It seemed to him that the worst was rewarded as well as the best. But that was a challenge as well.

And now this other thing, this history, this most intimate sort of disaster.

He had no idea where to find help. He still didn't have a clue as to how he had escaped Mac's fate. He felt as if he had dodged a bullet; someone, he suspected, was playing games with him.

This reaction was unexpected, since his religious education, a matter of kindly ladies with shiny shins boring him for an hour on Sunday morning, had never taken hold. The closest thing he had known to God was his own father, and that was long ago. If cornered, he would admit that you could speak of a divinity in things, in life itself, but to go from there to a person, a jealous parent who made up rules and pointed a finger at those who broke them — well, that would have been laughable if so many people didn't believe it.

Yet he couldn't shake the feeling that he had been singled out somehow, not by an unlucky conjunction of circumstances but by a will, an intelligence that meant to beat down his pride and teach him a thing or two. This was only the first step; there would be more. The things that used to comfort him — the vastness of time and space, the innumerable varieties of life, his own relative insignificance — no longer provided a refuge. The wheels were turning. He had been noticed.

So all the congratulations he offered himself for his safe return to the world had a hollow sound. He couldn't put himself at ease. He began to feel as if he were back in the office — as if here, in the midst of life, he was cut off from it by mistrust and fear.

He tried to compensate. If he was going to vanish again, he wanted to put things in order before he left. He wanted Carmen to know that he loved her. He told her so several times out of the blue, something he had never done. He started getting out of bed ahead of her and getting Cinda up himself. One morning at breakfast when she asked him why, he said he was just trying to make things easier for her. She thought about it for a moment and said, "You must have a better reason than that."

Poole looked at her uncombed hair and her sleepy face and

wanted to go back to bed with her. He let the urge pass; he was already dressed and had to be out in ten minutes.

He hadn't married her because he loved her. He had been in love with a lot of women. He asked her because he wanted a wife and family and he hadn't met anyone who suited him better. On their wedding day, when he stood up and said out loud that he would spend the rest of his life with her, he felt like Babe Ruth indicating the seats where he would deposit the next pitch; the element of bravado stunned him. But there was a great contentment with it, too. Never again would he spend half his time wondering whom he would sleep with next; he was going to know. Marriage also cured him of his old habit of asking himself whether he loved her. Sometimes he did, sometimes he didn't.

He could tell that she had noticed a change in him. She was biding her time, aware that something wasn't right but reluctant to come right out and ask him. They had secrets from each other, they had lies that were recognized and left undisturbed, but there was also a tacit understanding that a question posed in a certain way had to be answered truthfully.

Poole still wasn't sure whether he wanted to be approached that way. As time went on and he began to breathe a bit easier, the urge to involve her weakened but the feeling grew that there might not be any harm in it, that she could somehow absorb the news without much struggle. People believed what they wanted to believe; she was committed to him and would swallow any number of tall tales before she would admit to herself that she had married a lunatic. He thought of presenting it to her differently, as a sort of put-on, a bedtime story, something that might have happened but probably never had. He didn't want to burden her, but he wanted her to know.

So he gradually lost interest in concealment, at least as far as she was concerned; if he felt like referring obliquely to his recent experience, he did so and let her make what she would of it. He even mentioned Mac's name several times. When she asked him who he was, he said, "A guy I met at the office." He wasn't proud of games like these, but he couldn't resist playing them. They took the edge off his nervousness; they showed whoever was listening that he hadn't forgotten.

But he never got to tell her the whole story. Just over three weeks after his return, Poole vanished again.

It was a Sunday morning early in May. He had been out in the yard working on the lawn since ten, reseeding a weedy, sun-starved patch where he had never been able to build up a decent turf.

The air was warm and he was sweating a little when he went in the back door to wash his hands. Carmen was making sandwiches in the kitchen. He picked up the sports section and took it into the TV room to sit down for a few minutes before lunch.

By the time he had finished his first cigarette and wanted another, he noticed how hungry he was and wondered why Carmen hadn't called him. He was about to investigate when he stopped and held his head still, listening.

Normally, at this hour, even behind closed windows, you could hear noises from outside — kids shouting, a lawn mower, a car going by. Now, as he sat there, it sounded like three in the morning. It was the sort of quiet that allowed him to lie in bed and listen to the low rumble of the freeway to the north. But now even that was missing.

Poole felt like the transatlantic air passenger riding high over the ocean who hears the engines suddenly cut out.

He got up and went into the kitchen. There, at the edge of the sink, were two bowls of hot soup on plates with sandwiches tucked in beside them. The portable TV next to them was turned on, but it was hissing softly and the picture had gone off. "Carmen?" he said.

He went up to Lucinda's room. The crib was empty; there was nothing but a sweet, lingering odor.

He walked down again, pushed open the screen door, crossed the front lawn, and stopped in the middle of the street. Not a sound — not even a bird, an insect. Two houses down, a pair of plastic tricycles stood at the end of a driveway.

He went back to the kitchen and twirled the dial on the TV. Nothing. The same with the radio. Even so, he was not yet ready to believe. He returned to the den and sat down in the same spot on the couch. I was right here, he thought. He remembered looking through the window and seeing two teenage girls walk by. Just a little hitch, he told himself; just a moment of inattention. He waited, but nothing happened.

Poole sat there for twenty minutes. He smoked another cigarette. Tears welled in his eyes but he took no notice. He felt as if he weren't there at all, as if the person sitting on the edge of the couch was not actually himself but a bad reproduction, a botched copy.

His thoughts were interrupted by the thin whine of a battery-powered smoke alarm. He sat up and looked out through the window screen. The sound was coming from the Eastmans' house across the street, a white clapboard Victorian. He noted that both cars were in the driveway.

A minute later thick gray smoke began to sift upwards from one of the upstairs windows and gather under the crown of the gable. The alarm yelped and shut off. Then the glass in the sash splintered, fell, and slid down the porch roof into the gutter. He could hear flames crackling. Before long, black fumes were funneling out of every window in the upper story, and holes had opened in the roof. A projecting limb of the closest tree, a big maple, withered but didn't catch. It felt strange to be watching the spectacle without a crowd, without firemen and hoses. Poole went out again and crossed the street. At the edge of the grass he could feel the heat and the air being sucked past him. Now half the upper story was a black lattice swimming in flame; part of the attic fell in, and a shower of sparks cascaded into a rhododendron.

He walked around the neighborhood for the rest of the afternoon. The Eastmans' house burned to the ground, leaving a basement full of black rubble. There were other fires; when he climbed out his bedroom window a little later, carrying a bottle of bourbon, and scrambled up to the peak of the roof, he counted over a dozen motionless black plumes in the distance. It was one of those soft, hazy spring days when the air itself seems to glow. The tar shingles were warm and there was no breeze; a few wasps floated around the brick chimney. He drank from the bottle.

He knew now that it had happened again, that he had lost touch. In his stroll through the neighborhood he had seen sprinklers still going, soap drying on cars, a bag of golf clubs abandoned in a driveway. He had also noticed a worried-looking spaniel scratching at a door and heard something larger barking ferociously inside a garage.

The word *genocide* occurred to him. Not a cry, not a murmur — hundreds whisked away in a moment. Deep down, of course, he knew it was much more likely that it was he and not they who had disappeared, that this place was not what it seemed, and that his neighbors, wherever they were, had probably not noticed anything out of the ordinary.

The square-sided bottle of bourbon was now warm to the touch. He took another mouthful and waited to swallow it while he propped the bottle against the chimney. From this height, just above the trees, the town around him looked like a shrubby green meadow with a few slatey rocks poking through. He couldn't see more than a mile in any direction. His mood was such that he liked the idea of drinking in a place where a slip could be fatal.

He had already decided that he wasn't going to stay here, that he had to get away. Like the office, this neighborhood was probably one of those locales Mac had talked about, places that looked familiar and were therefore all the more unnerving. He thought of the pictures Mac had shown him — the eerie dawn, the empty house, the light in the window.

What he objected to most was the arbitrary rhythm of these trips to nowhere. Why this morning and not the day before? Why here and not that horrible corridor again? The process had no logic. If he could get a handle on it somehow, if he could anticipate, even predict, the next headlong plunge, then maybe he wouldn't feel so hollow; maybe he could even act, exert pressure, prevail. He could see now that he had been foolish to pretend that nothing had changed.

The afternoon lengthened. Every time Poole got restless he took another swallow of the bourbon. He stood up several times to relieve himself, one arm braced around the chimney, the long, lemony stream arcing down and splattering out of sight on the flagged terrace below. He could see a bit of the street from his perch and he spent much of his time watching it, ready to hail anyone who came along. The Eastman's house was still smoking, although a pipe had opened and was flooding the cellar.

The sun started to shine into his eyes as it slid toward evening. The smoke plumes on the horizon had dissolved, and the western sky brightened to a lovely pink-orange as deep shadows opened between the trees. Gulls in twos and threes beat their way to the south toward the water, their wings barely audible.

Tomorrow, he thought—tomorrow will be difficult, but this moment has a certain charm. To think that he was alone here; to think that this pleasant green bowl and the immense darkening sky overhead had no other observer but him. He didn't leave the roof until the sun was down and the color was gone from the trees.

That night he sat at the kitchen table and wrote a long letter to Carmen. He felt as if she were still somewhere nearby in the darkened house, and he was afraid, strangely enough, that she would creep up on him. The bourbon had poisoned him a little, and his ears were acutely sensitive. He threw water through the screen at an animal he heard snuffling under the window; it jumped and ran off.

He spent most of the night working on the letter, filling several dozen pages of a lined yellow pad. He wrote quickly, trying to stick to the facts, beginning with his arrival at the office and continuing through his struggles with Mac, his escape attempts, his early morning return, his decision not to tell her what had happened, his visit to Mac's wife, his gradual increase in confidence, and the latest disaster. He tried not to leave anything out. At the end he left a space and wrote the heading

TENTATIVE CONCLUSIONS

1) Reality is not uniform, but scattered in fragments.
2) These fragments are mutually exclusive but an individual may pass from one to another.
3) Passage between fragments is sudden and inadvertent.
4) Space and time are continuous within fragments, discontinuous outside them.
5) An individual can inhabit only one fragment at a time.
6) Fragments resemble dreams but are real.
7) Persons may inhabit a single fragment all their lives or travel regularly between them.
8) One fragment, the real world, is larger and more inclusive than all others.

9) Most people spend the first portion of their lives in this fragment and many never leave.
10) Departure from this fragment is difficult to reverse.

He put the pen down; it was after midnight. He stopped and read over what he had done so far. It seemed to him accurate but incomplete; a collection of facts, not a message to her. He decided to write a third and final portion.

Sitting back, he lit a cigarette. It was late enough now that the quiet did not seem so oppressive. He often worked at this table after Carmen had gone to bed, drinking tea and savoring the end of another day; he liked the clean counters and the dim glow of the appliances. But he knew he would not sleep much tonight.

In the morning he planned to get in the car and drive; the question that preoccupied him was how far he could go. According to Mac, it was rare to travel five miles without crossing a line.

But what, he wondered, if there aren't any? He imagined himself threading his way down a 95 littered with wrecks and shattered glass. Stamford a ghost town, Greenwich also, and not a breath stirring on the island of Manhattan — the bridges empty, the streets deserted, the high vault of Grand Central aching in the silence. An eternal Sunday morning. Just the tides lapping at the sea walls and the wind sucking at the cornices fifty stories overhead.

And what if he kept going? Driving all day, camping under bridges at night, cooking pilfered canned goods, siphoning gas from the hulks at the roadside, moving west across Pennsylvania, Ohio, Illinois, the Mississippi, the Plains, the Rockies, always looking for that one other survivor, slowly losing hope — there would be reason enough then to pray for a boundary.

If I knew, he said to himself, that this was going to be the last, that the next day or month or minute would not toss me into some equally impossible nightmare . . . He didn't finish the thought.

He picked up the pen again.

Carmen, I have lost you. I don't know why. I don't know for how long. And I can and will live without you — I am not about to give up. But when you see me again you must not expect to find the same person you used to know. Things have changed.

You are now for me a kind of dream, a dream of staying in place, of becoming a link in time. We were going to be together all our lives. We thought this was in our power. I am looking at the wedding band on my hand as I write this. I used to be afraid that I would get careless and it would slip off somehow, roll out of reach, and I'd lose it. But I don't think I was careless.

You know how I looked at the world — I didn't confuse it with paradise. There were certain things I considered worthwhile and I intended to make a place for them, a small place but big enough for the two of us and a few others. Beyond that, my concern faded rapidly. This was the bargain I made. Things could go wrong — accidents, disease, history. I didn't think they would.

But I was wrong. The life I wanted — our life — I can't seem to hold on to it. I am too light, somehow — I don't have the weight I need to stay in place. Maybe, then, it's pointless to fight it. Maybe the damage is beyond repair. How many times do I have to be reborn? I think of our daughter in the first ten seconds of her life, bloody and raging.

So I'm leaving my shelter. I have to look forward. There is a chance, I think, that I can learn to ride these currents — to steer across them. If there is a good side to these disasters, it is that I think I know the worst now and am ready to confront it. Yes, this is a contest of sorts. I feel as if there is a hand nudging me along.

I also know that you, Carmen, and I are not through with each other yet. There's still too much to be done. If I were to go upstairs now and find you in our bed, I wouldn't let you sleep — no, we would be up all night. I'd tell you more than

I've written here. I wouldn't waste any time. I've come back to you before and will do it again, I promise you.

How can I say this? What right do I have? Anybody can make promises. But consider — do I really have a choice? I have to go on as if there were a point to going on. I have to keep faith in something. What else if not you? Yes, I am using you, I am setting you up as a holy thing in order to drag myself out of this pit. I am pretending that our life together was the best of all possible worlds when we both know that it was far from it. But it was our life all the same, wasn't it? We chose it. We were going to make the best of it. Now that it's gone, now that I've got no one to talk to but myself, I say and believe that it was no favor to me to drive us apart.

I don't really think you'll read this letter. If I thought you might, I wouldn't be leaving tomorrow. But in a way it couldn't be more public. I address it to the silence that weighs on this house. I call on the power that made me to answer. I demand and expect an accounting. If I am not meant to live in the world I was born in, if everything I was led to assume is a lie, if the earth is not real, if history is not real, if men and things are not real, if I always have passed and always will pass through these shadows like a shadow myself — then why does it hurt to be alive?

Poole sat still for a moment and then tossed the pen down like a hot needle. He was shaking. It was nearly three in the morning. He folded the letter without rereading it, put it in an envelope, and left it on the bed upstairs. He packed a suitcase and carried it down to the front hall.

After that there wasn't much left to do. He didn't put many lights on. Restless, he moved around for a while, once venturing out to the street, and then went back to the deep armchair in the den. He was sitting there in the dark by the window when the streetlights went out. He had expected the current to fail eventually, but he was still sorry to see it. A faint odor of burning lingered in the night air.

He wasn't afraid to sleep anymore and he dozed off toward

morning. When he opened his eyes again the dark had just lifted. He got up, took a shower, and made himself eggs and coffee.

When he finished his first cigarette, most of the color had seeped back into the trees. He noticed a neighbor's dog, a white Labrador bitch, watching him through the window from halfway across the back yard, one paw lifted. He went to the door and tried to coax her inside. She wouldn't come but she stayed around; he would see her again later when he went out to the driveway.

He washed the dishes, left them in the rack, and went around the house, closing and locking the windows and doors. He had put his suitcase in the car and was about to close the front door behind him when he decided it might be a good idea to go up on the roof again and see what he could see.

He had to go out the bedroom window, cross to the driveway side, and follow a steep, narrow pitch from there to the peak. The shingles were a little damp, and he moved carefully.

At the top he straightened up and looked around. Yesterday's clear air was gone; a warm, glowing mist lay over the town, thick and shining in the low places. A few blackbirds flew in straight lines between the treetops. He shaded his eyes. The only blue in the sky was directly overhead, where the mist was thinnest. The landscape looked dark in the yellow distance, and metal glinted on the half-hidden roofs.

There was no reason to stay, but Poole was reluctant to go down again. The rising vapors carried sweet odors. He liked the warmth on the back of his neck. He knew that by this time on any other Monday he would have been in his office; the thought added to his melancholy without spoiling the impression. It was as if his vanished neighbors had entrusted this spot to him. He was the last — when he left, nothing.

Tired of standing, he went over to the chimney and leaned against its mortared edge. One more step and it was a sheer drop down to the flagstone terrace. He toyed with the idea, as he often had, but he did not take it seriously. He had too much courage, or too little.

Crossing his legs, he peered down the chimney's sooty throat, then looked up again, no longer interested in the glowing fog but content merely to stare. He was wondering what solitude was going to do to him. Time would accumulate. Certain portions of his mind might begin to stiffen. Sooner or later it was going to get worse than it was right now.

A sparrow dropped onto the TV antenna at the other end of the roof and twitched its tail, chirping. Poole watched it over his shoulder. When it leaves, he thought, I'll go.

It was still there when a hard-shelled, buzzing wasp flew into the corner of his eye. As he jerked back to swat it, it stung him.

The pain shocked him. It was sharp and dull at the same time. Blinded, he dropped to a crouch, the heel of his palm crushing the insect against his cheekbone, his other arm swinging wildly to grab the chimney. But he had miscalculated; it wasn't as close as he had thought, and his fingers only slapped its corner. The force of the motion carried his shoulder toward the edge. Poole forgot the sting. He knew that if he couldn't grab something now he was going to go over.

His swing carried him around; he tipped sideways into space. His last effort was a desperate, twisting lunge for the lip of the roof. But by the time he had gotten his body turned and his arms extended, he had fallen too far; his hands cracked against the side of the house. He saw the distance between them and the roof edge, small at first, begin to lengthen. He knew then that he was going down.

He was amazed by his stupidity. If he hadn't leaned the wrong way when he grabbed for the chimney, he would still be safe on top.

It didn't occur to him to cry out. Through his blurred eyes he saw the window of Cinda's room add itself to the growing height of the house. In a moment — in a certain brief interval — he was going to hit the ground. He felt a frozen, numbed terror balanced by a rueful satisfaction. Finally, he thought, all the teasing is over. This was the real thing.

Sometime later he noticed that he was lying on his side in a pool of water. Thirsty, he turned his head and drank, forcing a few gulps down his aching throat. He rolled onto his back and looked up.

A deep evening sky. A vapor trail like a child's scrawl. Some few clouds with rosy edges, others already gray and sinking. Directly above him an early star or planet shining faintly. A few leafless treetops at the edge of his vision.

Something else he recognized: a line with a slight kink in it blocking out a corner of the sky. A course of raised bricks led out to the kink — a chimney. A bit of window on either side. Eaves. The side of a house — the side of his own house.

So he was home. That was reassuring. He rested for a while, then rolled over and got up on his hands and knees, water dripping from him everywhere. He was naked. When he stood up, he saw that the puddle he had been lying in was about his own size and was outlined by a smooth crust of snow, as if his own warmth had melted it. He could just see the flagstones. It was as if he hadn't moved since he fell off the roof.

He looked around. Snow everywhere, blue in the dusk, glazed. Rutted slush in the driveway and a strange car behind Carmen's. Warm lights in the Eastmans' house across the street. The sky was still transparent, although it was dark on the ground.

He wasn't particularly troubled by the change of season. He had been through enough by now to know that he couldn't depend on time to unroll as smoothly as before. The important thing was that he was here.

He picked his way around the side of the house, his bare heels crunching on the snow. At the end of the street a flesh-colored sunset glowed through the empty trees. He saw the mailman's black footprints in an arc across the front lawn. Someone had shoveled the walk from the driveway to the front door — normally his job. The light was on over the stoop and the table lamp shone behind the living room curtains.

He stopped for a moment. He heard a truck spreading sand on the next street over, its chains beating the road. There was something wrong, unfortunately, with his head — it hung a bit to one side and rocked when he moved.

Carmen had put a Christmas wreath with a red velvet ribbon on the front door. He looked at the round button on the doorbell and tried the knob instead. It was locked; he went out to the garage and got the key he kept hidden there in an old orange juice can.

Inside, he shut the door gently behind him. There was no one in the living room, though he could hear a TV going upstairs. He took the big yellow towel from the downstairs bathroom, wrapped it around his waist, and started up.

The hallway was dark and no one saw him right away when he stopped outside the bedroom door. Carmen was sitting on the far edge of the bed in her bathrobe with one leg on the floor and Lucinda in her lap. Next to her a man in jeans, a sweater, and athletic socks was stretched out full length on his back with his head on the pillow and his fingers laced behind his neck, his eyes fixed on the TV across the room. It was her unmarried brother, Josie. A familiar voice was talking about the icy roads.

Josie noticed Poole first. His entire attitude changed, although nothing moved but his eyes. He must have alerted Carmen; she looked up and let out a small whimper. Poole smiled at her and took a step into the room.

Josie leaped off the bed as if in welcome, grabbed something that was leaning beside the headboard, and swung it at Poole, who heard it whistle. It was a baseball bat. It smashed into his side with a startling crunch, and he hit the floor hard on his knees. When he scrambled up again, holding his side, he found Josie crouched opposite him with his feet spread, the bat raised like a club. He pointed at the bathroom door a step away. "In there!" he screamed.

Before Poole could protest, the bat whistled out again and hit him in the same spot with another ugly thud. He scrabbled sideways along the wall, one hand raised, and retreated into the darkened john. Josie followed him closely and stopped just outside the door. Carmen had gotten off the bed and come nearer, still holding Cinda, who had started to wail; Josie motioned her back. The light was behind her and Poole couldn't read her expression. Just then the bat shot forward again, barely missing him. "Wait a minute!" he yelled, stumbling back.

Still crouching, the bat filling the doorway, Josie turned and motioned to Carmen with his free hand. "Get me the phone," he said. When she didn't move, he shouted at her.

Poole was trying to see over Josie's shoulder from deep in the darkened bathroom. "Carmen," he called out, "are you all right? Is it OK?" He didn't want to fool with that bat again.

Carmen moved out of sight toward the head of the bed. Josie turned back to him. His handsome face, in shadow, was twisted into something else. "You're poison, dead man. You touch them, they die. Got that? You touch them, they die. The fucking truth!"

He could hear Carmen sobbing now. She reappeared with the phone. Poole leaned forward and the bat snaked out again. "Come on!" Josie yelled at her.

Poole saw Carmen, still holding Cinda, put the phone down on the floor and crouch beside it. She raised her free hand and hesitated, looking at him past Josie's knees. "Did you want him to die?" she cried suddenly. "Did you?"

Josie ducked down and hit the buttons himself. In a moment

he was up again, the receiver at his ear, the bat still extended. "Yes," he said. "A dead man. He's here right now. Rocker Poole. Fourteen Rowland Road, Rowayton. Hurry up." He dropped the receiver and it thumped on the carpet.

Poole spread his hands, palms outward. "Hey, look — "

Josie's free arm lashed out and smacked the wall beside the doorway; the bathroom filled with bright white light. "See for yourself!"

Poole turned and looked in the mirror over the sink.

The face he saw wasn't his. It was the sort of face he had seen only in wartime atrocity photos or pictures of traffic deaths. The skin was the color of wet newsprint. The head lolled crazily to one side. The entire neck was mottled brown, and there was a large region of torn flesh on the upper side with a deep hole at its center, a ragged bite filled with grayish, stringy lumps of ripped muscle and some white cottony substance. Way down at the bottom a small blade of grayish bone stood out. The worst thing, however, was the eyes — they were his own eyes, and he saw them staring back at him.

Though Poole jerked away and brought up his hands, the picture remained. When his shoulder banged the wall, he poked his nose with his thumb and felt it give way like soft wax. Josie clicked off the light. Poole looked up to see him at the door with the bat raised. Carmen had moved out of sight again. He could hear her trying to quiet Lucinda. Both of them were crying.

"You don't belong here," Josie said. "You have to understand that."

Poole heard him but he wasn't listening. He looked out the window. The sky still glowed in the west above the darkened street and the blue, snow-covered lawns. He sat down on the toilet and patted his chest, feeling for a heartbeat — nothing. He tried his wrist — nothing there either. A shadow flickered; he looked up and saw Carmen carry Cinda out of the room behind Josie's silhouette. "What happens now?" he asked, strangely calm.

Josie didn't drop his guard. "They'll be here in a minute. They'll take you down to the center. Just remember that you can't touch anyone."

Very little light came into the bathroom and Poole knew that Josie couldn't see him at the far end. "What happened to me?"

"You died. You're a dead man."

"Can they revive me?"

"Don't even think about it."

He heard footsteps on the carpet, and Carmen came back into the room. She stopped behind Josie and looked in at him without saying anything. She was barefoot and he thought he saw her shivering. "Carmen — " he began. She started trembling violently, shook her head twice, and looked away, her face tilted up. Poole felt something contract in his chest.

Josie ignored her. "Just relax," he said, still peering into the bathroom. "You'll be all right."

Poole had been squeezing his knees with his hands. When he stopped for a moment, he felt the marks his fingers had left. "Carmen," he said again. He looked out the window. A half-dozen neighbors in overcoats had gathered in the street. Downstairs someone was banging on the front door.

Carmen had stopped shaking. "Go answer it," Josie said. Ignoring him, she moved closer to the door, gluing herself to the frame and looking in at Poole. Her nearness forced her brother deeper into the bathroom, the bat still raised. "Get back," he hissed over his shoulder. The banging continued downstairs, louder now.

"You answer it," she said gently. "I'll be all right." Poole could see a wide wet streak on one side of her face.

"Forget it. Go get the door!" Josie had inched back until he was almost flat against her, the end of the bat pointed at Poole's head.

"You go. I want to stay with him."

"No!"

An ambulance with a red flasher pulled up outside the house. Poole saw three men jump out and run up toward the door.

Josie hadn't taken his eyes off Poole. "If you even start to make a move . . . ," he said.

Poole knew that there was something Carmen wanted to tell him before the men came for him. "What is it?" he asked, looking at her. She was still clinging to the doorframe, her body outlined by the glow behind her. "Is it really you?" she said finally, her voice soft and tentative.

"Yes!" Poole said. Just then there was a splintering bang followed by footsteps pounding up the stairs. At the last second she pulled back from the doorway. Josie retreated with her. Poole heard several men come into the room. Then a bright light shone in his eyes.

He was told to walk toward the light and lie down on the stretcher he found beneath it. "Should I, Carmen?" he called out. He heard some scuffling noises and her voice again, raw and pleading. "Yes, Rocker — please!"

When he did, several thick blankets were thrown over his head and body. The stretcher was lifted and the blankets cinched snugly around him. He was carried down the stairs and across the lawn, footsteps crunching on the snow. Someone said, "On the left — one, two, *three*," and he was slid into the ambulance.

A short, quick ride. He was taken out, brought up some steps, and set down. He heard a door shut; it was quiet. No light penetrated the blankets. There was some soft and pleasant orchestral music.

The door opened. Someone undid the straps. A friendly female voice. "You can get up now, Mr. Poole." He heard her go out.

He lay there for a few moments longer. In the ambulance he had noticed that it was no longer necessary for him to breathe. He could fill his lungs, but there was no pressure to do so. Listening, he was impressed by the stillness of his own body.

He pushed the blankets away. A large, attractive room with a couch and several chairs. A belt-high maple strip on three sides. On the long wall a panoramic photo of a snowy mountain range. It was much like one of the better waiting rooms in a new hospital except for the floor-to-ceiling wire-mesh fence that divided it in two.

A door on the other side opened and a short, chunky man in a business suit with a zippered calfskin slipcase under his arm shut it behind him. Graying hair, fleshy ears. He came up to the fence and pinged it with a fingernail. "Quarantine," he said. "Ugly, I know, but unavoidable. I'm Dr. Mignoli. Dr. Ernest Mignoli."

He was clearly unfazed by Poole's appearance. Just to make sure, Poole got up and went to the fence. Mignoli was standing six inches back and didn't move.

"I see you're undressed," he said, smiling and glancing down. "We've got clothes if you want them. But you look all right." He had a small rapid voice, a juicy mouth, yellowish teeth. "You want to talk to your wife?"

Poole pointed to the wound on his neck and watched Mignoli's eyes shift to it. "Yes, I know," he continued. "There's not much we can do about that, I'm afraid." The smile vanished. "Were you aware that you have a broken neck?"

Poole didn't answer.

"That's why your head hangs over like that — a complete cervical fracture. But if you make an effort you ought to be able to hold it up straight. Try it."

Poole did so; the man was right. It took constant effort, however, and there were unpleasant noises at the juncture. He let it slump over again.

"Nice," Mignoli said. "Now I've got some bad news for you. You want to get it over with?"

After a moment Poole said, "Why not?"

"Good — here it is. We know for a fact that you have very little time left. You'll be dead by this time tomorrow. We can't save you — nobody can. That's just how it is."

Poole stared back at his open and intelligent face, looking for a clue. At last he snickered. "I'm going to die?"

"That's right."

"Then what would you call me now?"

Mignoli frowned. "You're a sick man, Mr. Poole, but you're not dead. You don't need an M.D. to see that." He paused. "Why don't you put some clothes on and pull up a chair? We've got some things to discuss."

Poole continued to study him. After a short interval Mignoli turned away, sat down at a low table, and pulled some papers from his slipcase. He started to whistle softly.

Poole went through the drawers of the bureau under the panorama. He found some underwear, socks, and a flannel-lined khaki jumpsuit. He put them all on. His hands were a little stiff and didn't seem to have any warmth. He noticed that there was a mirror over the sink in the corner but he avoided it. The door he had come through was, as he had expected, locked. Mignoli had spread his papers on the table and glanced up at him now and then as he dressed. Poole explored his side of the room thoroughly and pocketed the Marlboros and the plastic lighter he found before he pulled a chair up to the wire. A moment later Mignoli pushed up his chair, too. He left the papers behind.

"I see," he began, settling in, "that you were in the health business also — technology finance. Did you take much science at college?"

Poole stared back at him a little longer than was necessary. "Are you nuts?"

"Excuse me?"

"I mean what's going on? What are we here for?"

"What do you think?"

"I have no idea. It's like a nightmare."

"Yes, well, you're very ill. It's my job to counsel you."

"Why?"

"It's my work. I get paid for it."

"So you know what happened to me?"

"In a clinical sense, yes."

"So what is it?"

Mignoli seemed relieved to hear the question. He leaned back. "Mr. Poole," he said, "you are what's known as a returnee." He was watching Poole closely.

"What's that?"

"Don't you know?"

"No."

Mignoli considered the response for a moment. "Well, the theory goes like this. Some people, at the moment of death, react so violently against it that they don't actually die. It's a function of will power. The will can't save the body, but it can outlive it and later return to its old surroundings in a fleshy disguise — a disguise that mimics the old self. That's what your body is — not a living thing, but an expression of a stubborn wish. It's my sad duty to tell you that it will fail you very soon. We hope to reconcile you to this. If we can't, then at least we can be with you until the end."

Poole sat there dumbly for a few moments. "This is all news to me."

"Well, yes, it usually is."

"It doesn't happen where I come from."

"No?"

Poole could tell he was being drawn out. He didn't particularly care. He was troubled by the contrast between Mignoli's squat, ruddy, and well-kept hands, bristling with dark hairs, and his own grayish and dead-looking ones, white as chalk under the nails. "Not at all," he said. "As far as I know, never."

"So you don't believe me?"

"I don't believe that this is the place I came from. I admit I was fooled at first. But over there, you're either dead or alive. Nobody comes back. Anybody that's still walking around has to be alive."

Mignoli looked thoughtful. "Would you admit that you might have forgotten a few things? On purpose, so to speak?"

"Where I come from, if you had a guy wandering around with a broken neck and no pulse, it would be the biggest news in a century. You wouldn't have a room like this waiting for him and a guy like you to hold his hand."

"No?" Mignoli's eyes widened slightly.

"No!" Poole nearly shouted.

Mignoli turned and looked longingly at the sheaf of notes on the table. "Would it be fair then to say that you're not sorry to be leaving us?"

"I'm a freak, aren't I? Would you want me around the house?"

Mignoli's mournful eyes turned to him again. "This quarantine represents an ancient taboo that has a sound medical basis. You're a dangerous person — unwittingly so."

"Am I?"

"In most respects your body is indistinguishable from a corpse. Therefore it's a haven for microorganisms. Outside of freezing you solid, we have no way to arrest its deterioration further."

Poole remembered the fear on Josie's face. "Did you know I was coming?"

"Returning, you mean? Yes, there were signs."

"Like what?"

"Your body, though quite dead, spasmed occasionally. Your skin maintained electrical resistance."

"How did I die?"

"You fell off your roof."

"When?"

"Last spring."

Poole didn't answer.

"Your wife heard you cry out. She was the first one there. You were already gone. It may have been your anger at being taken from her that brought you back. At any rate, you looked for her first. It's been quite a trial for all of them, waiting for you. We can't predict these things with any certainty. When you see them, don't be surprised if there's a certain coldness — remember, they buried you months ago."

"They're coming here?"

"They'd like to, yes. There isn't much time."

Neither of them spoke for a minute or so. Mignoli went to the table. Poole didn't look at the other man. He was staring at a patch of the mustard-colored carpet.

He asked himself if this new life of his, this wandering, was really so different. He was still at its center. Worlds still dwindled to infinity on every side; past and future still blurred into the unknown. If anything, it was truer to his actual condition. It gave the lie to all those altars to permanence he had erected around himself. *Don't seek your kingdom here,* it said.

He noticed a loose flap of skin on his knuckle and peeled it back to reveal a flat fan of ivory tendons on the back of his hand. They tightened when he made a fist. There was no bleeding. He put the scrap back again and pressed on it.

"Mr. Poole?"

Mignoli again; he sounded tentative. Poole looked up.

"We still have some work to do. Are you interested?" He now had a lined pad in his lap and a pen in hand.

"Like what?"

"Just a few points to clear up."

Poole didn't argue.

"First of all, I have to remind you that you have no legal status. You can make no gifts or bequests from your estate — the will you signed is binding and will remain so. That doesn't mean your family won't honor any additional wishes.

"Second, it's our policy to allow no one into the room without your permission. There are probably at least a dozen people who'll want to see you — family, friends. I'll give you a list later. You can cross any of them off. Also, if there's anyone you want to see who's not on the list, let me know and I'll try and get in touch with them.

"Third" — he pointed to a standing burlap screen set up at one end of the wire on Poole's side — "if you'd rather not have people look at you, you can sit behind that. You won't see them either, of course." He paused. "Maybe this is a good time to remind you of the old prejudice against returnees. For centuries they were regarded as evil spirits who had captured the souls of the dead. They were hated and feared — they were even burned. So don't be surprised if you encounter some hostility. This wire is also for your protection."

"Doctor," Poole said.

"Yes?"

"What do *you* think? Do you think I died and came back?"

"Yes, I do."

"What would you say if I told you I came from another place entirely?"

Mignoli hesitated. "I couldn't prove you wrong. I've heard it before."

"But you don't think so."

"I think you're a strong-willed man who's suffered a great disappointment."

"You think I'm lying to myself."

Mignoli rested his head on two fingers and looked down at

the pen in his hand. His eyes flicked up at Poole. "Are you afraid to die?"

"I'm more afraid that I'll just keep going; that I'll never find my way back."

"Why do you have to? Why not just say goodbye?"

"Because I belong here."

"Who says?"

"I do."

Mignoli looked thoughtful. "This . . . loyalty. Who is it to?"

"My wife. My family."

"You don't think they can get along without you?"

"*I* don't want to be without *them*."

"They ought to be here by now. You want me to bring them in?"

On an impulse Poole got up, crossed the room, and looked in the mirror. The wound was as vile as ever. His nose was crushed and pushed awry.

"All right," he said quickly. "Go ahead."

It was Carmen first. Mignoli had gone out; she came in a minute later. Poole was standing at the fence with his hands in the wire.

She stopped halfway across the room and he stared at her narrow shoulders, her boyish hips, the handkerchief balled in her strong, delicate fingers. She had on a black sweater with roomy sleeves. Her face was red and swollen. She wouldn't meet his eyes.

"You look terrible," she said at last, half turned away. "Just awful."

"Carmen," he said softly, as if trying to wake her. "Carmen."

"Don't look at me like that!" She whirled around, clutching her elbows and trembling.

"It's OK," Poole said.

When she finally faced him again, she had mastered something in herself.

"I'm sorry," he said. "I didn't know."

"Didn't know what?"

"That I would hurt you."

"We can't hurt each other anymore." She looked away. "I didn't want Lucinda to see you."

"That makes sense."

"I'm going to sell the house. I wouldn't do it before."

"Where will you go?"

"I don't know. We'll be all right."

Poole searched her face as if it were a mirror. "Did you know I was coming back?"

"That's what they said — a fifty-fifty chance."

"I'm going to keep trying."

"No — you mustn't."

"How can you say that?"

She started to tremble again. He flinched, and the fence shivered like a tree full of tiny metal leaves.

"It's over, Rocker," she said, almost whispering.

"I want you."

"No. It's evil."

"It can't be helped."

"You were good to me. Be good now, *please*."

"Don't you want me too?"

She had bitten down on her lower lip and it was bleeding. He felt full of pity, a pity that made him cruel. "We're not through yet," he said. "I know it."

Her arms fell slowly to her sides. She moved closer and stopped right under him, shocking him with her wide, helpless eyes.

He backed off a few steps and lit a cigarette. It was tasteless; he threw it away. He paced around the room aimlessly, his head lolling on his shoulder. After a while he stopped in front of her. She was still clinging to the fence, motionless. "The worst is over," he said, reaching through the mesh and dragging the handkerchief from her hand. He hung it over the wire. Her eyes were dull and lifeless.

Now it was he who couldn't hold her gaze. He turned sideways, hiding the wound. When he looked at her again she was absorbed in tracing a square in the wire with one finger.

"I didn't expect this," he said.

Nothing moved but her hand. "What's it like?" she asked softly. "Is it bad?"

He wasn't sure what she meant. "No — I don't think so."

"I'm so *sorry* for myself."

He watched her for a moment. "The doctor said I was a returnee. Do you know what that is?"

"Yes."

"Are there a lot of them?"

"Not really."

"I swear I never heard of them."

She shrugged, her mouth quivering, unable to speak.

"You know what that does to me?" he went on. "It makes me think that this is a different place from the one I came from. That's why I'm not afraid to leave. That's why I think there's hope for us."

Her fingers slowed and stopped. She raised her head. "I wish," she said, "that I still had you. Is that such a crime?" She tried to hold his eyes but the sobs rose up in her again — harsh, metallic, painful. She hung her head and wept.

After she left, Mignoli came in again. He went straight to the wire, curled a piece of paper, and pushed it through. "Doin' OK?" he asked, an edge to his voice.

The paper was a typewritten list of names, beginning with Carmen and including his parents, his brother and sister, a few relatives, a couple of old friends, the man he worked for at the bank, and several others he didn't recognize. Mignoli's name was at the bottom.

"Only the underlined ones are here," Mignoli said. "The others are on their way. The ones at the bottom are a couple of my students. I'll be back in a few minutes." He waited long enough for Poole to say something and went out.

Poole studied the list for a few seconds longer, then crumpled it and tossed it in a corner. He hadn't asked Carmen to go, though he hadn't protested when she did. There was room enough in the couch and chairs on the other side for at least a half-dozen people. He imagined them all gathered over there, talking in low voices while he sulked or loitered by the fence — the dead man ashamed of dying.

He unzipped his jumpsuit and reached in to touch the spot where Josie had hit him. No pain — not much feeling at all. His ribs all seemed to be in place, though the flesh over them was like putty.

It was coming on again — the old doubt, the old fear. *This is no dream.* The faintest whisper, but he could hear it. How laughable, really, to be a dead man.

He sat down on the chair under the big photo. He didn't want to play this one to the end; everybody took it so seriously. He got up, retrieved the list, and smoothed it out on his knee. His parents' names, at the top, were underlined. After what had happened with Carmen he doubted he could convince them that he wasn't their son.

Mignoli came in again, opening the door just wide enough to step through. He clicked it shut gently and came up to the fence, frowning and abstracted. "OK so far?"

Poole made him wait a little. "Not exactly."

"Oh?"

"I want to call it off — I have this tremendous urge to end it right here."

"It's up to you."

Poole stared at him through the wire, wondering what he meant.

"Your body's not keeping you alive," Mignoli said. "It's just your will to live. If you let that lapse . . ." He shrugged.

"Then what?"

"Everybody goes home. We take care of the remains."

"That's it?"

Mignoli gave him a strange look. "As far as we know."

"Suppose I hang on? How long then?"

"Less than a day at most." He paused. "There's no magic here."

At that moment Poole began to hate him. "It's not what you think. It's not just one death — unh-unh, it's death after death, each one worse than the one before, each one teasing you into thinking it's the last."

Mignoli stared at him for a long moment. "What if you're right?"

WHEN HE WAS telling the story, Poole always cut it off right there, leaving out the ugly scenes that followed, the scenes that still troubled him even though he knew they weren't unusual. Nearly everybody could remember similar ones: violent frenzies, desperate appeals, sudden acts of self-mutilation. It was always a struggle; you had to exhaust all your strength before you could see that defeat was in fact a victory.

"Living in fear" — that was the customary phrase. You said, "When I was living in fear," and went on from there. Everyone knew what you meant — the fear of death. That fear included all the others — the fear of endings, the fear of failed beginnings, right down to the fear of hunger and the fear of ridicule. Not that it wasn't still legitimate to be afraid — no, there were plenty of reasons, good reasons, to cultivate prudence and a healthy suspicion — but the big fear, the fear that tied the rest of them together, had been laid to rest.

Looking back, Poole could see that the fear of death had been at the heart of all great institutions — religions, nations, families. They offered you an identity, a destiny; in return they demanded allegiance. If you refused, then you had to be shut out.

That was a powerful threat if you happened to believe in death; every minor sanction was a shadow of the big one.

Now death had lost its privileges. It had retreated; it lived somewhere beyond the edge of the world. Someday, it was said, the dragon would come back and spread its power everywhere. This was the threat — or the hope. In the meantime, life mastered all.

Poole still had troubles of his own, but he no longer imagined that they were unique. He had seen some ugly places; he didn't doubt he would stumble across worse if he gave himself a chance. For the moment he was in no hurry to go looking for them.

He had found an old dinghy in the long grass above the beach, and he liked to drag it down to the cove, row it out a way, toss out the anchor, and lie naked on the floorboards in the sun while the water sucked and slapped the old planks. He'd bring a beer or two and stay out half the day, dozing and sweating, rolling over the side now and then to cool off. Water leaked in slowly through the seams; when it got too wet, he would come in again.

Late in the afternoon, depending on the tides, he would wade out to the bar where the clams were thickest and the sand was so soft and fine you could dig for them with your hands. Jewel's dog liked to come with him and stalk minnows in the shallows. This hound — a long-legged mutt with short cinnamon fur and yellow-brown eyes — was more likely to step on a fish than to catch one. If Poole didn't feel like digging, he would go out anyway and throw a stick for the dog.

He was no stranger to the cove. As a boy he had often crossed it on slippery plates of sea ice that gained another thickness with each tide. In the springtime he had dropped nets into it baited with cracked mussels and drawn them up heavy with struggling shiners or a deep-green eel. He knew how it tasted; he had swallowed quarts of it. Though all the docks and sea walls and shoreline homes were gone, he had recognized it immediately.

It was sadder now; it was awash with memories. The hut he had built out of weathered boards and old plastic was just a short walk from the site of the house he had grown up in, now a scrubby tangle of oaks and blackberry canes with a low ledge of dark granite in back, a ledge in whose crevices his mother had once set out dozens of lily and crocus bulbs. This odor of the past made the silence more familiar, more companionable, and he liked to tramp through the woods and the salt meadows in search of more ghosts.

The cove was only a mile across at its widest and nowhere more than eight or ten feet deep. Through its mouth he could look out across the Sound at the low green hills of Long Island. He never found any trace of the rich old homes that had surrounded it; as soon as he pushed into the woods a few hundred yards, he lost all his old references and couldn't decide where to put the grade school and the commuter train station that had been the twin poles of the town. Its main street, Sound Beach Avenue, was now a cattail marsh full of blackbirds.

Poole had stumbled into the cove by accident: an untreated fever in his previous life had suddenly flared up and killed him. He had died several times by then, and he knew it was much like being tied up, blindfolded, and dumped across a line. There were some people, gamblers, who would slit their own throats just for a change of scene; Poole still had a lingering respect for death and tricks like this disgusted him.

The air was warm, and shelter was no problem; water was in easy reach. He found crabs, clams, and berries in abundance. Matches, however, were another story, and he spent much of his first few days fooling with bits of rock and wood in the hope of starting a fire. It was soon obvious that he lacked the skills; his hands were rough and raw. He decided to put the effort aside and explore the neighborhood.

He was looking for a line. Lines, as he had rapidly learned, were the chief arbiters of life outside the real world, a kind of universal currency that determined whether you would eat well or starve to death, stay warm or shiver all night. He had crossed dozens of them since his first encounter in Mac's office. They whisked you instantly between worlds; they guaranteed that no one could be trapped in any given locale. No matter how comfortable people might be, they rarely considered themselves at home unless they had access to at least one.

They weren't that easy to find; they were motionless, invisible, transparent. You could walk right by one for days without noticing it. Fortunately they were sensitive to light and would often glow faintly, like a window, provided it was dark enough on your side or bright enough on the other. The one in Mac's office was unusual in this respect, having been more opaque than most. The best time to look for them was at night. Poole found one at dusk on his third day at the cove.

It wasn't at all far from his camp, which he had set up on one edge of a rounded peninsula of fifty or so acres extending into the cove and pinched by marshes at its base. Until he went away to college, this island-like patch of ground had been his neighborhood, a private enclave of sixty or seventy homes with a single road leading in from the higher ground to the north. At its southern end a bar of coarse sand angled into the cove; on its far side there was a small spring where he went for water. Rather than walk all the way around the point whenever he was thirsty, he had started to cut straight through the woods, and the line was in a rocky hollow near the spring, a few yards back from the landward side of the trail.

It looked like a flat puddle of light stood on end, an inch or two shorter than himself and about a yard in width. When he first saw it, he stiffened and his heart began to race. He stood there, motionless; when it brightened as the twilight thickened, he knew he was not mistaken.

He picked his way toward it and circled it twice, studying it from every angle. Like all lines, it had a front and a back and was invisible from behind. He knelt down and examined the jumble of rocks and leaves underneath; there was no sign that it was in regular use. Trembling with excitement, he retreated a few steps to consider, although there wasn't much thinking to be done; he already knew he was going to try it, that he had to try it, that he wouldn't be able to sit still until he did. Crossing a strange line was like jumping out of an airplane — easy, but difficult. He dug up a pebble and tossed it through; it vanished without a sound.

As it happened, the line solved most of his problems. It led directly into a supermarket. Poole went there regularly, even though he considered it unsafe.

The supermarket had several peculiarities. It was quieter than a chain store ought to be. The ceiling was about two stories too high. When he climbed up one of the racks of shelves and looked around, he saw hundreds of aisles stretching away into the distance. What he didn't see was any boundary or horizon whatsoever; the room seemed to fade to infinity. If he ventured any distance from the line, he was careful to memorize each turn along the way, and he often marked them by knocking a few items to the floor.

There were people there too, though not many. In the first week he saw no more than a half dozen, and none of them twice. They were as wary as he was. It was much more common to come across the remains of a meal or a flattened carton that someone had slept on.

Though he eventually began to wander miles from the line, Poole never found the boundary he was looking for — the check-out counters, the electric doors, the parking lot. But he did discover certain internal divisions. Not far from the line the supermarket shaded into a department store featuring appliances and home furnishings. If he continued in that direction, past acres and acres of refrigerators and microwave ovens, the room abruptly opened into a vast automobile showroom. On its far side, not even visible until the halfway point, was a low green hedge where the house plants section began. He didn't know what was beyond that. It was a two-hour walk just to get there.

Poole didn't ask himself what sort of consumer public would justify an assemblage of this magnitude. The common forms of the real world were often carried over with no apparent logic; he had learned to approach them with an eye for utility. In his first few visits he found nearly all the things he was looking for — matches, tools, cookware, food, clothing, liquor, containers. He lugged them all back to his hut on the beach and stored them in a blue nylon backpacker's tent. Between the hut and the high-water mark he dug out a hearth in the sand, lined it with rocks, and equipped it with a circular rack from an outdoor grill. He stacked wood for fuel under a tarp nearby and often kept the fire going well into the night.

When he first saw Jewel, she was standing by a refrigerated meat case, holding out a steak for her dog to sniff. She noticed him immediately, even though he had just stepped out from a crossing aisle some distance away. She stared at him blankly for a moment and then tossed the steak back into the bin, turning so that he could see the long knife strapped to her hip. The dog jumped neatly into the locker after the meat and started rooting around. She settled back against the case and folded her arms, giving Poole all her attention. When she said something to the dog, his head popped up and he did likewise.

It was a standoff. Poole looked at her jeans, her black T-shirt, her heeled leather boots, her shoulder-length black hair. He had been at the cove for over a week by then and hadn't spoken to a soul. That was the main reason he kept coming back across the line.

He stepped out into the middle of the aisle and spread his hands. "Want to talk?" he called out.

After a long moment she cleared her throat. "Are you alone?"

"Yes."

The dog jumped out of the bin and took a few quick steps toward him, slowing suddenly and dropping his head to one side in order to feign interest in a spot on the floor.

"What do you want?" she asked.

"Nothing special."

"Where do you come from?"

"Across a line. It's not far from here."

"All right," she said at last. "Don't get too close."

Poole came up along the edge of the bin and leaned against its plastic rim a few steps away. The dog moved between them and sat down carefully, his gaze intense and yellow. Poole saw she had a roomy leather pouch on the hip opposite the knife.

"You're not carrying anything," she said.

"Not right now."

"Then why did you come?"

He shrugged.

She glanced down at his hands. "You've been getting some sun."

He nodded. "Every day."

They studied each other. She looked about twenty-five. Her black hair was thick and oily. Although not big, she was solid and powerfully feminine. She had a fierce, face-splitting nose, clear dark eyes, and a full, underslung mouth. Her skin looked healthy but it had a shadowy pallor.

"Who do you go with?" she asked.

"Nobody. What about you?"

"Can't you tell?"

He knew what she meant; if she belonged to any sort of tight group or clan, she wouldn't be out here alone. "This place is usually pretty quiet," he said.

"You're the first person I've seen."

"How did you get in?"

"The usual way."

This was a euphemism for some kind of death or killing. Poole was glad to hear that she wasn't a beginner, even more glad that she wasn't attached. "Still miss the real world?" he said. This was another formula, a sort of greeting.

"All the time."

He had no trouble persuading her to go back across the line with him.

Although he didn't expect any thanks for showing her the way out, he knew he wouldn't have done it for anyone. He had a certain kind of life in mind for himself at the cove and he needed someone like Jewel to complete the picture.

The sun was nearly down when they got back. He took her around the point instead of the short way through the woods. She followed a few steps behind him in the narrow, wrack-strewn lane of sand between the eelgrass and the shrubby edge of the woods, the dog hanging close by her side.

That night they grilled some chicken over the fire and drank a little wine. She cursed when the mosquitoes bit her and complained that she hadn't had a bath in a week. Before it got dark Poole showed her the hut, the storage tent, the trash pit. She wasn't at all eager to talk; when they finished eating and settled back in the coarse sand in front of the fire she seemed to forget him completely, content just to stare into the coals. The dog was restless and got up regularly to crash around in the bushes.

Poole had noticed her firm, attractive figure. He wasn't the dreamer he had once been; he knew that a woman's body operated on his mind in a predictable way.

He picked up a stick and amused himself for a while by poking at the fire. The light in the sky was nearly gone. Now and then a fish jumped in the inlet. He heard the dog come back for the last time and settle down next to her.

He was developing a past for her. All she had told him was her first name. He imagined a Greek or Italian family, a house in the suburbs, high school and college, maybe even a marriage and a child. Jobs, car payments, doctors, aunts and uncles — the works. Maybe she had liked to restore furniture or write poetry. A few secrets — a yen for a cousin, an abortion, a few thousand dollars put away. In short, a life precious to itself and a few others — a soul.

Then the break. Nightmare, panic, rage. Repeated rapes by other wanderers. After more journeys, after a death or two, she sees, in a vision, the world that made her — the mortal, vanished world. She sees it as it is — a memory. She takes a last look and locks it away.

Poole could tell at a glance that she had been through it — there was something hard and untouchable behind her eyes. He sat up with her for another few minutes, then went to bed.

When he woke up in the morning she was gone. She had slept in the storage tent; the blanket he had given her was still laid out. Chilled, stiff, he hobbled out to the edge of the cove.

She was way down at the spit, her figure gray against the blue morning, wandering beside the water's edge while the dog dawdled behind her. He went back to the hut and started building up the fire for breakfast.

He didn't see her again until late afternoon, when she trudged back to the inlet with her bag full of fresh supplies from across the line. Her hair was wet; he guessed she had washed at the spring. He was sitting in front of the hut, and she didn't look at him as she circled around the far side of the hearth.

For the next few days she was gone at first light, returning scratched and dirty shortly before sundown. "Find any?" he would ask. He assumed she was out looking for lines, the old traveler's reflex. As far as he knew there was only one. It looked to him as if she had decided this was a good place to stay for a while and was checking it for leaks. She still didn't have much to say to him.

While he was waiting, Poole mostly hung around the camp

and amused himself with his worthless fire-making equipment. He had tried every conceivable combination of rocks and he still couldn't strike a spark, though it was easy enough if he cheated a little and used an old piece of angle iron he had picked up — he learned to toss a white-hot speck with considerable accuracy into a little heap of tinder he made by crumbling dead leaves. Once in twenty or thirty tries it would singe a tiny spot — once in fifty or sixty he got a real burn. Then he bent down and tried to blow it to life. He actually produced a flame on several occasions. Jewel's dog, if they were back by then, would watch these operations with great interest.

While Jewel was away he was tempted to look through her bag in the storage tent but he never did. It seemed to him that she was playing a sort of game with him and that he would do better if he stuck to the rules.

On the fifth morning it was she, not Poole, who raked out the ashes and restarted the fire. She was squatting on her heels and warming her hands over the coals when he crawled out. "I want to live here," she said. "Do you think we can get along?"

That day he rowed her out into the middle of the cove in the dinghy. She sat facing him in a pair of khaki shorts and a light blue sweat shirt, both hands on the gunwales, her bare legs bent at the knee. The dog watched them from the beach for a while and trotted back toward the camp. It was a warm, hazy morning and the eddies from the oars barely puckered the flat water.

He showed her all the old landmarks — the mooring ground, the rocky islet, the beach where the seaplane used to come in, the site of the old yacht club dock. She rested her chin on her palm and looked where he pointed but didn't comment, only nodding and raking her hair back from her eyes. When he got tired of hearing himself talk, he shipped the oars and dried his hands on his jeans. They were well out from the shore. She caught his eye and he had the impression she was smiling at him.

"How deep is it here?" she asked.

"A little over our heads."

"I never drowned," she said. "I'm still waiting for that one."

After a moment he said, "How many?"

"Seriously?"

He nodded, feeling the weight of the heavy air.

"Several dozen." She stroked the tip of her nose gently with her ring finger.

"That's a lot."

She turned and looked out over the water, her arms crossed on her knees. "I keep hoping things will improve."

"You think so?"

She nodded, leaning over the side to dip her fingers. "This place, for instance, is an improvement. Of course it won't be summer forever." She straightened up and shook her hand dry. "How old do you think I am?"

"Early twenties."

"No — since then, I mean."

"I couldn't say."

"I've gone gray a few times. Once I was so old I went deaf and blind."

Poole didn't doubt it. A moment later, on impulse, he reached down and ran a finger along the inside of her smooth, dusky thigh.

They didn't make love that day. It was almost a week later — a dark, greenish, and interminable rainy morning. Poole had forgotten to cover the fire the night before and the ashes were soaked. They stayed in the hut and drank some brandy. The walls didn't keep the dampness out; none of his blankets was completely dry.

They had to sit up to drink. Jewel was wearing a hooded

sweat shirt, jeans, and a pair of his socks. Possibilities were mentioned and discarded — going for water, making another raid on the supermarket. It was clear that neither of them was much interested. The dog lay in the moist sand under the overhang with his head on his paws, looking up at the rain.

Jewel handed him the bottle and rolled onto her back with her arms over her head. She shut her eyes. As he looked at her, his head warmed by the brandy, he realized that this was the perfect time. He had wanted women more in his life — in fact, he felt a bit sluggish. But the rain made a difference — the steady drumming over his head sent him a powerful message, as strong in its way as her drawn-up knee or the sleepy look on her face. He was reminded of those sudden summer cloudbursts when he and a friend were working on the beach crew in high school; they would dash for the back door of the burger stand and the waitresses would let them in — the dimness, the damp clothes, the boss somewhere far away.

Something held him back; he couldn't name it exactly. A sense, perhaps, that this moment was the last of its kind — a reluctance, a sentimentality, like holding an old letter or snapshot over a wastebasket. He was still thinking about this when he noticed she was looking back at him — two dark gleams under the lashes. He knew then that he wouldn't wait any longer.

Often, in the following days, he would see her from a distance — wandering on the beach, playing with the dog, sitting on a rock at the water's edge. The mummichogs were spawning in the gravel at the spit and she could spend all morning watching them, still as a heron, the schools browning the ripples at her feet. The sun had turned her a deep tobacco color. She was never in any hurry. The bright noon light seemed to stupefy her; she stripped and stretched out full length on the sand for hours.

All the sun she soaked up came out again in heady waves that dizzied him when he touched her. Her skin was soft and thick and didn't bruise. Her sweat had a smoky smell. The middle of the day, when the sun was high and blinding, was the time when he wanted her most. His skin started to prickle; his head felt like an empty box; the glints on the water made his eyes ache.

She was always somewhere nearby, her body dark in the bright light, a motionless figure at the end of a trail in the sand. When she saw him coming, she would turn or roll over and stare back at him; if she was wearing anything, she took it off. They never retreated into the shade. Sometimes he stood over her for so long that she had to reach up and pull him down.

She had no sharp edges; she was as tight as a ripe plum. Once he entered her, he quickly became preoccupied with a certain flow of pleasure. Half blinded by the glare, drenched in her salty heat, he saw her only in bits and pieces — her stubby, childish hand, the supple curve of her hip and raised thigh. He procrastinated by turning her over and splitting her from behind, or rolling onto his back and guiding her down on top of him, her breasts dangling like big honeyed raindrops. He was always a bit shocked when it was over. The sun still beat down on him. He was aware of her weight and thickness again. If the tide was out, it was a long walk out to the water for a swim.

They barely touched each other after dark. She became a different person then — uneasy, preoccupied, never wandering far from the hut and the fire. She still slept alone in the storage tent, and she liked to have the dog right outside the entrance; sometimes he would hear her call it back if it got up during the night.

She rarely left the cove anymore; it was he who crossed the line every few days to bring back food and supplies, usually going just after breakfast and taking the dog with him. They were lazy about cooking and ate a lot of fruit and sandwiches. Poole became expert at catching blue crabs at dusk with a long-handled net and a fishhead on a string. They steamed them the same night and tossed their shells back in the long grass at the edge of the woods, where they were picked clean before morning.

He spent a lot of time rowing, and his hands roughened under his knuckles. In good weather he could get out of the cove in no time and he liked to pull well out into the open water and let the tides take him up and down the coast. There were dolphins out there, and bluefish running off the points — he once saw a brown, disk-shaped turtle as wide as the boat slide under his oar. Though he could see ten or fifteen miles in either direction, he never spotted any telltale flaw in the light that would indicate a line.

Sometimes Jewel met him at the beach when he came in. They dragged the boat up into the grass and flipped it onto the oars, then walked back to the camp together. She might have a can full of blackberries or a bucket of clams. They built up the fire and drank a little cold wine while the dog sat down next to the freezer chest where they kept the food.

The dog tolerated Poole but was clearly in love with Jewel. Sex made him nervous — so did trips to the supermarket. He never relaxed until he was back across the line and had located her again. After dark he frequently got into noisy showdowns with raccoons or opossums that came too near the tent. They learned to stay away.

Poole sometimes wondered if he was any better off than the dog. It seemed to him that Jewel was able to conceal most of herself from him almost without effort. She rarely talked about herself; it was as if she had lost the need to hear her own voice. She liked to spend all day roaming along the stretch of beach at the point, picking up shells and watching the drifting clouds of birds settle onto the flats. When the tide was coming in, she would settle down in its path and wait for it, barely moving. The sky over the cove, its changing clouds, the blues it shed on the water — these mesmerized her. She sought out the sun even on the hottest days. The dog didn't have her stamina; he could usually be found panting in the shade nearby. Poole concluded that she was intent on cultivating a certain kind of oblivion, and he left her alone most of the time.

He wandered farther; one day he rode the tide all the way down to Manhattan Island. It looked strangely flat and uninviting, and he didn't go ashore — he was more at ease on the water. His favorite occupation was following small creeks and inlets back through the marshes, their channels sometimes barely wider than the dinghy. If he went at high tide, he could often trace them all the way to their heads, those rare spots where the salt water ended and a fresh brook or streamlet bubbled in from a green tunnel between rocks. In the old days these places had mostly been buried under culverts and storm drains. Now he could see how their own forces shaped them, how the pale gray sand spread out in long tongues over their bottoms and the colder and heavier fresh water, often tinged amber, dived down and slid away just above. One morning he came upon a tight, silvery mass of alewives crammed into the last finger of the tide and milling crazily in their own excitement; when the dinghy floated over them they started darting up the stream like birds or flying knives.

Several weeks passed. The marsh grass got greener and thicker and the mosquitoes more vicious. Poole took down the hut and brought back another tent for himself, a larger one, high enough to stand in and equipped with a sort of netted-in porch. Out at the point he built a sunshade made of a light tarp lashed to a frame of trimmed saplings. He set a washing platform made of two-by-fours just above the pool at the spring.

These improvements, he was aware, were vain attempts to make the cove into something it was not. Jewel, on the contrary, didn't seem to need any further conveniences to make herself at home.

They got into the habit of rowing out to the mouth of the cove in the late afternoon, although the tides sometimes made it a chore to carry the dinghy in and out. They would bring along a bottle of wine or a few beers and drink them along the way. As the sun sank, the breeze usually dropped and the cove flattened into a perfect mirror around them; sometimes it was so quiet they could hear the wingbeats of birds passing high overhead.

He found it easier to talk to her then. Bit by bit, in no particular order, he told her his story — his first jump, the months in Mac's office, his brief return, his further wanderings. Its point, for him, lay in a certain rhythm of discovery, and in this sense he considered it far from over.

He could tell that she had heard it before. This wasn't surprising; it was everyone's story. What was different about her was that she didn't present herself as a victim or castaway; her own history or future didn't seem to occupy her in the least. What interested her were the sights and textures of the cove — the tides, the wildlife, the skies, and shorelines. He could rarely lure her into any discussion about what had happened to them or why.

This selflessness intrigued him. He wondered if it was as genuine as it seemed; he wondered if there were old wounds underneath. She wasn't entirely open with him. She wouldn't tell him, for instance, why she stayed away from the line or why she wouldn't leave her tent at night. She had a strong streak of sensuality, but it was almost totally passive. It seemed to him that she had adapted to adverse conditions with a sort of mental shell, a pretense; she had scaled down the world to the present moment and her immediate surroundings.

Poole could see how you might need skills like these after several dozen lifetimes. It was one way to recapture your own life. And although he never learned how to draw her out, there were times when his ramblings seemed to strike something in her, and she would offer something in his own terms.

One afternoon, while they were sitting at the beach at the opening and waiting for the tide to rise a little before heading back, she drew him a map in the sand. It looked like one of those time exposures of the night sky surrounding the polestar — dozens of short streaks circling a fixed center. Poole had never seen it before.

"I'm cheating a little," she said, showing him a rust-colored pebble and tossing it in the middle. "Can you guess what that is?"

"The real world."

She smiled. "We think alike. Now show me where we are."

Poole, sitting cross-legged, reached out and pointed at one of the streaks farthest from the center.

"What's that?" she asked.

"It's a line — the one we've been using."

"OK — now suppose you started there and wanted to get back to the middle. How would you do it?"

He looked at her for a moment. "You'd have to cross all those other lines in between."

"Have you tried it?"

"I actually did it once — when I came back from Mac's office."

"How do you explain that?"

He hesitated. "I think I was pretty close already."

"Wasn't it only your first line?"

"Uh-huh."

She reached out and made a wide stirring motion over the drawing. "Now suppose this whole thing is turning like a wheel. That means anything that's loose is going to keep sliding farther and farther out. How could you fight that?"

"You'd have to keep crossing lines in the opposite direction."

"Retrace your steps?"

"Sort of."

"You'd need some kind of compass; you'd have to know which way was in." She looked down at her work. "I knew a man who said he had done it. A long time ago."

"Huh."

"He said that as he got closer there were more and more lines. They were hot, too, so bright they blinded him. He said it was like trying to walk into a furnace."

"I've heard stories too," Poole said.

"Let me finish. Eventually he couldn't see anymore. But by then he was so close he could feel a wind blowing past him, and he just kept walking into it. His hair burned off — he actually caught fire. But just before he got swept out again, he said, he touched it — the wall, I mean. The wall between him and the real world. He just kind of grazed it. He said it was the scariest thing that had ever happened to him."

"You believed this?"

"Not really — but Rocker, you should have seen his eyes. They had this smoky, sooty color. Even the whites looked scorched."

Poole didn't answer. Her own, he noticed, were bright and clear.

She smoothed out the drawing. "OK, now you make me one."

He had to think about it first. When he was ready, he tossed out the pebble and quickly drew two stick figures standing side by side, their eyes shut. Over their heads he placed two large balloons and inserted the pebble in the space where they overlapped. He drew a line under the two figures. "OK," he said. "Explain."

Leaning on one arm, her legs drawn up, she twirled a bit of straw between her thumb and finger. "That's you and me," she said finally.

"Correct."

"We look like we're asleep, but we're thinking . . . we're thinking about the same thing, the pebble."

"Keep going."

"The pebble is . . ." The straw stopped moving. "The pebble is this place, the cove." She glanced up at him.

"Exactly. So where's the real world?"

She paused, frowning. "It's the space outside the balloons. We're still in it. But we can't see it. We're cut off — we're dreaming."

"So how do we get back?"

"We wake up."

"Sounds easy, doesn't it?"

She was still looking at the drawing. "This shows you haven't been here for long. I mean, you really haven't accepted it."

"Should I?"

"According to this, we never really left."

She had a point. He wasn't sure whether he wanted to pursue it. He looked over her body at the dark skin of the Sound.

"But we did leave," Jewel said. "We're different now. I don't think we're going to get back."

"So what are we supposed to do with our lives?"

"What were we ever supposed to do?"

He looked down at her again. And though he shook his head and snorted, as if her simplicity amazed him, he was beginning to wonder if he was the one who had more to learn.

Now and then she tried to sympathize with his sense of loss. She said it would never really go away, though as time went on he would probably get used to it — it would turn into something precious. Annoyed, Poole answered that it would be better if people didn't remember, that it was just this memory that made it impossible for them to start over, since they knew they could never be so alive again. He used the word ghosts. Ghosts, he said, are former human beings left over from the end of the world. Ghosts couldn't die or be born or give birth. We are ghosts, he continued, and we ought to just fade away. When he got into this mood, she didn't argue with him.

Poole still got the bulk of their groceries from a short block of aisles about a ten-minute walk from the line. No matter how much he carted off, there was always more; if he emptied a shelf onto the floor, he would come back and find it full. The whole place, he concluded, could grow back like a starfish. One day he took a hammer to a long row of glass freezer cases just to see how they would react. They all repaired themselves before his next visit. He found this less magical than irritating—just another reminder of how far he was from home.

He had a lookout near the line, a high perch on top of a steel rack full of five-gallon bottles of spring water. From there he could see over everything. The rectangular ceiling lights stretched away in even rows in every direction, as if he were standing at the center of an enormous spoked wheel. A sparse forest of thin white pillars, multiplying in the distance, grew out of the aisles. This was a different sort of infinity than a night sky full of stars. The silence was by no means complete. If he sat still for five minutes the faint and ubiquitous machine hum was sure to be interrupted by distant shiftings and settlings of merchandise. The thing he never heard was a human voice.

He didn't find nearly as many signs of use as he once had—it was as if something had driven everyone away. When he mentioned this to Jewel, she said that there was probably a killer in the neighborhood and that it might be a good idea to stay on the near side of the line for the time being; they had what they needed. Poole didn't take her advice, but he stopped bringing the dog with him and he made a point of removing all evidence of his passage from the area around the line, scattering the boxes he had stacked nearby and sweeping up the sand and dirt he had tracked in. If there was indeed a nut roaming around, Poole counted on seeing him first and not staying for a second look.

As it happened, she was right. One morning, wandering farther than usual, he found a man who had been shot through the chest sitting on the floor, propped up against a bank of shelves. Tall and haggard, he was dressed like a weekend athlete—sneakers, gym shorts, a T-shirt. Although his face had been hacked up and his gut cut open, Poole wasn't particularly shocked. This is a message, he thought, a protest lodged not so much against its victim as against a world that lent even the most brutal acts so little resonance. What disturbed him most was a pencil drawing he found on a scrap of cardboard by the man's knee — a fluid and expert sketch of a woman, a particular woman, arranging flowers in a pitcher and looking out a window, as if waiting for someone who was already late. It looked as if the man had been working on it when he was surprised; it was only half finished.

Poole spent the next hour or so wrapping the body in a couple of bed sheets and carting it back to the cove. That afternoon he and Jewel dug a grave in a small clearing just behind the point. None of this, however, eased the queasy feeling in his stomach, and he had a bad moment toward the end, after they had lowered the body in, covered it with a thin blanket, and scattered a few stalks of goldenrod on top. Jewel asked him if he wanted to say anything. As he stood there beside the drying heaps of sand, trying to remember the appropriate phrases, it occurred to him that the man in the grave was in essence no different from himself and that neither of them had been able to resign himself to life after death — hence the pencil sketch, hence this foolish effort to revive the old mystery. He began to feel ungrateful then — his throat thickened and he nearly blurted out a few choice sarcasms. Jewel surprised him; she had come up beside him. "Stranger," she said, her voice low and clear, "may you find hope and peace and an end to your troubles. Forgive us. We never knew you." She bent down, picked up a little sand, and tossed it in the grave.

The cove seemed different after that. The tides cycling through it, peaking an hour later each day, helped to convince him that time was passing. He spent hours sitting alone in the stone-filled hollow by the line, running a finger along its smooth inner rim.

Jewel had said that reality is what you get used to. Reality, for him, was the place he had come from.

He liked to take a stick and poke it across the line, watching the border of apparent nothingness swallow it right up to his hand, then give it up again, untouched. A line was such a small and harmless-looking thing, not much different from a door or window, and yet it was the mark of the plague, a tiny crater that contained whole catastrophe. It hovered there, passive and indiscriminate, waiting for whatever was pushed into it. Poole thought he knew why Jewel liked to stay away. A line, he had decided, was like an orifice or sphincter through which drained that sense of settled limits so necessary to life.

He could also see easily enough why Jewel liked the cove. He liked it himself and yet knew now that it was wasted on him. He wasn't yet ready for it; it asked too much. "Stay here," it said soothingly, "enjoy yourself, imagine that there is no other place than this." In that respect it wasn't much different from the world he had come from, where most people managed to live their lives within the apparent boundaries and it was considered misguided and even unhealthy to concern oneself much with what lay beyond them — good advice, no doubt, for those who had never left.

But now, whether he was floating in the dinghy in the middle of the cove, coaxing another crab to glide up to his net, or pleasuring himself in Jewel's sun-drenched and anything-but-ghostly arms, he was conscious of a certain displacement of effort, as if a part of him were saying, "This may be nice, but I am not deceived." He was like a sleeper disturbed in the middle of the night by strange footsteps in the hall. Or like a puppet who notices for the first time in his life the fine threads attached to his limbs. He could almost wish that there weren't any line in the hollow behind the spring. Soon, he knew — if it lasted — he would be crossing it for the last time. There had to be other lines in the supermarket; he would cross them also. This was his side of the bargain, his token of good faith, his proof that he would not now and maybe never step aside and say, "This is good enough — now let me be." Had he lived that way once? Maybe he had; maybe he thought he had sealed up all the lines. Now they all called out to him together, saying, "Get up and leave your comfort — why stop now?" Calling him deeper into the woods.

Once he had made up his mind, a deadly calm descended on him. He knew that he was afraid, deeply afraid, but his fear couldn't touch him. He deliberately allowed himself to stay a few days longer.

One morning after breakfast he asked Jewel if she wanted to row out to the opening with him. A short while later she met him at the spit in her khaki shorts, a lunch packed in a bag over her shoulder. The dog knew the routine; he danced around happily until they set the dinghy down in the shallows, then hopped in and clambered over the seat to the bow. Poole sat down at the oars and Jewel pushed off, stepping smoothly over the transom as they glided away.

She had just washed her hair and it was still heavy and wet. She sat sideways to make room for the oars, her body rocking a little with each pull, the shadow of her chin shifting across her throat. The shoreline slowly dwindled behind her. It was a bright day and the morning mist shone like exhaled steam on the water. Now and then Poole held the oars and looked over his shoulder to check his bearing.

They beached behind the bar at the entrance and dragged the boat up above the high-water line, then dawdled along the outer shore for an hour or so, talking about nothing in particular. When they came back, they persuaded the dog to dig for water at the height of the beach. It was about a foot down, cool and fresh, and they crouched down beside the hole and brought it up in their cupped hands.

Their usual spot was a broad shelf of peach-colored granite

on the ocean side of the low bluff that dominated the opening. Thanks to a few windblown pines it was partly in shade. After a quick plunge to cool off, they climbed up onto it. When the dog saw them settle there he nosed around for a minute and lay down just below.

"What was your wife like?" Jewel asked.

Poole was surprised; he had been thinking about her. "Small," he said. "Stubborn."

"Were you faithful to her?"

He glanced at Jewel. She was sitting a little behind him, leaning back on her hands with one knee drawn up. Her eyes moved into his.

"Yes, I was," he said.

She looked away. After a moment she said, "You're leaving, aren't you?"

"Yes."

"When?"

"Tomorrow morning."

"Why?"

"This place doesn't seem real to me."

She sat up and looked out at the water, frowning slightly, her arms wrapped around her knees.

"You want to go with me?"

She turned to him again. "I was an experiment, wasn't I?"

"Huh?"

"You wanted to slow things down. To see if you could start over." When he began to answer, she said, "No, no, that's all right — I'm flattered. And you know something? I liked it here too. I liked the smell of the creek at low tide. I liked the way your eyes got a little sugary when — " She hugged her knees and looked up into the tree. "Little things. Things you don't forget."

Poole waited a few moments. "What'll you do?"

She smiled crookedly. "Oh, I have a lover too. Only mine isn't as far away as yours. Mine is hot on my trail." She reached past him and over the edge of the rock to cuff the dog lightly. "Isn't that right, pea brain?" Annoyed, the dog sat up and gave her a reproachful look.

"You see," she said quickly, "I was using you too. This place is your place, not mine. So I hitched on and had a nice little time. Now I have to take my medicine." She crossed her legs under her and brushed the sand off her knees.

It seemed to Poole that the air had grown still. Above the scant shade overhead the sky was hot and white.

"If you stick around," she said, "you'll see what I'm talking about. Sometime after dark. Tonight."

After a moment he said, "I don't get it."

"No? Then you'd better leave before he gets here."

"Who?"

"My lover. Who else?" She seemed to enjoy his confusion. She leaned back and spread her arms, glancing down at herself. "Look at me — all summer fattening in the sun." She touched one of her full breasts. "Made to please, as Grandma would say." She shook her head, smiling again. "No, I won't be lonely tonight." She sat up and raked her damp hair back with both hands, exposing the egg-pale pockets under her arms. "I want you to take the dog — I'm giving him to you."

"Why tonight?"

"Because."

"Maybe I could help."

She shook her head. "You can do one of two things: you can leave before dark or you can stay. You'd better not stay."

Neither of them spoke for a few moments.

"I want to know what the hell you're talking about."

Something in his tone made the dog glance up. Jewel stared off to one side, then grabbed the lunch bag, pulled out a white T-shirt, and quickly put it on. When she saw he was still waiting, she leaned forward and rested a hand on his knee.

"Rocker, look," she said, "you used to live here, right? When you were growing up — and now it's come back to you. Well, tonight something's coming back to me. Get it? Only it's coming as a person and that person will be jealous if he finds you here. It'll be worse — much worse. So I'm asking you to stay away — come back tomorrow if you want. If you don't, he'll know you're here and you'll be sorry."

Her hand was still on his knee. "All right?" she said softly.

"Why tonight?" he asked again.

"Because you're leaving."

"But you said it didn't matter — you said he'd come anyway."

"He will. This place is yours, remember? It's part of you. But you're through with it now and so am I. I can feel it — that's how I know." She seemed to look for something in his eyes — an assent, a recognition. He didn't answer. Stymied, she sat back on her hands. "The guy who's coming tonight — he's part of me. I know all about him. He couldn't get in before, but now he can. He'll wait until dark. Then he'll come."

"What'll he do?"

"Take me away." Her voice was dull and precise. "Away from you. Back to myself." She looked sideways at Poole.

"Was he part of your former life?"

"Like this place?" She shook her head. "I'm not like you. I've been away too long."

Poole looked around, as if seeking help. Down the beach a clump of gulls were squabbling over something soft and stringy, their wings half raised, their cries indignant.

"You think I can do it?" he said. "Find my way back?"

"No — not really."

A moment later she sat up brusquely and unpacked the lunch bag, pouring each of them a paper cup full of iced wine from the thermos. She gave the dog a big hunk of smoked turkey.

"How old are you?" he said.

"I don't know. Many lifetimes, I guess. There's only so much you can remember." She dug into an orange with her thumbnail. "To me, for instance, you look pretty young. Not physically — it's a question of experience. You've still got that I-can't-believe-my-own-eyes look."

She started flinging bits of bright peel off the rock. "Look," she said, "just for fun, I'm going to pretend I'm you. You tell me if I get it right." She crossed her arms in her lap and gazed thoughtfully at a spot somewhere over the water. "OK, here goes." She returned to work, digging into the orange.

"In a way, nothing that happens here matters to me — I can't take it seriously. Endless supermarkets. Holes in space. It just doesn't make sense. So I say to myself, 'Well, I'll play along for now — I'll humor it.' But I know it's not right." She held out a piece of the orange for him; he took it. "This is a terrible thing, not being able to believe in my own life. A true nightmare. I can't get my feet on the ground. And yet I still have to go on. I still get hungry — I still need a place to stay.

"So it becomes a question of keeping faith. I say to myself, 'I know who I am. I know where I come from. I'm going to ride this out.' In other words, I reject all this — I deny it. None of it's real, I think, so why get upset?

"So I roam around, stretch my legs, see the sights. Deep inside me, where it can't be touched, is this refusal — I'm not really here. But as time goes by and nothing changes, I begin to get a little nervous. Nobody promised me a ride back. All I've got is my own confidence. I start to question it. Who's to say that the place I come from is still just around the corner? Maybe I don't have all the answers. Maybe I don't have any of them."

Poole wasn't tempted to interrupt. He watched her throat move as she swallowed a little wine.

"OK," she said. "So I'm marking time. I'm hoping something will turn up. Meanwhile I'm getting pretty good at making myself comfortable. I find this spot on the water where I lived half my life. I bring this girl in to keep me company. So we settle down together and pretend we're doing just fine. And you know what? It works." She smiled. "I actually start to like it." She picked up a paper napkin and started cleaning her fingers.

"But that's a problem too, isn't it? Because there's a little bargain I have with myself. It says that as long as I remember where I come from and put that above everything, then I still have a chance — I still might make it back. But if I let go, if I forget — even for an instant — then . . . who knows?" She paused. "So I'm torn. I want to stay, but I can't. I don't want to leave, but I have to. Finally I can't take it any longer. It's time to hit the road."

Their eyes met.

"What about you?" he asked. "Don't you want to go back?"

"Can't you tell?"

"No — I can't."

She looked down and chewed her lip, as if suppressing a private excitement. Then, abruptly, she straightened one leg and dumped it in his lap. She tossed her head back. "That's me," she said brightly. "Touch me." She had a playful, impish look.

When he glanced down at her tanned foreleg, she cocked it back slightly and slid her foot into his crotch, cupping him. "That feels good," she said. "Real good. You know why? Because I'm fading now — I'm going the other way."

She pulled her leg back and crossed it beneath her. "Rocker," she said, "you're different from me — a lot different. It's because you're still so close to the world. Get it?" She leaned toward him, her eyes large and earnest. "Time passes, even here. You only have so much. You get worn away — you get hungry for how it used to be. When you scent a little fresh blood, you just can't help but beg for it."

Poole stared at her. She looked out at the water, as if trying to settle herself. "It's all right," she said. "You see, Rocker, you're just starting out here. The past is still strong in you. You made this place out of what you remembered — it was your desire that put the flesh on my bones. This is a gift you have and you're going to have it for a long time." She turned to him. "In time, ages from now, you'll be like me — your light will fade out. You'll be a shadow — you'll live in the shadows. Like me, you'll need someone else to take you back again. That's how it is. That's how it's always been."

A moment later she hopped down off the rock and shaded her eyes, looking down the beach. "Let's go somewhere," she said. "I can't sit any more." The dog got up and watched her stretch.

Stunned, Poole swallowed the rest of his wine and climbed down after her. She pointed to a low bit of land floating in the grainy mist out near the center of the Sound. "What's that?"

"Captain's Island."

"Let's go there, OK?"

It was a mile or so out. He let her do the rowing. The tide carried them through the opening and they slid easily across the surface. It was one of the close, glassy days when the wind drops to nothing and every rock or bar lies beached on its own reflection. Jewel leaned into her work, her bare heels braced against the crossrib and the oarlocks clanking. Poole was quiet. He watched a pale bit of vegetable crud float in the half inch of water under her seat.

I don't believe in my own life. I can't take it seriously. Not at all — he took it much too seriously. That was the killer — this odor of real life that clung to him even here. He noted how Jewel's locked knees stiffened as she pulled. Very expressive knees, he thought, very lifelike, very attractive in their sturdy way. When she saw him watching her, she grinned and took an extra deep stroke.

The bow scraped to a stop and the dog leaped off. Jewel frowned at a broken blister and shook her hand. The beach was wide, hard-packed, and glistening. Five or six crows lifted out of the brush at the island's center and flapped away, complaining.

He and Jewel rolled a rock onto the painter and started across the flats, their shadows dim under the heavy sky.

"Here we are," he said.

"Uh-huh." She had rolled up her hands in her T-shirt.

"Here," he said. "Here is here and here is where we are."

They walked a little farther.

"You want to know something?" he said.

"What?"

"Bad news travels fast. But nobody ever told me what you did back there."

"Told you what?"

"That we just keep sinking. That we're drifting farther and farther from the world."

Her arm brushed his. "It's a gradual thing. You might never even notice."

The rippled sand was the color of old canvas. Poole started kicking at its watery skin, sending up showers of bright droplets. "Are you afraid?" he asked.

"Of what?"

"Of tonight."

"A little. It goes pretty quick."

"What's his name?"

"He doesn't have one." She looked around and spotted the dog way up at the top of the beach. "Maybe he did once." Poole became absorbed in watching the mirrored water shatter as his splashings dropped into it. "The thing to remember," she said quietly, "is that your mind is in charge now. It dictates. Any life you can imagine is the life you can live."

"Then there's nothing outside of me."

"No — I wouldn't say that." Her voice had a relaxed, patient quality. "It's just that your dreams are stronger now. They spread out around you. You can live in them — so can I."

"So I'm locked up in my own head."

"Weren't you always?"

Rather than agree, he said nothing.

"And the best thing," she went on, "is that the dreams stay real. Someone can live here after we're gone."

"I don't like it," he said. "It's like quicksand — it just swallows you."

He thought he heard her sigh. "What is it?"

"To me, this is what you are." Her nod took in the empty distances around them. "All this space, all this water, this stillness — this is what's inside you. I could never make a place like this."

"Why not?"

"I'm too old." She paused. "What you'll find is that your life is going to take a certain shape. Some things are going to haunt you — things you cared about, things you were afraid of. They'll catch up with you here."

"Like what?"

"You'd know better than me."

The rest of the afternoon had a strange, swollen quality. The sun sank behind clouds and reappeared, bloody and diminished, in a melon-colored sky. Although there was nothing left to do except get in the dinghy and row home, it was as if they had agreed to draw out the moment to its greatest possible length, guaranteeing by their mutual silence and slow circuit along the water's edge that not a minute would pass by without its weight being registered and felt. The dog followed a few steps behind, patient and incurious, stopping now and then to nose their footprints or gaze out at the empty water. The high part of the island wasn't much larger than a city block, and they circled it a half dozen times, glancing up with blank eyes at the same glassy horizons they had studied so closely and unseeingly the last time around. After a long lull the tide started to flow in around the bars. It probed the low spots, seized them, and spread inward, cutting off the higher banks and drowning them one by one. Poole was very much aware that before this water retreated again he would have seen Jewel for the last time. She had told him more than once that she couldn't go with him, that it was impossible even if she wanted to. She looked strange to him now, her figure dark against the weakening light — it was hard to believe he had spent so many hours touching her, kissing her, guiding himself into her in search of some still-virgin thrill, and watching her face as if it might tell him whether he loved her. At this moment her future seemed to him more seductive than his own. He knew where he was going: in a few hours he would cross into the supermarket, stay as long as it took to find another line, cross that one, look for another, not at all convinced he was heading anywhere in particular but unwilling to call it quits. In the meantime she would return to that place and that lover which had for her the same importance his own home had for him, the difference being that for her they were not the object of a search but, rather, untiring pursuers. She was, if he could believe her, the survivor of several centuries of exile and wandering. Maybe after all that time a certain pattern had begun to emerge. Maybe she knew what was coming because her life was like a melody or phrase that never ceased repeating itself. The choice, then, lay between resisting this current or trying to conform to it. She had apparently settled on the latter, judging by the thoughtful but not disquieted look on her face, as if she were remembering earlier and more traumatic encounters at this particular kink in the road.

Whatever the reason, he could tell that she was withdrawing from him now, drinking in this last glimpse of the mussel-blue water and the low shores opposite as if she had already left them far behind. Now and then she took his hand and pressed it between hers or stopped him and moved in between his arms. The thought that it would have to be the last time made him reluctant to give in. But she, for once, persisted, seeking out his mouth with her own and leaning her weight into his until his breath started to thicken. She lay down naked on her back in the dry, soft sand above the tideline and spread her legs. Poole pushed into her just once and came almost without moving. It hurt, and yet neither of them flinched; it was as if they were killing something. The dog lifted his head and let go a long, unearthly howl.

The dinghy was already afloat in two feet of water when they finally waded out to it. For a moment Poole thought she wasn't going to get in. The dog had the same idea and stood waiting, the water just up to his chest. In that moment Poole had time to imagine an empty island deserted in the deepening twilight except for a small figure sitting on the beach and looking off toward the mainland, her eyes fixed on the spot where a manlike shadow had just slipped into the water and was swimming toward her with long, steady strokes.

He left the cove shortly after sunset. He didn't go far. An hour later he was sitting on a stepstool in the supermarket, his back to the line, facing down the narrow aisle that led into it. He had put a chain collar on the dog and tied him with a piece of nylon rope to one of the nearby shelves. His pack rested upright on the checked linoleum floor; protruding from it, within easy reach, was a chisel-ended tire iron.

He had chosen this spot so that anyone who wanted to cross over would have to push past him to get to the line. He didn't know if anyone was coming. Jewel hadn't said that her visitor would have to enter here or anywhere else, and he had purposely avoided questioning her about it. He was wearing a watch for the first time in months, and every few minutes he glanced down at it as if to assure himself that it was still going.

The dog was tied a little farther up the aisle. Captive, unhappy, he nosed along the black rubber baseboards with the leash dragging along behind.

Poole didn't intend to interfere with whatever was scheduled to take place between Jewel and her guest, if in fact there was any such person. It was to relieve his anxiety on this second point that he had posted himself here. Much of what she had said to him in the past few weeks was difficult to believe, and not only because it contradicted his own experience. If she was right on this point, however, he would have to give some of the others more consideration. He was like a man who has been told by a likely-looking stranger that his house has been built over a soft spot and might collapse at any moment; though he could cite any number of reasons why this was impossible, he saw no harm in going down to the basement for another look.

He planned to sit in front of the line for the rest of the night. If nothing happened, he would cross back over in the morning and look for Jewel. Whether he found her or not, he could then leave for the second time without feeling that he had missed a chance to learn something.

He shifted his weight on the stool's ridged rubber cover, his back aching a little, and looked around. The aisle hemmed him in closely on either side. At both ends it opened into larger crossing aisles, each of them with a solid bank of display shelves on the far side. High over his head a row of plastic light panels glowed in the ceiling. The line itself floated invisibly only inches behind his back; he could look across it by turning and ducking his head through.

The aisle around him was devoted exclusively to household cleaning products. The three high shelves on his right held rank after brilliant rank of boxes of laundry soap in painful fluorescent colors, the names all familiar to him — Tide, All, Fab, Wisk, Cheer — and down below, the inevitable blue-and-white jugs of Clorox. These continued to the end of the aisle, their logos garbled by the narrowing perspective. On his left the middle shelf had been taken out, and the pegboard bristled with dozens of protruding hooks hung with plastic toilet brushes, pole-handled sponge mops, and packs of scouring pads, dust cloths, and rubber gloves. The air had a sweetish smell.

He picked up a weighty aerosol can of rug shampoo from a shelf next to him and examined the instructions. A cartoon panel showed an elegantly poised female wrist holding the can upside down and squirting foam onto a pile carpet. A warning, DO NOT PUNCTURE OR INCINERATE, was printed along the bottom. He flipped the can over once, swung it back behind his hip, and lofted it high into the air to his left, where it hung for an instant before crashing down unseen a few aisles over. He could tell it had taken several items with it.

No, Poole thought, I won't lack for anything here.

By midnight he had been waiting for over three hours. He had got up a half-dozen times to stretch his legs, never venturing farther than the end of the aisle. After he had a few turns like this, the dog realized that he wasn't going anywhere and lay down facing the stool, his head between his paws, his mustard-colored eyes mournful and resigned.

A series of yawns exercised Poole's stubbly face. Restless, he was tempted to cross over again and go back to the camp; it was possible that whatever was going to happen had happened hours earlier and that it was pointless to stew here any longer. Jewel had said that her visitor would know it if he was anywhere in the cove, and for this reason he had amused himself for a while by sticking parts of his body across the line, as if trying to bait something out. Nothing happened. It was dark over there; ducking in was like plunging his head into cool black water.

It seemed to him that his life had already taken "a certain shape," as Jewel said — a shape that hadn't changed in any significant respect since that first day in Mac's office. Something had happened to him there — after all this time, that was all he knew. He had hoped to piece it together. He had even imagined there was a reason behind it, that sooner or later a guide would appear to take him in hand and point the way forward. Delusion. The days piled up, the questions multiplied; nothing was resolved.

Some minutes later the dog lifted its head and looked at him in a curious way. It took a few moments for Poole to realize that it wasn't looking at him but rather over his shoulder. When he turned, he got a shock; he jumped backward off the stool and lunged for the tire iron. A moment later he was crouched low in the middle of the aisle, stiff and trembling, the iron pointed at the line.

It was acting very strangely. Masses of glowing yellow specks were rippling across its surface like pollen on water. Here and there they congealed into a glistening crust. They were thickest in the center but were nowhere too bright to look at. They boiled all over the line, hectic and weirdly sentient, like a swarm of bees. They didn't make a sound.

The dog had backed up also and was standing motionless behind him. Poole had never seen a line act like this before. He was convinced that something was going to come through and that when it did he would have to stick it with the iron. He retreated a few more steps, nearly stumbling over the dog. And while he stood there, fascinated, the brilliant dust started to fade. It showered less often to the edge of the line. The waves that rippled it lost their opacity. Before long, the glitter came and went in an area no larger than a dinner plate. Soon after, it vanished for good, and he was looking straight through to the other end of the aisle.

Poole dropped his shoulders and exhaled an appreciative obscenity. He thought he knew what had happened. Something had used the line — something had used it to cross into the cove.

He didn't react immediately. The question, of course, was whether he was going to go in after it. The longer he waited, the more reasonable it seemed to wait a little longer. There was no one watching him except the dog, and the dog didn't know what to do either; he shifted his feet anxiously and licked his nose.

Poole knew that if he stayed here and did nothing, he would

have to pay a price. Why else had he sat here all night if not for a chance like this? To go this far and stop, to take so many pains to set the stage and then turn and walk away — a few more showings like this, and he could give up supposing there was any doubt about what he would do.

He took the iron and the flashlight. When the dog saw that he was going to be left behind, he started barking savagely and lunging at the cord. Poole ignored him and stepped over into silence.

He stood in the hollow and waited for his eyes to adjust, the line glowing dimly beside him. In a minute or so he could make out scraps of starlight through the leaves overhead. He didn't hear anything beyond the usual nocturnal rustlings and his own measured breathing. The ground under his feet had a wormy, nighttime smell.

He groped his way past the spring and down to the edge of the marsh. His emergence alarmed some foraging animal; it snorted and shuffled back into the brush. The tide was ebbing but still covered most of the cove. It soaked up the little available light — it was brighter than the sky and outlined the low shore ahead of him. A few mosquitoes rose up toward his face. By every indication this night was no different from any other he had spent here.

He didn't hurry. He was already wondering if he had been wrong about the line — if the brief shimmer pointed only to a temporary imbalance. On occasion a line could reverse itself, giving access to several locales at once; that was what had happened to the one in Mac's office, so that he stepped across it into his own bedroom. He had assumed that the one in the hollow was doing something similar and that Jewel's visitor had taken advantage. He decided that if he found nothing moving at the camp, he would turn around and come back.

But as he was crossing the wide stretch of beach at the head of the point he noticed something that made him stop short and forget any such hopes. A few steps to his right, in hard, damp sand that must have been under water only minutes earlier, there was a set of tracks parallel to his own.

He had walked that sand often enough to know that it barely gave way even when he had a ten-gallon water bottle in each hand — and yet the tracks had broken deep into it. He looked up and scanned the empty beach around him. There was a feeling of exchange, of mutual recognition, as if this moment had been expressly prepared for him. He could see a long way, however, and there was nothing in sight. He went down to take a closer look.

He almost clicked on the flashlight, not so much for what it could show him as to file a similar notice of entry, so that anyone who happened to be watching would know that he also was willing to make his presence visible. He decided against it. He glanced up; the star-pitted sky glowed weakly at its edges.

Standing above one of the tracks, the flashlight and the tire iron weighing down his arms, he noticed that it looked not so much like the record of a shape pressing from above as the collapsed hole left after a small explosion. There was loose sand scattered haphazardly around the rim of an oblong crater conceivably faithful to the length and width of a foot and with a bottom, although in shadow and obscured by crumblings from either side, that seemed to shelve down in the direction of motion — away from the line, toward the camp. Bemused, conscious of an almost scientific detachment, he placed his own sneaker beside the track and pressed his weight on it. When he stepped away he saw that its kidney-shaped print, although clean and unblurred, did not even break the surface. He also considered it noteworthy that the tracks had several yards of untouched sand between them, as if whoever made them had the stride of a hurdler and was wasting no time. He looked up again. The dim water gently brimmed along the beach.

I ought to hear something now, he thought, staring at the low shoulder ahead where the tracks curved into the inlet. He was shivering, as if cold. Though he had been living on this beach for several months he felt as if he were trespassing on someone's private domain.

After he had stood there for a while without noticing anything further he began to get impatient. It was clear to him that he would soon have to pick up the trail and follow it into the camp, but he wished there was some more useful way to spend the minute or two remaining to him other than in waiting for some further cue or signal when it was obvious there was no reason to expect one. Do it now, he thought—just do it.

He didn't try to conceal his approach. Once he turned the corner he was in full view of the campsite, but he went on, steady and unhurried, staggering a little when he hit the softer sand, his eyes targeted on those pale shapes which he knew to be the tents but which at this distance looked more like old snowdrifts or boulders in high grass. Then the sand ended and his feet were loud and clumsy in the matted seaweed along the edge of the marsh. What he was doing wasn't walking; it was more like a continuous and repeatedly thwarted effort to fall on his face. Each time, at the last moment, his rear leg swung forward of its own volition to delay the catastrophe by one more step.

He was over halfway there when a few sounds began to reach him—sharp little mews and sighs that seemed to originate at the flat spot in front of his tent, where unless he was mistaken there was something struggling on the ground. He didn't stop to listen. He didn't stop at all until he was only a few steps away, when he was more or less certain that the little cries were coming from Jewel and that she was lying on her back under the pale, rocking body of her lover, who was propped up on his arms with his head hanging between his shoulders. Whether they saw him or not, they ignored him.

In normal circumstances Poole would have turned and

walked away, but he didn't do that now. It was so dark that he still wasn't quite sure what was happening. He wanted to get a look at the man's face, as if he had come for no other reason. And it didn't seem as if either of them was distracted by his presence. He could hear two voices now, two sets of lungs, one harsher and more raucous than the other.

So this, he thought, is what she meant when she said her lover was coming. Although their bodies were fluid as water in the dimness, he was sure that he wasn't mistaken. He could hear his hips slapping against hers like wake slapping against a sea wall. They were both breathing harder now, almost gasping, as if they had glimpsed the end and were racing to meet it.

He had retreated a step and was about to turn and head back for the line when he saw the man reach out to one side and apparently grab something that was lying there, then raise his arm high and bring it down hard near the base of Jewel's neck with an ugly meaty noise. He did it twice — the second time it cut short a gurgling cry that seemed to Poole to be different in quality from the others — there was a note of real distress. His hand tightened on the flashlight and clicked it on.

It threw a bright glare like a spotlight on both of them. Poole saw Jewel's knife, the same one she had worn that first day at the market, raised high in the man's fist. He saw it come down again twice into her slick and bloody chest. Her head jerked back each time and she coughed, choking. In the harsh circle of light her blood was a shocking red.

Poole dropped the flashlight and charged. There was no impact; he came down hard on his elbows and a moment later was standing crouched over Jewel, her body between his legs. The man had disappeared. Poole hadn't even seen him jump away. He peered into the dark, listening, the iron raised. Jewel was struggling weakly underneath him, one hand groping at his pants leg.

Poole started cursing mechanically and hurriedly unbuttoning his shirt. He tore it off and leaned down to tamp it around Jewel's throat; her blood soaked it instantly. He knew she was dying; there was no way she could live. His wrist bumped against something and he realized the knife was still in her chest. He stood up and started swinging the iron blindly, cutting the air, praying that it would hit something. Then he noticed the flashlight again. It was still on; it lit up a narrow spike of sand. He was about to reach for it when a hand landed flat on his chest and pushed him backward with such force that he tripped and fell over. By the time he scrambled up, the light had bobbed off the ground, advanced a step or two, and was shining full on the man's face — it took Poole a moment to realize he had pointed it at himself. Then he saw the knife, the same knife, come into the light. It leveled itself across the man's throat and slid away with a jerk. Blood jumped out as if vomited. He's dead, Poole thought calmly — he's killed himself. The man had fair skin and fair hair and was staring straight at him with his shocked blue eyes. Then he fell and dropped the flashlight. It landed between them and lit up a patch of empty sand.

A few minutes later Poole was still looking at it; there were tiny moths crawling over the bulb.

He had a vision then. It was very lifelike, very persuasive. In it he turned and left the bodies where they had fallen and started back toward the line. He walked stiffly, his feet awkward in the dark, the stars overhead jogging at each step. As he went, he thought how strange it was to have this sensation of motion, of forward progress, when in fact he was still standing over the flashlight and hadn't moved an inch. He was going to cross the line again, but this time it wouldn't take him back to the supermarket, where the dog was tied up and whining and pacing back and forth. No, this time it would lead him farther back. He would step across it into his own home, where his wife was in the kitchen making lunch, his daughter was asleep upstairs, and a soft breeze was blowing through the open windows.

It happened just as he expected. He walked into the hall, climbed the stairs, and went into the bathroom to shower and change. There were two people now—there was one motionless and fascinated in the dark at the campsite while the other soaped his chest and arms and listened to the loud water drum against his shoulder blades, each aware of the other but each creating an interior privacy for himself, like two prisoners sharing the same cell.

Some minutes later he sat down at the kitchen table in his bathrobe. There was a bowl of clam chowder on a plate in front of him and another full of toasted french bread beside it. Just across from him Carmen picked up her spoon, sank it into her soup, and lifted it to her mouth. She noticed him watching her. Her eyes sharpened, as he had known they would; she had seen his sunburn. Then they shifted up, meaning that his hair didn't look right either. But he had business in this world; he intended to live in it. He watched her confusion fix itself on her small, serious face. This was as close, he suspected, as she would ever come to knowing. She was looking at him steadily now. In a moment she was going to say his name.

A GLOW FROM THE CHOIR

AT FIRST she thought he was violently ill. His skin had darkened to a deep brown and his nose and cheekbones looked pink and raw. She took him by the wrist and turned his hand out; she pulled her chair closer and looked in his eyes.

He was willing to be stared at. He told her not to worry, that he knew he looked a little strange, and that if she just gave him time he would try to explain.

She didn't want it explained — there was something dishonest in his eyes. They looked too white, too prominent in his darkened face. She didn't like his hair either — it hadn't been that long at breakfast. She had no idea what he was talking about. She was too busy thinking, *This can't be right* and *What is this?*, her mind having suddenly clicked shut on itself and left her alone in the midst of a brutal silence, an outraged silence. And yet she was talking to him now, saying words, asking questions; she had been split neatly in two, one side frozen and speechless and the other moved out of reach and running on like a toy.

She got up suddenly and looked at the clock. She felt light on her feet, dizzy. He was talking about death now — he said he had fallen off the roof and broken his neck but that he hadn't died. She was barely listening. *A burst blood vessel? Some kind of poisoning?* They had to get to a hospital, she said.

He agreed to it immediately. She called their regular sitter, a fourteen-year-old, and they left as soon as the girl arrived.

In an examining room at the ER she stood by the door while an intense-looking man with red hair shone a penlight in his eyes, asked a few simple questions, and called in a nurse for a blood sample. Rocker had his shirt off and the doctor asked him where he had got his tan. "At the beach," he said. The doctor took a step back and crossed his arms. "Any drugs in the last forty-eight hours?"

"No."

"Has this happened before?"

"Yes."

"How often?"

"Once."

They started talking about it. The doctor jotted something down on a pad and handed it to the nurse, who took it out with the sample.

She didn't like his tone. The phrase she had used at the desk was "massive hallucinations." Rocker was talking about them as if describing a head cold. The doctor crooked a knuckle under his nose, the lab coat tightening across his shoulders, then snatched up the pad and started writing again. His eyes followed the pencil as he spoke. "I don't think there's any cause for immediate action. If you want to pursue this further, and I think you should, I recommend that you go and see this man." He tore off the sheet and handed it to Rocker.

Carmen stepped up then, the words spooling evenly out of her mouth. "Excuse me, doctor. This morning my husband had his normal weight and color. Now he's lost ten pounds and he looks burned all over. Don't you find that unusual?"

He was a young man, no older than she. "Yes, I do."

"Then why aren't you doing anything?"

"Because no action is indicated. He has all the signs of a healthy man."

"I assure you he is not."

"You may be right. But again, I don't believe there's an immediate danger."

"How do you know?"

"I can't know, Mrs. Poole. I can only make a judgment. My judgment is that you ought to see a specialist."

"What kind of specialist?"

"Neuropsychiatry."

She stared at him for a moment. Before she could answer, a nurse leaned in and called him outside.

Later that afternoon Rocker sat down on a high stool on the patio with a towel wrapped around his neck while she cut his hair. She had wetted it with a squeeze bottle and it had a sweet, smoky odor. She felt guilty, as if she were destroying evidence of a crime.

"You think I should go see that guy?"

"Yes," she said. "Tomorrow."

"He's not going to believe me." He took another bite of the apple he had brought from the refrigerator. Lucinda watched from her seat on the back stoop.

"I believe you," she said. Although the scissors were sharp and bit cleanly behind the comb, she wasn't getting much accomplished. "I believe that something happened to you this morning."

"Actually," he said, "it goes back to that first time in the bedroom. Early in April."

She had never seen his hair so ragged. There was sand caught in the roots.

"There was a dog at the last place. He didn't know the difference — he didn't care whether he was in the real world or Planet Z or any goddamn place. I admired that dog."

She didn't answer.

"That's the secret, I think. You don't go around asking is this real, is that real. It's all real. All of it."

His skin was cool to the touch. She tilted his head forward with a slight pressure. Three parallel and virtually healed scratches ran from his nape around the side of his neck. *Fingernails,* she thought.

While she sat at the kitchen table over the now-cold chowder, she watched him wander around the back yard with Cinda, holding her up to the lilacs blooming outside the garage and dipping her hand in the water in the birdbath. He moved carefully, as if protecting a string of delicate internal sutures. He spent the entire afternoon on his feet, looking at things and touching them, never straying far and coming back to her every few minutes. He reminded her of nothing so much as one of those confused, hesitant people you saw downtown now and then, people for whom the world is at every moment fragile and new-skinned and mysterious. "This is wonderful, Carmen," he said. "I just can't believe it." There were times when she thought he was going to burst into tears.

"It's like when you come back from a long trip," he said. "You let yourself in, put down your bags, walk through the place, and then you don't know what to do next — you're back, yes, you're back, but . . ."

He couldn't keep his hands off her. Each time their eyes met he had to move closer and crouch down beside her or touch her shoulder, his gaze open and wondering. Then, as if losing the thread again, he would turn away and start another circuit. She told him he was acting funny. "You would, too," he said. Her concern seemed to irritate him — as if she hadn't been listening.

"Don't misunderstand me," he said. "This is where I want to be — let's not forget that."

Before long she gave up pretending she could just sit and watch him and got up to accompany him, walking him from room to room like a scientist leading a just-captured sea creature around the floor of a tank. She started to cry and she didn't fight it, weeping slowly and continuously, the tears freeing her a little. He talked just as steadily, not trying to convince her of anything but simply touching things and naming them, as if amazed that they were all still in place.

She didn't argue or interrupt. He went on and on, thinking out loud, the sound of his voice providing a connection between them. After a while he steadied a little and seemed more aware of her presence. "I know you're upset," he said. "I know why. But it's not as bad as you think. I can handle it — I know I can."

She agreed, of course. But it was clear to her now, in spite of his assurances, that things were not going to be the same.

That night, after dark, he took her upstairs to the bedroom. He'd been talking about lines. Lines, he claimed, were the key features of imaginary landscapes — therefore if there were any lines around here, this could not be the real world.

He shut the door, pulled the shades, and turned out the light. She heard him come up beside her in the grayness. After a few moments he said, "Well that's something, I guess."

He asked her to stay where she was and went out, turning off the hall light and starting downstairs. When he reached the bottom she heard him moving around on the ground floor, more switches clicking as he snapped them off. There was a silence before she heard him again, much fainter now, pulling open the cellar door in the kitchen. His footsteps faded as he went down. The house was quiet again.

Would I feel safer, she wondered, if he weren't here? She could just make out the familiar shapes of the dresser, the linen closet, the cane-seated rocker where he habitually tossed his clothes. Lucinda was asleep in the next room.

Now he was coming up again, his feet heavy on the cellar steps. She heard him shut the door behind him and move down the hall to the foot of the stairs. He wasn't turning on any lights. Halfway up he stopped short, as if listening. His head would be just level with the bottom of the railing. "Rocker?" she called out. She reached for the table lamp and turned it on.

"It's all right," he said. She heard him continue up to the landing at the far end of the hall. She leaned out to look through the door and saw him coming toward her, the whites of his eyes startling in his darkened face. When he came in, he pulled up all the shades again and leaned against the wall by the front window, looking out.

"Why did you stop?"

"Sorry." He shrugged. "So quiet, I guess."

"Did you find anything?"

"No."

She moved up next to him. The sash was open and the newly leafed trees floated heavy and odorous in the stillness outside the screen.

He sighed that uncommon sigh of his and moved into the center of the room, rubbing his face with both hands, then sat down on the edge of the bed and lay back heavily, his arms over his head. He looked at her for a moment before his eyes turned up to the ceiling.

She sat down next to him. "You feeling OK?"

"I'll be all right."

"If I were you," she began, hesitant, "I would want to know — I mean, I couldn't just pretend it didn't . . . *happen*."

"So what would you do?"

"I'd try to connect it . . . somehow."

He reached across behind her and turned out the light again.

A car went by; a series of pale rectangles floated across the ceiling.

"Uncontrollable dreaming," he said. He lay there motionless for a few moments. "What do you think — you want to be married to a nut?"

"It's been pretty good up to now."

"That's all? Pretty good?"

She didn't answer. In the restored dimness she was much more aware of the hushed and scented summer night outside. Down the street a dog collar clinked.

"Rocker?" she said. Her own voice sounded naked in the dark.

"Yeah?"

"I'm afraid. I'm really afraid."

"Then be afraid," he said.

They talked for most of the night. When they weren't talking they lay awake beside each other. He tried, again, to tell her what had happened to him. This time she found that she could listen to him without having to decide whether any of it was true. A car went by at one A.M.; another, sometime after three. He told her about a man named Mac and an office with no exit, the same story he had told her several weeks earlier as something he had dreamt. She had a feeling, hard to justify, that it would all be different in the morning — at any rate, morning was still difficult to imagine. During one of the silences she turned to him and moved closer; a few minutes later they undressed and made love. She was glad for it; it was like a prayer, a wordless, bodily prayer, and although she made no effort to respond to him, she did, which made her start crying again. To have his weight over her, to have him inside her — that was a way of having him.

*

"A secret?" she said.

"That's right, Mrs. Poole," he said. "An open secret — he tells us, but we don't believe him. He knows we don't. That's quite a burden to carry. We're all in the dark, while he alone knows the truth. So we all look more than a little pathetic to him. He doesn't have much patience with us — it's hard for him to take us seriously."

She didn't answer. She was sitting hunched over the kitchen table, the receiver tight against her ear. It was Monday afternoon, the next day; Rocker had called her at work at lunch and told her he was going to see the specialist at two and would have him call her at home at five. She had asked him to go; he'd made no secret of his opinion that it was a waste of time.

"The joke's on us, apparently," he went on. "Now he's the doctor — he's trying to help *us* adjust."

There was another silence. "Do you know what's wrong with him?" she asked.

"Physically, no. I want to do some tests — extensive tests, as a matter of fact — but frankly I don't expect to find anything. There are some forms of epilepsy that are remotely possible, but . . . What I'm saying is that I'm almost certain that your husband's condition is functional, which means that it can't be traced to any neurological source. That's not to say that it's untreatable — not at all. But in a case like his, where the problem doesn't seem to have hindered his normal routine, I would hesitate to try anything." He paused. "I don't want to minimize your concern — your very legitimate concern — but it seems to me that his main symptom is that he believes certain things that can't be proved. And who doesn't?"

She was thinking again.

"Mrs. Poole?" He had a quick, penetrating voice.

"Yes — I'm sorry."

"I don't mean to alarm you. I'm not saying that there's nothing we can do — I'm saying that as of now there may not be any *need* for action. Do you follow me?"

"I think so."

"Your husband has told us — quite sincerely, I think — about this other world that exists alongside our own. Fine. The question now is which is going to be more important to him. This is the major concern."

A sensible man, she thought. And yet she was afraid of him, afraid of what she might say.

She had left work early that day, at lunchtime, just after the third or fourth person had asked her if she was feeling all right. But instead of going home, she had driven straight to the public library, where she had sat at a table in the reference area and burrowed through dozens of weighty books full of Latin terms and tangled anatomical drawings, and though she wasn't able to penetrate much beyond the summaries and generalizations, she knew by midafternoon that her suspicions were correct — that although some illnesses, such as hypertension or asthma, could be brought on or aggravated by psychological states, there were limits to the mind's influence and that what had happened to Rocker far exceeded them. Tanning, for instance, took time; without it the skin could not protect itself and merely burned. Hair also needed time, a lot of time, to form and harden. And it was only later in the day, after she had pushed aside all the diagrams and cross sections, that she began to read things that spoke to her directly.

These books had no pictures. Their tone was different; a certain hesitancy crept through. Phrases like "many researchers believe" or "current studies suggest" stood out on page after page. The writers took great care to balance contrasting explanations; they hastened to say that the word *schizophrenia,* for instance, did not belong to the same class as words like *malaria* and *pneumonia* — it had much more in common, they said, with words like *cancer* and *senility*. But in spite of all their ponderous distinctions, she found them describing, in their less self-conscious moments, precisely those beliefs or delusions which Rocker himself had so earnestly laid out for her the day before — in a word, madness.

The construction of a private universe. Grandiose claims. Failure to recognize contradictions. Obsession with fantasy. Proliferation of symbols. Vertigo. Disorientation. Tyrannical dreams.

She hadn't written anything down. She had raced ahead almost despairingly, riffling through book after book, her head warm and painful, the book dust raw in her throat, all the learned authors blurring into a single impitiable drone like the buzz from the lights overhead while a few girls giggled somewhere nearby and a cherry-faced alcoholic drowsed over a newspaper. Here is a label then, she had thought, a box or package where she could fit him if she pleased and where she herself had some claim to enter, having herself seen or thought she had seen the color of his face and skin, not to mention those wet cuttings from his fragrant scalp she had swept off the flagstones or the spot on the bedroom floor she had already stepped around a half-dozen times. So she had shut all the books and left them on the table and walked out into the abrupt and street-noisy afternoon, thinking, *What now?* and *Where is he taking me*?

And now this voice on the phone, this smooth Dr. Waxman, probing for her secrets. Under the surface there was another message, a seductive and treasonous appeal — "You and I are here and he's over there and together we're going to bring him back" — asking her already to ally herself with common sense and medical authority, asking her to see the man she lived with as a problem, a dilemma, just as you might remove a faulty part from a machine and hold it up to the light. And the horror was that the same treatment awaited her if she dared to confess that she couldn't find the necessary distance, that she believed everything he had told her, or, if she did not believe, at least was unable to dismiss it. Rocker had known this when he asked the doctor to call. He had known how she would sit here, speechless, with the receiver locked against her ear. This was his message as well, his way of saying, *How do you like it*?

"Yes," she said. "Of course."

"Would you like me to call back?"

"No . . . no really, it's OK." She straightened on the edge of the chair, forcing herself to speak. "So you want to see him again, then."

"Yes, I do. Of course he's got to decide whether the effort's worthwhile. At the moment he doesn't seem convinced. Tell me this — do you think he ought to be seeing a doctor?"

"Oh no . . . well, from what you've said . . . I mean, he seems pretty good right now."

"Back to normal?"

"No, not exactly. But I thought it might be something else, something . . ."

"Organic," he said. "Yes, but I don't think so. The fact is, I really don't know what to think — he may not need any help at all. So I asked him to schedule these tests and come back later in the week."

"Could you call me when you see them?"

"Certainly. But as I said, I don't expect to find anything. I don't want to make any promises here, but I suspect this problem might not be as serious as it looks — it seems to me that your husband is a long way from becoming a fanatic about it. For instance, when he was telling me about his experiences in these other worlds I got no sense that he expected me to believe him — I think he would've been insulted if I said I did. That shows he can see things through our eyes as well, which is out of reach of a lot of people who've never been near a psychiatrist's office." He paused. "What I'm saying, I guess, is that I don't think this is a crisis, either medically or psychologically. That's about all I can offer right now."

"Well, I'm glad to hear that," she said. And she was, in a way.

"One more thing," he said. "The man at the ER told me that you'd mentioned other symptoms too. Physical symptoms."

"Uh-huh."

"Your husband told me that naturally there were some changes in his appearance, since he'd been away so long."

"Well . . ."

"Were there any differences?"

She cleared her throat; it was time to lie. "I may have exaggerated a little. I was pretty upset — we were being ignored."

"What made you think he should go?"

"He didn't look right. He looked shocked, sort of. As if he didn't know me."

"But he recovered quickly."

"Oh, yes."

He waited a few moments. "Well, that's it, I guess. Is there anything else you think I should know?"

She looked down at the pad in front of her, where she had written the word NO in letters two inches high, blackening it until the paper shone. "Well . . . like what, for instance?"

"Do you think he's hiding anything?"

She immediately thought of those scratches on his neck. They made it difficult to answer at all.

"Give it a few days," he said. "It would be nice, I realize, to have an explanation for all this, but explanations are a dime a dozen — what matters is whether you can adapt. In that respect I think the outlook is good, very good. But you be the judge. I'll call you at the end of the week."

That was it. When he hung up, she slumped back and spent several minutes just sitting there and dangling the receiver over her finger, wondering what kind of victory she had won.

For the next day or two she tensed whenever the phone rang; she knew she wasn't a good liar. She was afraid that it would be

Waxman again and that he would want to know what she was trying to hide. Or if not him, someone else — her mother, Rocker's boss, anyone. And people did call, but all they said was *How've you been?* or *Can you do me a favor?* or *Let's get together soon.* No one asked her why she hadn't done anything about Rocker.

They were long, busy, suburban days, the kind of days she had once believed she had every right to expect. Anchormen joked on the evening news; bluish smoke floated up from outdoor grills; her eyes stung over the cutting board as she chopped an onion. She was usually halfway through a glass of wine when she heard Rocker open the front door. He stopped in the hall, put down his briefcase, looked through the mail. She turned when she heard him come in behind her. Their eyes met; he kissed her on the neck, hugged her with one arm, took a beer out of the refrigerator, and tasted it before he ripped open a bill or a magazine offer with his thumb, frowning slightly or shrugging as he tossed it on the table or tipped it into the garbage. Then he went to the back door, his tie loose around his throat, and looked out for a few moments, his shirt wilted from the ride home. If he hadn't already noticed, he would ask what she was making. Maybe something on the TV would catch his eye; maybe he would start up immediately to change, lifting his jacket off the banister on the way.

And now this other thing was there also, bringing them even closer together whether they discussed it or not, hanging silent at the end of every look or half-uttered remark. He was the only one she could share it with. It was like a secret, a conspiracy, the two of them alone at the center of a vast ignorance.

His footsteps were heavier on the carpeted stairs as he came down, stopping in the living room to lift Lucinda out of her playpen, she over a year old now and adding a pound or so every other week. He wouldn't put her down for another ten minutes, holding her in the crook of his elbow while he snitched tidbits off the counter and leaned against the wall, watching

Carmen move from the sink to the stove, from the stove to the icebox and back again, Cinda reaching out for whatever he was eating. Within a mile or two there had to be at least a hundred other couples spending this hour in exactly the same way, nearly indistinguishable from them in every respect except for this *thing*—she didn't know how else to describe it; she was afraid to name it any more exactly—this *thing* that had entered their home and now stood like a wall between them and what they used to be.

She believed him now. She believed that he had discovered a means of entry into another, separate world. She believed him simply because, as the shock wore off, she realized that she had to believe him, that if she did not, then she would have to admit that she didn't believe her own eyes either, and that what she had seen Sunday morning posed such a threat to her view of things that it simply couldn't penetrate.

There was a price, of course. It might be more accurate to say not that she believed him, but that she doubted a thousand things she had formerly believed without effort. Even the most ordinary facts of her life seemed suspect to her. Something important had happened at that moment when he walked into the kitchen, something so important that a week later she still felt as if she hadn't moved an inch beyond it, as if her life had stopped dead right there and what she was living now was a sort of persistent memory, a stubborn routine that simulated normality but actually couldn't have been more unlike it.

He treated it as a joke. "This is a game," he said, standing in front of the dresser while he knotted his tie. "You take a man, knock him down, and watch him try to get up again. After a while he gets sneaky—he sees the punch coming. Then you have to lay off him for a while. Give him a breather. Wait till he starts to relax."

He wouldn't admit that anything very noteworthy had happened to him. Though he never said so, she suspected that he regretted telling her about it. He seemed to see it as weakness, an embarrassment, a private difficulty. This attitude had its effect on her. She didn't want their life to change. In marrying him at twenty-seven, in having his child two years later, she had made a choice for a certain kind of future — the first genuinely permanent choice, she believed, that she had ever made. She took it seriously. It meant that she had exchanged all the men in the world, imagined and otherwise, for one faulty individual. They defined each other now; their daughter defined both of them.

She could tell, just by looking at him, that he hadn't for a moment doubted the truth of what he had told her. He was so sure of himself that he didn't seem to care whether she believed him or not — it was as if he took a kind of grim satisfaction in knowing that he wouldn't be believed, in knowing that no one who hadn't seen this thing could possibly believe in it. She was no stranger to this side of him. It was typical of his darker moods, those times when he confronted himself and his own life with a sort of wonderment mixed with scorn.

No one seemed to notice any change in him. Actually, that wasn't true — they noticed, but they drew their own conclusions. He looked better than he used to — trimmed down, deeply tanned, with a buoyant and sardonic gleam in his eye. He looked older, distinctly older, but there was nothing that couldn't be put down to a few days in the sun.

They went out to dinner with his parents the following Friday at one of those roadside inns in Westchester with creaking floorboards and tasseled menus and a gravel parking lot full of new-minted sedans. Rocker didn't tell them anything. She had thought he might surprise her; he did not. It occurred to her that if she mentioned it herself, she would only confuse them; it was becoming more and more obvious that if he wanted to conceal this thing, he had the whole world on his side. And yet everything in her told her that this was suicidal, that something had to be done, to the point where she could barely stand to look at him, since every glance made it harder to remember the old Rocker, the Rocker who had made his escape. She had nothing solid she could cling to, nothing she could touch and say "This proves that my eyes didn't lie and that I saw what I saw"; she went so far as to pull out the trash pail in the kitchen and dig through to the bottom, looking for those cuttings she had swept off the flagstones — not that they would settle anything, either, but it would have been some help at least to have them safe in plastic someplace where she could take them out and look at them, maybe even point them out to him when she got the feeling that he wanted her to forget, that he would be perfectly content if she never mentioned it again. That was his style, of course: *Don't say a word, it's my problem.* And she hadn't found them, just as she had known she wouldn't even before she started lifting out the eggshells and coffee grounds and greasy paper towels. That was his style also, to remember, in spite of everything, that the garbage had to go out on Tuesday nights.

They continued to live together. That was what he wanted; that was where his fear showed most — he seemed to think he could save the situation by re-creating down to the smallest detail the life of the man he had replaced. It hadn't worked before, of course, but that didn't stop him. And it was already a failure, as far as she was concerned.

It wasn't that she couldn't talk to him. He never tried to deny any part of what he had told her. He seemed to like having a listener who was obliged to believe him; if she let him, he would go on for hours, story after story, each one more bizarre than the last, as if discovering for the first time that he could see them from the outside, as parts of a colossal and preposterous fairy tale. Bit by bit he built a picture for her, a picture of an endless labyrinth of alternate worlds where former human beings wandered like lost dogs and sniffed at the ruins, no longer quite believing that they were real. Over and over he came back to a man named Mac and an office with no exit; the place, he said, where he had first begun to understand what freedom was.

It was like listening to a child, in a way; he had a child's naïve faith, a child's self-absorption. But in his eyes, she knew, it was she who was innocent, she who was lessened.

Because there was no way she could participate in this other side of him, this wandering side which he had renounced temporarily but which had obviously hooked him for good. Strange that he hadn't mentioned any lovers over there — not so strange, in fact, not so simple to admit betrayal. And she had had him once — that was what hurt worst, to know that there had been a time when she knew he was hers for life, not because he was weak, but because he was strong.

All the tests came back negative. He had a CAT scan, a serotonin sample, a check for heavy metals — nothing. Waxman apparently wasn't interested in grilling her further; when he called back Friday he said he would tell her if anything truly unusual came up but that in general he preferred not to discuss treatment with family unless the patient requested it. She didn't object; she didn't see that it made any difference. Rocker had apparently taken a liking to him and was talking about going back indefinitely — "comic relief," he called it.

She often imagined what he might say if she confronted him directly, if she said that the reason he traveled to these other worlds was that they gave him the perfect place to cheat on her. Actually, she wasn't really that interested in his answer, whatever it might be, but rather in the outcome, the dénouement, the definitive break. Three decades of modern life hadn't convinced her that there was no such thing as adultery. They used to hang people for it in Boston, the town she grew up in. He was ready, she knew, to make his excuses — he wouldn't lie to her; he would admit the fact and even produce details if she insisted, a lie being worthless unless credible — but in his own mind, she knew, he was still pure as could be; not guilty but bewitched.

Therefore she chose to swallow her outrage and meet his silence with more of the same, each of them knowing what the other knew but saving it up for some more distant reckoning when it might prove more valuable. In the meantime they still slept in the same bed, although his body revolted her, burned a deep unlikely brown and carrying the foxy scent of strange females pursued and enjoyed in who knew what kind of infantile circumstances — revolted her, yes, but aroused her as well, as if it were a battleground where she could meet those intruders and wash away their juices with her own more bitter products. So she went a little crazy herself, playing the whore or the bitch in heat, nagging him daily for sex and not giving in until he surrendered. And he always surrendered, since short of kicking her away there was nothing he could do; sooner or later he always wound up with his belt down around his ankles and his prick standing up like a big rubber thumb. If she walked away at that point, he would get up and come after her, striding bowlegged from room to room with an irritated look, shirttails flapping over his bare ass. Sometimes she led him down into the back yard or the driveway, mostly dark at night but not completely shielded, where he screwed her against the car or flat out on the lawn. She was waiting, of course, for him to lose patience and confront her, this reduction to basics being the point of the whole degrading exercise, but it seemed to appeal to him too, and it continued for several days.

All the apparent continuities were still in place around her — her job, the house, Lucinda, right down to the neighbor's cat, which dug up the ivy, and the shy kid in her nine o'clock class who'd been sending her notes — no evidence here that everything wasn't as it should be, no grounds for any suspicion whatsoever — and yet in her mind they were all on the strictest probation. A gap had opened between herself and her own existence; she trusted none of her former certainties. She knew that Rocker understood this: the other night, out of the blue, he had said to her, "Carmen, I want to apologize for something — I want to apologize for the sadness of life." Not for leaving her, not for sleeping with ghosts — "for the sadness of life." He was serious. He got this look on his face sometimes, this mild, almost beatific look — the look on a rabbit's face as a snake suffocates it. He had accepted what happened to him. He considered it beyond his control.

What he had learned in that other place was that he didn't need her anymore. She could forgive him many things; she couldn't forgive him this. It meant that he was readying himself to leave her again, that neither she nor the world could hold him back much longer. He was afraid as well, she could tell, but it wasn't losing her that scared him — it was what he might find over there. And as he had stepped back from her, she stepped back, imagining how she would get along without him — a teacher's salary, the house put up for sale, new men in her life. Not long ago — only days, in fact — any such thoughts would have seemed shameful to her. She didn't resist them now. He had told her that he never wanted to go away again, that he had never stopped thinking about her, and that now that he was back he considered himself the luckiest man alive. She knew better. As he had said himself, he was different now. If you leave again, she had thought, don't come back.

So there was a sort of armed truce between them, each agreeing to maintain certain semblances, to pretend that the wound might heal over again; in short, to give the world a chance to regain its solidity. They still went out to parties now and then, they still paid the bills, they still took Lucinda for walks in the leaf-heavy dark after dinner, that bluish and dreamlike hour when the lights came on in the neighbors' houses and the fireflies rose up from the lawns in soft ascending streaks. Maybe they weren't married anymore, maybe they were like children who had stayed out too late and would be found next morning slack and lifeless at the edge of the road — but the hope was still there, the hope that this was not the final word. Because she shared his guilt, she had trusted in appearances; she had thought that the world belonged to her simply because she believed in it. Now that confidence was gone and it was like the moment long after midnight when footsteps stop outside the door and the knob begins to turn — wake up, wake up, your dream of life is over; your nightmare has arrived.

POOLE sat in his gray-carpeted office on the eighteenth floor with his back to the wall and his feet stretched out alongside the window, enjoying his triumph. He was in the midst of writing the quarterly report for the high-growth mutual fund he managed, always a pleasurable job when it lived up to its name, and his desk was littered with the printouts and transaction reports that attested to his good fortune. These figures would feature prominently in the bank's next promotional mailing and would funnel many thousands of additional dollars into his care, those lustful and elusive dollars which floated like a golden froth from one hot spot to the next.

Although it was a warm day, the half-inch sheet of tinted glass beside him felt cool against his knee. Below him the city of Stamford lay spread out like a full-size model of itself. He couldn't see any part of his own building, which was one of eight or ten crystalline giants set in a row facing southward across the Connecticut Turnpike. Together they formed a high and abstract rampart of steel and glass that made the rest of the city look crushed and trivial. For the last three weeks he had spent most of the daylight hours sitting in this little open-ended cell suspended several hundred feet in the air.

Across the turnpike lay the dark cindery rail yards, the freight cars always motionless on the sidings, although tiny figures with orange helmets could sometimes be seen picking their way among them. Beyond them stood a low row of billboards walling off the poor neighborhoods on the south side, a dark band broken by a few smokestacks and gas tanks and enclosing several wreckers' yards and razed blocks strewn with rubble. Then more greenery again and the edge of the Sound a mile or so away, several new developments and office complexes outlined against the water. At that distance the perspective flattened and the horizon rose to meet his eye.

He sometimes wondered if the builders who had pushed these steel boxes into the clouds had imagined what it would be like to work in them. It seemed to him that you couldn't look out a window like this without developing a certain distance from life at ground level. There was nobody perched high over *your* head, quickly becoming bored with your antlike predictability, but only a few hundred dizzy souls in airy niches like your own, some of them actually visible behind the sky-colored glass of the adjacent towers.

On the wall outside his door there was a little aluminum bracket holding a black plastic strip with his name stamped into it. This indicated that he had arrived. A visitor walking around the perimeter of the floor would see several dozen of these nameplates. It had taken him five years to acquire his and it was currently worth about $60,000 a year, a buoyant figure but not nearly enough to make anyone rich in Fairfield County. That would depend on how well his own private fund performed, the carefully balanced handful of issues that had grown steadily over the years in spite of a few conspicuous turkeys and ill-timed sell-outs.

He was still amazed at how easily he had fit back into his job.

Of course it didn't hurt that nearly half the stocks he had chosen over the winter had been creeping steadily up the charts, part of an overall surge in the health manufacturing sector, but there was more to it than that; somewhere along the way the game had lost its terrors for him. He had noticed that he didn't start to sweat every time one of the senior v.p.'s cleared his throat and looked him in the eye. In fact, there were times when it was all he could do to keep from breaking into the broadest of smiles.

Jewel was right: he no longer believed in his own life. No, that wasn't it — he believed in it, believed that it was still his and still in progress, but he had lost his trust in the world around him. It didn't convince anymore — it was like a movie he had stumbled into by mistake, full of familiar sets and actors and surprisingly realistic here and there, but ultimately a mirage. And not just any fantasy either, but the most elaborate and cunning deception ever conceived. It had to be — otherwise people would see through it in a moment.

He had been thinking this over lately. It seemed to him that reality suffered from a kind of demented extravagance. Four billion human beings on earth, perhaps a million different species of animal life — who could believe this if it wasn't so? But let that pass. All right, given this unimaginable swarm of interrelated awarenesses, how likely was it that he should be what he was and not something else? Out of the infinity of possible lives, why Rockland Randall Poole? Life, it seemed, was a disease of matter, a process by which various chemical compounds became aware of their own unlikelihood. But somehow they survived the shock; they immediately got busy making more of themselves. This was their inheritance from nonlife, from the rocks and gases they were made of — that they were able to continue without having to know why.

And that was what the world did for you, and had done for him until lately: it washed you in a constant stream of reassuring detail, endlessly reaffirming what you were and how you were situated, like a mirror that tracked you everywhere, until in the end you became habituated and the fact of your own being seemed less miraculous than the shape of a young woman's buttocks or the way a certain man in short pants dropped a ball through a hoop.

He noticed that the afternoon traffic had started to build up on the highway below him, noiseless behind the glass. He picked up the phone and punched his own number.

While he listened to it ring he stared at the steel-framed picture of Carmen at the corner of his desk, as if doing so could make her answer. She was standing beside a tree with feathery red bark in a campground in New Hampshire, one hand resting lightly on it and her head in profile while she gazed at its crown with a sober, self-conscious look on her small and serious face.

"Hi," he said. "You're back."

"I just got in."

"I wanted to remind you I'm going to see Waxman tonight. You'd better go ahead and eat."

"All right — don't get lost on the way home."

Fair enough, he thought, hanging up.

Waxman's office was a few blocks off Atlantic Street in a former middle-class neighborhood that had changed color in the sixties and was bulldozed ten years later to make room for corporate offices, leaving a sort of high-gloss wasteland strewn with newly minted four- to six-story cubes and shoe boxes, each of them squatting in the middle of several acres of leveled rubble. Here and there a few brick row houses clung to the sidewalks, their exposed sides showing the scars of their former neighbors, along with a handful of forlorn and denuded single-family homes. One of these ghosts, Number 28 Selkirk, still had glass in the windows and a healthy horse chestnut shading a half-columned porch. It stood across an intersection from a weedy gas station that sold no gas but hadn't been completely abandoned. The other corners were empty and there was nothing else standing for half a block around.

The house itself looked as if it had withstood some half-hearted attacks by inexperienced wreckers. A few shingles had flaked off its high gray walls and a half-dozen bricks were missing from the stoop below the porch. The steep-banked mound of earth it stood on raised to eye level the police notices taped to the cellar windows. Under one cornice a section of gutter hung down at an uncomfortable angle. Solid, ugly, and obdurate, it looked as if it could easily survive another fifty years.

Waxman had three rooms on the ground floor on the right side. His car, an aged caramel Cadillac with a white vinyl roof and a slight backward tilt, was parked out front with several others not worth stealing. By the time he rang the doorbell on his initial visit, Poole had noticed the dandelions gone to seed on the meager lawn, the loose knob on the entryway door, and the muffled barking of the dog locked up in the gas station, so that the first thing he asked Waxman was whether his car would be all right out front.

Waxman didn't answer right away. He was well over six feet tall and had to duck his head to look out the door. A flat-sided man with tangled dark hair, big nocturnal eyes, and a bold and bony high-kinked nose, he stepped out past Poole and stalked up and down the porch once, peering into the empty plain around them, as if looking for a telltale cloud of dust. He was dressed like a snowbound lumberjack in a plaid flannel shirt with turtleneck, jeans, and heavy socks, and he held a thick, jacketless book between his thumb and fingers, a knuckle inserted to keep his place. After a moment he turned to Poole and fixed him with his intent and steady gaze. "As you can see," he said, "nothing much happens around here. But if I had a car like yours I'd pull it up into the side lot. Then we can see it from inside." A moment later, apparently reacting to something in Poole's face, he held out his huge and none-too-fleshy hand. "William Waxman," he said.

Poole heard the door move behind him. He turned and saw a young black girl of eight or nine wedged in the opening and glued to the jamb with a sort of innocent lust. She had shy eyes and a pretty face. "Is that another crazy man?" she asked, her accent broad and sulky.

"Does he look crazy to you?" Waxman said.

"Ah oun't know."

"Then why don't you ask him yourself?"

Her eyes drifted past Poole without meeting his. "Mistah, are you crazy?"

"I don't think so," Poole said.

Just before she slipped back in, she looked straight at him for a moment. They heard her sneakers slapping up the stairs.

"I had the cops here once," Waxman said.

Poole had been expecting a smart address, a well-kept waiting room, artwork on the walls. "You're Dr. Waxman?" he said.

"That's right."

"Then why here?"

"Various reasons. One is that I only get people who really want to see me."

"I'm surprised you get anyone at all."

"So am I, sometimes."

Poole looked out again at the baked plain around them reddening in the afternoon light. A mile to the south his own offices rose out of a mass of new construction. "You could land a plane out here," he said.

"How badly do you want to see me?" Waxman asked.

Poole glanced at him. He had already decided that he had nothing to lose by telling Waxman the truth.

"Every time you come here it's going to cost you a hundred

dollars. All we're going to do is sit and talk. If you think I'm wasting your time, or I think you're wasting mine, then we'll drop it."

Poole was again struck by the deadpan, utterly serious look on his face.

"I'm not in the business of curing people," Waxman said. "Most of the patients I see can't be cured — not by me, not by anyone. A few of them recover on their own."

"Then what good are you?"

For the first time Waxman looked as if he might think about smiling.

The apartment surprised Poole. It didn't look as if it had been inhabited by a long string of tenants without money. Waxman immediately asked him if he wanted a beer, and Poole followed him through to the back.

The three rooms were large and clean and stood in a row, connected by archways. The first one had a fireplace and a big bay window and was lined with floor-to-ceiling bookcases on three sides. The second was a bedroom, the third a kitchen. The walls were mostly bare and furniture was scarce. On his way through, Poole spotted several adult toys: skis, an aqualung, a video camera. The kitchen had a back door with three heavy locks and a window that looked out onto a fire escape. Some sort of stew was cooking in a pot on the stove.

Waxman also took a beer and leaned against the refrigerator with one arm folded across his chest. "Now you know how I live," he said. They were both drinking out of bottles.

"Been here long?"

"A couple of years."

Waxman was studying him again.

"What're you looking at?" Poole asked.

"You."

"Is that the routine? Just stare at 'em and see what they say?"

Waxman turned away and tucked his chin down to deaden a

belch, looking a bit owlish as it arrived. He towered over the refrigerator.

"I may as well tell you right now," Poole said. "There's no way you could have what I need."

"What's that?" Waxman asked, still looking at the floor.

"I've been places. I've been to other worlds. I've come back from the dead."

"You expect me to believe that?"

"Not at all — that's just what I mean."

Waxman looked up at him. "Why should I believe you?"

"Exactly — why should you?"

"You have any proof?"

"None whatsoever." Poole hadn't brought along his pajamas.

"Too bad."

Poole snickered. "Not really."

Waxman had already finished his beer. He put his empty down. "Let's go in the front room."

There was a table there, a sturdy slab of blond wood that made the room look like an alcove in a private library. It had three matching rail-back chairs with splayed legs and paddle-shaped armrests. Poole took the one that faced the bay window and found himself looking south toward the turnpike across several empty blocks, nothing interrupting their vacancy except a few patches of high weeds and a row of streetlights. This was to become his regular seat. Waxman usually took the one across the corner, facing the front window and its heavy green curtains, which he always kept drawn in the late afternoon. On bright days a little sun filtered around them and shed hazy gold streaks on the floor and bookcases.

The room was quieter than any bank Poole had ever worked in. The street outside wasn't a through road and few cars passed. Now and then other tenants clumped in and out, their shadows looming briefly behind the curtain over the glass panel in the door to the entryway, but no one ever knocked and the phone never rang. Poole noticed that many of the encyclopedia-size volumes on the surrounding shelves were printed in Hebrew. Waxman nodded when he asked about them.

"Scriptural commentaries — I was going to be a rabbi. Or if not a rabbi, at least an educated man. I still like having them around."

"You changed your mind?"

"You can find a lot of things in those books, but you can't find God." He sat back, easily filling the chair.

"So you gave it up."

"I became a tennis player. I'm still a pretty good tennis player." He unlimbered one arm and reached behind himself to lift a clean plastic ashtray off a bookshelf, shoving it across the table toward Poole. Poole had been wanting a cigarette but didn't remember having touched his pocket.

"So you're a banker," Waxman said.

"I used to be. Now I run a mutual fund."

"Stocks?"

He nodded. "Medical technology. Small companies that look like they might take off."

"You like it?"

"Sometimes."

"Mentally unbalanced people usually operate best in sales or P.R. work, where a little mania pays off."

Poole waited a few moments, wondering if he was serious. "So you think you can help me, then."

"Possibly. I'm sort of a free-lance researcher. I like to poke around in other people's minds."

"Why?"

"It interests me."

"That's all?"

"That's plenty, as far as I'm concerned."

"I thought you had to put the patient first."

"I try not to do any harm."

They were quiet for a moment. "Got any mental problems yourself?" Poole asked.

Waxman nodded. "Many. You could say all my problems are mental problems."

"Like what?"

"Ingratitude."

Poole waited, but he didn't elaborate. "Ingratitude to whom?"

Waxman sat thoughtfully for a while, his long wrists dangling over the armrests. He looked up at last. "You want to get started?"

Not once, either on that visit or any of his subsequent ones, did Poole catch Waxman suggesting that anything he had told him might not be true. And it wasn't as if he were humoring him either; he seemed genuinely willing to take it all on faith. In the beginning this made Poole intensely suspicious, not wanting to have any allowances made for him, and he repeatedly tried to get the other man to admit that his credulity wasn't quite so elastic. This Waxman refused to do. The question, for him, wasn't whether Poole had lost touch with reality, or even whether these other worlds had any existence outside his delusions. He took a more practical approach: "Given that all this actually happened to you, given that it might happen again, what are you going to do about it?"

This seemed to Poole a remarkably adult attitude. He decided that Waxman was a worthy opponent.

He went to see him twice a week, on Tuesdays and Fridays at five. On Fridays he brought a check for $200 and left it on the table on his way out. The money served a useful purpose: it confirmed that the time spent at Waxman's had a certain value. As it took only minutes to get there from downtown, there was no need to make any excuses at work.

There was an element of flattery, Poole discovered, in having your mind poked and prodded by a skilled investigator. He was no longer just another young executive trying to get an edge; he was mentally distinct in an interesting way. In his former life he would have considered it a sign of weakness, or at least luxurious self-absorption, to pay someone like Waxman to fish for monsters in his psychic depths. Now he had to admit that he liked it.

Not the least of the attractions of these afternoon meetings was his sense that they were irrelevant to his main concerns, like the daily card games he used to play at college. He enjoyed looking at himself through Waxman's eyes, as a sick man in a world that was still basically intact. It would be pleasant, he often thought, to go over to this outlook, to admit that he had gone nuts and be able to dismiss everything he had seen as fundamentally unreal. But he never for a moment believed he was going insane, if insanity meant retreating to a private mental universe. He had Mac and Carmen to vouch for that — Mac whose traces he had followed back to reality, and Carmen who was unfortunately going through the same sequence of shock and outrage he had experienced in Mac's office. That was serious, painful stuff; seeing Waxman let him escape from it now and then. Going to Waxman was almost like crossing a line; it took him out of a world full of threats and uncertainties and put him in a place where his own life turned into a clever and intriguing puzzle.

They didn't always stay in the front room. On hot afternoons Waxman produced a couple of squeaky wooden church-basement chairs and they took them out to the porch, where they set them down on either side of an old cable spool used as a table and looked out over the peeled gray railing at the street and the vacant lot opposite. Sometimes there were three or four black men in short-sleeved shirts standing around a car at the gas station across the intersection. Poole took off his shoes, jacket, and tie and rolled up his cuffs. Waxman might be wearing as little as a T-shirt and a pair of shorts. He never offered Poole beer again, but brought out a red plastic pitcher full of water and ice and a couple of tall glasses. Poole smoked his Winstons down to the filters and threw the butts over the railing.

Waxman was apparently the only white person in the building. He nodded at the other tenants, who seemed to be mostly women, but they didn't stop to talk. It was clear to Poole that they all knew what Waxman did and that they regarded him, Poole, as a lunatic in spite of his pricey car and downtown clothes, watching him closely if unobtrusively from the moment they started up the steps. Waxman always had Poole take the seat farthest from the double door.

He didn't talk about his other patients. He apparently spent several days a week at a psychiatric hospital in Bridgeport; Poole saw the parking sticker on his car. He was bright; there was no doubt about that. After the first couple of visits he knew Poole's story forward and backward. He liked it; he said it was "interesting." Poole thought it was more than that, of course, but he didn't argue. He was still trying to figure Waxman out.

Here was a man who clearly might have achieved some position in life but instead had chosen to hide out here and play host to lunatics. And not out of a spirit of sacrifice, either; he told Poole he had abandoned a job at a local clinic because he couldn't say yes to everybody. If he had any friends or relatives, he never mentioned them. So he had deliberately drawn the circle tight around himself; whatever he was looking for, he had taken pains to make sure he wouldn't find it in the usual places.

As a matter of temperament Poole didn't trust people who were unusual. In his brief career as a loan officer at another bank, he had once given several thousand dollars to a man in red-white-and-blue cowboy boots, and when the loan went bad he knew that the boots were at fault. A man like Waxman, a man so determined to set himself apart, would normally have struck him as a lightweight, a person of no genuine originality. He apparently had money and could afford to play games.

Poole hadn't yet abandoned this prejudice. Having seen how delicately the world was put together, he was, if anything, even more conservative. But he didn't get the sense, with Waxman, that the act was designed for its effect on an audience. In fact, he saw a resemblance between Waxman's rejection of ordinary life and his own forced detachment from it.

Poole lived permanently now in the greenish half light before a thunderstorm. He didn't know how much time he had. Several times a day he was invaded by a sense that Something Was Going to Happen — namely, that he was losing his grip again. It froze him in place; his heart started to pound; he searched the walls for the first signs of dissolution. And though it was all over in a matter of seconds and there was no evidence that anything at all had taken place, he always felt as if he had barely escaped. Sooner or later he knew that the thing he feared was going to come back.

So he was always tempted to take a few steps in its direction, as if to dare it to show itself. And Waxman's place, it seemed to him, was a sort of advance outpost of the unreal.

On a Tuesday late in June they were sitting out on the porch watching the parking lot in the distance empty for the day when a car Poole didn't recognize cruised past the house several times. It was a big car, a beat-up station wagon, the kind a carpenter or electrician might use to get around to his jobs. On the third or fourth circuit it pulled up in front with the motor running. The driver was on the far side and Poole couldn't see him.

"This is a friend of mine," Waxman said. "He's a little unpredictable."

A minute or so later the engine shut off, and Poole, watching through the railing, saw the door open and a big man in a green army jacket get out. He was careful not to look at the house. "Waxman?" he called out.

"Up here."

"Who's the other guy?"

"A friend."

"You sure?"

"See for yourself."

After another silence the man pushed the door shut, circled the front of the car, and came up the steps, stopping at the lip of the porch. He looked like a bouncer at a Port Chester bar — a fat, humid face, a droopy mustache, bleary red eyes. He was staring at Poole.

"You think he's going to hurt you?" Waxman said.

"Get him out of here."

"You want to sit down?"

"I said get him out of here."

Poole was less than comfortable. The man's gaze had a peculiar intensity.

"Got any weapons?" Waxman asked, bland as butter. The man looked at him for the first time.

Poole watched the man cross the porch, reach into his jacket, and produce an automatic pistol, a switchblade, a hand grenade, two gun clips, a handful of bullets, and a hypodermic wrapped in plastic. He laid them all out on the cable spool.

"That's all?" Waxman said.

The man's eyes narrowed. He hesitated, then reached behind his head and lifted out something that had been hanging around his neck — a short length of bare steel wire with a wooden handle at each end. He gathered the handles together and laid them down also. "What about yours?" he said harshly.

Waxman sat up, undid his belt, pulled it off, and dropped it on the spool. He eased back again. "That's all."

The man returned his attention to Poole.

"I already checked," Waxman said.

"I don't like his face. He's a faggot, isn't he?"

"Why do you say that?"

"He's got faggot clothes and faggot hair. That makes him a faggot." He stuck out his lips and made some juicy kissing noises.

"What if he is?"

The man was still staring at Poole. His chest rose and fell evenly. "Did you get that piano yet?"

"No, I didn't."

"That's too bad — I was going to play you some good music."

"I'm working on it."

"You ever hear 'The Flight of the Bumblebee'? The Flight of the *Faggot* Bumblebee?"

Waxman waited a few seconds. "Yeah, I have."

"Well, get moving then." He spat over Poole's legs and left, the porch creaking under his weight. Poole watched him get in the car and pull away.

"That guy is clearly fucked up," Poole said, trying to breathe again.

Waxman got up and went inside. He came out with a canvas bag and an old cotton sheet. While Poole watched, he started ripping up the sheet, wrapping the weapons in it, and packing them in the bag. "We've got a deal going," he said. "He needs a hiding place." Squatting beside the bag, he picked up the grenade and hefted it, then shook his head.

"What're you going to do with that?"

"Good question." He rolled it up carefully and put it inside.

"What's he so afraid of?"

"No one wants to feel helpless. To his mind he's just taking a few sensible precautions."

Poole watched as Waxman pulled the bag's drawstring tight, pushed it against the wall, and straightened up again. "So you go along with it."

"I try to make him feel safe." He squinted into the flat brightness surrounding the porch, his cheeks drawn up under his eyes, then sat down again. He tilted his head back against the shingles. "Some people, when they get nervous, start taking pills. This guy goes out and buys guns." He watched a wasp drift lazily across the ceiling.

"But you can't tell him what you really think."

"What's that?"

"That he doesn't need guns."

"Why would I want to do that?"

"Because it's the truth."

"You think you could prove it to him?"

Poole didn't answer.

"It takes a certain amount of courage to be a nut," Waxman said. "You have to believe in yourself."

"So you pretend to believe him."

"I don't pretend anything. I just said he could keep his stuff here and come get it whenever he wanted." He rubbed his eyes and blinked. "You'd be surprised — these guys can usually tell when someone's lying to them."

Poole looked at the patch of clear spit on the dusty floorboards beside him.

"He's not like you," Waxman said. "He wants people to think he's weird. Then maybe they won't mess with him."

"Why do you do it?"

"I told him that also. I told him that if he went along with me, I'd try to keep him out of the wards. That's something he can understand."

"So you think he's harmless?"

"No — I just think he needs a little breathing room."

This was standard Waxman. Delusions should be accommodated, not attacked — permit the madman his madness.

Poole watched a bright yellow bulldozer heaping up dirt several blocks away, the sun glittering on its blade.

"So how've you been?" Waxman said. He sat with his chair tipped back and his head cushioned on his hands.

"Pretty good."

"No mental traveling?"

"Nope."

"Do you miss it much?"

After a moment Poole said, "Sometimes."

"I'd think reality might get a little stale after a while. Like hanging around in a college town after you've graduated."

"Yeah, but what can I do?"

Waxman didn't answer. "How's your wife doing?"

"She's trying to adjust." Poole hadn't told him what Carmen had seen.

"I'm surprised she hasn't called again."

"What would you tell her?"

"That you're not any worse."

"What do you mean, worse?"

"Well . . ." Waxman rearranged his lengthy arms and legs. "What you might expect, I guess, is some low-grade panic. As the situation became less tolerable in your eyes."

"I disagree. I think I'd be more likely to withdraw . . . to pretend the whole thing is a kind of joke."

"Yes, but you're not the type."

"No?"

"You'd get tired of it. Deep down, I think, you're a serious man."

After a moment Poole snorted.

"The world didn't ask you to be a hero," Waxman went on. "It asked you to make your peace with your own time and place. You thought you could do that — you intended to try, anyway. But you missed something. You got taken by surprise.

"The whole thing lacks drama," Waxman continued. "We've been taught to think that the really important struggles are historical — against disease, injustice, ignorance. Yours is nothing like that. You don't even know who you're fighting."

Poole watched the bulldozer cough out a little puff of black smoke as it reversed direction.

"So you're getting fed up with reality," Waxman said. "It's all right by itself, but it just doesn't speak to your concerns. You can't understand how people get so worked up over it."

Although Waxman was only rephrasing what Poole himself had said over the past few weeks, it was still a little disconcerting to hear it thrown back at him so readily.

"But consider," he went on. "Sure, things look flat to you now. But aren't you glad, in a way? Do you really want those other worlds to start breaking in here?"

"What're you trying to say?" Poole lit a cigarette, cupping the lighter.

"I'm saying that your sanity depends on a certain inviolable retreat — the real world. Your imagination, dangerous as it is, can't be allowed to poison it."

"I *like* the real world," Poole said.

"But don't you think it lacks something?"

"Like what?"

"Answers. It can't tell you, for instance, what happened to you."

"That's all right."

"In other words, you accept your isolation. You've been to hell and back, but it doesn't signify."

"What choice do I have?"

Waxman tipped forward again and looked around. After a few moments he said, "So what do you think of the rest of us?"

Poole turned and found Waxman's wary dark eyes looking into his.

"We haven't seen what you have. We don't know — we don't even suspect."

Poole didn't answer.

"You pity us? You wish you could clue us in?" Waxman squinted up at the light. "Or maybe you feel privileged. Now you're exempt, sort of. You're different.

"Because when you get right down to it," he continued, "we're out of the picture. We're there, but we don't really matter. This thing is between you and someone else."

"Like who?" Poole said.

"I thought you might tell me."

"I don't usually think in those terms."

"Yes, but it's unavoidable now, isn't it?"

"Do you think I see this as a personal message?"

"I think this trip put the fear into you. I think you saw something there you didn't want to see."

They watched a black kid walk down the middle of the street, tossing a rock and catching it.

"So you think," Poole said, not looking at Waxman, "that I really didn't go anywhere. That I imagined the whole thing because I have this unacknowledged need to threaten myself, to make myself suffer. Because I had gotten away too easily, somehow."

"Did I say that?"

"You're the expert, right? How else do you account for it?"

"By taking your word for it. You don't think I'm capable of believing you?"

"No."

"Then you underestimate me."

The statement opened a little hole between them. Usually, at this point, Waxman would go on to say that since he couldn't disprove Poole's story, it didn't matter whether he believed it or not — he had no basis for either opinion. But Poole sensed that it was different this time.

"All right," he said. "I'm listening. I underestimate you."

"I believe, for instance, that there are many worlds and that most of them are invisible."

"Go on."

"I believe that the material world is a residue or ash that contains but doesn't define us."

"Uh-huh."

"I believe that the real world is a womb that some people never crawl out of."

Poole decided to keep quiet.

"I believe that your so-called delusions are evidence of remarkable powers. Not only do I believe that these other worlds exist, but I believe that you visited them. I believe that what makes you special is exactly this power to transcend your surroundings. I believe that you have brought back something valuable and that your message ought to be heard."

Waxman turned his head sideways on the shingles and looked at Poole for a long moment. "Surprised?"

"Yes."

"Maybe you want a second opinion."

"Who else do you believe? You believe that guy who was just here?"

"He's not as crazy as he looks. He's pretty ordinary, as a matter of fact. Not like you."

"What's the difference?"

"You can't tell?"

"I'd like you to explain it to me."

Waxman hesitated, as if tempted to object, then settled back again. "It's pretty obvious, isn't it? The main point is that he's shut himself off — he doesn't take reality into account. He's got a system, a certain way of seeing. Say we're sitting here and he says someone is listening behind the doors. So we get up and take a look. There's no one there. So he says the person must have run up the stairs. I point out that we would have heard him. He says no, the guy was real quiet. I point out that the door at the top is locked. He says of course, the guy had a key. You see what I'm saying? He can't correct for errors. He takes things and warps them to fit his script. Whereas you're still attentive. You're still open to new facts." He stopped and looked at Poole.

"I didn't think I was nearly so convincing."

Waxman didn't smile. "I'm not kidding. This is what I believe."

Poole was thinking that no M.D. who had a regular-type office with a leatherbound appointment book and a Persian rug would ever have tried this particular gambit. "What've you got against reality?"

"Nothing. Absolutely nothing. I just think it's incomplete. It's made to be surmounted. It shouldn't become a prison. It should take whatever shape we choose to give it."

Twenty minutes later Poole was calling Carmen to tell her he was going to be late. Waxman was still out front on the porch. While he waited for an answer, Poole opened the refrigerator and looked inside. Several plastic jugs of spring water. Bacon, eggs, cream cheese. He spotted a few beers on the door and took one.

"I don't know," he said. "Another hour, maybe."

"Is something happening?"

"Waxman got a little weird. I'll tell you about it later."

"Weird?"

"He says he believes me now."

"Huh." She was quiet for a moment. "But how could he?"

"I don't know. It's funny, actually." He put the beer on the counter and popped it with one hand.

"Did you tell him about me?"

"Not yet, no."

She waited again. "He must be testing you."

"Could be."

"Maybe I'll call him tomorrow. See how he explains it then."

"That's an idea."

It was her turn to say something. Poole traced the can's cold rim with a finger.

"He's still living in the real world," she said. "I think I've forgotten what it's like."

"It's a lot like this."

"Not for me it isn't. In the real world you wake up after a while. You don't just keep on with it."

As he hung up it occurred to Poole that he was spreading weirdness wherever he went.

When he went back, Waxman was bringing the bag full of weapons inside. Poole stepped out onto the porch. The shadows had lengthened and the bulldozer had ceased operations. Two blocks away a city bus stopped at an empty corner, and a heavy woman with a stiff leg climbed down and started hitching along in his direction. A half-dozen seagulls stood beside a milky brown puddle in the lot across the street. Nothing was moving at the gas station. Some of the low heaps of rubble were beginning to throw shadows.

Waxman came out and joined him at the railing. After a moment he grabbed the edge of the roof with both hands and leaned against it, his oversize body broad and flat as a kite. "You think I'm putting you on," he said.

"Maybe not."

"Why should I do that?"

"To see how I take it?"

Waxman had to lift his head to look at Poole over his shoulder. "She believes you too, doesn't she?"

"She says she does."

"It's more than that. Why not tell me about it?"

"I want to hear from you first. I want to know where you get your ideas."

"Your problem is that you don't want to be believed." Waxman let his head hang for a moment, then straightened up, threw a leg over the railing, and straddled it with his back against the pillar by the steps. "You keep mistaking me for someone else, I think. The guy who's supposed to lead you out of the woods."

"What are you, then?"

"An independent investigator. A student of illusions." He turned and squinted at the emptiness around them. "You grew up around here, right?"

"The next town over."

"People usually develop a certain loyalty. Do you feel that?"

"Yes."

"We're less than thirty miles from New York City. That's the center of the known world."

"So what?" Poole watched the stiff-legged woman step down off the curb at the intersection and start toward the house, puffing visibly. A chocolate-colored dog with a cropped tail lifted its head from the base of a phone pole and watched her too.

"I'm just trying to orient you. You do want to get oriented, don't you?"

When Waxman heard her feet on the steps, he turned and nodded at the woman, who had a large, weary face, graying hair, and round shoulders. She glanced at him once but didn't answer, using one hand to drag herself up the rail while she clutched a black pocketbook under her bosom with the other. At the top she stopped to catch her breath, then went in the doors at the other end of the porch.

"You still haven't satisfied me," Poole said, cupping his hands around another cigarette.

"What do I have to do?"

"Tell me why you believe me." He moved over to the wall of the house and leaned against it.

"That could take a while."

"I've got time."

"Let's hope so." Waxman watched him for a couple of moments, then unfolded his long limbs and went inside.

Poole believed he had every reason to be suspicious. He was jealous of his singularity. He didn't want to be told that there was anything normal or reasonable about what had happened to him. He considered Waxman an intelligent man, a man like himself, for all his eccentricities — not the kind who was attracted to bizarre ideas. But Waxman was subtle also. He had made a career out of delicate transactions with damaged minds. It was easily possible that he had sensed why Poole considered these visits a harmless pastime, why he found it so relaxing to tell the truth and be taken for a helpless liar. But it all rested on Waxman's assumption that Poole was indeed severely deluded. For him to admit that there could be other possibilities took all the zip out of the exchange. It made it serious again.

A minute later Poole was sitting at the big table in the front room with his beer, an ashtray, and his cigarette. Waxman turned on the hanging lamp overhead and pulled out a cardboard file box from one of the tightly stuffed bookcases, then slid it onto the table and sat down. The windows were open and the curtains hung still in the blue afternoon air.

Inside the box's green marble-patterned sleeve was a bulky gray carton much like the ones Poole's bank used to hold securities; coverless, it was held shut by four triangular flaps, each equipped with a metal button. When Waxman undid the cotton tie wrapped around them and opened it, Poole saw what looked like a stack of large black-and-white photos. Waxman was watching him closely now, like an attorney about to expose some privileged documents. He had said barely a word since they came in. Then he tilted up the first dozen or so photos and started going through them slowly, his lips clamped a little tighter than usual. Poole saw that several of them had official-looking stamps and handwritten notations on their backs.

Waxman lifted one out and pushed it across to him. It was a picture of a dead man, a priest, hanging by the neck from the crossbeam over the door of a shed. One foot trailed on the ground; the other was bent back and tied to his wrist. His free hand was at his throat, its fingers caught underneath the noose. His face was turned away and unnaturally swollen, almost balloonish.

"That was taken in Spain in 1936," Waxman said. "The reason his hand is caught like that is that he wasn't really hanged.

He was stood up, tied, and left balancing on one leg. You can't stand forever on one leg. Eventually he got worn out and hanged himself."

He handed Poole another one. It showed a boxcar drawn up on a siding in bright daylight. There were soldiers in shirt-sleeves standing around with their guns pointed down, and a group of barebacked laborers were prying timbers off the side of the car. Its door was open and it was filled to a low height with a crushed, confused mass like a heap of frozen garbage.

"Check out the guy to the left," Waxman said. "The guy scratching his head there."

Poole saw a Nazi officer who had taken off his visored cap to do just that.

"That guy's in deep shit," Waxman said. "He's got a car full of several hundred Polish Jews that he was supposed to deliver to Auschwitz. But it was a hot day and the train got held up too long and they all collapsed and died and and stiffened up. Now they're hard as rock and he can't even get them out of the car without taking it apart. So he's already late and he's destroying government property. He knows he's going to get hell from somebody."

Poole was still looking at the picture when Waxman slid another over it. This one was in color. It showed five or six Cambodians or Vietnamese standing around a small hole in the side of a muddy hill. They were all men but they looked too weak to be soldiers and several of them had large, unbandaged wounds. Two of them were holding cans that they had apparently been using as scoops. All of the men were looking in the hole, where parts of a body were beginning to emerge.

"That group has been napalmed over and over," Waxman said. "Those are burns you're looking at. But their biggest problem is food. That's why they're digging out that corpse. They need something to eat."

On the reverse side Poole found a neat oval stamp in black ink containing the letters USIA and a number. It seemed to him that Waxman was reading too far into the picture.

He handed Poole another one that looked as if it came from the same roll—a makeshift hearth surrounded by some charred and familiar-looking bones. Poole felt a little dizzy.

"You see my point?" Waxman said.

"No."

"You can't depend on your prejudices. Certain things that might seem unlikely are far from impossible."

Poole looked at the stack of photos still remaining in the carton. There must have been forty or fifty of them. "You collect those?"

"Uh-huh. Atrocity pictures."

"Why?"

"I'm like you, I guess. I'm interested in boundaries."

Poole glanced at the top photo again.

"I'm almost superstitious about it. As if as soon as I draw a line somewhere, anywhere, it becomes inevitable that I'll have to cross it."

"That's a pretty crackpot idea."

"Maybe. But what bothers you, I think, is that I don't immediately assume that you're lying. That's what you expect."

Poole didn't answer.

"I used to work at the admitting office of a psychiatric hospital in Middletown. We'd have people walking in all the time saying, 'I'm a nut, let me in.' They weren't kidding. They'd lost confidence in their own sanity, but at least they knew that we, the M.D.'s, still knew which end was up. This was important to them. Now you think I'm going soft on you."

Poole sat back and pushed the photos away. "So you believe me. So what?"

Waxman reached into his shirt pocket and produced a small black-capped bottle, the kind used to fill syringes, and put it down on the table between them. It had a white label with lots of fine print and a clear liquid inside. "You could try this."

Poole didn't reach for it. "What the hell is that?"

"A common research isotope with a half-life of about six months. The body excretes it along a well-established curve. It counts heartbeats, in effect. If you went away again it might tell us exactly how long you were gone."

Poole picked up the bottle. Down at one corner he noticed a little exploded windmill, the radiation symbol. Waxman took advantage of his silence to start packing up the photos.

Poole lit another cigarette. His forehead and cheekbones felt heavy and numb, meaning that he was starting to get a headache. It occurred to him that he was tired of listening to Waxman talk. He always talked about him, Poole, and Poole was tired of hearing himself talked about. It wasn't clear to him what good it would do to have this colorless radioactive juice in his veins.

"What is it?" Waxman said.

"I think I need another beer."

Waxman went out to the kitchen and came back with two cold Heinekens. They drank them.

"Feel better?" Waxman asked.

"A little."

Waxman went out again and brought back two shot glasses and an iced bottle of vodka. He filled them both level and they knocked them back. "One more should do it," he said, filling them again.

A minute or so later Poole said, "Right about now I start to get restless."

"Want to go for a walk?"

"Definitely."

Poole's legs felt nearly weightless as they thumped down the porch steps. The sun lit the sky from just under the horizon and the streetlights had started to glow.

They headed south, toward downtown, through several empty blocks. They passed a construction trailer with lights on inside, several abandoned cars, a pile of rolled-up fencing, and a billboard announcing a new office building. The occasional clang of a basketball rim floated in from the distance.

Poole unzipped his fly and stepped into a patch of weeds to relieve himself, the curved stream spattering on the edge of a broken cinder block. He was swaying a little.

"I'm drunk," Waxman said, hands in pockets.

"What'd you expect?" Poole smothered a laugh.

"You think it's funny?"

"No, not at all, it's very serious."

Some yards back from the road they noticed a portable traffic sign with a molded concrete base. They picked up rocks and started desultorily bombarding it. It wasn't easy to hit. Poole noticed that the wrist snap and follow-through made his stomach tighten and slosh. "Enough," he said, knocking the grit from his hands.

Poole walked on the sidewalk, Waxman in the street. It seemed to Poole that his feet were a long way from his head. Several streetlights cruised by at the usual altitude. The sky had turned the color of low-fat milk. He stopped and turned around, hoping to spot Waxman's building, but it had shrunk down somewhere in the distance. "Some doctor you are," he said.

When Poole turned, Waxman had disappeared. Someone said, "Over here." Waxman was sitting on a bench on the edge of the road, a wooden park bench that looked as if it had been dragged there for their especial use. Poole had been wanting to get off his feet. When he dropped onto it, he noticed that his surroundings weren't so eager to settle down; there was a slight but unmistakable drift to the right.

Off to the left an office building with strip windows blocked part of the western sky. The lights had come on inside and there were people moving around. Poole looked at his watch; it was after eight. His banker's shoes had collected several layers of dust.

"You want to know something funny?" he said.

"What."

"For a while there I thought you were going to be it."

The ground had risen and darkened around them, and Poole's cigarette glowed like a tiny orange meteor. A bright sliver of day still lingered on the horizon. Higher up a few stars had sparked into the deepening blue.

"It?" Waxman said.

"Yeah. The tour guide. The messenger. I've told you about this."

"How do you know I'm not?"

"You would've said so by now. Besides, I know better."

"You might have to invent one," Waxman said.

"Either that or stop waiting for him."

"What was he going to tell you?"

"The usual stuff. Who I am, what happened to me."

Waxman didn't answer. Poole smoked several more cigarettes. He had meant to say something more but his mind wandered and it no longer seemed important. When he looked up again it was nearly dark.

A police car turned onto the street two blocks down and advanced slowly, its headlights picking out the chunks of rubble in the road. It slowed down as it passed them, and Poole got a glimpse of the green glow of the dashboard and the two faces inside. A little farther down its searchlight flicked on and probed deep into a construction site.

"It seems to me," Poole said, aware of an oddly solemn note in his voice, "that my life has turned into a series of failed distractions. As if my real business lay elsewhere."

"So what's going to satisfy you?"

"Good question."

The air was cool and still. The nearest streetlight had burned out and they were sitting deep in shadow.

"I see you differently," Waxman said. "In my eyes, you're a lucky man."

"For what?"

"For your vision. For your freedom."

"You call that lucky?" Poole leaned down and crushed out his butt under his heel.

"You think you have a lot to lose," Waxman said. "I respect that — I can even admire it. But I have a different outlook."

"You're nuts," Poole said without much heat.

"I'm self-absorbed — there's a difference. I'm an idealist. You could say I'm in love with what I can't see. So you won't catch me making any rules for creation in general. It's bigger than I am. It doesn't have a human face. It manufactures shits like me by the billion." He paused, unhurried. "But it's the special cases that interest me — the rebels, the cripples, the madmen. Each one sees himself as the world's first man, the original Adam. Of course some of them have just been terrorized by various inner demons. But there are others, I'm convinced, who are more than that."

Poole wondered if he was serious. No matter how many times he told himself that this man didn't know what he was talking about, a small leaven of doubt remained. He wished he could see Waxman's face.

"These other worlds — they exist. They are within reach. Speaking for myself, I'd say there's a certain built-in masking effect, a sort of mental buffer, that prevents me from fully entering them.

"This isn't what you want to hear," he continued. "You're divided. On the one hand you have this power — or illness, as you would say — and on the other you have this loyalty to ordinary life. You'd like me to flatten out the conflict somehow. But you picked the wrong man — I can't do that. We're more alike than you think."

There was no need for Poole to say anything. He knew what was coming next. He wondered why he hadn't suspected it before, since it was the natural result and culmination of everything Waxman had said to him over six weeks. It was an obscenity, an outrage, and yet it was necessary somehow. All he felt now was a hunger to hear it actually spoken, just as the body of a piece of music creates an almost painful need for its last few bars.

"So I'm asking you a favor now," Waxman said. "You have the power to open these doors that lead outside our world. I'm asking you to open one for me."

There it was, exposed at last. Poole sat quite still and watched a pair of headlights thread their way through some low, darkened buildings two streets over.

"I'm asking you the way you asked Mac."

It was as if there were something evil in the air, something powerful and malevolent that had nothing to do with Waxman and yet was speaking out of his mouth.

"I can't," Poole said simply.

"Have you ever tried it?"

"No."

"You mean you're afraid it might work."

Poole was still following the car with his eyes. As it turned, its headlights swept across a vacant lot. "You don't know what it's like," he said quietly. "You don't know how horrible it is."

"That's right, I don't."

"Then why are you doing this to me?" Poole heard the rising, pleading curl in his own voice and it sickened him.

"It's your choice. You have to decide. But it would be interesting to see if you can control this thing, because it owns you now."

Poole didn't answer.

"We're talking about fear," Waxman said. "The worst kind."

How pleasant, Poole thought, to step back across — to say goodbye for the last time. No more waiting for the axe to fall. To do honor to his former life — not to dig it up over and over like a corpse that wouldn't die.

"No," he said. "Out of the question."

"This world," Waxman said, "is already contaminated. It breeds its own nightmares."

"I said no."

Waxman ended it there. It took a few moments for Poole to realize that he was finished. He began to breathe again. Waxman's feet scraped on the gravel as he shifted his weight. Something like normality started to seep back into the quietness and the low hum of the city around them.

But it wasn't the same as before. Poole sensed it. And so it came as no great surprise to him when, twenty minutes later, they approached the house and saw a small crowd gathered on the porch. The sodium lamp over the intersection lit the whole area with a strong rusty light, a false daylight. Four or five men were coming over from the gas station and a figure leaned out of a lit window on the third floor and called down to someone by the railing. A woman in a bathrobe, one hand holding it shut at her throat, ran down the steps to a car that had just pulled up. It looked like a fire; the whole building had emptied.

But there were no flames, just a weak whitish glow screened by a knot of bodies on the porch. Poole knew what it was as soon as he saw it. After a minute he and Waxman continued on their way, threading past the kids on the sidewalk, the clump of people on the stoop parting to let them through. Even in the inner circle there was no jostling for position, no reluctance to give ground. It was as if the line itself shed a certain decorum.

It hung quietly in midair, shivering a little from time to time like a butterfly still damp from its chrysalis. A soft, nacreous glow shone on the faces of the onlookers. Unlike any other Poole had encountered, it gave off light from both sides. It looked as if no one had tried to touch it yet.

Its edges, although clean and sharp, were rippling here and there. Someone clicked on the bare overhead bulb and it faded instantly, though it remained visible. The light went off after a few seconds and it brightened again.

Poole looked around at the circle of sober, diffident faces. Waxman was standing right next to him. There were shouts in the street and more cars arriving. The line was about six feet high and half again as wide; it seemed to have a separate anchor or focus in the upper left-hand corner, where a slowly pulsing bud or polyp interrupted its symmetry.

Poole stepped up beside it, rolled up his sleeve, and thrust his arm in up to the elbow, alarming the crowd. He could see his hand dimly; when he peered around the edge he saw that it had emerged untouched on the far side. Then he tried to run a finger along the inner rim but felt nothing at all — it was as thin as smoke. A woman at his back said, "Git away from there mister, you gone hurt yourself." Either the line hadn't finished forming completely or was a dud of some kind; it didn't seem to lead anywhere. Poole went around to the other side and tried the same experiment. By then other people had stepped closer and were reaching out for it, still leaning the other way, as if ready to bolt. The denseness of the bodies tightening around him began to bother Poole and he pushed his way out of the crowd to a free spot in the corner by Waxman's door. Waxman joined him there a moment later.

The mood of the crowd lightened; it became almost festive. The kids who had been held back up to then got loose and started racing around. Poole lit a cigarette, sat down on the railing, and rubbed his moist hands on his knees. Several more clumps of people were hurrying down the street from an apartment house a block away. The porch creaked like a ship in heavy weather and the voices blended into a steady hubbub.

Poole had an urge to flee. In spite of what he had said to Waxman on the bench down the street, he felt directly responsible for this event. That familiar odor of panic was thick around him again, that sense that reality was dissolving right before his eyes.

Waxman kept turning back toward the line, as if to make sure it was still there.

"Seeing is believing," Poole said.

A skinny gray dog yelped and ran out in the street, pursued by a stiff-tailed mutt. Two kids on bikes were swooping under the streetlight like moths. Somewhere in the crowd a deep, resonant voice said, "It's glory, people, it's glory that's come in here tonight." There were giggles and a few catcalls. Down by the sidewalk a half-dozen boys with bare legs and high socks were sitting on Waxman's old Cadillac. A police car pulled up across the street.

"It's going to be busy around here for a while," Poole said.

"No kidding."

"You might get chased out. Lots of people — *lots* of people."

"You think that thing'll last?"

Poole glanced up at Waxman's troubled eyes. "It's like no line I ever saw."

They both turned to look at it. The blue-white glow shone up over the heads and shoulders of the spectators and left a halo on the ceiling.

"It's not that bright," Poole said. "It'll vanish in the daytime."

"But will it ever open up? Will you be able to cross it?"

"I don't know."

Poole watched two cops, one white and one black, get out of the cruiser, their T-shirts showing through their collars. They stood together on the driver's side and studied the crowd.

Poole watched them cross to the sidewalk and start talking to a stocky older man with a checked hat and a bow tie. He leaned back from the waist and traced a large oval with his hands, then pointed up at the porch. It looked to Poole as if he was laughing. The white cop, who had a thumb hooked in his belt, cocked his head and glanced at his partner.

The crowd around the line was more fluid now; some people were drifting away and others were coming back for a second or third look. The flow from down the street had dried up for the moment.

The cops climbed up the stoop and entered the crush. Off in the distance, along the built-up edge of Atlantic Street, tiny groups of dark figures were turning into the cross streets and starting toward them, clearly visible under the lights. More cops arrived, raising the temperature. One of them parked to block the street at the intersection and turned on his blue flashers. Up on the porch, people had stopped looking at the line and were glancing at one another. A fat girl in pink stretch pants took several pictures with a cheap flash camera.

"We're going to get herded off of here," Waxman said.

"I'm not that anxious to stick around."

"We've got to talk about this."

"I know."

Their eyes met. Somebody threw a bottle and it shattered in the street. The police lights rocketed clockwise across the crowd.

Poole saw something in Waxman's eyes. It was an admission of sorts, an acknowledgment, and it made a claim: it asserted that the two of them had a special relationship to what had happened here tonight. Once that look had passed between them there was no need for assurances; they knew they could trust each other. As soon as a man with a bullhorn got up and ordered everybody off the porch, the two of them retreated into the apartment and Poole went out the back way, got in his car, and drove home.

As he heard later, the police had trouble with the crowd. By eleven o'clock there were a dozen patrolmen facing three or four hundred neighborhood people. A cordon had been set up around the now-empty porch and the uniformed men inside it made easy targets for rock throwers hidden by the crush. A window shattered, spraying glass. The department answered with mounted officers and used them to push the crowd back across the street, the first few rows recoiling from the animals' huge flanks. People drawn in from the more distant neighborhoods downtown found a confrontation in progress and added to it simply by being there.

Waxman later told Poole some of the things he had heard inside the crowd — that the cops had shot someone, that there was an armed man in the house, that a drug factory had been raided. The line was visible from a distance but didn't look that unusual.

After several arrests — two or three kids were shoved into cruisers — it became apparent that the cops had the upper hand, and the onlookers got tired of waiting for something to happen. The crowd shrank rapidly and by midnight there were only fifty or sixty people loitering behind the barricades, mostly those who lived close by and had been there from the beginning. The police started to relax and people moved around freely again.

When Waxman got back up on the porch he recognized the mayor, a tiny woman named DeCastro who dressed like an attorney and had brought two of her sons along. The police chief and the fire marshal were conferring quietly in a corner. Among the gawkers surrounding the line were several white men in open shirts and nappy shoes who turned out to be academics called in to have a look. They stood out of the way when a camera crew from a local station moved in, trailing wires. The line disappeared as soon as their lights came on, and they had to make do with a few interviews, though they seemed remarkably unbusinesslike about their work, as if they knew they were settling for a distant second best.

Now that the crowd and the drama had dissipated, the line

quickly recovered its fascination. People lowered their voices in its vicinity. They were drawn to it but kept a certain distance, all except a few kids, who made a game of dashing through it. Pale and bluish, it rippled noiselessly in midair and cast a cool, snowy light over the darkened porch. Waxman talked to a professor of physics who had spent five minutes shining a flashlight on it and fanning it with a piece of cardboard. Clearly mystified, he muttered about ionized fields and plasma dynamics for a few moments, then admitted that he didn't know what the hell it was and that he felt as if someone were pulling his leg. When he heard that Waxman lived inside, he said, "Move out now," and laughed uneasily. He left a few minutes later.

The line lasted through the night without incident. The mayor went home, as did the professors, the camera crew, and the police, who led their horses into a van at one A.M., leaving a pair of patrol cars stationed across the street. Some of the tenants brought out chairs and gathered in small groups to talk it over, including a few older men with tired faces and rumbling voices whom Waxman had never seen before.

At around two, Poole came by with Carmen and Lucinda in Carmen's car, the compact. Waxman was sitting on a corner of the balustrade, talking to a cop. By then the neighbors had gotten used to the line and were staring at it much as they might stare into a hearth or a campfire. Poole was recognized as the man who had first touched it and his arrival caused a little stir. He was carrying Lucinda, who was awake and restless. He and Carmen stood beside the line for a minute or so before the cop came up and asked them to move back.

They joined Waxman at the railing. He told them what had happened in the last few hours — the near riot, the police reaction, the moment when everyone seemed to remember how late it was and started home.

"It'll be different tomorrow," Poole said. "This place is going to get serious attention."

Waxman glanced at Carmen, who had taken the chair against the wall. She was a small, dark-haired woman in jeans with a boyish figure and watchful eyes — eyes that coolly regarded the entire scene, as if the glowing intruder weren't necessarily its most significant feature. Poole hadn't introduced her. Though she made no great point of it, Waxman could tell she was watching him carefully. She sat well back in the chair, composed and alert but a little chin-high, as if she were used to a more wholesome environment.

"Mrs. Poole," he said firmly, "I'm William Waxman. We've talked on the phone."

She gave him her formal attention. "Yes."

"I'd like to ask you some questions. May I?"

After a moment she said, "Certainly."

"Do you know what that thing is?"

She stared back at him briefly. "Well, I know what Rocker thinks."

"What's that?"

"That it's a line."

"A line meaning a sort of hole or doorway."

"Uh-huh."

"Do *you* think that's what it is?"

She paused. "I don't know."

"Well, it's not a commonplace object, is it?"

"What are you trying to say?"

"Nothing, except I find it very odd that it shows up on my porch just after I ask your husband to produce one."

Poole laughed. "Remarkable, isn't it?"

Waxman watched a big late-model American car pull into the gas station across the intersection and switch off its lights. He turned to Poole. "You once said that the hallmark of the real world is that it has no lines in it. Remember that?"

"Yes."

"Well, I'm just the slightest bit alarmed by the sight of this thing. Aren't you?"

Poole's chair creaked as he turned toward it, its undulant glow framing his stillness. He seemed to be in no hurry to answer. When he finally did, his voice was low and distinct. "It looks like more than a line to me. It looks like the fucking end of the world."

Waxman decided not to argue. "So why'd you come back?"

"I wanted to see it again. And I wanted Carmen to see it."

"You could've waited till tomorrow."

"Unh-unh — this is my last visit."

"Oh?"

"Look," he said quietly, "it doesn't belong here. If I knew how to get rid of it, I would. But I don't. So I'm going to count to ten and hope it goes away. That's it — that's my entire program."

Waxman didn't answer. He had spent a good part of the last six hours staring at the thing and it still hadn't become familiar. Any moment now, he had thought, I am going to get used to it — any moment I am going to recognize that just because I've never seen one before doesn't mean that it signifies anything in particular. But he hadn't gotten used to it. The longer he looked at it, the more threatened he felt. It was uncanny the way it engaged all his defenses.

And now he had Poole sitting right in between, Poole, who wasn't exactly the angel Gabriel but who wasn't quite Joe Blow either — the same Poole who had softened him up for this moment with his twice-a-week mushmouthed Scheherazade — and though Waxman usually favored the conservative approach, this time he wanted to operate directly. He wanted, in fact, to grab Poole by the neck.

"Doctor," Carmen said, "I think we ought to recognize something."

"What's that?"

"That we're in over our heads. That we don't know what we're facing."

"Fine. So what?"

"So if we're going to admit that that thing has any importance at all, then Rocker's the expert. So the question is now, do we trust him? I say yes. I say yes, we trust him."

Poole didn't look at her. He was sitting slouched back with his daughter curled on his chest.

"Of course we trust him," Waxman said. He saw a black kid in a nightshirt approach the line, his wary face paled by its glow.

"You say that pretty easily."

"What choice do we have?"

"Well, you've seen tonight how risky it is to take him for granted. He steals things, doctor. He steals them and won't give them back."

Poole looked uncomfortable. Waxman didn't like her tone. "Tell me about it."

"Now I can, can't I? Now that it means something to you."

This girl is no lightweight, Waxman thought. She was holding him down with those dark, humorless eyes. "So you think we're in trouble."

"I don't think anything. All I know is that certain things changed when I wasn't looking. They've changed me, all right."

And they'll change *you* too, Waxman thought.

Poole watched another squad car pull up across the street. "We'd better go," he said.

"Not yet," Waxman said.

Poole had started to get up. He stopped.

"This thing is our baby. We've got to take it into custody."

"How do you propose to do that?"

Waxman turned to Carmen. "Maybe you'd like to stay."

She didn't look away. "Doctor," she said finally, "I didn't even want to come here. I was afraid I'd see what I'm seeing. But to be honest with you, it doesn't change anything."

Poole laughed and stood up. He looked back at the line, resettling his daughter on his shoulder. Another police car pulled up across the street.

Waxman stared at the line. Tiny months zipped through it unhindered. "This is bad," he said. "This is no time to back off."

"Go ahead then," Poole said. "Do your worst."

"But you're running away."

"We could sit here all night. We wouldn't be any wiser."

"Are you going to sleep now?"

"I'll tell you what — I'm *not* going to hang around until that thing owns me. I'm not going to give it that chance. That's not what I came for."

Waxman looked at Carmen. She had nothing to add. He turned back to Poole. "Well, I'll tell *you* what — I'm not through with you yet. Your treatment's just getting started."

Poole looked out at the street. "No kidding."

"Believe it — I'm going to squeeze that thing *hard*. In my book you don't stop just because there's a little blood. You finish the job."

Poole looked over his shoulder at the line again.

Waxman lowered his voice. "I saw what happened tonight. I was there, remember?"

Poole turned toward him. "You might call me if you notice any change. I'd be interested to know."

"You would, huh."

"I'm not suggesting you stay here. But if you decide not to leave."

"Why should I leave?"

"Because you and I messed around and we took it too far. Maybe there's no permanent damage — maybe we were that lucky. But you're a fool if you can't see this is a dangerous place." He looked utterly serious.

"I'm not leaving," Waxman said.

"Well, then, you'd better hold on to something, because you

can go a long way without even trying." He turned to go down the steps.

"Look," Waxman said quickly, "as far as I'm concerned you and I are buddies for life."

That stopped him. When he looked back a certain complex recognition showed in his eyes. "Well," he said softly. "I guess I can't complain about that." He turned and left.

Waxman was still watching him when Poole's wife touched his elbow. "Doctor," she said, "you have to trust yourself too."

He looked down at her. "What? More advice?"

"You're alone with us now. That's how it is."

He didn't answer. He felt like the butt of an elaborate joke; they'd be howling with laughter as soon as they turned the next corner.

"I won't call you here," she said quietly. "But you know where we live."

She joined Poole on the sidewalk. He watched them walk down the block, get in their car, and drive away.

FLASH AND BLAST

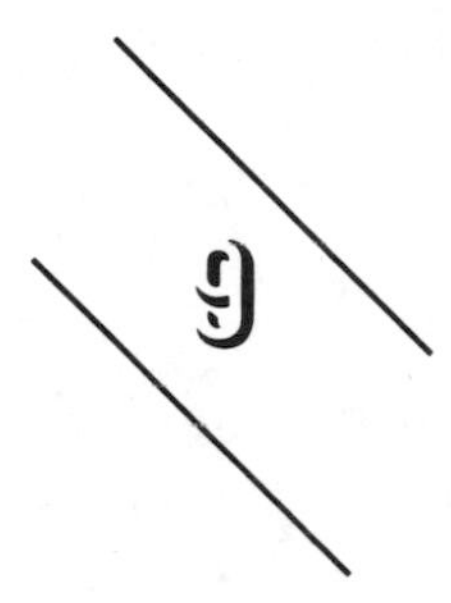

WAXMAN dozed for an hour or two later on but was awake again at five-thirty with a thick head and gummy eyelids. The sky had just started to lighten and turn watery. He lay in bed for a few minutes, listening to the pigeons coo on the fire escape, then pulled on a pair of jeans, unlocked the front door, and stepped out into the damp morning stillness.

The line was still there, though not as bright as before. Several of his neighbors were still wrapped up like shrubs in burlap at the far end of the porch. He stared at it for a few moments, his throat dry and his face rubbery, then went in again and sat down to think it over.

In the daytime, as Poole had predicted, the line vanished. This made work difficult for the crew of researchers who arrived just after nine. By midafternoon they had brought in a portable darkroom tent made of black nylon and set it up around the line. In the next few days Waxman watched dozens of visiting experts duck inside and come out blinking a few minutes later. The tent came down every night and was stored in a trailer across the street.

According to the landlord, a man Waxman met for the first

time that week, the city of Stamford had impounded the property and could therefore toss out all the tenants any time it pleased. He had also heard that the mayor had been promised federal subsidies for the extra police work required to keep the site secure. As the building's owner, he had tried to find out who exactly was pulling all the strings and had received answers ranging from the Army Corps of Engineers to the Environmental Protection Agency; he was still working on it.

At any rate, the takeover was a success and Waxman wasn't allowed to park out front anymore. He had to leave his car on the next block, beyond the gas station, and identify himself to a cop posted between two sawhorse barricades before he could approach the house. Once he was past, no one paid him any attention and he could go where he liked.

The initial TV and newspaper reports brought in crowds of onlookers, who were admitted in groups of twenty or thirty at a time, so that anyone willing to stand and wait until one or two in the morning was guaranteed a close look at the line. It became known as "the Stamford Bubble" and incited widespread skepticism and derision. The most popular theory claimed it was a stunt designed to draw attention to some new optical or electronic technique; at any moment, it was said, the people behind it would step forward and announce their discoveries, now that sufficient interest had been aroused. It was no accident, supposedly, that it had appeared in a city where dozens of major corporations were headquartered.

What it meant for Waxman was a constant parade of footsteps past his front door at all hours of the day and night, the sweep of headlights across his interior walls, and a raft of unintelligible murmurs floating in the front window. The researchers paid homage to the line by surrounding it with all sorts of sophisticated monitoring equipment. It was impossible to get his patients past the barricades with any speed and he had to move his practice to the clinic in Bridgeport. Needless to say, the relative peace and quiet that had first attracted him to 28 Selkirk were long gone. He went to look at a few apartments across town and nearly decided to move out.

He never did, however. The fact was that he regarded himself as a kind of personal envoy to the line, or at least a necessary witness. Poole had convinced him that there was more to it than was immediately apparent. He went so far as to believe that it was intimately linked to his own future. The line answered something in him; it was like a door opening suddenly in the room where he had lived all his life.

He could see that this was a naïve, irrational, and primitive idea, exactly the sort of notion that made life difficult for his patients and kept doctors like himself in business. An idea like that, once it became a motivating force, was a sure recipe for what clinicians called "inappropriate behaviors." He was loyal to it just the same. Thanks to its influence, he spent most of his free time within shouting distance of the line. He expected more from it; he believed that it was going to dazzle him again. He made a habit of coming out to the porch at dusk for its daily unveiling; two or three men started undoing the snaps that held the tent together, then pulled the fabric off its aluminum frame, revealing the still-faint image floating weightless inside. They were careful to collapse the entire structure without letting it touch the line at any point, as if it were fragile as smoke. Waxman enjoyed this delicacy; it gave the whole operation a ceremonial aspect. Shortly after dawn every day the same ritual was performed in reverse.

By the end of the week there were six construction trailers in the lot across the street, and a chain-link fence strung with barbed wire enclosed both them and his building in a compound of several acres. Outside the fence the area around the gas station had been turned into a parking lot. Every day, weekends included, there were at least a dozen technicians inside the fence, going back and forth from the trailers to the porch on their more or less obscure errands. The scene reminded Waxman of an anthill — the same disorganized haste, the same leaderless efficiency. At mealtimes food was set out on a table across the street, shaded by an improvised awning. Most of the people wore nothing more formal than jeans and sneakers; they all had little pocket badges printed with their names and pictures of themselves.

Waxman was there every day and nobody seemed to care that he didn't have a tag. One man — Waxman instantly marked him as a recent product of a grad program in psychology — had been assigned to interview the tenants and invited them one by one to an office in one of the trailers. When Waxman's turn came, he kept quiet about his experience with Poole, a not entirely unselfish gesture, but the last thing he needed was an unfavorable bill of mental health.

Although his grounding in the physical sciences wasn't particularly strong, he enjoyed picking up what he could about the experts' deliberations. By the end of the first few days they were all in agreement that the behavior of the line was, strictly speaking, impossible. They had separated its glow into its various components and found that most of them clustered toward the blue end of the spectrum, in the region of dwarf stars, lightning bugs, and magnesium flares, but the variety of wavelengths observed suggested no single heating or combustion but instead a complex of elements and temperatures influenced by any number of additional factors — in short, something not unlike sunlight itself. Since there was no way any such effect could be produced by a surface less than a micron in depth, this gave rise to the mirror theory, which explained the line as a sort of reflective membrane that altered and refocused available energies. The mirror-theory partisans assembled a magnificent arsenal of portable x-rays, strobes, flash bulbs, lasers, and ray guns of every description, pointed them at the line, and fired away. All their bullets passed through it untouched — as if the line neither gathered its energies from its surroundings nor produced them internally — as if it transferred them intact from some totally foreign and separate location.

Another group pinned its hopes on periodicity: they wanted to demonstrate that the line's hypnotic swellings and shrinkings, expressed as a calculus of intensity and surface area, followed curves dictated by externals like temperature, pressure, humidity, and so forth. Trained model builders, they quantified factors, linked equations, collected numerous readings, and when all was ready upended their data into the hopper of a high-speed computer in a lab in New Haven. When the smoke cleared, the machine announced that each of their indices varied randomly as a function of all others.

Waxman got to know several of the younger researchers, including a lively, outspoken woman with long milk-white legs, big plastic glasses, and ashy black hair. She was a mathematician and spent most of her time back among the trailers working for someone else. After they had caught each other's eye several times, it was plain to both that there was an interest and they cloaked it behind a superficial frankness. They contrived to run into each other several times a day and she told him exactly what she thought of the project and its personnel, while he professed to find her opinions both original and instructive — which, more often than not, they were.

She pointed out the man in charge, a heavyset, deliberate, and self-effacing chemist named Salmon, who could often be seen wandering around the compound with a bemused and tentative air, nodding wisely when spoken to and taking notes with a cheap ballpoint in a blue notebook. It was he who presided over the daily meetings that took place twice a day inside one of the trailers. Only a dozen or so attended — Waxman's friend rarely among them — but she seemed to know what took place.

Over and over, she said, Salmon had emphasized that their job was to *describe* the line rather then explain it and that no one should be surprised if it didn't behave naturally. That was why they were there: it was an exception. He reminded them that the history of science was littered with the wreckage of former certainties. He had heard the talk, he said; he had read the newspapers; there was a feeling that this was some kind of competency test, that they either had to wrap the thing up in a tight little package or go home with egg on their faces, even though everyone knew that good work took time and plenty of it.

In other words, she said (her name was Zabel Hand and she was twenty-eight), you have a group of people who have spent most of their lives cultivating their bent for consistent, systematic thinking, and you've shown them that the object of their scrutiny, the material world, is neither consistent nor systematic. So of course they were worried — it was like sending hemophiliacs to a knife fight. As for herself, she was a mathematician, a symbolist; she studied marks on a blackboard and therefore didn't insist that reality conform to her schemes, although she had to admit that the whole thing was a little spooky.

The weather had turned hot and sticky, drawing luminous fogs off the still-cool Sound in the morning and burning them away by midafternoon. Waxman's end of the porch had been marked off with a steel rail and converted to a sort of holding pen for the tourists who came every night to look at the line — young couples, sleepy kids, retirees on vacation. After having waited for an hour or more in the parking lot, they were none too impressed; the sight was less than spectacular. There was no young man hired by the owner to explain it to them, just an armed cop in a folding chair on the other side of the stoop and perhaps a couple of shadowy figures with plastic tags mumbling to each other.

Waxman toured the compound at least once a day, feeling both exposed and invisible, like one of those would-be assassins who are recognized only after the fact, when the films are examined. There was plenty to look at; the street in front of 28 Selkirk had been turned into a construction site. A crane mounted on muddy treads sat in Poole's old parking spot at the side of the house and lifted crates full of machinery off flatbed trucks that backed through the gate — they were building a power plant. Another crane was ripping up the sidewalk to lay cable. Behind the trailers a little garden of chalk-white dish antennae pointed at the sky. Men with clipboards and pencils bawled at one another over the staccato roar of jackhammers; distorted voices crackled through loudspeakers; stacks of lumber rattled as they hit the ground.

The back entryway, where the fence ran closest to the house, was the only quiet spot left, and the other tenants had taken to gathering there in an oblong space of dry, beaten earth just beneath the rusted ladder that hung down from the fire escape. There the aunts and grandmothers sighed for an hour in the early evening with a half-dozen kids scrambling at their feet. They had their own ideas; they didn't expect to be told what the line was or where it had come from; any day now the landlord's agent would be coming around to tell them to move out. Through the fence, a block away, another office building was rising out of a cloud of dust and skeletal girders.

Waxman had seen one of their grown daughters on TV accuse the city of destroying the neighborhood — their homes had been invaded, they couldn't get to their cars, barbed wire and gasoline were stacked up all over. Ain't no wonder, the women said, she can't get her man past that gate no more.

Waxman didn't doubt that they were right and that in a matter of days they would all be moved out of the compound. It was obvious that the project was gaining momentum almost hourly, now that people in high places were starting to realize how freakish the line actually was. He could sense it in the crowds in the parking lot every night, the newsmen who no longer felt comfortable with their own jokes, the new gripes about discipline he was hearing from the researchers. The old first-come, first-served system for visitors had broken down after a week and was replaced by a mail-order lottery that nobody seemed to win. People gathered anyway; after dark the head of the parking lot turned into an open-air rendezvous for carloads of barhoppers and high school kids who drove in, looked around, and drove away again.

The line itself continued to defy inquiry. It looked the same as it had from the beginning, calmly rippling in place, fading every morning at dawn and brightening again at sundown. New rumors sprang up almost daily but they didn't last long. The project spokesman refused to make predictions. "We rule nothing out" was his standard rejoinder.

The woman Waxman regularly talked with didn't see any mystery in the general hardening of attitudes. The project, Zabel said, had failed to perform its priestly function — it couldn't explain the line. This was good science but lousy politics, because nowadays most people believed — mistakenly, of course — that scientists ought to be able to explain nearly anything.

So what we have here, she told him, is a textbook case of holy dread. The men who were running the show, the invisible men that Dr. Salmon talked to every night, had it worst of all. They gave the orders; if there were mistakes made, they would make them. That's why they were building this googol-volt transformer right on the site. They were nervous, they wanted options; she knew for a fact that the idea hadn't come from inside the project.

Her own feeling was that the original governing committee, with Salmon at its head, was no more than a shell by now; an entirely new group was already in place. It acted in secret; it would remain out of sight. Meanwhile she and all the other nobodies would be allowed to keep trying to redeem themselves, just so long as they didn't talk too much.

She and her colleagues were paid $700 a week and were expected to be either at the compound or the motel around the clock. A few days into the project they were all issued white cotton jumpsuits and safety shoes and were forbidden to wear anything else. Each of them was assigned to a research team and expected to take orders like a soldier. Their duties weren't that demanding; the point, Salmon had said, was to create a "climate of discovery." A plywood bulletin board across the street described each team's assignment and its findings to date. Zabel was writing programs for a group headed by a physicist whom she described as "ornery, witless, and dangerously weird."

In the debate over whether the apparition represented a crisis of some kind she came down firmly in the negative. In a crisis you had to act quickly or face the consequences — but what consequences? The very thing that made the line unique was that it had no apparent relation to its environment.

As time went on Waxman leaned more and more toward this opinion. Maybe that was why he couldn't bring himself to get in touch with Poole again, although not a day passed when he didn't look at the phone and think of his pale eyes and endless cigarettes. There were plenty of reasons to call him. In fact, Poole had asked Waxman to do so if anything happened to the line; he hadn't said "if and only if." And yet he couldn't do it. It had become almost unthinkable.

This was a personal quarantine based on the deepest convictions, because he could think like Poole now and Poole believed that the line was his own offspring. He also believed that it was a deadly threat to reality itself, which he equated with his own sanity. To approach it, to give it the comfort of his presence, would be a crime of the highest magnitude. Because the line was a sort of madness, a madness that didn't limit itself to its host but could reach out to infect the ground he walked on.

At times it seemed to Waxman that he lived inside Poole's mind. This wasn't a new experience for him; he had been trained to cultivate exactly this sort of clairvoyance. And yet in the past the return route had always been open; no matter how deeply he had burrowed into the mechanisms of a psychosis, he had never had any trouble detaching himself; the typical curse of his profession was not identification with illness but rather a withering lucidity. This time, however, it seemed that he had stayed too long.

Poole was the key, he believed; even now Poole's absence here was stronger than the presence of so many others. Because it wasn't really a question of insanity anymore; it was a question of a little blue-white puddle that might or might not represent the end of the world.

Late at night, lying in bed, when the light and noise of day could no longer compete for his attention, Waxman liked to stare up at the ceiling and lay out his meager handful of certainties. He had chosen each of them with care — they were all that separated him from complete vertigo. First, there was something out on the porch, something new to the world, at least to ordinary eyes. Second, prior to its appearance Rockland Poole had spent several weeks describing an experience to him, an experience that included many encounters with objects seemingly identical with the one on the porch. Third, the object appeared immediately after he had asked Poole to show him some evidence for his claims.

Waxman hoarded these facts. No matter what he might think of what he had seen and heard in the past few days, they couldn't be denied.

His mornings had fallen into a certain routine. He might walk over to Atlantic Street and buy a newspaper; he might hunt up Zabel and pester her for a bit; if he had to go to Bridgeport, he went to Bridgeport; he might even go back inside and write a few more pages of his study, *Religiosity in Schizophrenics*, knowing that none of these things was going to reconcile him to his essential inaction. The line had made him its prisoner; he considered it his duty to stay close. This was one way — the only way — of not giving in to it. He didn't think it was harmless. It had a narcotic effect; it made you say to yourself, "This can't actually be," but it wasn't harmless. He saw it through Poole's eyes now, but with this difference—he could not believe that it would draw strength from his nearness. Whereas Poole, he was convinced, stayed away not so much because he feared the line but because he feared himself and his effect on it. In a certain very real sense, Poole *was* the line. He had brought it back with him; it represented a power that did not exist before.

So of course Poole was scared; so of course he had retreated into his former life, which had now become a sort of lost kingdom, a ghost dance. Waxman imagined him riding the elevator, nodding at secretaries, packing his briefcase for a meeting—ritual acts performed in devotion to that greatest illusion, reality. In Poole's mind the line had become a symbol for temptation, evil, and death, for that portion of nothingness he carried inside himself.

That was how it stood at this moment; that was how it had stood for the last week and a half. The line didn't move and Poole didn't go to it. Each balanced the other; each remained dormant. Waxman watched both out of the corner of his eye. For a nickel, he thought, I would be a reasonable man.

The machines picked it up immediately. They stood in a broad half circle around the line like dogs waiting under a tree, some mounted on tripods, others clamped to wheeled carriages, all pointing their electronic muzzles at the same square yard of empty air. The black nylon darkroom tent had come down for the night and a strip of duct tape on the floorboards delineated the forbidden area; they loitered just outside it, patient and witless, each sending its own version of events down a cable under the road to the steadily filling magnetic reservoirs in the air-conditioned trailers across the street. They had all protested in unison when a boy of eight snuck between them to touch the line; since then they had noticed nothing out of character.

A man drinking heavily sugared coffee and reading a paperback sat facing a bank of brightly lit video monitors. The last time he had looked it was after two A.M. He was used to being alone with the machines; they kept him company. Every now and then he glanced up at the screens.

Between one moment and another he sat up and let the book fall. Eleven tiny amplifiers, each attached to a monitor, were beeping at him simultaneously. He reached forward and pushed a clear plastic button on a phone console, then another one beside it that started a tape rolling in an adjacent trailer. The machines could easily have done this job for him and would have done so within seconds if he hadn't beaten them to it — the idea, however, was to get him involved.

He was looking at the monitors when the phone buzzed and he picked it up. "I don't know," he said. "Like a thirty percent flicker across the board. It's still happening." He tapped the side of his face with a pencil. "No . . . no . . . just brighter, sort of . . . All right." He hung up.

A minute later there was a knock on the door at the far end of the trailer and another man came in. He walked down the narrow aisle toward the first and joined him, staring up at the screens. Each screen displayed energy output against a vertical scale and on each a greenish luminescence was spurting well above it usual ceiling. As the second man reached for another phone he said, "Turn off that damn noise, would you please?" The first flicked a switch and the beeping stopped.

By the time the cops let Salmon in at the gate, there were three men standing on the porch and looking at the line, their white suits reflecting its stuttering glow. One of them noticed Salmon and said, "Here he is." The others turned and watched the heavier, older man come down the empty street in shirtsleeves and khakis, his figure obvious and unhurried under the stark rusty light of the sodium street lamp. After he climbed into the shadow of the porch he nodded once and said, "Williams, Duncan, Bodine." He paused. "Something new, eh?" A moment later they all turned and looked at the line.

Rocker wasn't one of those people who would just lie in bed if he couldn't sleep. Beds were for sleeping in; he had better things to do than stare at the ceiling. The house wasn't so large that she couldn't hear him moving things around in the refrigerator or turning on the TV. She usually woke up again when he crawled back in.

Once upon a time she might have wanted to know what was bothering him. No more; she knew too much already. It seemed to her that all his comings and goings were just another part of his campaign to unhinge her. Because she was different—asleep or awake, she wouldn't leave the bed until it was time to get up.

She needed a good night's sleep. At least she definitely needed something, whatever it might be. Something other than what she had now, which was a secret urge to be a long way away from whatever this was. Even if she couldn't quite imagine what relief would feel like, she believed she'd know it when it came.

On this particular morning it seemed to her that Rocker had been even more restless than usual. When she woke up for the last time, it was because he and Cinda were standing fully dressed by the bed. It was after seven and broad daylight. "Get up," he said. He wasn't wearing a tie, she noticed.

Neither of them would be going to work, he announced. They were going to spend the entire day together. Something had happened during the night. He said he'd tell her about it at breakfast.

A few minutes later the phone rang. They were sitting in the kitchen over tea, Lucinda clamped to the table in her plastic seat and munching dry Cheerios one-handed. Carmen had dressed for work; she still hadn't called the school. As she got up to answer he said, "It's Waxman. He'll want to talk to me."

He was right. She handed him the phone and he sat back, the cord stretched halfway across the room.

"Yes, I know — I felt it here too. It started about two o'clock and lasted ten minutes . . . Scared the shit out of me . . . Surprised? At the time, yeah . . . Let me tell you something — this is it, this is the big one . . . I mean something's going to happen — no, I don't know what. More lines, maybe — maybe I'll cross over again . . . It's just a feeling, that's all . . . Probably sometime today . . . Look, there's here and there's there, remember? I'd say something's building up over there and I'm feeling it here . . . Well, yeah, but they aren't so far apart anymore . . . Could I be wrong? Sure I could." He glanced over at her. "I hope I am . . . We're going to stick right here and wait it out . . . That's the thing — if there's anyone you want to be with after today, then you'd better find them now — otherwise . . . otherwise forget it. I told you, it's just a feeling . . . No, I'm not giving in to it, I'm being perfectly realistic . . . I couldn't say . . . I have no idea . . . Yes, of course it's insane, but so what?"

He lit a cigarette. "Look, I don't care what happened to the line — that's just a reaction, a telltale. It's like me, it's sensitized. It could've vanished completely. I'd be saying the same thing."

Cinda had stopped eating and was watching him. "Look," he said, "you don't have to believe me — seeing is believing. But just keep it in mind, all right?"

Earlier, they had crept down the stairs in a tight little group, Rocker testing each step as if it were thin as cardboard, one arm groping out front for invisible holes. In the kitchen he had left Carmen and Cinda at the door while he slid out across the patterned tile like a skater trying a dangerous piece of ice. After he had examined the whole room, he straightened up and looked back at her. "They're not here," he'd said. "Yet."

She tipped in another gulp of tea. People, she knew, would

accuse her of abandoning him. But she just wasn't equipped to live with this man; if she didn't bend here, she would break.

She watched him hang up the phone. He was in love with it, this sickness. It made him king of the world — heartless, untouchable. And though he had told her that it was she he wanted most, that it was in order to protect her that he had to battle these monsters, she wasn't deceived. In his eyes, she was just a hostage, a blind.

She believed contradictory things. She believed that he was mentally ill; she was also convinced he was sane. She believed he was both the old friend she had married and the stranger who was going to kill her. This, to her mind, was intolerable — black should not become white, up should not become down. And yet what had she done about it? Nothing. She had been waiting for a moment just like this.

He seemed glad to finish the call. When he leaned forward again he was rubbing his hands and glancing back at the clock. "All right," he said, "we go out, we do a little shopping, and we come back here."

After they got in the car, Cinda strapped in back, he remembered he had forgotten something and they all had to go inside again. He found the item, a receipt, under the phone in the den.

They walked into the ShopRite on the Post Road just after it opened, and the aisles were empty except for a few clerks putting out produce. Cinda sat at the top of the cart while he packed it solid with canned goods — beans, vegetables, tuna. "Anything that keeps," he said. He emptied whole shelves into the basket. When they rolled up to the check-out he pulled Cinda out of the cart, told the girl to start ringing it up, and grabbed another one, this time going for rice, pasta, and lentils, topping it off with a dozen cartons of Winstons and as many boxes of salt. At the last moment he grabbed a couple of gallon jugs of vegetable oil and several ten-pound boxes of powdered milk. "This is what they send to Upper Volta," he added, "where millions face starvation."

When they got to the register a kid was already bagging the first load. The girl ringing it up looked bored and had to keep pushing her glasses up her nose. "Cash," Rocker said. The tape was two feet long and the bill came to over three hundred. He paid with fifty-dollar bills; his wallet was stuffed with them.

They went to Caldor's next and bought flashlights, tape, and nylon rope, moving over to sporting goods for a couple of Coleman stoves and fuel. They had to put the back seat down in the Honda to fit it all in and Cinda moved up front to Carmen's lap. He drove as he usually did — a little too fast. The last stop was a hole-in-the-wall place in Springdale, a dank wooden storefront on a side street with a copper bell over the door and a couple of secondhand TVs in the window.

A musty old man sitting on a stool over a workbench strewn with electronic parts got up when they came in. He seemed to recognize Rocker; he led them back past the cellar stairs to a plank-floored alcove, where he jerked on an overhead light and slid behind a glass case with a worn maple top. The cubbyhole had shelves on all sides that rose high into the dimness; a rack behind him held twelve or fifteen rifles.

Rocker pushed across the counter the receipt he had taken out of the den; Carmen saw it was a printed form from the Stamford Police Department. The man coughed throatily, nodded, and stole a quick glance at her and Cinda before he coughed again and turned to the corner behind him.

"Mister," she said evenly, "we don't want any guns."

He kept rummaging in the corner; he didn't seem to have heard her. Rocker faced forward and said nothing, a finger tapping the counter.

"We changed our minds. I said we don't want any guns."

When the man turned around he was holding a rifle by the

end of the barrel. He didn't look at her; he had a rag and was buffing it here and there.

Just then Cinda reached out from her shoulder and grabbed for something on a shelf; it fell and smashed on the floor. Rocker stooped, gathered up the pieces, and piled them on the counter — the remains of a model locomotive. The man leaned forward and looked them over. "Piece a junk," he said, shrugging. After a moment he lifted up the rifle and passed it over to Rocker. They leaned together and he began to point out its features with a stubby pencil.

Lucinda had seen something else and was squirming to reach it. Carmen turned abruptly and started back for the glow of daylight at the front of the store. The bell rang; she was out on the sidewalk and he hadn't followed. The leafy, little-used street was empty except for a man in white sitting on the back lip of a laundry truck, smoking. When she saw him, she noticed that there was a Stamford police cruiser parked just beyond. She got in the car and waited, watching the mirror.

Rocker came out a few minutes later carrying two long packages in brown paper and a heavy cardboard box. He opened the hatchback, slid everything inside, and slammed it shut, then threw himself in beside her. He didn't look at her as he turned the key. "That was an incredibly stupid thing you just did," he said. "I don't think you realize."

After he turned the first corner she asked him if he had seen the cop.

"This isn't Texas. You buy guns in this town, you get noticed."

They followed a big green sanitation truck down Hope Street, a few scraps of paper dangling from its grimy back end. He pointed at it. "That," he said, "is civilization. Civilization is what's going to get scarce around here."

She didn't answer. He had committed himself now; he had said today was the day. Better to go along with him then and let his own predictions do him in — provided, of course, that he didn't start fooling with those guns.

When they got back to the house they took everything in through the garage. It filled an entire corner of the kitchen — almost two dozen bags. "What I anticipate," he said, "is a repeat of my prior experience. Only now it'll take place right here. Here, where the three of us live."

Later, after they'd been sitting for a while, he relaxed toward her a little. Slowly, and without much in the way of preparation, he began to describe to her the new world they were going to live in — a sort of infinite shoal of islands in time, each of them separate and bordered by lines.

"It'll be hard for you at first. You'll think everything is gone — everything. You'll be right, in a way. You can't make plans over there. Things change from one moment to the next. The way we live now — always moving forward in a certain direction — that won't work at all. But you can't cry about it — it changes you, that's all, and you can't go back. Your life is over — everything is over — but you're still there."

It was a bright, sunny morning and the neighborhood was quiet around them, just a car sighing by out front every now and then and the mailman's shoes on the porch at ten-thirty. When her friend Beth called from work to ask how she was, she said it was just a bug and she'd be back tomorrow — as if there'd be a tomorrow, as if this was not the end of the world. It wasn't clear to her which result Rocker was hoping for. Something had happened to him during the night; he had felt, as he said, "everything slip a little."

He wouldn't be any more specific; he was much more interested in talking about their future together. "All this stuff," he said, waving at the groceries, "is just to tide us over the first week or so. People will panic — they'll be dangerous to be around. You're going to see some horrible things, I promise you. In this neighborhood, for instance, I'd guess that ten percent at most will make it through the first three days — all the rest are going to stumble into lines. That's what we have to avoid — if we get separated, that's how it'll happen.

"Later, when things start to cool off, we'll be able to look around a little. It won't be like before. It won't even be like it was for me last time, when I still had a real world to get back to. We'll be living, you see, in a series of private landscapes — places that exist only because someone happened to imagine them. They'll be connected by lines. That's the main thing — to find out where the lines are and where they lead."

She understood him perfectly; this whole effort was an attempt on his part to save their relationship, to put them on an equal footing again. In his eyes she had become a wingless, earthbound creature, and out of some obscure combination of guilt and nostalgia he had decided to take her flying. He didn't seem to realize that she would never be able to follow him. She knew herself; she knew what she was. All the stuff he had collected this morning — it was an offering to her, an attempt to coax her out of her stubborn sanity and let him carry her away. Tomorrow, however, it would still be here and so would she — there was a prophecy she could believe in. As for him, he might or might or might not be able to reconcile himself. That was an interesting question — whether, having destroyed her world by discovering he could leave it, he would keep trying to put it back together again.

The day lengthened slowly. By two-thirty, when the sharp cries of eight- and ten-year-olds coming back from school began to filter over the hedges and back lawns, they had been in the kitchen for over five hours. She had graded a few dozen tests; she had read most of the *Times*. All the bags they had brought home were still in the corner by the dishwasher. Although each passing minute weakened his case, she was determined to let him be the first to make excuses. He showed no particular impatience. He sat with his back to the screen door and had a cigarette now and then; for a man who was about to be shown up as an ordinary mortal, he seemed remarkably relaxed. Sometime soon, she hoped, he would turn to her, shrug, and admit that it was beginning to look as if he had been mistaken and that maybe neither of them would be going anywhere today. She would settle for that; she wouldn't ask any more.

When she looked up again it was almost three. Rocker had eaten an apple right down to the seeds and was pushing them around with a fingernail. She could tell he knew he was beginning to look like an idiot; he would have to say something before long. Cinda was sitting on the floor by the bags and talking to herself in her usual singsong way. Out by the back fence the spidery new tomato plants were drooping in the sun.

She watched him pick up the dark, tear-shaped seeds one at a time and drop them in the ashtray. The long brown packages were still leaning up against the dishwasher like stage properties, untouched. The grocery bags made a compact bulwark around them. She was reminded of those pictures from the fifties of back yard bomb shelters, little underground vaults full of bottled water and Chef Boyardee. It was as if he wanted to put her in the mood, to create a sense of expectation.

Suddenly it fell into place: the difference between last night and those other times was that last night the thing had come for him and failed. He had fought it and won. And that was what he couldn't admit, not even to himself — that he was stronger now, that he could beat it, and that if he vanished again it would be by his own choice and not because he was simply swept away.

Yes, something had "slipped" — but it wasn't, as he claimed, the world they lived in, but rather the grip of that other place, his precious imaginary playground. And when he had realized this, when he recognized at a gut level what had actually happened, he had immediately denied it. He didn't want to be ordinary again. That was what all this stuff was for — not preparation for a possible disaster, but an attempt to bring one on! Calling it down from heaven, more or less.

She watched him lean over and take Cinda under the shoulders, lifting her onto his knee. Her breathing had shifted to a new, deeper rhythm.

The phone rang. She got up to answer; it was Waxman. "Is Rocker around?" he asked.

"Yes."

"Can I talk to him?"

"Maybe. What do you want?"

She felt him hesitate. "I'm at my place — I just learned something. The line disappeared."

"Well, of course."

Another pause. "You already knew?"

She looked at Rocker. "It's over now. That's all — no big deal. The danger has passed, as they say."

"Is he all right?" Waxman sounded a little panicky.

She kept looking at Rocker. He had leaned forward, ready to get up, but he wasn't moving.

"Yes, doctor, it's over. It's time to get on with our crummy little lives."

He started to say something but she pressed the hook down and hung up. She was still looking at Rocker. After a moment she walked over, lifted Cinda out of his lap, and took her down the hall to the front door. We can't afford to be separated, he had said. Let him prove it, she thought.

She had her back to the hallway. Cinda reached out for the screen and dragged her tiny fingertips across it, frowning. She heard his chair squeak back and his footsteps quiet on the carpet behind her.

When she finally turned around he said, "You don't believe me."

"Should I? I don't think you believe it either."

"I swear to you, Carmen — I do." He had a weary, almost hopeless look in his eyes.

"Then go, why don't you. Only don't take me. Don't bother."

"It's not like that. We're all in it now."

"That's what you keep saying. Maybe if you say it enough, it might come true."

He didn't answer. She looked out the door again. Neither of the Eastmans was home yet across the street. A kid rattled by on a bike, his white shirt flashing in the leaf-prismed light.

"Rocker," she said finally, "if you want to go, go. Don't let me keep you."

He moved up beside her.

"Door's open," she said.

"Carmen — " he began.

"Be honest — you like it over there."

He didn't answer.

"Because if you're not going," she said, "then let's drop all this. Let's just get on with it."

"Carmen," he said again. He turned and stared out the screen for a few moments. "Carmen," he said, facing her, "I can't leave you. Not even if I wanted. Don't you see?"

"No."

"Imagine," he said, "that I did go away. What would you lose? Not me — you can never lose me. That's what it means to love somebody — you can never lose them."

It wasn't what he said that bothered her, but the tone, the pleading note.

"Look," he said, "believe it or not, most of what you do over there is remembering. But remembering should come at the end, right? Not in the middle. I don't want this to be the end — I want it to be the middle."

She didn't answer.

"You think I want the sky to fall," he said. "You're right, I do. You know why? *Because I know it's going to happen.* Which is better — to go out and meet it or to keep running away? And when it happens, I want you with me. That's why you're here now. If I had my way, it would've happened hours ago."

"So what do you want to do?"

He looked at his watch. "Just a little longer. Humor me."

"Nothing's going to happen."

The phone rang again. "I want to answer that," he said. "Will you come with me?"

She followed him into the kitchen.

It was Waxman again. "Look," Rocker said, a new urgency in his voice, "I could be wrong, but I think this is it. The main thing is to stay cool and not start rushing around. Just stay where you are — if nothing's changed a half hour from now, I think we'll be all right."

So this is it, she thought — this is the moment. An odd notion occurred to her then. It approached her not as a fact but as a possibility, as sudden and distinct as a drop of cold water on the back of her neck, startling but not unassimilable: Suppose he was right? She was more intrigued than alarmed. Maybe then she would find out what had made such a fool of him. Her lack of fear convinced her that she was in no particular danger. Maybe the thing wouldn't come unless it was invited; maybe it was up to her to let it in the door. She watched Rocker heap a few further cautions on the unfortunate Dr. Waxman. His eyes had a life of their own, moving uneasily around the room and stopping short several times a second, as if hunting for the first signs of collapse. The more she thought about it, the more she became convinced that the choice might indeed be hers and that all that stood between her and rampant unreality was a mere germ of acquiescence, a consent that could change everything and needed only to be offered freely. And it would be a way of keeping him as well, of getting out from under the rock he had laid on her with his secret knowledge and his ghostly lovers. Brooded too long, certain kinds of innocence turned to poison.

The call was over. She watched him hold the receiver for a few moments and then reach back to hang it up slowly. He sat down at the table, leaning forward heavily on his elbows and avoiding her eyes. He knew he couldn't hope to hold this off alone; he also knew that they had no future together unless she welcomed it too, no matter what he said.

"Carmen," he said, facing her again. "This is it. Right now. Come with me."

Waxman clicked off the phone and looked across the street. The porch was empty except for the black nylon tent and the machines that surrounded it, their electronic snoots thrust under its skirts. Beneath the awning beside him a monitor showed the faintly luminous interior where the line had vanished. The sun was bright overhead.

A wild-eyed kid in a white suit ran up, snatched the phone from him, and shook it. "Does this work?" he asked.

This isn't right, Waxman thought. A knot of people stood just outside the gate, looking in. Only a moment earlier there had been nothing special going on.

A candy-red van pulled up in the lot. Its doors cracked open and everybody but the driver got out. They were from the A.M. shift; they had only just left. But they didn't come in; they were all staring at the porch.

Irritated, Waxman glanced to his left. More and more white suits were popping up from behind the trailers. They stopped dead at the edge of the sidewalk.

He looked at the porch again. Whatever was up there was screaming at him now. *Get away*, it said. *Run for it.* Strange that he couldn't hear a thing.

He was still wondering whether it might not be wise to move off when he saw the tent crack in several places like an egg. A huge brightness emerged. Too late, he thought, watching it. He had never seen anything so bright.

DREAM SCIENCE

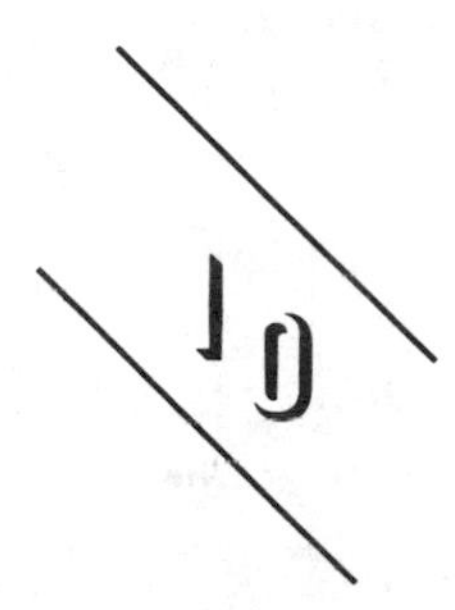

Poole and his wife were sitting in the kitchen surrounded by groceries when Stamford went up. It was a sunny day and their windows faced east, so the flash barely lightened the room. It traveled six miles and bounced off the sky above the lilacs along the back fence, whitening for an instant and quickly decaying. Then a deep thunderous rumble approached on the ground, building until the bulb covers on the hanging lamp tinkled in their cups. About two minutes later the last item, a tide of hot air, moved through the trees.

There was rain the next day and it washed most of the ash off the leeward towns. By then people had begun to realize that there hadn't been any war. Bits of Waxman's building were floating down on Labrador and Galway.

No one came to Poole's house. Even he found it difficult to put the blame on himself.

But the world wasn't unready for Stamford. Generations of experts had meticulously prepared for much greater disasters. And so within a half hour there was a white van rolling down Poole's street with a loudspeaker warning everyone to stay inside and shut doors and windows. Those needing medical attention were advised to display a bed sheet. After it passed, a woman two houses down ran her kids into the car and drove away.

Poole was still in the kitchen. Thanks to a maverick news director who would later be fired, the first aerial pictures were coming over the TV. Like thousands of others he sat and watched the lens travel past the long sea cliff of charred steel overlooking the highway, each corporate megalith swirling with dust and funneling black smoke into the sky.

He spent most of the next seventy-two hours hunched over the set, filling an ashtray with Winstons. He didn't wash or change or leave the house. He wouldn't answer the phone or go to the door. When neighbors came over he barely acknowledged them. From their street alone nine people had vanished in downtown Stamford.

Subsequent network reports showed the world what had happened that afternoon. There was now a mile-wide crater in the heart of the city; in aerial shots it looked like a dish full of sand. Close-ups from the periphery displayed some of the lesser results: a truck melted down on its hubs, two burned corpses entwined, a charred high-rise lying on its side like a brick. With the aid of maps and newspaper photos Poole established what he already suspected — that the blast had centered on a spot just east of Atlantic Street and about ten blocks north of the turnpike. Waxman's neighborhood; a bull's-eye. There was nothing there now.

More pictures — Soviet and Japanese delegations deplaning in daylight. An antinuclear demonstration at the UN Plaza. Stock shots of the White House. Rows of hospital beds. Satellite images of a pill-shaped cloud. Nothing but pictures.

Carmen and Cinda moved in with a friend across town. Poole didn't object; he didn't even ask why. He made no secret of his opinion that he was responsible for Stamford's destruction. People quickly gave up arguing with him; it was his wife they pitied.

They didn't come over unless they saw her car in the driveway. Rowayton had received very little fallout and the nearest condemned area was three miles away.

When the Bank of Connecticut learned that he was alive, alone out of seven fund managers in Stamford, they tried to bring him to Hartford to sort out records. "Can it wait?" he asked. "Not really," they answered. He said he was under great personal pressure. They offered to send a counselor — they sent a vice president instead.

When the man came to the door, Poole reached into a metal box on the stoop and handed him a small chunk of cement rock in an open bag of lead shot. "What is it?" the man asked, suspecting a joke. "It came from the office," Poole said. "You'd better handle it carefully — you've already received the x-ray equivalent of four hundred CAT scans." The rock was warm; he had baked it in the oven. The man dropped it like a snake and jumped back onto the lawn, clutching his wrist. "You're nuts!" he screamed. Poole's shrug implied that the point was debatable. The man crab-walked back to his Volvo. Poole went in the house. He heard no more from the bank.

But antics like that passed largely unnoticed, given what the authorities had to face: thousands of bodies to dig out and identify, hamstrung power and telephone grids, sniper attacks, brushfire panics, and above all a terrifying inability to account for the event. The first word from the experts was that the temperature curves indicated a thermonuclear blast but that fusion products were remarkably scarce; one even ventured to say that nine tenths of the forces had apparently escaped inward, as if at the moment of ignition they were sucked down a tube. That day dozens of papers ran a picture of a fire hydrant eight feet tall.

Poole didn't like anything he heard. It seemed to him that the entire world still believed that nothing had changed. And it was far from clear to him what he was doing, sitting at home reading newspapers. He had grown immune to the horrors on TV. The idea of blowing his brains out was just that — an idea. And time, the deceiver, was creeping forward again.

Carmen came over with Cinda in the late afternoons. Watching her move around the kitchen, he would think, *This is my wife.* She didn't try to get him to talk. She said plenty by what she did, washing whatever had been left in the sink and adding fresh fruit to the basket on top of the icebox. Meanwhile Cinda toddled around, laughing and pointing. They had played this game before; it was called Imitation of Reality.

Clearly he was paralyzed by this matter of definitions. Was this or was this not the so-called real world? On its face it might seem a trivial question, but it wasn't — it was anything but. The funny thing was that he couldn't even imagine a solid proof either way; he was becoming too good a dreamer. And while he was dreaming, thirty thousand people had gone up in smoke.

To suppose that he personally had had nothing to do with it tortured the facts. And yet, like every true criminal, he considered himself innocent. He hadn't come to this place as a stranger, an outcast. It wasn't his wish to see it destroyed. For that he held those other forces responsible, those shadow masters who couldn't stand to see him escape. But if he wasn't meant to be here, then why did he keep coming back?

Thoughts like these made thinking almost impossible. Poole didn't want to die; he didn't want to see any more Stamfords. At the moment he had just enough room to sit still. And since he had to believe something, he chose to imagine that when the walls started thinning again and the next moment approached, he would know it. Then he would have to decide.

On the third day he showered and shaved and went for a drive. The morning was brilliant; the roads were dry. The trees had finished their growth and the town was all shut up in green.

He went over the creek past the boatyard and into Norwalk. Coming out by the highway he noticed a faint stink in the air, like a chemical fire put out with water. He turned onto the ramp and headed for Stamford.

The road ended a few miles away in a wall of trucks shielding a tank and an antiaircraft gun. Long before he reached them he was steered off the last exit. He parked on the long grass of the embankment and climbed up the shoulder. There was a crowd there and some cameras and a dozen state cops beside portable barricades. Several people held handkerchiefs over their mouths. The pavement was empty on the far side of the trucks; Stamford lay around a couple of other bends. Now and then a closed trailer or van came from that way and went by without stopping. A helicopter gnawed the air overhead.

He had seen all this on the news. He sat on the guardrail and watched a party of longhairs in T-shirts share a six-pack. The crowd was large but fluid. A sweaty man with a bullhorn was reading from the New Testament. Poole spotted what he believed were several undercover cops.

He lit a cigarette. Down the slope behind him a kid was walking down the row of cars. He stopped by a vent window and looked both ways, then snaked an arm in and released the door. After poking around inside he came out empty-handed.

Poole heard a shout and saw a man in white standing halfway up one of the barricades, waving a sheet of computer paper like a flag. "People!" he called out. "Listen! They've been lying to you! There is no radiation! There is no radiation!"

Poole got up and moved closer. The man was a cheerful-looking type in his thirties with an open, intelligent face and a photo ID clipped to his shirt. Now that he had an audience, he stepped down off his perch and lowered his voice. "Look," he said easily, "it'll be announced any moment. It was an honest mistake. But I saw the figures myself. Normal levels. No heat at all."

Everybody looked doubtful. A cop watched with a thoughtful expression. Poole noticed more sheets of green paper lying around. The man had on one of those hooded beekeeper outfits volunteers wore in the crater.

"Who told you this?" someone demanded. It was a stocky gray-haired man with a heavy accent.

Though his anger seemed to take the young man by surprise, he didn't answer in kind. "Hey." He shrugged. "Does it matter? But try watching some of these trucks coming out — see if the windows are open. That ought to tell you something, right?" He paused, then said, " 'Scuse me," and went out through the group.

Poole watched him sit down on the guardrail and run a dusty hand through his hair. The cops didn't move. More advice from Jesus came through the bullhorn.

A yellow dog ran up the embankment and started dancing around. The stocky man had a grim, thwarted look, as if he'd exposed himself to no purpose. A woman came up and said, "What'd he say?" to no one in particular. Someone started to explain. Poole watched the dog squeeze past the barricades and bound off toward the trucks and the tank, seduced by the bright beachlike expanse of the road.

What now? he wondered. He had, it seemed, an adequate disguise; these strangers didn't sense what he was. He preferred their view of him to his own.

A well-dressed blonde from the camera crew toe-stepped across the road in heels and started talking to the man in the jumpsuit. He tapped his picture card and pointed away toward Stamford. Another pair of cars slid down the exit — one parked below and the other crossed underneath and climbed the opposite ramp, the driver's face turning in the window as he passed.

Poole could see by now that although he had plenty to look at around here, the kind of information he wanted wasn't apparent. There was a pressure, instead, to let his guard down, to call off the search for his monsters.

That was what he was afraid of, no doubt. Not of what happened to this place.

Hands in pockets, he drifted to the edge of the overpass and looked down. It was quite a drop. The spotted pavement below was the closest thing he had to a line.

What amazed him most was that he had ever thought he could pick up again here. That job of his, for instance — twenty, thirty years in an office trying to guess which way the same old nickel would fall! And his wife, his daughter — step by step, hand in hand, forever. Forever!

But the hardest thing was that he knew even now that once upon a time he could have lived it, that he had truly believed it was his greatest desire.

Die once, people said, and you're ruined for life.

He turned around. A little breeze was coming up from the west. A truck went by with its windows down and its crew bareheaded. The crowd waved; the driver lifted his hand.

It was ignorance that made scenes like this possible. Nobody here was thinking about where to find the next line. This world was a prison, and because not one of them had ever been out they had lavished all their strength on it. No wonder it was an incredible place.

He went back to his car. He drove north and west on the local roads, probing toward Stamford. A tremendous hygienic machinery encircled the wound, its outer fringes marked by loud warnings slapped on trees and phone poles, blockaded streets, and ambulances loitering like taxis. A lot of neighborhood people were clustered around tank trucks getting water. At one point a man in street clothes stepped out and stopped him, saying, "Wait here, please." Moments later a trio of blue-black sedans swept through the intersection like missiles.

All this merely impressed on him the immensity of the world's still-unblemished innocence. It terrified him; he was thinking of what it would take to destroy it.

Several times he stopped the car and turned off the key, dizzied. The walls of his chest felt dangerously thin. Perhaps he wasn't in the absolute best mental condition. Maybe he barely knew what he was seeing.

At Bull's Head in Stamford, largely untouched, thanks to the high ground around Ridgeway, the police line split several large parking lots. The National Guard was using the lower ones as a main staging area, and a crowd had gathered up above to watch. When Poole saw it he turned around and parked behind the liquor store at the top of the hill. He borrowed a quarter from a stranger and called his wife.

"Where are you?" she asked.

"Stamford. I went for a drive."

"What is it?"

He paused. "I just thought I'd call you."

"Well, I'm fine. Cinda is fine."

"Do you think I'm a dead man?"

No answer. He didn't have to see her face to know how it looked.

"This is pointless," she said finally.

"You're right."

He waited. It was this silence of hers that he craved.

"Rock," she said, "you wrecked my life."

He laughed.

"What'd you decide about that letter?"

"Which one? the one where I tell the world that I opened the line?"

"I wrote it myself. I've got it right here."

"Huh." A well-dressed older woman with a bag of groceries was standing ten feet away and staring at him, waiting for the phone. "What's it say?"

"Just the facts."

The facts, he thought.

"Rock, your problem is a lack of information. This might produce some. Suppose there's other people like you?"

"There aren't any."

"What if there were?"

He took a deep breath. "Listen — if some asshole actually decides to take me seriously — in other words, if it *succeeds* — I'm fucked. They'll bury me so deep — "

"I didn't say who you are."

"If you say anything, it's obvious."

He heard her draw breath. "Well, why'n't you come over here now and look at it." She was losing her voice; she was crying. He hated that.

"Look," he said, "if you want to blow the whistle, fine. But don't ask me to do it for you — I won't. And tell me — do you really think anyone around here is equipped to hear this? Seriously? *Now* who's dreaming! You know it's true and you *still* can't take it!"

More sobs. That meant she was probably alone. She was, in fact, a wreck — red-eyed, raw-throated, feverish. In her calm moments she seemed a lot less lucid. It was as though she needed these fits to bring herself out.

"Are you coming?" she asked.

"First you leave our house, then you want me over there."

"No! You left first! You never stop leaving!"

He hooked a finger in the change cup and bore down hard on the edge.

"What is it you *need* over there?"

"The responsible thing would be to kill myself, wouldn't it?"

"Go ahead!"

"You mean that?"

Her voice rose into a wail. "Well, you're not worried about *me*, are you?"

He was flustered. "Carmen, I've got a lot — "

"Admit it! You think God is about to tell you his greatest secrets and you can't figure out why I keep harping on this goddamn marriage!"

Poole's ears rang. The woman had put down her groceries.

"Look," he said thickly, "it's all mixed up, isn't it? I don't know why I left. I don't know why I'm back. Are you going to tell me?"

She was quiet again. "Say something!" he shouted.

A mousy mechanical voice demanded more change. He heard his daughter ask, "Mommy?" Then, very deliberately, the button went down and the line went dead.

Carmen looked at the three-page letter she had typed on her friend's cheap electric. It began:

> Three days ago Stamford was destroyed in an explosion of mysterious origin. I propose to deepen that mystery.

She laid it down and lowered her face in her hand. A moment later she picked up a pen, hesitated, then crossed out "Dear Commissioners" and wrote "Dear God." Then she curled her finger around it and bore down on the barrel until it snapped.

Her face burned. She got up and went to the window. Over the top of a lattice fence a woman in the next yard was hanging up sheets, her mouth full of clothespins. Cinda abandoned her pile of toy magnets and demanded to see also.

Forty minutes later Poole pulled into the parking slot behind his wife's car and looked up at the apartment. It was a second-floor unit in a boxy row of pale yellow aluminum-sided condos backed by the railroad. He hadn't prepared any arguments. He was still trying to make out the situation. If he was as damaging to this world as he believed, it seemed to him odd that he could move through it so freely. Maybe that was why he was drawn to one of its few sensitive points.

She let him in quietly. They sat for a while in the sunny, low-ceilinged front room. It had a piano in one corner, two windows clogged with house plants, and five or six overlapping Persian rugs, which gave it a dry, warmish odor.

"Here I am," he said. Cinda was trying to tug his keys out of his hand.

She didn't answer. It seemed to him that she wanted to force a certain weight on the moment. She was slumped in a corner of the couch with one hand arched on her forehead.

"I don't know," she said. "I just don't."

He got up and walked through the apartment. There were plants everywhere on plates and saucers speckled with dirt and dead leaves. A long-haired cat jumped off a pile of old newspapers and went out a window to the balcony. He saw the letter she had written on the kitchen table.

He picked it up and read it. There was nothing in it he hadn't told her himself. Its tone was modest; its claims, horrendous.

He went back to the front room. She hadn't moved. Her hand protected her eyes from him. After he had stared at her for a moment she let her arm drop. "Did you know," she said, "that Waxman was in Stamford?"

"Course he was. That's where he called from."

"He was listed as missing this morning."

"So?"

Cinda was watching them both from the floor.

"If Waxman's gone, then it's just you and me. That letter's not going to convince anyone."

"Then why did you write it?"

"I'm tired of being alone with you."

He smiled.

"So how would you like to treat this? As an emergency? A put-on? An excuse to consider yourself nuts?"

He grimaced and plucked at the skin under his throat. No such luck, he thought.

"Well, it's obvious you're worried about it. I'd like to hear what you've got in mind."

He took a few steps toward the window and looked back at her. He didn't know if he wanted to have this conversation. But on the other hand he couldn't possibly have it with anyone else. "I guess," he said, "I'm scared to death."

She looked at him closely. "Of what?"

"Things are coming apart."

He could tell she felt what he did — that merely putting these thoughts into words gave them a certain legitimacy.

"You're afraid of me too," she said.

"Yeah, well, who shouldn't I be afraid of? Name one person."

He could see she was breathing quite evenly.

"Don't think I'm trying to turn the clock back," she said. "I'm not."

"But you think that whatever's started ought to be stopped."

"Absolutely."

He didn't answer.

"Look," she went on, "the problem is that these . . . *events* . . . seem to be connected to you."

"So it seems."

"So we have to expose that connection. See if it actually exists."

He couldn't let her off there. "Suppose it turns out I'm the problem?"

"You don't know that."

"Suppose I ran in here to hide? Suppose my old friends are looking for me? You want to tell people that?"

She didn't look up. "All the more reason to find out for yourself."

"Hah!" He took a step toward her, stabbing down with a finger. "*You're* ready to buy it, I see! That's one thing *you* can believe!"

She made a knot with her fingers and frowned into it. "Don't shout at me."

He started walking up and down. Cinda crawled onto the couch beside her like a small animal leaving the water.

Carmen spoke first. "It might be that it's finished already.

The thing in Stamford is gone. Maybe there won't be any more."

"Sure," he said. "Wonderful."

"Maybe you have to decide. Maybe it's you who's letting them in."

He stopped and looked at her. "Maybe I'm goddamn Satan come from hell to blow up the world."

She made a face and glanced away.

"What's Stamford?" he asked. "There's hundreds of Stamfords. But there's only one me."

Cinda burrowed into her mother's side. Carmen lifted an arm to receive her. "You don't know what you are. Neither do I."

After a few moments his anger collapsed. She was merely telling the truth. He went out on the balcony and lit a cigarette.

He stayed for another hour or so. She didn't press him anymore. It was clear now that she wasn't going to make herself responsible for what he did or didn't do. This surprised him at first but it wasn't so unselfish. Like moving over here, it was a way of limiting the damage, of removing herself from the line of fire.

So he had taught her something after all — he had shown her how to think like a ghost. To accept a certain helplessness. To make no pointless conditions.

When he came back inside, he sat on the floor and watched his daughter dump beach pebbles out of a clay pot and put them back in again. She wasn't too expert — she laid her hand flat on the pile, closed it, and held it shut tight high over the target. When she let go, half of the pebbles bounced out.

He could feel his wife's eyes on both of them — the one she had lost a little too close to the one she was determined to keep. Her weak or her strong point, depending on how you looked at it.

The long-haired cat came in, gray with green eyes, and sniffed the air with exquisite distaste, then went over and stared at the doorknob, its tail high and curling. Poole could see that there was more than enough world for him right here in this room, provided he could hold on to it. Then why did there have to be any future at all?

"You coming over tonight?" he asked, still watching the cat. He had been careful not to say "home."

"Probably. Why?"

"I may not be there."

She was thinking. He could almost hear it.

"Don't do anything stupid."

"Like what?"

"Like not say goodbye."

He looked up at her. "You really think I'm ready for that?"

Once again they examined each other.

"Seems like you always come back. Only it's worse every time."

"I'll tell you something," he said, his voice roughening. "If it comes on like before, if it really gets close . . . otherwise, forget it. I've come too goddamn far."

"Good," she said. "Good."

He shut the door quietly. At the last moment the cat ran over and stared up through the doorway, as if there really were something different about him.

He drove around for the rest of the morning. Everywhere he looked he saw more of the world. It was a like a trap without walls; it positively welcomed his scrutiny, daring him to unspring it. And this seamlessness itself became an argument against him: if he still belonged here, then why couldn't he breathe?

He had a gun wrapped in plastic in the trunk—his only hedge against too much reality.

On the radio the newsmen were talking about a forthcoming announcement. It was going to be carried live from the governor's headquarters in Norwalk. He listened to it from a parking lot barely a mile away. There was some kind of checkpoint just up the road.

"I can tell you today," the governor said, "that there is virtually no danger from radiation in Stamford."

He sounded hoarse but vigorous. Poole watched a blue-and-white patrol car slide through his mirror.

"It appears," he went on, "that the initial figures were much too high. We were misled by erroneous reports."

The patrol car stopped at the checkpoint. Poole lit a Winston. An arm emerged from the car and handed the guard a white doughnut bag.

". . . and I pledge this to you now — all the injured will be cared for. All the homeless will be sheltered. I met with the President this morning and we agreed that this tragedy, which in one afternoon took more than half as many lives as the war in Vietnam, must become the number one priority of his administration."

Poole pressed the scan button. The speech was all over the dial.

Now the voice was subdued, almost chastened. "As you're probably aware, the explosion centered on the site that was so heavily publicized. There was nothing brought to the area. We have no reason to believe any weaponry was involved."

Oh no? Poole thought, examining the ash on his cigarette. At the checkpoint the guard handed back the doughnut bag, doughnut in hand.

". . . I ask you to keep this in mind when you hear people say that we're helpless. I've heard a lot of things in the last couple of days. In that time we've evacuated tens of thousands of people without injury and provided medical care for as many others. We've put out hundreds of fires and made food, clothing, and shelter available on a truly massive scale. And the truth is that we're only just gearing up. Those are the facts. I say look at the facts."

Poole had slumped down in his seat. He wasn't unaffected. He had heard of murderers weeping at the graves of their victims.

The car started easily. He pulled out and drove off.

About an hour later a helmeted man on a big chestnut horse laid his hand on his holster and ordered Poole out of his car. Then a heavy steel-walled van pulled up and a cop got out and unlocked the back door. Poole looked at the horse, which was watching him with its wary billiard-ball eyes. "What about my car?" he said. "Get the fuck in," he was told.

"Criminal trespass," the marshal said, transferring numbers from Poole's driver's license. They were in a trailer placed across the entrance of a chain-link enclosure topped with barbed wire. He pointed at the phone with a long regulatory finger. "You can make one call and one call only."

Poole didn't stir. He believed it would be a few hours at most. He still felt like an idiot.

The marshal handed him his license and waved him out the door. "Next."

Poole stepped down into an unroofed pen full of strangers. A half-dozen portable toilets stood in a row. Water splashed down continuously from a hose clipped to the fence. This was in a gas station parking lot off the Post Road. It was outside the blast damage but well within the prohibited area.

Nobody seemed in any great hurry to be released. The other prisoners stood around in clumps. They were mostly young and surly. They all looked as though they had just arrived.

About ninety minutes earlier the governor's announcement, combined with a determined incursion by a few dozen protestors, had unsettled the crowds by the gate behind Strawberry Hill and they had started moving up to the barricades and squeezing past by the hundreds, swamping the checkpoints. Poole had been watching from up the street in his car; seeing his chance, he had backed up and circled around to a quieter spot where the perimeter ran behind several half-finished construction projects. There were places where it thinned to a single strand of barbed wire. He found one of them and forced his car underneath, gashing the windshield. Soldiers yelled and ran toward him from half a block away. He pretended not to notice.

He still didn't know how close he had gotten to the line. After scooting too quickly down several unrecognizable streets bulldozed through rubble, he had come out on a rough slope of pulverized ash leading down to a sort of dried-up lake bed crisscrossed with tracks — the crater itself. Far off in the middle he saw a squat group of trailers. When a helicopter buzzed him, he stepped on the gas.

But when he pulled up in his own dust behind the trailers, he had no clear idea about what to do next. There was no sign of the line. He couldn't even locate Waxman's building. Several guys in white suits with shovels were standing around like clamdiggers. Within moments the cop on horseback appeared, his hand on his gun.

The van had taken him directly to this place. Poole walked up and down the pen a few times and heard several people talking about a similar exploit before he realized it was his own. When he looked out the front fence, there were two men dressed like civilians standing across the street watching him. Suddenly he knew he had made a serious mistake.

He went back to the trailer and poked his head in. "I want to make that call," he said. There were certain papers in his house he didn't want anyone seeing. The marshal looked up, inscrutable. "Hurry up," he said.

Poole dialed his wife at her friend's apartment. Nobody answered. He let it ring for a while without hope. Bad luck he had learned to expect, but his own stupidity continued to amaze him.

Two kid soldiers appeared and escorted him down the road. They took him to an evacuated nursing home just a few blocks away and put him in a room with a bed, linoleum, floral prints, and a tiny bathroom. "Don't leave," they said, and went out. A sealed window overlooked a hedged-in strip of lawn with a frail dogwood and a bird feeder.

Poole stayed away from the door. He found the amount of traffic in the hall ominous. It seemed he was quickly losing his margin for error.

Three days later he was still in the room. Certain things had become clear. Number one, the image of the world as it presented itself was as lifelike as ever — there were no releasing flaws, no giveaway breaks. He felt like a fly in a puddle, caught in a perfect mirror of the real.

The other item was that his efforts to throw the burden of truth on his captors hadn't changed anything. He'd seen a total of three people. One was obviously a shrink. This one had come right out and admitted that he didn't think Poole's story was a matter for public concern. Why not? Poole asked. Should it be? the man said.

They had taken away the curtain rods, the coat hangers, and his belt — even the plug for the bathtub drain. When he complained about this, the same man said it was nothing personal. No, Poole replied — it's a hostile act. We don't agree and you're showing me whose opinion matters. Suppose it was you locked in here? Suppose it was me with the notebook? Then who'd be the nut?

Well, it's not like that, is it? the man said.

Poole wasn't too concerned about what this idiot thought of him. He had no compelling reason to be anywhere else.

If he had to guess, he would say they were holding him because they hadn't yet decided he was totally useless. They'd placed him in Stamford on the night the line opened up. They had a lot of questions about Waxman. *Did he receive any mail from abroad? Were you aware he collected pictures of Hiroshima? Can you recall seeing anything odd in his apartment?*

He missed having a TV. Question Man Number 2 had given him a transistor radio but late the first night he had smashed it on the bedstead. This was his only violent act and yet it had cost him his shoelaces.

He'd been having a dream. The announcer came on and said that new lines had appeared in Bridgeport, Hartford, and West Islip, Long Island. Somehow he knew he was dreaming but he kept listening anyway. He didn't like the calm in the man's voice—he sensed some ridicule there. Suddenly he realized that he was awake and that this wasn't a radio but a tape player—it had been rigged to insult him. Enraged, he jumped up and smashed it. Then he woke up completely and recognized his mistake. Though he asked, he didn't get another one.

He spent most of his time sitting on the bed and looking out the window. A tall hedge limited the view. In the afternoon a blue shadow slid up the glass. The feeder was empty and no birds came to it.

After the first day he stopped hearing noises in the rooms on either side. At mealtimes there was a knock on the door, the lock turned, and an aide handed him a cafeteria-style sandwich wrapped in plastic. It was hard to get a good look at these people because they stood well outside; a chain on the door prevented him from opening it more than a few inches. He discovered that if he stuck his foot in that opening he was permitted to stand there and look out for as long as he wanted, although someone always shut it eventually. The building sounded inhabited; he heard footsteps and smelled food. He seemed to have this little end of it to himself. There was a guard around the corner who kept people away.

He didn't particularly mind. Now that he was a prisoner, he didn't have to worry about getting caught. He had told all his secrets; he had no more to confess. He didn't even have any sharp objects to play with. So he was free to consider his predicament at leisure.

Was he insane? At last this had become an almost frivolous question. Here, in this room, it was unlikely that he would ever gather enough evidence to decide either way, and it was foolish to try. He and the shrink, for instance, regarded each other as badly deluded, but did that mean one of them had to be wrong?

He didn't know. That was just it, that was what he was discovering — this not-knowing wasn't necessarily a weakness, a trap. Who said he had to know? Why this death-grip phobia about being mistaken?

Because if in fact he had helped to destroy Stamford, it was the least of his crimes: he had destroyed whole worlds full of Stamfords, over and over, on the day he took leave of the real. Now they were all ghosts. Every one of them. No matter how solid they looked.

So what business did he have trying to decide whether this one was indeed the one he had left? If it wasn't, would that let him off? If it was, would he ever know it for sure?

Of course not. The real world was the biggest phantom of all.

Sometimes he wondered if they were giving him drugs. He felt a little too relaxed, too lucid. He was never bored; he could spend hours watching the smoke curl up from his cigarette. The shrink was like an entertainer. He came in at odd hours, knocking softly before he unlocked the door, as if visiting a dangerous reptile. Sometimes he stayed for ten minutes, sometimes forty or fifty. He never looked comfortable.

"I murdered them all," Poole liked to say. "I murdered them all."

The man often seemed preoccupied. After the first couple of meetings he stopped taking notes. It was his associates who had asked all the questions about Waxman; he acted as if he was merely a caretaker. He was a young man with a bad complexion and gold-rim glasses — a novice, a worrier. He wore wide-wale corduroys in green or burgundy and suede oxfords. He seemed to have exhausted his curiosity; sometimes he just sat without saying anything.

Poole was grateful for the space he was given. He also tried to keep the questions to a minimum. Every hour that went by seemed to make this world a little stronger, a little more safe to believe in. If he could, he meant to protect it.

Yes, he was expecting a visitor. The bear might have gone back in the woods but the bear was still around. Next time it came for him he wasn't going to turn his back. That was his mistake; that was why Stamford was history.

He realized now that each time he had crossed over he had been fully warned in advance. If he had dismissed the signals, it was only because he hadn't understood them — they came from outside certain boundaries whose existence he still didn't suspect. But now, after three separate trials, he was sensitized — he knew that the enemy approached gradually, from the deepest part of the unreal, and sent tremor after tremor toward the surface. And even when it reached striking distance, it paused, hesitant, as if awaiting some small encouragement, or even just a moment of inattention.

But that was exactly what it didn't get the last time. He had felt it coming the whole way, hours ahead, and when it finally stopped and was right there, right beside him, an arm's length away, its silence itself asking the inevitable question: *Are you coming with me?* — just like that, *Are you coming with me?* — he, for once, had said no.

And in that same instant the flash at the window, the tinkling lamp, and thirty thousand dead.

He didn't feel threatened right now. In fact it seemed to him that this room was an ideal place to await the next confrontation. That was what he cared about — not what might or might not be in the newspapers — because he finally understood the nature of his position. It was *his* stubbornness, *his* persistent backtracking, that had exposed this world to destruction, and if he wanted to prevent it, he merely had to give himself up. Sooner or later the bear would come again.

Was he afraid? Yes. Was he bitter? Not anymore. He felt reprieved. He spent a lot of time thinking about those weeks he had spent on the beach with Jewel. Though he hadn't understood it at the time, she also had strayed back toward the world, leaving a telltale trace in her wake. And when she felt that unmistakable stirring behind her, the notice that her hour was waning, she had announced her own murder with astonishing calm. She hadn't tried to run away—she hadn't tried to hide behind anyone. That had been his idea—that was why, just a few days ago, he had locked himself up with Carmen and Cinda and six months' worth of groceries, trying to fade into his surroundings, knowing that the skin of the world was about to break and pretending he wasn't the target—a sorry performance!

And now he was the intruder, the stowaway, the spirit blown deep into the real.

So he let the hours pass. Though he stared out the window at his little hedged-in strip of lawn, he was looking elsewhere—toward his partner, his brother, the blind angel dissolved in his veins. At the moment he felt nothing. The air was slack; the sun shone undimmed. But he didn't expect to be surprised.

On the third afternoon he was standing at his usual post with his foot in the door when he heard a commotion around the corner—hurrying steps, the guard's keys as he stood up, someone calling out, "Ma'am. Ma'am!" Then a chair got knocked over and he heard Carmen shout his name.

"In here!" he answered. He rattled the door and yelled as she was hustled away.

When the guard got back to his post, Poole did some more shouting and gorilla pounding. At last the man stood up and came around the corner. Poole had never seen him before. He had a pouchy black face and a cop's uniform — and a cop's fishy stare. He stopped just out of reach.

"That was my wife," Poole said.

He didn't answer.

"You think you can beat her up?"

"She beat *me* up."

"Where is she now?"

"Don' know. Talkin' to somebody."

"When am I getting out of here?"

"Don' know that either."

"Would you take her a message for me?"

The guard appeared to think about it. But after a moment he turned and went back to his seat without answering.

Poole lit a cigarette, took several puffs, and tossed it onto the rug. But it didn't catch; it burned down to the filter and went out.

"You have to understand," the man said, "that your husband doesn't believe in us anymore. We're like actors playing roles from his past. He'll go along up to a point, but in reality there's only one person he's concerned with — a sort of elusive counterpart, a mysterious Someone Else."

"I don't have to understand anything. I want to see him and you won't let me. Why not?"

"There shouldn't be any problem once you get clearance."

"Good. How do I get clearance?"

The three men looked at one another.

"I want to see him," she said. "Right now."

Two of the men got up and went out. The other one, much younger, avoided her gaze. He looked tired, like a student who had written too many papers.

"Why are you hiding him?" she asked.

He slouched a little deeper in his chair. "I've spent a lot of time with him, Mrs. Poole. He hasn't asked to see anyone. I think he feels comfortable here."

"Is that why you didn't notify me?"

"We've been grasping at straws, I admit."

She didn't trust this character. He was camouflaged somehow.

"Is it true," he said slowly, "that he convinced you he's mixed up in this?"

"In what?"

"In what happened to Stamford."

She waited. "I humor him sometimes."

"But you're confident he's just a person like anyone else."

"Of course. Aren't you?"

He ground his teeth a little and looked up at the ceiling.

The other men came back a minute later, asked her to follow them, then led her quickly down several noisy, cluttered corridors to a room with a blank sheet of paper taped to the door. The friendly, almost obsequious one took the knob in his hand and touched her arm. "Your husband has a fragile personality, Mrs. Poole. He could get excited. If you get in trouble, make some noise — we'll come in." He paused. "Ready?"

She stared at him for a moment, then nodded.

He let her in.

Rocker smiled when he saw her. He was standing by a window at the far end of a bright, bare room with aqua walls and a huge tin can — a whirlpool bath — in a corner. "You found me," he said.

He was wearing the same clothes. He looked distinctly uneasy, though willing to please. He hadn't shaved and was barefoot.

"This just gets worse and worse," she said.

He crossed the room and handed her a crumpled piece of paper. He'd scribbled *Place is bugged* on it in pencil.

While she was putting it in her bag, he took her in his arms and brought his mouth to her ear. "I'm glad you came," he whispered.

She didn't lower her voice. "Tell me something. Do you want to be here?"

"As long as I can."

"What the hell does that mean?"

He pulled back and looked at her. He had a melting, piteous expression. "They know everything — I told them."

The thought flashed: *Crazy.* "So what?"

He pulled her close again. "Course they don't believe me," he muttered, stroking her hair.

She looked over his shoulder at the ceiling. There was a little camera up there, pointed down. "You haven't been away again, have you?" she asked.

"No."

"You like being locked up?" She was standing quite still — playing dead, more or less.

He stepped back, lifted the bag off her shoulder, and fished his scrap of paper out of it, then went to the wall and started writing. He handed it back and she held it up to her eyes. *Let's say goodbye forever,* it said. *Now.*

She let her arms drop. "Rocker — what is this?"

There were tears in his eyes. He didn't want to speak. "I always loved you, Carmen."

"What?"

"I did. I still do."

"Stop it! Just stop it!"

"I would, but I can't. Goodbye, Carmen."

He was already at the door. She knew it was locked. She was sure it was locked.

But instead of reaching for the knob he began pounding it with his fists. It swung open immediately. He let the first man step in, then attacked him. Two more ran in to help. In a moment all three were cursing and struggling. They bundled him out; she last saw him banging backwards through the double doors, heels dragging, looking back at her with the sweetest kind of pain in his eyes.

She eventually gave up the whole story. She didn't take much persuading. She was afraid that if she didn't tell it soon she wouldn't be able to anymore — it would all fade, lose outline, become unimportant. What they did with it once they had it — that was their problem. They didn't seem like dangerous people. If they were what they claimed, then they needed to know. But for herself it was just no longer possible otherwise.

The three of them heard her out in the same room as before. She still didn't know their names. There was the hefty, ingratiating one — he smiled a lot and had a barking laugh — plus his thinner, more diffident buddy, spotlessly dressed and doodling on a notepad — and then the young one, the brooder. Before long it was evident that they knew the whole story from Rocker. They seemed to think she deserved some sympathy for being married to him — as if she were still normal, as if she'd merely skirted the hole he fell into.

They were nobodies, she realized. They were just three more bloodhounds let loose in the wreckage. They had no idea that they'd found anything important.

All except the young one, it seemed. After the other two finished with a few polite, pointless questions, he sat up, took the table under his elbows, leaned close, and asked her why any sane person would believe a word of what she'd said. She agreed that they wouldn't. Then how do you expect us to believe it, he asked. I don't, she admitted.

That was his opening. He leaned even closer and stared at her pointblank. "But if all this is true, then hadn't you better make sure we believe it? Considering what might be at stake?"

She remained cool. "He can convince you. I can't."

"So you're just kissing him off. You're turning him over to us."

"Is that a mistake?"

"Hell, you're *counting* on not being believed, because if we believed you, we'd have to revise our opinion of him. In pure self-defense. We might even have to do something drastic."

She waited a few moments. "I don't think you will."

"Maybe not, but it's obvious that if we made the decision, we wouldn't let you slow us down. You knew that when you came in here."

She glanced at the other men. They looked cowed, almost shamefaced. The young one sat back and cleared his throat. The others got up quietly and left.

After the door closed he tipped back and wedged a foot against the table. "You can't believe you're hearing this, can you?" he said. "You're running out of credulity. A couple more bumps and you'll just stop paying attention."

She forced herself to study him again. He had coarse, spotty skin, a mat of dark curls as stiff as an Airedale's, and small, inconspicuous eyes.

"You said he could convince me," he went on. "But is that what I want? Look what happened to Waxman. Look at you, for chrissake!"

She got up and went to the window. Down below, a bed of wood chips and ornamental evergreens sloped off to the parking lot, where a couple of tow trucks were parked. "I'm not crazy," she said.

"Yeah, but you wish you were."

She had one hand curled tight on her chest. Although she didn't swallow his act for a minute, she still believed this was a dangerous moment.

"You want to say something?"

"He knows he can't stay."

"You mean you've resigned yourself to losing him."

"No. I mean there won't be any more Stamfords."

He nodded. "I get it. You're hoping for the best."

Leave now, she told herself. *Just leave*.

"So what do you do now? Go home? Have a drink? Call your mom?" He paused. "Have you done everything you can humanly do?"

The room seemed to lengthen behind her. Around the side of her head she saw him sitting at the far end. His voice filled all the space in between.

"I'll tell you this — I'm keeping him. I'll decide whether you see him again. And if you try to make trouble about that, you'll soon find that nobody's listening. So you don't have to worry about his barging in on you and saying, 'Honey, forgive me.' That's not going to happen."

She left the window, walked down the room, and stopped opposite him. "You had better leave him alone."

"What?"

"I told you what I know. It's not the whole story. You'd better keep that in mind."

He waited. "Are you threatening me?"

"No. I'm just not lying to you."

"Huh." He sat back a little. "Well, that's different, I guess."

After a moment he took out a handkerchief and started cleaning his glasses. She could do nothing with him, she realized. He knew nothing.

Poole smoked ten cigarettes in two hours. The door was locked and he tossed the lit butts at the jamb. He thought he had outgrown remorse. But he was still thinking about how Carmen had looked as the double doors shut on her face.

His keeper came in around dinnertime and looked at the pattern of burns on the linoleum. Then he pushed the door closed, put a sandwich on the night table, and handed Poole a half-open paper supermarket bag. "From your wife," he said.

Poole looked inside. Clothes — balled athletic socks, underwear, jeans, and shirts. All washed and packed neatly.

His keeper lowered himself into the padded motel chair and let his head back on the wall. The shadow of the hedge settled onto his chest; tinted sun mottled his face.

"Where is she now?" Poole asked.

"She went home."

"You guys are all coldhearted bastards."

The kid started rubbing his eyes, his wire-rim glasses riding up on his forehead. He didn't disagree. He didn't say anything.

Later that evening, after he'd left, Poole emptied the bag onto the bed. In one of the pairs of jeans he found a wallet snapshot of Lucinda. It was painful to look at. Even so, he was glad to have it, because in spite of the evidence, once upon a time he had known how to live.

He propped the photo on the sill and looked out the window. The dogwood's leafy shadow slanted down on the glass, cooling his eyes. Golden light crowned the tree from behind and shifted in razory gleams on a dozen tiny threads strung underneath. Just above the lawn, the air itself seemed to glow brightest; a few gnats or specks of dust floated like sparks.

This would be a good moment, he thought, even though he knew he still had some way to go. Nothing stirred in the blue dusk under the hedge. Where are you? he asked silently, wondering if he could be heard. But there was nothing — just the space for an answer.

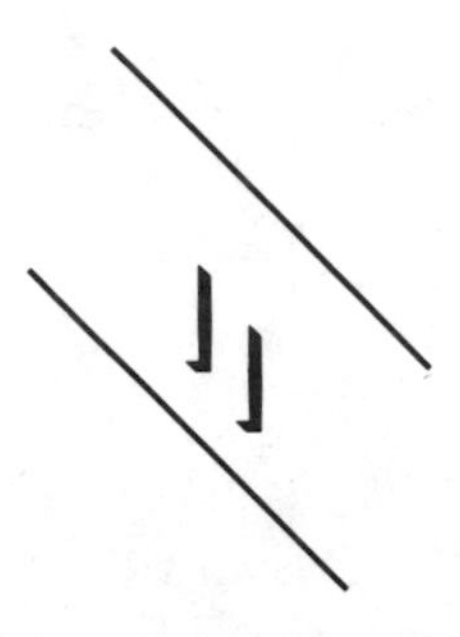

Now, when Cinda asked where Daddy was, Carmen knew. She had several more meetings with his custodian. He allowed her to wait in his office and watch on a closed-circuit TV while he went in to see Rocker. She didn't insist on going along. For the moment she preferred being out of the picture.

This was, she realized, a well-guarded place. There were always a half-dozen cops loitering outside. It was evident that they had deliberately let her in.

Rocker looked cramped on the little bluish screen. His voice sounded muffled and colorless. But she could tell, just by watching him, that he still regarded himself as in charge of the situation, prisoner or not.

She never saw the other two men who had questioned her earlier. It was just this kid now, this raw and arrogant stranger who seemed to think it ironic that he had become God. Any time you want, he said, you can come here. But you can't take him out and you can't do without me.

She made sure he knew that she considered him dirt. This was to offset the hold he had on her, since she used his office as a place to let out that part of herself which knew exactly what she had seen and refused to deny it. Keeping the truth intact there allowed her to go home and deal with the rest of her life, which had somehow gone on regardless.

She was due back at work in two days. Rocker's mother was staying at the house. A lawyer was trying to get him a hearing. Both of their families considered him a victim of bad luck and official hysteria. If he'd said he was Jesus Christ, would they have believed that as well?

No one even asked her what she believed. They simply assumed that Rocker's increasing weirdness had left her more and more isolated. She didn't complicate things by telling the truth. And what was the truth? That her husband was as sane as ever and the world had gone nuts? That she'd believed him when he said he'd doomed Stamford? Or had he just "overreacted to certain coincidences," as his father so generously put it? A lot of people, after all, had discovered vast meanings in the event.

And so in the endless phone calls and kitchen discussions everyone took it for granted that she, his wife, had never been converted for long by his talk about coming and going and ducking through lines. Hadn't she made him get help? Hadn't she tried to protect him? As for the angry scratches on his neck when he came back that other time, or his inexplicable sunburn, or the hundred other small things that no one else had noticed — they slid right by in the telling, as if everyone understood how to take them.

After several sessions like this she realized that she had said everything. The picture hadn't changed; she had merely shifted it slightly, so that it took its color from her entire conscious life and not from those few hellish moments when doubt had seeped in. And she could still see it that way, she discovered — she could still easily imagine that she had allowed her own disturbed state and fears about Rocker to twist her perspective.

What was infinitely harder was to keep the other possibility, the private and terrible one, from simply rotting away in her mind.

Under these circumstances the air at home quickly became unbreathable. Every morning she turned Cinda over to Rocker's mother and drove straight to Stamford. The soldiers at the various gates took her driver's license, punched it up in their booths, and handed it back without comment. At Basswood, the former nursing home, she had to leave it at the desk. To the right a pair of steel doors with glass insets opened to the corridor that led toward Rocker's room. They were always locked and there was a guard just inside.

There was another man by the elevator, and several more blocking other passages. She was confined to the ground-floor common areas, including the cubbyhole on the other side of the open-air courtyard where she met with Rocker's keeper.

He wasn't often there. This "office" was just a room with a desk in it, but the monitor was always on and she could watch Rocker smoke, chew his nails, and stare out the window. He didn't seem aware of the camera. Once in a while he would swear a little or pace around, but for the most part he seemed relaxed. He kept Cinda's snapshot on the windowsill and often took it down, handling it with exaggerated care. His keeper pointed that out. "Pictures are powerful magic," he said.

This nameless individual became a different person when he went in to see Rocker—droop-shouldered, fidgety, self-conscious. If he was trying to draw him out, he had no success. "It's important," he told her, "that he get no pressure from outside. Just a little feedback, a routine. So he knows where he is but doesn't feel threatened."

He managed to appear remarkably frank while telling her almost nothing. She didn't know what his aims were or who he reported to or whether he took her at all seriously. Maybe he represented a major behind-the-scenes effort; maybe he was just a nursemaid on an extra-long leash. In the second case she could forget the frantic meetings upstairs, where dozens of badly spooked Einsteins were going over Rocker's every word.

She knew now why he had gone back to the crater. Both of their lives had fallen into that hole. And the idea lingered that it wasn't too late, that even worse blows could still be avoided. She pressed his man hard on this point. She accused him of a lack of imagination, a deep unseriousness. Here you are, she said, pretending that he's the only issue, as if all this happened on Mars. You think just because you're not looking there's nothing to see?

Talk like this ran right off his back. He admitted that he didn't like Stamford much either but he questioned how ready she was to do anything about it. And when, he asked, did it become my responsibility? When you started in on this fairy tale? Do you know how it sounds?

She couldn't answer that. He always made sense, in his insulting way; he was the ideal inhabitant of this unspeakable new world.

Watching Rocker relaxed her somehow. The man's visits never upset him. He amused himself by constructing tiny balloons and airships out of the plastic his sandwiches came wrapped in and sending them aloft over the vent on the windowsill. He spent considerable time writing, using a pencil about an inch and a half long. He didn't seem at all hurried. When his keeper asked what he was doing he cheerfully answered, "None of your business."

It was possible, of course, that he had reached an entirely new level of disconnection. But she didn't think so. For the first time since that wet morning in April he had dropped his concealed manic edge, his grim buoyancy. He had discovered something, she believed. He knew exactly what he was doing.

Maybe it was fear of spoiling this impression that kept her

from trying to see him. But she needed this secret intimacy, this sense of a still-unbroken thread. And he needed her more where she was than inside his cage with him.

So she wasn't disappointed when the lawyer said he had hit a brick wall. The details didn't interest her. The time for Rocker to get out was when he wanted to — no sooner. And each hour she sat watching him seemed to make the world a little more solid under her feet.

At the start of her third morning in front of the TV the curly-headed kid showed her a copy of a report he had written entitled "The Lazarus Effect: Rockland Poole and the Destruction of Stamford." It set out Rocker's entire account in plain language without once implying that there was anything difficult or unusual about it. The line on Waxman's porch became "an incomplete hole or doorway generated by the presence of a 'dead man' in the real world." Her own reaction was described as "a step-by-step movement from outrage and disbelief to near-total conversion." It mentioned that Rocker was now in custody and in excellent condition.

"Who's seen this?" she asked.

"Several people."

"No one's asked you about it?"

"If you want a story to convince, you've got to at least make it plausible."

He hadn't answered the question, she noticed. "The truth isn't always easy to believe."

"Absolutely. That's why there has to be evidence. And when people are prejudiced, even that doesn't work." He nodded at the paper. "The problem, you see, is that I could've gotten that from any ordinary crackpot. I can't visit the next world and confirm it."

She looked at the little bluish screen. Rocker was lying back on the bed in his socks, his hands under his neck.

"I've got a request to make," he said. "Would you be willing to go before a larger group? To tell them what you've told me?"

This took her by surprise. "Why?"

"Because I think you should be heard. This might be a good time."

"What kind of group?"

"These would be people from the investigation. Ten or fifteen at most."

She looked at him. His eyes told her nothing useful. "Isn't that a lot to ask?"

"I thought you might jump at the chance."

"Suppose I say no?"

"Then we don't do it. Obviously."

"Obviously."

After a moment he turned away, frowning. "You know, Mrs. Poole, I think you underestimate our, uh . . . *willingness* to face facts. Stamford is gone. We can't explain why." He cleared his throat. "So while we're waiting for the spacemen to demand our surrender, we're trying to keep busy . . . and there's some pretty heavy pressure to develop ideas. *Any* ideas."

She didn't answer.

"I mean it genuinely looks as if nothing like this ever happened before. Right? So why be pedantic about it?"

He sounded uncomfortable. She was still having trouble believing her ears.

"Look," he said, hurrying, "people have this curious talent—have you noticed? They don't need explanations for everything. If they're cornered they'll say 'will of God,' 'hand of fate,' or any damn thing, and then it's business as usual. Believe it or not, that's the going attitude around here—*some*body knows, so why do I have to know? Look at me, for instance. I volunteered for this shit, but do I really want to know why there's a stinking ash heap where Stamford used to be? Of course not. What I want is for it not to have happened. Only it *did* happen, Mrs. Poole. That's the hard part. It did happen."

After a moment he pried his gaze away, wincing, and looked at the floor.

She tried to imagine herself in a room with fifteen cabinet-level executives, attempting to convince them of Rocker's satanic powers. "But why?"

"Why?" he nearly cried. He waved at the report. "But that's worthless, don't you see? No one's even going to listen to it unless it's in person, dead on, and stone cold sober. So they can judge you and it both."

"No," she said finally. "I don't think so."

He didn't answer. He sat wedged in the back of his seat, his small eyes fixed on her.

"You don't trust me," she said. "Why should I trust you? Not to mention these others."

"Of course I trust you."

"No you don't. You use me. You're still trying to use me. You don't have the slightest idea what you're doing."

He waited again, studying her.

"Look at that," she said, pointing at the TV. "That's a person in there. What do you know about him? Nothing. What're you likely to find out? Nothing. But do you care? Not much — and why should you? You can still lock him up like an animal! You can still make deals with me!"

He chewed his thumb for a few moments, then got up abruptly and went out. He came back with a manila envelope and handed it to her.

They were pictures — brutal pictures. Heaps of charred corpses. A surgeon in scrubs holding up a big piece of replacement skin. She looked at only a couple and threw the envelope on the floor.

"It *happened*," he said. "Remember? It *happened*."

"Of course it happened!"

Neither of them spoke for a few moments. Someone walked past the open doorway.

He sighed and sat forward, ready to stand. "All right, Mrs. Poole. Maybe I do trust you a little. Maybe we can come back to this later." He got up and went out.

She opened her hand. Her nails had cut a row of crescents into the base of her thumb.

That afternoon he agreed to take a sealed message to Rocker. In it she wrote, *I haven't forgotten. If you need me, let me know. Carmen.*

Just moments after he left with it he reappeared on the monitor. He gave the note to Rocker and went out. Rocker opened it quickly and immediately went back to what he was writing. She waited an hour; he didn't look at it again.

She didn't go back to work on schedule. To all intents and purposes she moved into the room off the courtyard, returning home only at night. She started taking Cinda with her and equipped the room with a foam pad, diapers, and toys.

Her parents objected to this; she let them object. Once she was through the gates, she was out of reach.

Inside the building no one paid her any particular attention. As far as Cinda was concerned, the whole place was filled with charming strangers. She seemed perfectly willing to get used to seeing Rocker only on TV. His keeper spooked her, however. She got very big-eyed and quiet when he came into the room.

In the mornings, before it got hot, they went out in the courtyard and Cinda squatted by the edge and arranged the damp wood chips in impenetrable designs on the flags while Carmen sat in a white mesh chair and drank coffee from a thermos, watching clouds slide out fully formed into the open square overhead. A family of sparrows cheeped in a loose spot in the flashing. By then Rocker was already up and waiting for his breakfast.

At the back of her head she had a little thimble-size cup with her sanity in it. If it fell over, she knew, she would begin to misinterpret the simplest events, and she didn't have that luxury now — she had seen enough to know that she was exquisitely placed.

She gave no speeches to rooms full of responsible men. Even Rocker's keeper stopped bullying her. He came around three or four times a day and sat down to watch Rocker on the monitor. "How's he doing?" he would ask. She made a point of not saying much. She was here at his discretion.

She never saw him talking to anyone else. He spent considerable time in the other, forbidden parts of the building. What he did there was mysterious. But she didn't permit it to worry her much; she had already made her decision.

She took her cues from Rocker now. She believed that as long as he kept quiet, no further disasters were imminent. Whether this was true or just wishful thinking was a question she simply didn't have the resources to investigate. But even a stranger could tell that he was a different man from before.

He wasn't scared now. Any yet he was waiting for something; he clearly didn't anticipate being in that little box forever. His intent was transparent: he expected another attempt to uproot him. That was why he had tried to say goodbye — because he meant to let it succeed.

Crazy, of course. But not like before — not with no end in sight. A different kind of dementia — not opposed to itself, but in earnest.

So she watched him very carefully. It was as if she also were locked in that room.

Meanwhile the rest of the world ran on. Burn cases from Stamford were causing work stoppages in New York–area hospitals. They were "contaminated," it was said; even breathing the same air was considered dangerous. Photographs of the line were published and republished. The superpowers, it was reported, had put their strategic forces on alert almost in tandem, then taken them off, then put them on again.

Stories like these didn't alarm her. If anything, they were reassuring — they implied that she was right to be concerned. The line between the real and unreal had dissolved, and she had redrawn it herself; secretly she knew that the whole effort was preposterous, and that real life had ended long before, but that didn't relieve her of the need to continue.

She looked to Cinda for help. At home she moved her crib across the hall and right up next to the bed. She took baths instead of showers so that the curtain wouldn't separate them. Cinda was so small, so clumsy, so *babyish* — certain to suffer, it seemed. But if life was meant to be cruel, then how could she be so delicate?

Changing her, holding her, washing her — over and over, like a sleepwalker. Her knuckleless hands were always a little colder than her own. Every human feeling showed in her large, strangely adult eyes. Of course she had no idea what had gone wrong. She was still new to the world — she got carted around like a handbag. But that didn't mean she was powerless. Not at all — day and night, all by herself, she proved that not everything had turned to ashes. And so keeping her close made it impossible to lose touch completely. Or at least that was the hope. Because she wouldn't be here at all without mighty allies.

Two nights after Rocker's mother left, Carmen got a call very late. It was his keeper in Stamford. Something had come up and he wanted to see her. He wouldn't say what it was.

Waxman was watching the house from his rented car in the shadow of a clump of old hemlocks across the street. It was after two A.M. and he heard the phone ring distinctly. He knew what the call was about. He could easily cross over, ring the doorbell, and tell her. A mosquito fat with his blood whined along the rim of the windshield.

He had spent three days watching her. He knew approximately where Rocker was. He might have known exactly by now if he had been willing to take a few risks.

A light went on in two windows upstairs. The raccoon perched on a plastic trash barrel down the block rocked it till it fell over; a pale bladder spilled out. Then a light in the front hall, the light out upstairs, and a small figure around the back of the house and the noise of keys by the car. In his mirror a pair of high beams steadily brightened on a phone pole until a darkened car scooped them up.

As her rear wheels hit the street, her backup lights colored one side of his face faintly. After the corner her engine climbed through three gears and faded out. In the silence the insect's floating whine reapproached and pinpointed itself, begging for murder. He didn't move. *It's as though*, he thought, *I want it to happen*.

"Why should you care?" she said.

As if trying to wear down a difficult child, he started the tape again. The picture was reddish and obscure. Rocker's head and naked back stood out darkly against the sheets. He looked asleep. At the corner of the screen the box read 12:49A. "Just watch," he said.

In the next instant Rocker flipped over and sat bolt upright, clutching the blanket. He didn't cry out. He leaned forward, as if listening. After a few seconds he uncovered his feet and eased them onto the floor. He stayed like that, motionless, for another full minute.

The picture switched back to real time. Rocker was sitting naked in the armchair nearest the camera, smoking. The lights were still off. The little box read 2:46A.

"Want to see it again?"

She had never been here this late. The hallways were dim and the phones were quiet. Only this room was bright. Cinda was half asleep on her back in the corner, talking to herself.

"You'll have to explain it to me," she said.

"What don't you understand?"

"Everything."

"You may as well relax, Mrs. Poole. We're going to be here awhile."

He got up and left the room. She heard him talking to someone down the hall. Every now and then the ember on Rocker's cigarette curved toward his mouth and glowed brighter.

His keeper came back a minute later with a stack of videotapes. He took out the one in the machine and put in another. He looked nervous to her. "This is from a camera in the lobby," he said. "I'm going to show you about ten seconds."

Rocker vanished and she saw the empty glassed-in vestibule, a box full of light.

"Notice the time," he said.

Down in the lower right corner it said 12:49A.

Then he showed her similar snippets of another set of doors, an elevator landing, a long hallway, and a section of roof. He stood by the machine and watched her. When the last one popped out, he put Rocker in again. "As you can see," he said, "these others don't mean much without this one."

Lightning? she thought. A short in the basement?

The machine played the same sequence over and over. There was Rocker lying on his face, then the split-second glitch — the picture snowed over for an instant — and then Rocker jumping out of his skin.

"Like he touched a live wire," he said.

All the tapes showed the same damage at 12:49A.

"I was here at ten of one — I didn't notice anything. But these cameras did. And so did he."

Every six seconds Rocker bolted up again, quivering. "Turn it off," she said.

He did so. Rocker the night owl reappeared, standing naked at the window and looking out, his hands spread on the glass.

The man looked down at the screen. "What's he see out there?"

She felt as if the walls of her head were spreading away from each other. "I don't know."

He handed her a folded paper from his pocket, then stepped over the wires and sat down across the doorway. He stared at the screen and started chewing his thumbnail.

The paper looked like a telex that had been recopied several times — faint, eroded, and splotchy:

CMC HILLTOP IV. IDIOPATHIC ELECTROMAG PULSE RECORDED 12:49:493EST. VOICE CONFIRMATION HILLTOP II, SENTINEL, STASAT CONTROL.

"What's this?" she asked.

"Another glitch. The same one. Twenty miles high."

She looked up at him.

"You know why I called you?" he asked.

"No."

"On the night before Stamford, your husband noticed something, didn't he?"

"Yes."

"So what do you think? Are we in trouble?"

She looked at the screen. Rocker stepped back from the window and started hunting for his cigarettes. When he found them, he lay back on the bed and lit another. "You'll have to ask him," she said.

"I'm not asking him. I'm asking you."

Her face felt hot. A bean-shaped area at the back of her head began to hurt. "Be serious."

"I am serious."

"Rocker had nothing to do with Stamford."

A long, ominous pause. "Really?"

"I'm not always crazy, you know."

"Then what did we just see there?"

"He woke up in the night. Don't you ever do that?"

He didn't answer. She risked looking at him. He was staring right back, motionless, his flat, unhandsome face the color of oatmeal. "I get it," he said. "Now I'm the loony."

She looked away. In her mind's eye she saw Rocker jerking upright again.

"Mrs. Poole," he said.

"Yes?"

"I can be as warped as I please."

She didn't answer.

"I can lock you up here. I can take your daughter away. You know why?"

"Why?"

His voice was low, almost soothing. "Because people are scared. A lot of people are scared. A lot of people are dead."

"You keep saying that."

"These are facts. You know what facts are, don't you?"

"Yes."

"Here's another fact. If I had to balance your husband's welfare against another thirty thousand people, it wouldn't take me long to decide."

"You think he killed them?"

"I think it's wrong to suppose that the worse things get, the less they matter."

She didn't answer.

"You're asking a lot from me, Mrs. Poole. You hand me the facts, and then you expect me not to believe them. Do you even know what you want?" He paused. "Maybe you're hoping I'll do something you don't feel able to do."

"Like what?"

"Like send this so-called husband of yours back where he came from."

She looked at the screen. Rocker was lying with his feet crossed at the ankles, his head on the pillow. Her heart was skittering wildly. "How?"

"By killing him, of course."

"Are you nuts?"

"How many more Stamfords do you think we can take?"

She was quiet.

"You're wedged in tight, Mrs. Poole — look at what you've said. If your husband *is* a fugitive, and if his presence *does* provoke these events, then hadn't we better throw him over the wall? Do we have the *right* to do nothing?"

"What — you want my permission?"

"That's exactly it, Mrs. Poole. I want you to say it's all right for me to go in there and provide him with this." He showed her a little bottle of green pills. "And if that doesn't work, I want your approval to go further."

She stared at him. "No! Of course not!"

"Why not, Mrs. Poole? Are you going to tell me you don't believe what you've been saying? That you've been *lying* to me?"

"It was an accident! He didn't know!"

"All right — so this time he *does* know. He knows that things are getting shaky again, he knows that the lid is about to get ripped off his hideout, and he knows that if he doesn't play things exactly right, we may see a fire that will make the last one look pitiful. Look at him, Mrs. Poole. Does he seem anxious to you? Would you say he's aware of his awesome responsibilities?"

Rocker had drawn up his legs, propped his hips on his hands, and was doing a sort of cycling routine on his back.

"You don't know what he's thinking."

"No, I don't. And if I ask him he won't tell me. So what do I do, Mrs. Poole? Nothing? And with no help from you? Are you really prepared to sacrifice the whole world to your conscience?"

Cinda had started to cry herself awake, kicking a little and tossing her head.

"He knows what to do," she said, the monitor filling her eyes.

"He knows what's going on."

"Then why did you tell me at all? Was it just panic? Or did you feel, maybe, that it's unfair for us not to know? That we at least ought to *hear* the truth, even if we'd never believe it? As if we were real human beings, Mrs. Poole. As if someday someone might discover, nightmare or not, that all this actually happened."

He went out again a few minutes later. He didn't reappear on the monitor. Cinda got up and tried to crawl into her lap, then drowsed for a while at her feet. In the lighted entry across the courtyard Carmen saw people going in and out hurriedly, often gathering in little clumps by the desk. Rocker was restless too.

Sometime later his keeper came back with another manila envelope. He clicked the door shut and sat down beside her. By then Cinda was back on her pad in the corner, awake but quiet.

He watched Rocker for a little while, tapping his knee with a pencil, then turned to her. "Mrs. Poole," he said, "there's a reason why your husband got so little attention. I just found out about it." He opened the envelope and handed her three large photos. "These were all taken in the crater a few hours after the event. Very close to the center of the blast."

The first one showed a sort of husk or cocoon made of several charred, soggy sleeping bags. It was lying on the ground. The next showed a small oxygen tank and mask, also apparently discarded, and the third a set of tracks half buried in dust leading across a field of gray ash.

"As you can see," he said, "these show that someone survived the explosion, then walked out of the crater while it was still hot. The theory is that there was some kind of basement or shelter nearby that was uncovered but not destroyed. The wet bags protected his body. The mask allowed him to breathe. He left before anyone saw him. And since it appears that he knew what was coming, there has naturally been a tremendous interest in locating and identifying him — a great effort, in fact. Your husband seemed unimportant beside it."

She handed the photos back. Let him talk, she thought.

"I wasn't told about this — hardly anyone was. But I saw them tonight, and something occurred to me. Could this be the visitor your husband's expecting? His so-called nemesis? And what if he came from outside? What if he survived the blast not because he was buried somewhere but because he entered *after* it peaked? *What if he came through the line*?"

She stared at the monitor. She wished he would go away.

"There *is* someone here, Mrs. Poole — they're right about that. Maybe your husband knows it. Maybe that's why he can't sleep. Do you have any idea who it might be?"

She remembered a story Rocker had told — something about a girl who was pursued and killed by a mysterious intruder. It seemed to her she had more than enough to think about as it was.

"You're very quiet, Mrs. Poole. Are you OK?"

"Yes."

"Well, I wish I knew what to do. I feel like all the pieces are here if I could just put them together."

"Oh?"

His voice sounded less distinct after that. It was as if the pressure had increased in her ears. He went on about how the two of them had to bear down and make decisions. This seemed to her honest but ignorant. It was like arguing that they ought to suspend the rotation of Mars. He was right, of course, but that didn't make him any wiser.

Something was going to happen. She too could feel it coming. And it was a mistake to give way to impatience, to start working from fear. This talk about killing was exactly that — fear. As if to say *I am helpless*.

But he wasn't ready for murder yet. Murder was a little too real. Reality was the last thing he wanted to get into now.

That was Rocker's secret: he set people adrift. One peek at his world, and they fell in head first. Right away they began to lose confidence. They didn't know how far to believe their own eyes. Men like this — thinkers, problem solvers — didn't have a chance. The harder they pushed, the quicker they fell apart.

It was quiet in the room. The man had left and Cinda was asleep. Rocker had returned to the armchair. His head lay back; he seemed to be dozing.

Night was already fading when Carmen got back to the house. In a chilly dusk dense with bird music she lifted Cinda out of the car and onto her shoulder. A foghorn called somewhere and the still air was heavy with the rich stink of low tide. It had rained and nothing had dried out.

A light glowed greenishly over the back door. Streaks of wet hung from the windowsills. She crossed quickly to the patio, cushioning her steps. She had got the screen door open and the keys out of her mouth when she saw the envelope taped to the window square nearest the doorknob. She pulled it off, unlocked, and went inside.

A minute later Waxman saw a cluster of lights go on upstairs. He was sitting at a picnic table more or less in plain sight, although deep in the leafy corner by the tool shed. He was wearing a dark-colored sweat suit, a ski hat, and a pair of gauze gloves from the burn unit at Norwalk Hospital. He hadn't moved for a long time; he was cold and the grass had sprung up in his footprints.

He hoped she wouldn't come out of the house and get back in the car. He doubted very much she would call the police.

More night melted away overhead. Open spaces acquired a grayish, fetal solidity. A badly tuned station wagon cruised down the street behind him, tossing out newspapers. After what seemed like enough time he got up and started across the noiseless lawn toward the house.

She must have been watching him; before he had gone three steps her figure moved in behind the screen door. He stopped when he was close enough to see the shape of her face. She had his note in her hand.

After a moment she reached over and snapped off the overhead light. In the restored dimness a moth fluttered up from the foundation.

"What do you want?" she said finally.

"I need to see Rocker."

"Why?"

"I'll tell you. It's very important."

Her face was a mask. She had pushed her sweater up on her elbows. The height of the stoop put their eyes on a level.

"Aren't you supposed to be dead?" she asked.

"Maybe I am."

She just watched him then. It was as though she were waiting for the next thought to enter her mind.

"All right," she said at last. "Come in."

He stopped just over the threshold. He saw brick-colored tiles, a refrigerator, and saucepans gleaming in the dark.

"Sit there," she said, pointing.

He took a chair at the table. Arms crossed, she was standing in the door to the next room.

"You're not going to see Rocker unless he wants you to," she said. "And maybe not even then."

He was barely listening. The long wait seemed to have stupefied him. And yet there were no gaps in his awareness — he understood exactly what was at stake.

"Where've you been?" she asked.

He looked up at her, his gloved hands flat on his knees. "Can I have some coffee?"

She started to make it. He hadn't talked to anyone for over a week.

He didn't feel the thing now. It hadn't lasted that long to begin with. Just a hint, really — the doomed man's discomfort as his murderer pencils an *x* by his name.

He didn't plan to explain it. All he knew was that at a certain moment shortly before one A.M. he had felt the shadow of extinction lap the edge of this world. The fact that he'd never felt it before didn't prevent him from knowing what it was. In that moment the entire earth was his body and it had shivered like the moon in a puddle.

"It's about what happened just before one," he said. "That's why they called you, isn't it?"

She poured water in the machine, turned it on, and laid her hands on the counter, motionless, her head slightly bowed.

"He felt it too, didn't he?"

"Felt what?" she said at last.

"The next time. The beginning."

She turned around and looked at him. She stood so still she was almost invisible. "I don't know what you're talking about."

Now he waited. "You ever heard of Stamford, Connecticut?"

She thought about this. "Where've you been?"

"I went over and came back. A lot of people went over."

"What people?"

"People who were close to the line when it happened."

Something moved in the next room. After a moment he realized it was her child.

"Did they come back also?"

"Nope. Just me."

She appeared to think about this, as well. Or at least she didn't look away. Maybe she was studying the raw patches where his eyebrows had been.

It wasn't a good time, he knew, to start explaining things. How he had seen Rocker's world. How he had found his way out. How he'd returned when he left, at the height of the blast, and how he'd spent eight days in a motel trying to convince himself that this was really and truly the place he had come from.

"Do you think Rocker made Stamford happen?" she asked.

"Yes."

"On purpose?"

"I think there was an effort to uproot him. Only Stamford got it instead."

"There's been talk about killing him. Were you planning to kill him?"

"Not unless I have to."

He didn't know why he said that. He had prepared various stories. But there was no sign he had surprised her.

"Unless you have to," she repeated.

"He can't stay here. Neither can I."

The coffee had stopped gurgling. She got down a mug, filled it, then stopped.

"Just milk," he said.

When she opened the refrigerator, light spilled onto the floor. After she poured from the carton she held the mug out to him so that he had to stretch to reach it. Then she was back in the doorway. "I don't know that Rocker'll want to see you after he hears this."

"How is he?"

"Good."

"Have you talked to him lately?"

"They keep him locked up."

"Why?"

"He's made some claims."

He hesitated. "What's this talk about killing him?"

There was a moment, then, when he thought she would tell him.

"I need some rest," she said suddenly. "Why don't you go out for a few hours. Come back around nine."

"Are you kidding me?"

"What's wrong with that?"

"I have to see him."

"I know — you told me. Are you going to threaten me too?"

She amazed him. It occurred to him that he had put himself at a disadvantage. "Do you think I'm nuts?"

"I don't know. Are you?"

"I'm afraid not."

Silence.

"Look," he said, lowering his voice. "I don't know how much time there is left. So I have to assume there isn't any. Does that make sense to you?"

"You think you're going to tell him anything he doesn't know?"

"He's got to understand his position."

"What is his position?"

"Delicate. Very delicate."

She didn't answer.

"Look," he said again. "I spent some time over there. I learned a few things. Number one, everything he's told you is true. There is such a place. People here go to it. They don't come back — they *shouldn't* come back. When they do, bad things happen. Like that thing on my porch. It should never have been here — *I* shouldn't be here. Neither should Rocker. When you come back, you beat a path — you create a hole, a weakness. Forces act on it, forces collect at it. That's what Stamford was. And more people will come back, and more Stamfords will happen, unless he and I let go and leave here. I'm willing to do it. And if he isn't, I'll take him with me. That thing last night — that was only a warning. It means we have to go. *Now.* Today."

"I'm sorry," she said finally. "You're just going to have to leave."

"I can't accept that."

"Didn't you just say you were planning to murder my husband?"

"If we work together, it might not be necessary."

Several seconds went by.

"Mister, I'll be honest — you worry me."

"You let me in, didn't you? Did you think we were going to talk about the weather?"

She didn't answer.

"I'm a serious person, Mrs. Poole. I realize that there's no forgiveness, ever — believe me, I know it — but here I am."

He could see her breathing now. Her chest rose and fell evenly.

"That shocks you, I know. Because up to now you've been saving yourself — nothing's been allowed to become real. The line wasn't real. Stamford wasn't real. The whole world could go down — that wouldn't be real. But you know, you *know*, that if you were to go along with me now, if you were to permit this . . . *crime* . . . then that at last would become real. Then everything else would turn real. And that scares you to death."

The room was still dark. He looked at her pale face, waiting.

"But the funny thing is that you *are* going to help me, Mrs. Poole. You already know that. Because if you don't, then you become a part of Stamford and of as many more Stamfords as it takes to put an end to this world. And that's just too much responsibility. Because how many worlds are there? Just one, Mrs. Poole. This one."

She walked over to the screen door and looked out. The birds were still loud. Her calmness seemed to him particularly dangerous.

"I'm not afraid," she said quietly, then turned and looked at him, her arms crossed on her chest. "I'm not afraid of whatever it is he's going to do. And if you knew him, you wouldn't be afraid either."

He didn't answer.

"Don't misunderstand me — I believe you. I know that if it weren't for him — but he's different now, really. He won't let it happen."

He waited a few moments. "But it's not up to him."

"No?"

He sat up. "Look — there'd be no threat at all if he weren't here. Don't you see that?"

"He's already come back twice. Do you think you can keep him out?"

"There won't *be* a next time if we don't stop him now."

She gave him a long look and then answered softly, as if talking to herself, "You don't really want to kill him, I think."

Maybe this is hell, he thought. *Maybe this is the place.*

"How about this," she said finally. "Why don't you stay here — I'll go in again. I'll call as soon as I see him. Maybe he'll want to talk to you."

"No."

"No?"

"I get in your car and you take me there."

She shook her head. "No."

"You don't seem to understand how serious I am."

She didn't answer.

He surprised himself then — he got up, crossed the room, and grabbed her by the throat. Her head banged against the wall. When he pressed his thumb on her windpipe, her hands dropped away. "If you don't breathe," he said, "you die." He banged her head back again. "What I am doing to you is what Rocker is doing to the rest of this world — killing it." He banged her again. "And I don't give a fuck what he's thinking. He's death. So am I." He squeezed tighter. "So what happens now is that he and I are going to leave here. Without being asked. So we won't get a chance to say no."

He dropped her. She sagged against the wall, clutching her neck. He felt a sort of bitter satisfaction, as if brutality were a riddle he had solved.

Then she started shaking her head in big, uneven jerks. He towered over her; he couldn't see her face. Her child was sitting up on a couch in the next room, shrieking. The noise irritated him. His mind kept drifting toward it.

When the phone rang, he merely gritted his teeth. He frowned and looked around the room. Just then the little girl ran in with her chubby arms held high. Her mother scrambled upright and grabbed her; they clutched each other and rocked. The phone was still jangling. He couldn't stand it anymore. He went over in two strides and picked it up.

A man's voice said, "Who's this?" He recognized it immediately; it was Poole's.

"Poole," Waxman said.

That was the magic word. The child stopped wailing. Her mother straightened up and stared. The receiver felt absurdly precious in his hand.

"Waxman?" Poole asked.

"That's right," Waxman said.

For a moment nothing seemed able to happen. Then, like a bird bursting from cover, Poole's wife snatched up her child and bolted down the hall. He heard the screen door in front bang its frame.

"Where's Carmen?" Poole asked.

"She just left." Waxman's head felt unsteady. "Where are you?"

"Let me talk to her."

"I told you — she just left." Through the window he saw her jump in the car and pull out.

"Why'd she leave?"

"I think I make her nervous."

They waited again. It wasn't as if they could actually see each other.

"How long?" Waxman asked suddenly.

After a considerable silence Poole's voice dropped. "I don't know. A few hours, maybe." He paused. "What're you doing there?"

"I got news for you, Rocker. I went over. I came back."

More emptiness hissed in the wire.

"That's right," Waxman said. "I'm a dead man. I was in Stamford. I found my way back."

At last Poole said, "That's impossible."

"And you know what line I used? The one on the porch. The one that started it all. It's still open for business. Thanks to you."

Poole was either very surprised or very deliberate.

"Aren't you going to congratulate me?"

When Poole finally got his voice back he had almost none left. And yet he couldn't have been clearer. "I take it you saw what happened to Stamford."

"Yes, I did. I'd like to discuss it with you."

"Why?"

"Obvious reasons."

Poole waited a moment. "Then you know, then."

"Know what?"

"That we can't stay."

"Yes, I do."

"Good. It's good you know that."

Waxman didn't answer.

"Listen," Poole said. "Go down in the basement. Look behind the water heater. You'll find a shotgun and shells."

"And?"

"Use them."

Waxman teetered a little; he could see it too clearly. "But what about you?"

"Don't worry about me. I'm just about ready."

"That didn't make any difference last time."

"Last time was a mistake."

"Suppose you make another mistake?"

"That's not going to happen. I don't even like it here."

They both waited again.

"Suppose I come over there," Waxman said.

"Why?"

"I want to see you. I'm not ready yet."

"You'd never make it. This place is a fortress."

"I'll find a way."

"They're probably listening right now. They're probably sending someone to get you."

Waxman looked at the door to the basement. He felt terrible. "Rock, you don't know . . . you have no idea what's going on over there. All the lines are falling inward. All the spaces between — they're starting to fade. There's no *room* there anymore. It's bad, real bad."

"It's not so great here either."

"Rocker, listen. I came through the line. Everyone over there is piling up at the far end. You want to let them in here? *Here*?"

"That's not my intention."

"So get out now. Make it impossible."

"Can't do that."

"Why not?"

"Just can't."

Waxman reached up and laid a fist on the wall. "Rocker, this isn't personal. Understand? Other people come into it. Lots of people."

"Why don't you trust me?"

"I do trust you! But you're only a goddamn human being! That's all!"

Poole remained calm. "I know I can count on you, Will. Why can't you count on me?"

Waxman sat down at the table. "Rocker," he said, "I was in Stamford. Stamford blew up. Remember that?"

No answer.

"Stamford blew up and I crossed over. A lot of people did. One moment we were here, the next we were there. Only you know something? We didn't know it. Believe it or not, it looked just like this place. The only difference was that there were lines everywhere. *Everywhere*, Rocker — you could barely turn around. We thought that's what happened to everybody else — they had fallen into them, because the whole place was empty except for us.

"So we just sat tight for a while. We were about forty altogether. We tried to get organized. We didn't know what the hell had happened. And about three days later, just as it was getting obvious that we weren't at home anymore, we began to have visitors. *Visitors*, Rocker. Can you guess who they were? Can you?"

At last Poole said, "Tell me."

"Pilgrims, Rocker. Missing persons. Dead men. When they saw us, they laughed. They knew where we'd come from. They meant to retrace our steps. For the first time any of them could remember, they could see their way back to the world."

Again no answer.

"And you know where they saw it? Do you? You do, don't you?"

"The line on the porch."

"That's right. The back side."

Waxman went on. "Course they couldn't cross it. If they could, they'd all be here. So they sat down to wait. I heard their prayers, Rocker — they didn't know it, but they were praying to you. *They were praying that you'd keep the door open*."

Poole cleared his throat. "So what's your point?"

"There were a lot of them, Rocker. More than you ever saw. They swamped us."

"Huh." Poole had become thoughtful.

"Why don't you let them in, Rocker? They're like you and me, right? Haven't they been out there long enough?"

"I already told you. I'm leaving."

"Yes. Why is that? Because you don't want them in here? Because they don't belong in this world? Because you came back yourself, and you didn't like what you saw?"

"What's your point?"

"Look, Rocker — they weren't all so eager. They weren't all dying to go home. There were some, believe it or not, who wanted the line shut down. They knew you were here. They knew you had opened it. They even knew what was happening to Stamford. And they sent me — are you listening, Rocker? — they sent *me* to make *sure* you were *removed* in a *hurry*, because even though they don't live here, they set a value on this place. They think lines will destroy it. And you know what, Rocker? I agree."

"Who were these people?"

"From Panlogo, Rocker. Friends of Mac. They knew you."

"But they couldn't get over either."

"That's right. Just me. I was still fresh, so to speak."

No answer.

"Well, we can't wait for next time, Rocker. Tell me where you are. I'll get there — I'll bring what we need. That way we can be sure that we both check out in time. I'll tell you something — I'm like you now. I can feel it coming too."

Something rustled at Poole's end. "No," he said finally. "I don't think so."

"What!"

"I told you, I'm not ready. I want to see it in person."

"Rock, this isn't a game — this is fucking important."

"You're right — it's very important. But you don't hold all the cards."

The rest of the conversation accomplished nothing for Waxman. Poole meant to wait until the moment actually presented itself. He wouldn't even say where he was. In the end he simply hung up.

Waxman held the receiver for a few moments, then put it back gently. His throat hurt from shouting. He couldn't believe he had failed.

He stood there for several minutes before he noticed the motion — or rather noticed that he had noticed it. When he did, he dropped to his heels and laid a hand flat on the tiles. Unsatisfied, he did the same on the refrigerator, the countertop, and a windowpane. Then he filled a mug from the tap, set it on the table, and sat down beside it. The water's surface showed no vibration. Even with his hand around the rim it stayed flat.

But he wasn't reassured. Every few seconds another tremor passed through him. As soon as each one died out, he felt the next one begin. It was as though every tenth cell in his body were quivering in time to a queer, surging rhythm.

He turned his hand over and looked at his palm, plucking at the skin with his thumb. *He must feel this also,* he thought. It would probably become more noticeable as the moment approached.

He felt calmer now. Maybe the call hadn't been a disaster — maybe it was even necessary. He knew now that if he got his chance, he would take it.

A moment later he looked up and saw a graying, unshaven, and barefoot neighbor standing outside and trying to peer in. He was wearing only pajamas and was holding a snow shovel *en garde*. Waxman laughed out loud and went out the front door. *I'm learning*, he thought. *I'm learning*.

After he hung up, Poole felt his way back to his room. It was still unclear why his door had been left open. The guard had returned to his seat, his outstretched legs just visible around the corner. Poole had already decided to sit tight and hope Waxman wouldn't make any trouble.

He had no problem seeing the enemy now. It was a black, roaring ocean standing on end and swirling around him like smoke; he seemed to be caught on its surface. He couldn't fall in; if he edged toward it, it retreated. He stayed on its side of the room in order to keep the rest of the space clear. It was like balancing on the edge of a pit.

He tried looking straight at it. It had no apparent bottom; his eyes quickly lost focus. After a few moments the endless flashing and churning began to work on his stomach.

A visit to the guard netted him a couple more cigarettes. It was still the night man, the easy-tempered one with the Samoan physique. He didn't look too happy but seemed unaware of any problem. He apparently already knew the door was unchained.

One cigarette lit, the other safe in his pocket, Poole retraced his steps and herded the boiling darkness back in his room, then shut the door and started smoking in earnest. Though there was some new activity upstairs, he barely heard it. What concerned him now was what he would do when the intruder called his name. There was only one answer, and he intended to make it — after all, it was inconceivable that he would make any other — but would that be enough? The brutal truth was that as much as he wanted to submit, as much as he needed to submit, he didn't like the damn thing.

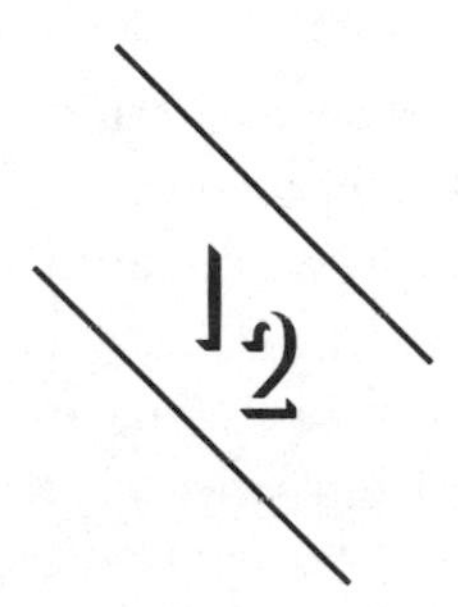

Carmen looked at her watch again. She was sitting with Cinda in her cinnamon-red compact at an Exxon station about two hundred yards from a little-used gate just south of the highway.

She had arrived there just after eight. At eight-ten a big red oil truck went by. It stopped by the gate for a minute and went on.

Traffic was light. Just around the bend the road veered away and the fence butted on a greasy arm of the harbor. The gate itself blocked a tunnel under the highway. This was where you had to turn around if you tried to circle the enclosure.

They hadn't let her in at the usual place. She had spent almost an hour trying to get hold of Rocker's keeper. Now she was waiting for the soldiers to abandon the gate.

She knew they would leave. Everyone was running from Stamford this morning. On her way over she'd seen thousands of people heading the other way — in cars, on bicycles, even on foot. It was as if they'd all got the same message at once. She'd had the westbound lanes on 95 nearly to herself.

Another red tanker stopped outside the gate. A minute later she saw a canvas-topped army truck pull up at the guardrail above. A man appeared and shouted down. The oil truck blocked her view below.

It was no mystery to her why all these people were scattering. Even Cinda knew why. The whole area had become uncomfortable. You could feel it; it was as obvious as anything so uncanny could be.

She looked at Cinda again. She was strapped in like a spaceman in her car seat, her arms limp at her sides, her eyes huge and drifting. She knew it better than anyone.

The soldier on the overpass was still leaning over the rail. He pointed at his wrist and pointed back toward Stamford, then made an arch with his arms over his head and spread them suddenly, indicating an explosion. He did this several times. Someone in the truck up above honked at him. She wished they would hurry up and go.

The soldier dropped out of sight and the truck rolled away. A minute later the red tanker rumbled and the two remaining guards ran around to the passenger side and climbed in. It puffed smoke and pulled out. She started the car.

They had left the gate open. On the far side of the tunnel she saw a splash of sunlight. It seemed to sway a little, like a flower on a stalk. She drove through.

She was about a mile from the hospital. The streets were deserted. As she went on, they began to flex and twist slightly at the edge of her vision, as if trying to lift free. *Please*, she thought. *Please*.

At the edge of the Post Road she stopped again, dizzied. Cloud shadows rippled over the ground like submerged nightmares. The whole landscape was struggling to remain intact, heaving and pitching noiselessly. But she couldn't feel any motion. A block down, an army truck had crashed into a wall and caught fire. She heard it before she saw it; it was hopping around like a cricket.

She went on. At the hospital there were only a half-dozen cars left in the lot. She parked, got out, and lifted Cinda onto the ground. "Listen," she said, "We're going inside — we're going to see Daddy. I don't know what to expect. But no matter what happens, we're staying together. So we're not going to be afraid." *Liar*, she thought. *Liar liar liar.*

Cinda's gaze slid away. She was trying hard to be somewhere else.

The doors opened quietly. The lobby was dim and empty. A dozen flickering monitors had been stacked by the windows on the courtyard. They were the only sign of life.

She tried the double doors on the right, the ones that led to Rocker's wing. Locked.

She went over to the monitors. There he was on his bed, smoking a cigarette. On the next screen the President sat behind a desk, his lips moving soundlessly. Several other screens showed scenes of the exodus.

She returned to the reception area and started looking for keys. There didn't seem to be any.

She went out again and circled the building. She found him sitting on the bed, his back to the light. At least, she believed it was Rocker. She rapped on the glass.

He started and turned around. He didn't look in the right place. He didn't seem able to see her at all.

She rapped again, harder. He got up on his knees and leaned closer, mouthing the words *I can't see*. He looked like a fish drowning in a bucket. It was awful the way his naked eyes searched for her.

She didn't try screaming at him; she took a step backward.

"Carmen?" he mouthed, incredulous.

By more pounding she managed to convey that yes, it was

she, and yes, she wanted to come in. "Front door," he mouthed. When she didn't answer he said, "Dah? Dah?" After a moment she saw he meant "Locked?" He seemed to think she should try again.

She didn't know what else to do. Arms raised, he was spread out on the glass, pale as a frog, his eyes bright and staring. He obviously didn't know whether she was still there. And since she didn't leave right away, she was still watching when his shoulders sank and his arms slid down. His head drooped, exposing his neck, and his hands curled into fists. He was suffering, clearly. She might have stayed even longer if he hadn't jerked up suddenly and started savagely beating the glass.

As she went through the front doors again, she saw a man across the lobby standing and watching the TVs. When she hesitated, he turned around; it was Rocker's keeper. "Hah!" he crowed. "Come on in!" He went back to the screens.

She approached cautiously. There didn't seem to be anyone else.

"Couldn't sleep, eh?" He was still facing the screens, his arms crossed on his chest. "You ought to see some of this stuff."

He must have been here before, she thought. She saw that Rocker had got down from the window and was sitting on the bed again.

"Sorry about the reception. It's getting worse by the minute." He touched a button on another set, and a voice started describing the image — a highway flooded with people. Though he had no keys in his hands, there was a likely bulge in his pocket.

He pulled out the bunch and handed it to her. "Try the skinny one in the middle. I warn you, it's hard to get his attention."

On the low magazine table she saw a cordless phone, some photostats, and a stack of videotapes. She could feel Cinda's heartbeat through her shirt. She didn't move.

"What's the problem?" he asked.

She didn't look up. The window *must* break, she had thought. "So you don't think he's responsible."

"Of course he is. It's been him all along. You know it, I know it — we all know it. Don't you think we can admit that now?"

She discovered that he was smiling at her — a relaxed, disarming smile.

"It was the other stuff that fooled us. All the stuff that still seemed so normal. No wonder we got excited." His smile broadened. "Your man's got the right idea. Full speed ahead."

She just stared at him then.

"You look puzzled."

Her eyes dropped to the keys in her hand.

"Don't tell me I'm making sense. Don't tell me you'd rather listen to me than go mop his forehead." He laughed.

She remembered that laugh. She glanced up. "It's not him who needs help. It's us. You and me."

"So you do understand."

She let her eyes rest on his face. His gaze was sly, even friendly. As if the worst had already happened.

He held the door open for her. A dirty yellow-gold carpet stretched down to the next corner. It was left and then right, then the second room on the left.

She started down. Maybe she had thought she wouldn't get this far — maybe she had thought that if she showed this much stupidity, someone or something would rise up to stop her. Of all people, she had the least excuse not to know — Rocker was different. Rocker was the end of the world.

His door was shut. A chain hung across the jamb. Cinda was whimpering. Carmen didn't hear anything inside.

She took the chain off and went in.

He was sitting on the bed, his head in his hands. He looked up slowly. She saw by his eyes that he could see her.

He said her name.

The room stank of him. The floor was littered with butts. A

huge spiderweb fracture spanned the window. The water was running and his hand was bloody. He had blood on his pants and along his hairline. He lowered his head.

She shut the door gently and put Cinda in the armchair. She already knew that he was going to ask her to leave. But she wasn't going to leave. She wasn't even going to argue about it.

"Carmen," he said again.

She dragged Cinda's chair over to the bed and sat down on the sheets alongside him. He didn't turn toward her. "Yes," she answered. "I'm here."

He was quiet. He seemed to be looking for a way to say something difficult. Something told her she had better let him.

He cleared his throat finally. "Waxman'll be here in ten minutes."

"Oh?"

"He's coming to kill me."

"He won't do it."

He didn't answer.

"I saw him,' she said. "He's not . . . he's not together enough."

After a moment he lifted his arm and pointed at the door. His head was still down. "Would you mind sitting over there?"

"Why?"

His fist boomed on the bed frame. "So I can see you, goddammit!"

She moved, taking the armchair. Even then his forehead stayed on his palm. His eyes were squeezed shut. Cinda turned over in her lap and burrowed against her.

"Look — just give me a minute," he said.

She waited. The room seemed steady enough. There was a lot of movement, however, outside the window — a tall hedge jumping and twitching wildly. Somehow it made no noise at all.

She noticed a long strip of bed sheet tacked across the far wall. This was like the last time — he had struggled then also.

But she didn't feel the weight of it. She was thinking about something else entirely.

"Look at me," she said suddenly.

He lifted his head. His face looked like a battlefield. He was exposing himself, she knew — he was taking his eye off the main object.

"I'm not here for you," she said quickly. "I mean I am, but — " She shook her head. "I'm here because I couldn't stand being anywhere else."

He was still watching her.

"So if I'm hurting you now, I say that's — that's the price."

He didn't answer. Something in his eyes made her voice start to fail. "I don't hate you," she said. "I don't. I just don't want to — I mean what am I supposed to do, run *away*? Run and hide? Why should I — I hate this shit! I'll *never* accept it!"

His face didn't change.

"Why don't you say something!"

His voice was stone cold. "Waxman just turned off the Post Road."

"What about the other thing?"

"It's here already. It's slowing down."

"Is it the same as before?"

"Sort of."

He sounded terrible. Cinda was picking carefully at a scrap of tape on the chair arm.

"What's it like?" she asked.

"It's big — it's fading. I could see it better before." He sat up and slid his hands down his thighs, his face tilted upward. "Take Cinda into the next room. You'll hear Waxman come in. You can come back if he's reasonable."

"No."

"I don't want Cinda to see this."

"You don't know everything."

Someone knocked on the door and stepped in—Rocker's keeper. He glanced at them both, his hand on the knob. "Everything all right in here?" he asked pleasantly.

"Get out," Rocker said.

"All right." He went away.

Cinda tried to squirm off Carmen's lap. She picked her up and went to bolt the door. The lock had been taken out. She sat down again. Rocker was silent.

She knew that he was right, that Waxman was dangerous. She was dangerous too, dangerous to herself, because she understood perfectly why she couldn't leave—she meant to force a decision, to make something become real.

"You're still here," he said.

"That's right. And you won't throw me out. You can't even stand to touch me."

"I don't know what's going to happen."

"Are you afraid?"

"Yes."

"Well, don't be. Don't be so damn . . . amenable."

After a few moments he said, "Can you see it at all?"

"What?"

"It's here in the room. Can you see it?"

He was still looking only at her. He was sitting quite still. "No, I can't."

"It's moving. It can't seem to get oriented."

She looked out the window. It was all a blur out there now. Reflected sunlight shimmered on the leafy greens swarming in the middle.

"This is all bullshit," she said, loud enough to be overheard.

"You really can't see it?"

She looked around the room. It wasn't so much what she could see as what was inside her. An awareness—a self-awareness.

"Here comes Waxman," he said.

She heard footsteps in the hall. The door opened and Waxman stepped in.

He was empty-handed. He glanced at them both and shut the door firmly. "OK," he said. "Time to go."

Rocker stared back at him. "Is it?"

Waxman turned to her suddenly. "Out. Now." He pointed.

She didn't answer. She was looking for something in his eyes. It wasn't there.

With astonishing ease he reached down, yanked her to her feet, and thrust her and Cinda out of the room. The door slammed in her face. When she ran into it, a little daylight showed and it clapped shut again. She heard him dragging the chair behind it.

She couldn't put Cinda down. She couldn't dig through with her nails. She was howling as loud as she could but not loud enough.

She ran into the lobby. Rocker's keeper was standing by the TVs. She grabbed him and explained that a murder was about to take place.

He seemed unimpressed. "None of this is for real," he said. "You can't kill anyone here." When she continued to argue, he turned up the sound on the screen. "All right," he said. "Look."

She saw Rocker sitting on his bed, watching calmly as Waxman unzipped a pocket on his nylon jacket and took out a chubby little gun. Rocker didn't comment when he followed it with a handful of bullets and started pushing them in. "Am I too late, do you think?" Waxman asked.

"Look at that," her friend said. "He's trying to restore order. Incredible."

"So you're really going to do it," Rocker said.

Waxman nodded, still loading. "You first, then me."

"We're not alone, you know."

"So what?"

She ran down the hall and assaulted the door. Of course it wouldn't move. All her rage couldn't fill the silence — there was more than enough left for the gun to go off. And only that could release her, she knew — only that could make resistance no longer necessary.

Then she noticed that the door was giving a little. She forced it all the way in; it carried the armchair aside. Waxman had his back to her, the gun dangling by his leg. He was talking to Rocker. "I'm not crazy," he said.

"Course you aren't," Rocker said.

She went out again. In the room across the hall she found an earthenware vase on the windowsill. It was suitably heavy.

When she got back, though, she found Waxman watching her. She walked right past him and sat down on the bed. She kept her hand tight around the vase, her other arm around Cinda. "Don't be an idiot,' she said.

Waxman didn't hear her; he had returned to Rocker. "How can you tell?" he asked.

"It's not moving," Rocker said. "It's positioned. What, you think it went home?"

"I don't feel it anymore."

He laughed. "Lucky you."

Waxman seemed no longer aware of the gun in his hand. He was gazing over Rocker's head at the window. She could tell that something was different out there. She turned to look.

The real world had come back. Sunlight streamed through the crown of the dogwood. The building over the hedge sat perfectly still.

"You bastard," Rocker said quietly. "You incredible bastard."

"You know," Waxman said, still looking outside, "this doesn't change anything." He didn't sound convinced.

"Suit yourself," Rocker answered. He turned to her suddenly, showed her his hand, and touched her face as gently as a wound, then touched Cinda. There were tears in his eyes. Cinda hugged Carmen a little closer.

"Wait a minute," Waxman said. "*Wait a minute.*" He held up both hands, the gun outlined on his palm.

She threw the vase at his head. It flattened him; the gun went off with a bang. She heard it skitter under the bed. When everything stopped moving, she put Cinda down and scrambled after it.

It was way back against the baseboard. She jumped up, jerked the bed aside, and stepped on it, then picked it up. By the time Waxman got up, she had Cinda at her waist and was backed against the window, fumbling with the gun. He looked merely amazed.

"Are you finished?" She sobbed. The gun wouldn't turn the right way. When she got it straightened out, she pointed it at him. Her eyes stung and her chest was heaving. "OK?" she said. "OK?"

Rocker looked up at her. "Relax," he said. "Please."

Waxman strode down the hall. In the lobby he found a man in a white shirt and tie watching the TVs. He walked up to him. "Is this the real world?" he asked.

The man seemed to think this was funny. "How real do you like it?"

Stupid, Waxman thought. He went out through the glass doors. He stopped just outside.

The sun shone in his eyes. A few trees gathered pockets of shadow. Nothing looked any different from the way it had when he came in. But of course everything was different.

He went back in and approached the man by the TVs. "Did you notice anything just now? Just a minute ago?"

"Well, of course. Didn't you?"

"Like what?"

He pointed at the screens. "These've cleared up. They were pretty bad earlier."

Waxman examined them. He saw several tense-looking newsmen reading from sheets of paper. "That's all?"

"Well, I wouldn't want to exaggerate. But it seemed like everything stopped jumping around."

After a moment Waxman realized that he was being laughed at. He glanced up. "What's so funny?"

"You are. You look disappointed."

"Things aren't always what they seem."

The man grinned. "I disagree — they're never anything *but* what they seem. At least until they become something else."

Idiot, Waxman thought. He found himself staring out into an open courtyard at a half-dozen white mesh chairs. They looked harmless. What he really wanted to do, he realized, was go insane.

He walked down the hall. When he appeared at the door, Poole's wife pointed the gun at him. "I'm sorry," he said. "I don't see it."

Poole remained motionless. His voice seemed to come from the center of his chest. "Nobody wants to kill me."

"I've seen them before, you know. I'm not new to this shit."

"Maybe I'm the one. Did you think of that?"

"What the hell does that mean?"

"Maybe I'm my own killer. Maybe it's right in here." He nodded at himself.

Waxman just stared at him then.

"Don't make my mistake," Poole said. "Don't think you can start over."

He sounds, Waxman thought, *as if he hates the idea.*

"Look," he said finally. "I didn't find you by accident. This place was *occupied*. There was *movement* coming out of here. Now there isn't. And you're saying that's nothing?"

Poole didn't seem to hear.

Waxman glanced out the window, then took a step back and looked down the hall. It was uncanny how much this madhouse resembled the world.

Nothing happened for a few moments. Poole's wife still had the gun pointed at him. He could see the red-purple marks he had left on her throat. Poole apparently didn't think there was any more to be said.

Waxman's attention strayed toward the window. The fracture partially obscured a piece of lawn, a small tree, and a tall hedge shielding the boxy end of a brick-faced modern building. He felt like a man dumped out of a spaceship; he had dropped the thread finally — he had lost his connection to what this place was and how it fit in. He didn't even want to have it explained.

He crossed in front of the bed and sat down in the chair by the bathroom. It was unlikely that he'd kill anyone now. But he took no particular credit — living here was like having to watch while surgeons opened your chest and replaced all your major organs with dish towels and old newspapers. It strained belief; there was a distinct odor of mockery. But the worst part was that all the wreckage retained the appearance of value; if the future had become laughable, the present didn't give an inch.

He looked at the group on the bed. Poole sat leaning over his knees with his head in his hands. His wife, in profile, was sitting up a bit too straight. Only the little girl seemed ready to make room for surprises.

Right about now, he thought, *would be a good time*. For what, he didn't know. For whatever it was that came next. Because it seemed to him that he was truly burned back to the roots, and that after today he would be less and less likely to concern himself with resemblances.

"Hey, Rocker," he said.

No answer.

"Let's pretend this is bullshit. Let's pretend we know better."

Poole didn't reply. He seemed to think a great deal depended on his powers of concentration.

Sanity, Waxman thought, isn't a game everybody can play.

He didn't feel so great. This thing that was supposedly nearby — he didn't want any part of it. He was sitting right next to the window; less than ten days earlier hundreds of people had been blinded by looking out windows.

But if his friends across the way and everyone else were still waiting for him to finish the work and send Poole back where he came from, they had overestimated his flexibility. It seemed he could stand by while whole worlds were erased but he could not stomach the simple intimate act. What pride! What courage! What a lamb for the slaughter!

It was puerile, he knew, to suppose you could take revenge on God by forcing him to destroy you.

The room was quiet. The door stood open. All the silent shaking and jostling had stopped.

An amplified voice started up down the hallyway. ". . . as you can see from these pictures, the panic appears to be losing force . . . The crowds are spreading out . . . fewer people are joining. This area, I'm told, is about five miles from Stamford . . . Wait a minute, I think we have our man in the helicopter now . . . Jerry, are you there?" A much noisier signal cut in. A rotor blade whickered; a garbled voice buzzed like a plastic panel.

Poole didn't react. *It's important,* Waxman thought, *that I stay in the room.*

The announcer was back. ". . . repeat, we have no word as yet as to what may have caused the stampede. You've heard what our people said. A premonition — an overwhelming urge to get out . . . As to whether there may be anything out of the ordinary happening in Stamford right now, it's hard to know, since we have no one on the spot. But we haven't seen anything on the skyline . . . It could be, some are saying, that this is nothing more than a massive attack of group hysteria. But let me emphasize that this is pure guesswork. Personally I find the whole thing completely astounding."

He went on in the same vein. Waxman wished he would shut up. It was painful, the way this nightmare kept trying to make sense.

He watched Poole's wife press her hands to her temples. She hadn't looked at him once. The gun was probably next to her leg. She also seemed to understand that only Poole could dig them out of here now. But he was still doubled over, his eyes squeezed shut, as if he were trying to hold a tiny flame steady in the center of his head.

Something cut off the announcer. The man from the lobby appeared in the doorway. "Guess what?" he said brightly.

Nobody answered.

He nodded at the window. "Take a look."

Waxman did so. He didn't see anything.

"Keep looking."

A moment later a head popped up on the roof opposite—a soldier with a gun. Two more ran up and took cover at the base of the hedge some distance down.

"There's more out front," the man said. "They're surrounding the building."

There were at least three on the roof, Waxman saw. Poole's wife picked up her child and backed away from the window.

"They're headed for trouble, getting mixed up with us," the man said.

Waxman saw two more run for the spot under the hedge, their hands flat on their helmets, their gear bouncing.

"Abuse of reality," the man said. "Incitement to nonsense. We're guilty, no doubt." He laughed.

Waxman began to work quickly then. "I'm taking this apart," he said, and yanked the bed frame out from under the mattress, forcing Poole to his feet. The frame was adjustable; loosened, screwed tight, and tipped onto its side, it was just long enough to brace the door shut.

No one else moved. When he finished, they were all corralled on the far side. Poole hadn't even noticed; he had sat down again.

"Hey, Rocker," Waxman said.

No answer.

"Rocker!"

Poole started moving his lips. "Please," he was saying. He was clearly talking to someone else.

Waxman didn't like what he saw — all that pain had to mean something. Though Carmen was on her knees at Poole's side with his shirt in her fists and her face blotted with rage, howling with a voice to scar granite, Rocker couldn't hear her; he was staring straight ahead and saying, "No. No. No." as steady as a heartbeat and blinking wetly and often, his eyes much too bright and his fingers curling like burning paper in his lap. *Don't lose it now*, Waxman thought, although what 'it' was and what losing it meant were matters entirely beyond him. All he knew was that something major was happening, something that centered on Poole but wasn't limited to him, so that he watched his face like a miner watching the wall of rock over his head.

He had started to think about what he could find to wedge the frame tighter when he noticed that the man from the lobby had gone to the window. He looked out too and saw why. There were people out there, eight or ten of them, only, unlike the soldiers, they weren't always solid — they had the ghostly habit of fading in and out without warning and were milling around like fireflies, present one moment and absent the next, as if not quite equipped to come all the way in.

Not here, he thought, chilled. He recognized their soft edges, their dark centers, their elusive faces. He could see more of them down near the end of the building. It was obvious to him that if they actually took root here, this world would become something entirely different — if it could survive them at all.

And yet in a way he was glad to see them. They removed all doubt; they showed that he was going to be pursued to the end.

Under the hedge one of the soldiers straightened up and looked around wildly. Another backed away from the edge of the roof. There was a whole nest of would-be individuals right under the window.

The man from the lobby banged on the glass, trying to get their attention. "This is more like it," he said. "No mistaking *these* guys." He grinned once at Waxman, then strode to the door, pushed the bed frame aside, and stepped out.

The hallway exploded with gunfire. Surprised, he fell in a bloody heap on the rug. A little acrid smoke drifted down from the direction of the lobby.

At that point Waxman shouted something that even he didn't hear, slammed the door shut, and barricaded it again. Then he ducked through the frame and approached Poole.

Poole seemed to know him. His face was moist and lacked color. He looked as if he'd been hit by a truck. "It's happening," he said.

Waxman didn't answer.

"We have to leave now."

Of course, Waxman thought. He saw the defeat in Poole's eyes.

"You ready?"

Poole seemed to think they both were. Even his wife's strength appeared to have run out.

OK, then, Waxman thought. And yet he didn't move right away. He and Poole were looking straight at each other.

Just then the soldiers started to break down the door. He heard them swearing and saw it leap in its frame, forcing the hinges. Poole had stood up — they were all up now and watching.

"The real world," Waxman said, his voice oddly solemn.

The gun was in plain sight on the bed. They could all see it. And yet none of them moved, since they were watching a spot just this side of the door where a line was forming.

It grew rapidly from a pale, wobbly spot at knee level, swelling until it was as tall as a man and twice as wide, glowing all the while with a soft bluish light. There it stopped, hovering, a plain invitation, and when the door blasted open and the soldiers rushed in, they hit it and vanished. At the same moment the line itself hiccupped and disappeared. Then it was quiet in the room.

Poole was the first to react. He eased over to the window and looked out, then crossed to the empty doorway and peered down the hall. He glanced back at them once and stepped through.

His wife and Waxman shared a look before she followed carefully, her child on her shoulder. Waxman followed her. He saw no one on the lawn outside the window. The man who'd been shot had disappeared from the hall. The silence amazed him.

Poole stopped at the first bend, then stepped around the guard's chair to where the corridor straightened again. But down at the far end, where the doors to the lobby should have been, there was only another corner like the first, with a couple of sunny rooms at the angle.

Poole didn't comment. His pace quickening, he led them past that corner, and the next, and the next. None of them was notably different. It seemed that the hallway didn't go anywhere but merely continued.

After several more turns Poole stopped and looked at them both. It was clear what he was thinking. "Well," he said at last, carefully filling his chest. "We did it, I guess. We did it."